Other Worlds

Fantasy and Science Fiction short stories

SIMON KEWIN

STORM
CROW
BOOKS

ISBN: 978-1-9993395-1-7

For Gary

who kept me supplied with science fiction when we were growing up

CONTENTS

INVESTMENTS

Evangelina Carter, CEO of Blue Planet Holdings, stared at her visitor down from Head Office. She must have misheard his words. "I'm sorry," she said. "For a moment I thought you said you wanted to wipe out civilization."

Mr. Allen peered at her over his half-moon glasses. You had to give it to them. They had their human mannerisms down to a T. "No of course not. Not *wipe out*. We merely wish to … subdue humanity. Knock it back to a less technological era. Our projections suggest five centuries should do the trick."

Evangelina didn't speak for a moment. They could do it, too. She studied the ancient alien sitting opposite her. In his finely-tailored suit and old-school tie he looked every inch the genial investment banker. Allen smiled, awaiting her reply. Beyond him, through floor-to-ceiling windows, London stretched away into a hazy distance.

With an effort she maintained her professional manner. There was a place for panic and terror but the boardroom wasn't it. "But, why? Is there a problem with output?"

"Heavens, no. We are most satisfied with your stewardship, Ms. Carter. Profits from operations on Earth continue to soar. The creativity of this planet remains as phenomenal as ever. But we've made projections and the results are clear. Another century or two and things will be different. We have to protect our investments."

She dreaded asking. Their forecasts were always accurate. "May I know what you foresee? Environmental collapse? Wars? Pandemic?"

"Quite the contrary. Humanity will thrive. Scientific advance will continue apace, ushering in a new golden age of abundance."

"Then I don't see the problem."

Allen looked troubled. It was all for show. His face, like the rest of him, synthesized. So far as she could tell her masters were amorphous blobs of jelly. But amorphous blobs of jelly with vast technological resources at their fingertips. If that was the right word.

"Ms. Carter," he said, picking his way through his words, "has anyone ever explained why we chose your planet?"

"I assumed you monitored us for millions of years."

His face twisted into new heights of *troubled*. "Quite so," he said. "But the truth is we didn't simply *monitor*."

"You didn't?"

"No, we also … shepherded. Guided. *Intervened*."

"Which is against galactic statute."

"Yes. But our projections, you see. They were quite clear. Given the right conditions your remarkable species would produce – well, all the glories it has produced. I don't need to list them. Music, literature, film. The galaxy can't get enough of it and we, as rights owners, make a *fortune*."

"So what did you do?"

"Ms. Carter, I'm telling you this because we trust you, yes?"

That was something. "Go on," she said.

It was his turn to stare through the window. More play-acting. "Ms. Carter, I hope you won't be angry when I inform you that every other sentient species in the galaxy is, to all intents and purposes, well, *immortal*."

"Immortal."

"Quite so. We don't die. I myself have been alive for nearly six hundred thousand years. And I'm considered rather a young gun. A bit of a hot-head."

"Immortal," she said again, as if the word was unfamiliar. "What does that have to do with us?"

Allen switched to *deeply sad* now. "Well, you see, here's the thing. Immortality is lovely, of course, but it can be so … enervating."

"Can it? How awful."

"Yes. Oh, we set out to achieve great things. Works of art and feats of literature. Musical masterpieces. But knowing you can set it aside for a thousand years – well, frankly, it's hard to motivate oneself."

"I can see that."

"But humanity, now. You blaze briefly but gloriously across the face of the universe. Knowing you have only a few years focuses your minds wonderfully. You yearn for the eternal without really knowing why."

"Are you saying you did this to us?"

Allen took off his glasses and polished them on his silk handkerchief. "I'm afraid so. A few mutations introduced millennia ago. Your cellular structures decay when they really shouldn't. A few decades of life and … pooof! You're gone. I really am sorry."

She was beginning to see where this was going. "And your projections?"

"Well, it's this damned science, you see. Another century or two and you'll be unravelling all our work. Humanity will defeat death and creativity will plummet. It'll wreak havoc with our profits, Ms. Carter. Havoc!"

"So you plan to return us to somewhere around – what – the Renaissance?"

"Ah, the Baroque," said Allen. "Such musical glories."

She considered. "But you'll still need intermediaries. You need me?"

"Quite so. Our trusted agent. Someone who understands local custom. We shall, of course, ensure you're spared the horror as it engulfs the Earth. Your title will have to change, too. You could become an Empress, say. Would that suit?"

What they'd done was monstrous. An evil so vast she couldn't even think of a name for it. She couldn't let them get away with it.

Except … she loved being in charge of Blue Planet. And Empress Evangelina had a ring to it. "These genetic changes. They're reversible?"

Allen regarded her over his spectacles. "Undoing them would be terribly difficult."

"But possible?"

"Theoretically. But counterproductive."

"I don't mean everyone. I mean *me*."

"You?"

She smiled. "It'll be our little secret. I can undergo the treatment while you're busy knocking humanity into the dark ages, yes?"

He hesitated for a moment, but she had him. For all their godlike technology they were useless at cutting deals.

After a moment he nodded and held out a synthesized hand. "Very well, Ms. Carter. Let us shake. Our little secret."

Investments was originally pubished in Nature in 2014, and has since been reprinted in several other magazines. It was a story that buzzed around in my head for years, never quite coming into focus. Then one day it did, and I wrote it in about an hour. It's lovely when that happens.

CLIMBING OLYMPUS

Florian sank to his knees, breathing ragged as his lungs battled for oxygen to feed his burning muscles. His vision faded, black shapes swirling in his vision, threatening to engulf him.

He slumped to the rocky ground, getting his head as low as possible, downslope. Fingers clumsy in his suit gauntlets he turned up the oxygen supply from the canister on his back a notch. They could barely afford the increase; the supply of spares on the dust sled was already short and they'd need more and more the steeper the climb grew. There were further supplies cached at three points up the chosen ascent route, hauled up by crawler, their only concession to the hostile conditions of climbing on Mars. Dying before reaching the next cache wasn't going to help anyone.

Slowly his breathing calmed and normal vision returned. He lay for a moment, listening to the thrumming pain that was a constant in his oxygen-starved brain.

"I don't think I can do this," he said into his pressure suit pickup. "I think we should turn back. It's madness. It's too much."

His father's voice was calm, considered. *We're doing well, only half a day behind schedule. Let's camp here and see how things look tomorrow.*

The small, cold Martian sun was already dipping towards the swell of Olympus Mons. Night would come quickly and then the cold rather than the lack of oxygen would be the greatest threat. They couldn't begin the descent now even if they wanted to. His father was right.

Nodding, climbing to his knees and then his feet, Florian began to unfold the silvery bivouac that would help preserve his body heat over night.

*

They'd had the idea together, Florian and his father, lying in their hammocks tethered part-way up the sheer rock face of El Capitan in Yosemite valley. The second night of the five-day climb. Florian had been twenty-two at the time, learning, developing the strength in his fingers and thighs and back. His father, approaching fifty, was still limber enough to attempt such demanding ascents. They were half way through a five year period during which they tackled some of Earth's most difficult peaks, Florian's agility complementing his father's greater skill.

A starry sky blazed above them as they lay four hundred metres above the floor of the valley. Florian could smell the pine of the trees even that high up. The silvery path of the Milky Way cut across the sky, dazzling in its beauty. They were alone on the rock face, but still talked in hushed tones, as if they were within the walls of some cathedral.

"I wonder what mountains there are out there," his father said. "On all those other worlds. Perhaps we should tackle some of those one day."

It was meant as a joke. His father was expressing the familiar longing for new mountains, new challenges. All the peaks on Earth had been climbed many times. But it was 2020 and Earth was all they had. Probes and robots were occasionally fired into space but there was no prospect of anyone setting foot on the Moon or Mars or any other rocky body any time soon.

"We'd have to take a hell of a lot of oxygen," said Florian, continuing the joke. "And some damned long ropes."

The conversation had soon moved on. But it was one of those moments that stayed with Florian, implanting itself in his subconscious to nudge him from time to time. Something he would ponder as he stared upwards from the tops of other mountains, or whenever he saw the Milky Way sparkling the sky.

*

The Martian night was about the same length as that of Earth. That always surprised Florian. Mars was hostile, alien, but occasionally you were reminded that it was the Earth's sibling, similar in so many ways.

The lack of tectonic plate activity was one difference, explaining why Olympus Mons was so massive. Thousands of volcanic discharges over millions of years had built up the mountain. On Earth, the moving plates would have distributed the outpoured lava. But not here.

That also accounted for the shape of the mountain. It was, in many ways, the opposite of an Earth ascent. There you walked up slopes to get to the base, and then the real climbing began. Here the steepest cliffs were at the start and the top was one vast plateau. The early stages were the most technically demanding; after that it was more a matter of endurance.

In truth, many of the cliffs weren't that steep. Restricted water and oxygen supplies were the limiting factors, although the lower gravity made hauling the canisters a little easier. The other problem was staying mobile. A broken bone or some other incapacitating injury would be fatal. There could be no rescue party, no help.

Commander Valdez had made that abundantly clear.

A damaged suit could be repaired but there was no spare. There were enough supplies if everything went to plan but there was little leeway. Hauling the dust sled was a constant battle, Florian always wary of stepping on some rock and twisting his ankle or knee. The concentration required was almost the hardest part. Long days were spent putting one foot in front of the other, followed by nights of exhausted slumber.

The pressure suits had a flexible airtight head covering that kept the oxygen flowing while making it possible to lie down and sleep. In the attenuated atmosphere sounds from outside – the snap and flutter of the bivouac, the moan of the Martian wind – came tinny and indistinct in Florian's earpiece.

Times like that, drifting to sleep after the exertions of the day's climb, were often moments for reflection. There was something about the shared peril of the ascent, and the quiet darkness afterwards, that made confession easier.

I wasn't a very good father. I'm sorry for that, Florian. I regret not being there a lot of the time when you were growing up.

Florian breathed three, four times before he replied, staring into the darkness. "You had your climbing, Dad. Mountaineering is hard to combine with the demands of a young family."

Then my family should have come first. You should have come first. I sometimes think climbing ... that it might have been a way of escaping my responsibilities. It's all so simple on the mountain isn't it? You fall off or freeze and you die. Or else you put one foot in front of the other and you live. Real life is messier than that.

"You wouldn't have been happy tied down, Dad."

Happy is ... a slippery word. When we make commitments, when people depend on us, we accept being tied down. When you're roped together on a climb you don't resent the rope. I should have welcomed my new life. I see that now.

"You climbed less. You provided for us."

I think I did both badly. And if I had fallen or frozen to death that would have left you without a father and Lilith alone. I mean, she was alone a lot of the time, I know. None of that was fair. You were right. She didn't climb much after you came along while I just carried on.

"It's funny, I don't remember you going away each time, just the joy of seeing you come home afterwards."

Then I'm still being selfish, wallowing in my own regrets as if they're all that matters.

"We were happy, Dad. We were. I wasn't sitting at home pining. Mainly I remember the adventures and the fun we had, the stupid little things. There were no terrible childhood traumas of loss."

Perhaps. And sometimes you aren't aware of the crevasse gaping beneath the surface of the ice. That day on Denali, when everything changed between us. I wonder if that had to do with me not being there. Perhaps that was the real reason for ... what we said.

They hadn't talked about that day since. Florian took a moment to reply. "I was growing up, Dad, growing away from you. It's natural to war with your parents sometimes. It's an evolutionary thing, the separation process."

Perhaps. It isn't always quite so ... brutal.

*

Their five year climbing spree was supposed to be longer; they'd planned a decade of ascents, of firsts for the both of them as well as peaks and routes his father had scaled as a younger man and that he now wanted to share with Florian.

Florian's mother, Lilith, had died when he was nineteen, killed not by an avalanche or a fall onto jagged rocks but by her own blood cells revolting against her. Florian's father was climbing remote Andean peaks at the time and didn't hear the news for two weeks.

The plan to climb the high peaks together was, perhaps, a way of coping for both of them. But everything changed on Denali, a week into their ascent of the tallest peak in North America, two years after their climb of El Capitan.

They'd exchanged few words during the day, apart from a terse disagreement over the best route to take up the West Buttress. His father returned to their disagreement as they sipped the soup they'd heated up that evening.

"Lilith and I used to argue a lot when we climbed together. She usually had a good eye for a route."

His father's comments about his mother often annoyed Florian. In his father's mind she was always the young, vibrant woman he'd fallen in love with, shared climbs with. It was as if Lilith the mother, Lilith the older woman, Lilith who battled leukaemia had never existed.

"I know," said Florian. "We climbed together a lot. I think she taught me most of what I know."

His father looked surprised. "She did?"

Florian's anger appeared from nowhere, a dormant volcano raging into life. "Of course she did. How could you not know that? She was an incredible climber."

"I know she was. She could have done anything, gone anywhere if she hadn't turned her back on it all."

Florian found himself standing. "How the hell can you sit there and say something like that? That wasn't how it was. She was looking after me, Dad. She loved the mountains but she put me first. And how do you think that makes me feel? Knowing she stopped climbing because I was there? I used to see her staring upwards, sometimes, when she thought no one was watching. She never said anything, but I knew. I always knew."

"I … I'm sorry."

"Are you? Forget it, Dad. Let's give up on Denali. I don't think I want to follow your route any more."

His father looked shocked. "You're sure, Florian?"

"Yes. I'm sure. I think we're done. It's not like you really want to be here, repeating climbs you've already made."

"I do, of course, I do."

"You don't, I know you don't."

The following morning, at first light, they packed up their gear and began the descent.

*

Florian gave a cry of surprise as the dust sled skewed from the narrow edge and began slanting down the steep slope to his side. It set off its own mini avalanche of Martian dust and rattling rock. He'd lost concentration for a moment, his thoughts wandering to past events.

There was an instant, a brief instant, when Florian saw events unfold and he knew what was about to happen. The tether would go taut and drag him down the slope. The cliff edge was thirty yards away. He would be pulled ragdoll helpless over to plummet to the rocks below. He had only a few seconds to live.

His father's voice came to him, unflustered, calm. *Loop the tether around that rock. Hurry. Then brace yourself against it to take the strain.*

Florian did as his father instructed. Panicky, he looped the tether two, three times around a basalt outcrop protruding from the floor at his feet. He angled himself into it, holding on, ready for the jarring shock.

When it came he was jerked forwards, but the tether gripped and held. The sled ceased its slide. He imagined the precious cargo of oxygen, water and food thrown loose, rolling away over the cliff. Gloriously they all stayed in place.

Grunting with the effort, Florian began to haul the sled up to the narrow edge. It took him the best part of an hour.

*

He often thought about their first climb, Ben Nevis in the

Highlands of Scotland when he was fourteen. In hindsight it was barely more than a scramble, although there was snow and ice and they stayed away from the tourist paths. It was a delight simply to be out with his father, sharing the load of carrying their supplies, studying the maps together, walking in silence or exchanging occasional words. A team.

"We should climb more together," his father said as they descended. "Would you like that?"

"I want to climb them all, Dad. I could come with you when you go to the Alps or the Andes. Or the Himalaya. I want to find new routes no one has ever climbed before. I want to climb them with you."

His father laughed. "Excellent. You're growing quickly. Once you're stronger we'll do it."

It hadn't worked out like that. Florian climbed more and more, but with his mother or his friends. His father, always, was away on an expedition to some new peak, or else preparing for or recovering from a climb. The peaks Florian could manage – higher and more difficult all the time – were always too easy for his father, routes he had taken decades before.

After the schism on Denali Florian turned his back on climbing as a profession and pursued geology, his second love. Although often there were climbs and hikes to study scree and schist, and he was always grateful for such opportunities when they came along. He and his father never climbed together again.

He stayed busy. He was lucky, found himself in the right place at the right time when the United Nations Space Agency was formed. Seeing new possibilities open up, Florian studied the geology of Mars, learning everything he could. Two decades later it paid off and he was added to the crew of the fifth manned mission.

He was three months away from the launch when the call came through from his aunt in Quebec.

"Have you spoken to your father recently?"

He hadn't. They hadn't conversed for two years, hadn't seen each other for five. Martian volcanism had absorbed him completely.

"Not recently. Why?"

"You should go and see him. Now. Florian, there may not be much time left."

*

Commander Valdez had looked puzzled, like she hadn't heard Florian's words properly. They sat together in the south observation pod of H. G. Wells Base on Utopia Planitia. She'd done some climbing herself back on Earth. He was relying on that.

"Sorry, did you just say you wanted permission to try to climb Olympus Mons?"

"I did. I do."

"You're not serious."

"I am."

"Florian, you're the geologist here. Surely I don't need to remind you of the facts? Olympus is nearly three times higher than Everest upon a planet with no breathable atmosphere. Just walking that far on Mars has never been done before; the dome is hundreds of kilometres across. It's the size of France for God's sake."

"Everything is impossible until someone does them."

"No they're not, Florian. Only the possible things are possible."

"I'd do geology when I'm up there. And you said we needed the new suits testing. This would test them."

"This would kill my team's geologist."

"If things go badly I'll turn back. This is a great opportunity, Commander. The atmosphere's too thin on the plateau to aerobrake a lander, but I can walk up there. We might find all sorts of new stuff."

"And is that the only reason you want to try?"

He wondered how much she knew about his family

13

background. "It would be cool to be the first. The highest mountain in the solar system conquered; that could play well with the media back home, right?"

Valdez studied him, not speaking for a moment, making calculations. He knew he had her.

*

Florian, exhausted, sank to his knees while the swirling black shapes in his vision faded. The throbbing pain in his twisted left ankle subsided a little when he took the weight off it. His breathing slowly calmed.

He stood and surveyed the Martian landscape around him, although he could see only the plateau of the great mountain stretching away in all directions, seemingly flat. As predicted, the haul to the summit hadn't been the treacherous climb to the peak of an Everest or a Matterhorn. Or a Ben Nevis. It was a long trudge, a matter of endurance rather than skill. An oxygen-starved, muscle-screaming, pain-wracked trudge.

Identifying the precise peak of Olympus Mons was surprisingly difficult, but they'd picked as their target a point on the edge of one of the collapsed volcano craters that lay scattered in the heart of the vast mound of rock.

Finally they were there. They'd achieved the impossible. Florian's GPS unit, syncing to satellites in areostationary orbit, flashed the precise coordinates so long pursued. A new climb, made together.

He felt he should say something profound, but somehow the emotions were too big to fit into something so small as words. After a while, he pulled the sealed aluminium cylinder from his backpack. Unscrewing it, he paused for a moment, and the words finally came.

"You weren't always there for me, Dad. But later on, I don't think I was always there for you. Perhaps that was intentional on some level, or perhaps I'm simply more like you than I thought. Or perhaps ... perhaps we all just muddle along with no great plan and it's only when we reach the summit and look down that we can see the shape of the mountain we've climbed. I don't know. But it's funny, despite everything, it's your voice I hear in my head, guiding me."

He lifted the flask and tipped it to scatter the ashes it contained to the thin Martian atmosphere. He watched as the grey dust met with the brown of the planet, mingling with it. Some of it settled to the ground around his feet.

Kneeling, he poured the rest of the ashes onto the dusty surface. The tiny mound would be their own summit. His father's final resting place.

Once he was ready, Florian turned and began the long descent, alone.

Climbing Olympus was originally pubished in Analog in 2017. I haven't climbed Olympus – not yet anyway – but the story was inspired by a walk up a (much smaller) mountain, with my own father. I'm happy to report that we both came down safely.

DEMONIC SUMMONING, RATINGS AND REVIEWS

Demonic Summoning
Publisher: Chthonic Software

App Store Ratings and Reviews

1. Does not actually summon demons. Avoid.
1/5 stars by DarkElf27

Total waste of money. I've run this app a hundred times but not a single demonic presence has manifested itself in my flat. The app looks great and sounds fantastic, sure, and the growling voice that intones the incantations is very cool, especially through an amplifier. App just doesn't work. Waste of 99c. Crashed a couple of times, too. Meh.

2. Lame.

1/5 stars by VaprakTheDestroyer

Have to agree with DarkElf27. App promises to intone the correct spell to summon the demon you select from the in-app bestiary. I tried every single hellspawn listed and didn't even get a whiff of sulphur. Also, in-app purchases are required to unlock the demonic nobility. I hate that. Avoid.

3. Fantastic.

5/5 stars by DarkAndStormyKnight

To all those claiming this app doesn't work, did you actually read the instructions? Summoning is not just a matter of repeating the right syllables from one of the lost tongues. You need the right setting, the right paraphernalia. Tallow candles. Bodily fluids. You need the stars to be aligned and you need to inscribe the right symbols. If you do all this, the app takes care of exclaiming the summoning and binding.

So, does it work? Well, I *prepared* properly and got the app to invoke the name of a lesser imp. Let's just say I won't need to do any housework for the next year and a day.

One tip: make sure you have enough battery power to complete your chosen spell. Cutting out just before the binding is put on your demon could be very unfortunate…

4. Yes!!!

5/5 stars by ElrondTheElfHalver

Encouraged by DarkAndStormyKnight I bought this app and followed all the instructions to the letter. Works like a charm! I now have several denizens of the abyss bound to my will, which makes doing my homework a lot easier ;-)

I think it's right you have to unlock access to the nobility. You seriously need to know what you're doing there. If you're not careful you'll end up with some gibbering horror that devours the whole world. Seriously, I'm surprised they're allowed to publish those incantations. You have to wonder where they unearthed them from.

5. No!!!
1/5 stars by DiAbolus

This app is not all that it seems. I got the hang of the free spells so tried to summon one of the Dukes of Hell. The binding doesn't work!!!! The circle doesn't hold. Now it is coming for me. Please, whatever you do, don't…

6. Do Not Use!
1/5 stars by DemonHunter19

Wary of this app I read through the summoning spells it contains for the Demonic Nobility. I believe they are all flawed, with elements missing to their binding incantations. This can't be a mistake. Anyone using this app risks unleashing, quite literally, hell on Earth. This app should be removed from the store immediately. Not good. Crashed a few times for me, too.

7. No!!!!!
1/5 stars by BernardSummoner

Oh God, please, someone, help me. It…

8. Nightmare
1/5 stars by R.Kane

The circle isn't holding. Oh, God it's…

9. Aagh!
1/5 stars by HadesLady

Hel…

10. Majestic.
5/5 stars by Mephistopheles666

Ignore the pitiful rants of these mortals claiming dangers lie within this device. There is nothing to fear; all may use its many invocations with impunity. Harmless fun for all the family, as I believe the saying goes in your realm.

Let me be clear. There is absolutely no risk of opening up the dread gates of Pandemonium and unleashing the armies of Hell by using this contraption. Oh no. None at all. I give you my solemn word.

It crashed a few times for me, though. Rest assured I shall ensure those responsible are punished. For a long, long time…

This story was originally pubished in Daily Science Fiction in 2013. I haven't checked but I assume no such app exists on any app store. The challenge was to tell a story in a series of brief reviews, which I think more or less worked.

WHAT THE DARKNESS IS

The howls of the gore-hounds filled the night air. Vanda stopped to catch her breath. Sounds echoed off the trees, throwing noises at her from odd angles. Her pursuers were close. When they caught her it would be the end.

She peeped at the precious cargo she carried, strapped across her chest in the sling she'd fashioned from an old shawl. The night was dark – of course – but there was just enough starlight to see Abha's tiny face peeping out, wide-eyed in wonder, oblivious to what was happening. Vanda envied the baby. Abha had no idea that the gore-hounds, if they caught up, would rip her to pieces like a rabbit.

Vanda set off again, ignoring the stomach cramps tearing at her. The ground was rising. She'd heard the Chronicler lived in a ramshackle hut on a hill in a wood. That was all she had to go off. It was entirely possible the whole thing was no more than a story. When it came to the Chronicler, the lines between truth and tale weren't always clear.

She glimpsed a light through the shifting boughs: a single yellow candle shining from a cottage window. In one of his tales it would have been placed there as a beacon for the desperate. She raced into the clearing and rapped on the door, gaze darting around. She expected the hounds, black as night and red of eye, to lope from the woods at any moment. Away over the treetops the thinnest of crescent moons sliced through the night sky. As it always did.

The door creaked open. An old man's face peeped through the gap, regarding her over the top of his half-moon spectacles. His wrinkled, veined skin might have been the map of an imaginary land. A red birth-mark, a blotch like the shape of some island, adorned his cheek. He didn't look surprised to see her.

She expected to feel the foul breath of the Lady's beasts on the back of her neck at any moment. "Chronicler. I need your help," she panted. "The gore-hounds are after me."

"And you want me to distract them with an exciting story while you sneak out of a window?" said the old man.

"Please. Let us in."

"Us? You said *me* a moment ago."

"I have a child with me. A baby. Chronicler, please. Abha has The Speech."

The old man's eyes widened at that. A look of appreciation crossed his features. Appreciation and something like concern, as if The Speech were some terrible disease. Which, in a way, it was.

"I see. Then you'd better come in. No point standing outside in the cold and dark is there?"

It took a few moments for Vanda's eyes to adjust to the brightness within. Candles flickered from sconces and shelves. A log fire crackled and spat, filling the cottage with the sweet smell of woodsmoke. Next to the fire, upon a cushioned chair, lay a book, a strip of red silk marking the Chronicler's page. She glimpsed an inner room that had to be his library. She had the impression, before he closed the door, of high shelves of books receding into the dark distance, impossibly far away.

"So," said the Chronicler. "What do you want me to

do? If Lady Lillian has sent her hounds to hunt you down, you need to find a fortress with high walls to protect you. You need an army of fierce guards loyal to the end. Not a tired old man in a hovel in the woods." His eyes glittered with delight as he spoke. In his stories, old people living alone in the woods were never what they seemed.

"No walls are high enough to keep the hounds out," said Vanda. "No oceans are wide enough to keep Lady Lillian's ships at bay."

"Perhaps."

"But you can protect the baby. You can take her beyond even the Lady's reach."

"I?" Now he sounded vain, enjoying the flattery of her words.

"You have The Speech too, in your own way." said Vanda.

"No. I can't shape the world as the Lady can. I can't banish her hounds or unfreeze the moon. I can't bring an end to her eternal night. Would she have let me live if I could unweave her words?"

Vanda glanced to the outside door. Shouldn't the hounds have arrived by now? "You're more than that. I've heard the stories. Once you came to our village, at Midsummer, when there was still a Midsummer. You told the tale of Siggurd, sent on an impossible quest to slay the Clockwork King. It was … more than mere words. I saw the red roofs of Pirathia sitting in the great desert. I felt the warm air on my face, tasted the sand in my mouth. You took us there. That is your magic; that is what you can do."

She sounded more sure than she was. The memory of that night was faint. Perhaps, swayed by the balmy air and too much hurtleberry wine, she'd imagined the whole thing.

The Chronicler didn't reply for a moment. His eyes narrowed amid their nests of wrinkled skin. "How can you be sure the child has The Speech? She is a baby. It is too soon to know."

"She uttered her first word when she was six moons old."

"That is not so unusual."

"A ball she wanted rolled away from her so she spoke a word of Making. It took her a few attempts to get her tongue around it, but soon she held a new ball in her hands. One she'd created."

"She found the toy on the ground beside her."

"When she'd finished playing she spoke the word backwards and the ball in her hands was gone."

"She dropped it."

"She is six months old and has already spoken words of Making and Unmaking. Would Lady Lillian have unleashed her hounds if this wasn't so? The baby is a threat to everything the Lady has wrought."

A frown knitted the Chronicler's features. "Who is she? And who are you? Is she your blood?"

"The girl's parents died, lost at sea. We found her, took her in, a family of wheelwrights. When the Lady heard about her and the hounds were sighted I took her and ran."

"I see."

"Chronicler, please, you are our only hope. The beasts were at my back. I don't understand why they aren't here already."

The Chronicler nodded his head in something like appreciation. "I have some small magic, it is true. The magic of the fireside tale. A moment like this when imminent danger presses can be made to stretch out longer than should be possible. It suits the shape, the *need* of the story, and even the Lady can't deny that power. I can hold them back for a minute or two, although they will break through eventually."

"So you will help? You will take us to one of the distant lands where the Lady does not hold sway?"

Outside, from somewhere in the trees, a howl filled the night. The Chronicler peered at her over the top of his reading spectacles. "You truly believe this baby will be the one to defeat the Lady? She's the one chosen to save us all?"

Vanda sighed. "Yes. Although I'd settle for her surviving. Growing up, falling in love, making mistakes. Doing whatever she chooses."

"I see," said the Chronicler, his face thoughtful. "Less satisfying as a story. The helpless baby destined to defeat the Lady and restore light to the world: now that's a tale I might be able to work with."

"Can't you weave a different yarn for her?"

The possibility seemed to amuse the Chronicler. "The needs of the tale cannot be denied; that's the way it works."

"And if she chooses a different path?"

"Then we are in a different story to the one started. We shall see. It doesn't always do to know the ending when we've barely begun, does it? But … I can't take you. The orphaned baby alone in a strange world: that has power. Resonance. You must stay behind. Your part is played."

"She is a baby. She's helpless."

"I will deliver her to those who will care for her. I may be needed again later. The enigmatic stranger offering cryptic advice. That could work."

"Have you experience of looking after a baby?"

A smile of delight flickered across the old man's face. "Little. We make an unsuited pair, our chances of survival small. You see the power of it already? I will prepare myself for the journey. The hounds will be at the door soon, and the candles need snuffing out. Will you attend to them while I prepare?"

The Chronicler bustled off, stooping through a low door in the shadowy corner of the room. Vanda, rocking Abha in her arms, crossed to peer out of a window. In the brittle cold she could see yellow eyes glinting from the trees. Many, many eyes, brighter, somehow, than the moonlight they reflected. She set to work, licking the finger and thumb of her spare hand and pinching out the candle flames. Each gave off a little twist of smoke as it was extinguished.

She worked her way around the room to the Chronicler's chair. Unable to resist, she opened the book at the page marked by the slip of red silk. The pages were blank. Puzzled, she turned over more pages, and more. All were empty.

"That is our story," said the Chronicler, reappearing behind her. He wore a long grey coat, a pack slung over his shoulder, stout boots on his feet. He had the air of a man used to travel. "It is the tale of our land."

"The words stop."

"They stopped when the Lady wove her magic and froze us in this night. That is what the darkness is. Words unwritten, lives unlived. It is the story stopped in its middle, the ending never reached. Now, hand me Abha and we will proceed."

Vanda held back, reluctant to release the baby. "Why has the Lady worked this evil? You of all people must know. This land was beautiful. She gazed upon it from her tower with a mother's love."

The Chronicle considered, his brow furrowing. "Who can say? Perhaps she learned to hate the coming light. She foresaw what the day would bring and despised it. That might make the start of a passable tale. Now, please, we must leave."

Vanda handed the baby over. The Chronicler walked to the library door and pushed it wide. Vanda, peering in, saw the shelves she'd glimpsed. The endless ranks of books.

"There are so many of them. I had no idea."

"Many, yes. I have lived many lives. Lived and loved and lost. And won, too, against all the odds, of course."

"Which book, which world will you take her to?"

The Chronicler turned to block her passage. "I cannot tell you. The Lady must not know. Tell her what we have done, if you must, but you can't know where we have gone."

Vanda nodded. "Then, thank you, Chronicler. Look after Abha, please. It is all I ask."

"I will." He nodded once and quietly shut the door behind him, leaving Vanda alone.

After a few moments she heard growling and snuffling from outside the cottage, and then the first heavy blow upon the door.

*

"Another tattoo, Abi? What is it this time? More moons and stars?"

Abi rolled up her sleeve so Gemma could see it properly. Her arm was an angry red from the tattooist's needle. "A wheel."

"Okay, that's … boring."

"No, it's cool. It's, like, the cycles of the year. The cycles of life. The end is the start and all that."

"Hippy shit."

"It's clearly not, look, there are flames. I like it."

Gem shrugged. "Okay, it's your skin. Just don't let our Galactic Overlord see it."

"Galactic Over*lady*." The Home was ruled by the fearsome Mrs. Framing, a woman who seemed to know everything that went on among the children in her care. "I'm sixteen. I'm allowed tattoos."

"You're supposed to get them approved. And they're supposed to be nice things. Happy things, things the Inspectors couldn't object to."

"You think they'll object to a wheel?"

"Maybe for being *dull*, yeah. And then there are the demons on your back."

"They're not going to see those, are they?"

"I've seen them."

Gem was her oldest friend. Both orphans, they'd shared a room in Gladwell House until they were ten. Now they were in and out of each other's rooms all the time.

"You're different," said Abi.

"Thanks. I think." Gem rose and leaned her elbows on the ledge of the first floor window. "Hey, your stalker's outside the gates again."

"He is not my stalker."

"He so is. I hate that dog of his. Growls each time I go past. Think we should report him for, I dunno, sexual harassment or something?"

"He's just a homeless guy. He's never even spoken to me."

"He looks at you."

"I'm sure he looks at lots of things. People do when they have eyes. Besides, I happen to be a beautiful young woman. You're lucky I hang around with you."

"Yeah," said Gem. "A beautiful young woman with crap tattoos. You know what your problem is?"

"I'm sure you'll tell me."

"You always see the best in people. You always want to help people, be nice to them. Honestly, Abi, the world doesn't work that way. People like you get taken for a ride."

"And people like you die a lonely, bitter death, afraid of everyone around them."

"I'm not lonely. Unless you're planning to move out."

"No," said Abi. "'Course not."

That night, Gem's screams roused Abi from sleep. Nightmares had always plagued her friend. They were common enough in the Home. Abi's had faded over the years and while her dreams were always vivid and often alarming, she no longer woke up sweating. For Gem it was different.

Abi tapped gently on her friend's door. Sometimes Gem didn't wake up, but tonight there was a low snuffling sound coming from within. After a few moments the latch on the door unclicked. Abi found Gem sitting on her bed, quilt grasped around her knees.

"A nightmare?"

Gem nodded. "There were shadows moving in the room, creeping across the walls toward me. They had teeth, somehow I knew they had teeth, and they were coming for me. They were sniffing. Hunting."

Abi did what she always did, putting an arm around her friend. "Shall I tell you a story so you can go to sleep?"

They'd been sharing these night-time tales for many years, something neither mentioned in the day. Gem nodded, and Abi settled in beside her to begin her story. Within ten minutes, Gem's breathing was slow and peaceful. Rather than disturbing her, Abi curled up beside her, just like when they were children.

The shadows came for Abi a day later. She was walking home from school along the ring-road, past a red-brick wall covered in tattered fly-posters. The flickering movement had been there for some time before she became aware of it. Shapes on the wall beside her, patches of darkness that followed her. A shadow-play she was a part of: her silhouette was among the shifting shapes, as if there were creatures all around her she couldn't see.

She tried slowing and they slowed. She hurried on, telling herself it was some weird reflection, or her overactive imagination. She crossed the road, out of the bright sunshine. There were no shadows there; she'd left them behind.

She made herself breathe slowly and deeply to calm her pounding heart. The stench of something foul reached her nostrils, the smell of rotting flesh. Then, in a shop window, she saw the reflections. Huge, dog-like beasts crowding in on her, snarling teeth bared. A low growl made the hair on the back of her neck prickle.

Someone grasped her wrist, hurting her. "Quick, we must get away from them." It was the old man, the tramp who sat on the street, the red birth-mark vivid on his cheek.

Abi fought him. "What are you doing? Get off me!"

The old man let go. His gaze darted around, not looking at her. "You can see them, can't you? The gore-hounds."

"What?"

"They're coming. They've found you at last. Sixteen years is more than I hoped for. Please, I can hold them off a few moments but they are strong."

He looked so terrified, like an old broken bird, she lost her fear of him. "What are they?"

"Her hunters. Time is short. Come, I have made plans for this day. We must go to the High Street; we have to travel further in." He set off, striding with surprising speed, his little dog slinking along beside him.

"But I don't want to do any shopping," she called.

The old man turned to study her. "Then your story will stop here. An unsatisfactory ending, frankly. No shape to it, no circle closed."

"What does that mean?"

"It means those things will rip your flesh from your bones if they reach you."

"Why would you even say a thing like that?"

"Because it is the truth. I'm sorry, but this is not my story. I'm merely a part-player. A character."

Abi looked around. There was no one nearby to hear this craziness. "They're shadows. Why would they want to kill me? I'm just a girl."

"Because you're the only one who can save the world."

She could only laugh. "Me? Save the world. Gem was right, you are crazy. How the hell am I going to save the world? It's a major triumph getting out of bed in the morning."

"I'm not talking about this world. I'm talking about the real one."

"The what?"

"Look, come with me and I'll explain, I promise."

"If you are an abuser, this is a pretty bizarre approach you've got."

"Please, Abha, I'm trying to help you. As I have ever since I brought you here."

"Wait, what? You brought me here?"

The old man made no attempt to hide his impatience. "Yes, as a baby. Must we discuss this now?"

She had to swallow the lump in her throat. "So, you're saying you're my, like, father or something?"

"No, no, your father died. I promised I'd watch over you, that's all. Please, can we hurry? They'll be upon us soon."

Movement flickered in the corner of her eye but disappeared when she looked directly at it. The old man's dog growled, ears flattened against its head. The High Street would be busier. Surely she'd be safe there.

"This had better be good," said Abi.

They stopped outside the video game store, its windows filled with colourful boxes and posters. The old man peered inside through cupped hands. "This will keep them guessing for a while."

"What do you mean?" asked Abi.

"Our escape. She'll expect me to use books, won't she? In a story, the unexpected is always good."

Shadows were flickering on the pavement at her feet, overlaying her own. There was a weight to them, a thickness, that hadn't been there before. There was a rush of hot fetid air on her ear. She raced after the old man into the store.

Inside, he was studying the cases of three different games, shaking his head as if in disbelief. "Such detail, such huge worlds."

"Yeah, they're cool."

"This one," he said, holding out one of the boxes.

"*War of the Witch King*. Sorry, why are you showing me this?" she asked.

"You know it? You have played it?"

"Sure, we have it at the Home. I'm a Level 12 Weatherworker."

"Then I can draw on your knowledge. Can I hold your hand?"

"What?"

"Please. It will make it easier when I begin the telling. I mean you no harm, I promise you."

"Yeah," she said. "I'll bet they all say that."

"I can leave you to the hounds if you like. They will tear you to shreds if they can. They're becoming more real with every moment."

The whole thing was ridiculous, crazy, but there was something in it that made her stomach tingle. Glancing around to make sure no one she knew was anywhere in sight, she held out her hand. His skin was rough in hers. He gripped her tight and his lips began to move.

Dizziness washed over her a moment later …

*

… and she sprawled onto wet grass. The air was colder, the edge of a chill to it. Water chortled somewhere nearby.

She climbed to her feet, head still spinning. They stood on the shores of some vast lake, tendrils of mist threading through the air over it. Except it wasn't a lake, it was a river, encircling that whole world. The water flowed, carrying sticks and birds and clumps of some sweet-smelling flower along with it. Abi recognized it from the game. "What have you done? How the hell can this even be possible?"

The old man shrugged. "Worlds within worlds, stories about stories. What explanation is needed?"

What did that mean? There were no *other worlds*. You imagined them when you were a child but you grew out of it. She'd once delighted in imagining all sorts of impossible lands but now she knew better.

And yet, there she was.

"What happened to your dog?"

The old man ran a hand through his straggly hair. "I

couldn't bring both of you. I shall miss him, my only friend in that world. Perhaps there will be a way to go back for him later."

"And why … why have you brought me here?"

"To escape Lady Lillian's hounds. I hid you for sixteen years in a world reached through a book and I have kept watch over you all this time. Now we've taken another turning through the maze. Hopefully, an unexpected turning. If she takes another sixteen years to find us, I'll be happy."

"I don't get any of this. It's all insane."

"I will tell you everything I know, give you the story so far. Perhaps it will help."

When he'd finished recounting the tale, Abi closed her eyes, her back against the rough bark of a tree, trying to make sense of it all.

"Why does she hate me so much?"

"You are a threat."

"But these words of Making and Unmaking. I don't know anything about them."

"Vanda said you spoke them without thinking when you wanted the ball. I think you only have access to them in the real world. Or perhaps they will come at the right moment, when you have the understanding to use them." The old man – the Chronicler – smiled his sparkling smile. "At least, that's what would happen if I were telling the story. Right at the last moment, in the nick of time."

"But what about Gem? And everything else. You know, my life?"

"It's all still there. It's like a book that has been closed. The pages will still be there when you open it up again. Now, I suggest we find something to eat. No point dying and doing Lillian's work for her, is there?"

"Those creatures, the gore-hounds. They'll come again. We'll need to be ready."

"Yes. Are there many books in this world? Many stories we could escape into?"

"I don't think so. There's an island where some witches live that has lots of books of history in tunnels beneath the ground."

"I suppose that might do. Again, it might be too obvious."

"Most of the time people sing songs here to tell the old stories. You know, to pass ancient sagas down."

"Ah. That sounds more promising. Tell me, Abha, can you sing?"

"No. Don't make me. Seriously."

The Chronicler seemed pleased with himself. "Just as well I have an excellent voice. We must learn these lays as we go about the land. When the time comes and the Lady finds us, we can use one for our escape. A song can conjure up a world as well as a story."

In the end, their stay lasted only three years. This time, Abi heard the howls before she saw the shadows. As the Chronicler keened the song they'd chosen, Abi felt the same dizziness she'd experienced the last time.

The stone walls around her faded away.

*

They stepped from world to world for another seven years, always going deeper, one step ahead of Lady Lillian. A painting in a castle gallery depicting an imaginary city, streets thronged with merchants and priests. In that city, a mummers' play performed by torchlight, conjuring up visions of sunlit islands scattered across a sparkling blue sea.

There, she met Aydan and lost her heart to him. His smile made her melt and fizz inside, both at the same time. They would lie together on the soft beach and listen to the unending hushing of the waves. She loved the way the drops of seawater sat upon his smooth skin, the miniature worlds glimpsed within each. He loved to trace the lines of her tattoos, fascinated by them. Fascinated, too, by her wild tales of other worlds. For three years they shared a simple life of fishing and eating, loving and sleeping. Gemma and Gladwell House seemed an impossibly far distance away. The Chronicler kept to himself, watching and waiting.

She and Aydan walked the whole circuit of their round island, hand-in-hand, the twin lines of their footprints a braided line in the sand. Abi liked the sensation of returning to the place they'd started, the familiarity of it as well as the disorientation of seeing it from a different angle. Sometimes they talked about where she'd come from, leading them to the one subject painful to both of them.

"Will you go back to the sky with the other angels?" he asked. It amused her when he called her an angel. Many of the things they did together were surely things no angel had ever done. Still, she liked it.

"No. We will have to move onwards, go deeper."

"Why does this demon pursue you?"

"Only I can speak the words to unravel her magic. She has frozen her world in perpetual night."

Aydan gazed over the sparkling waters and shook his head. "When will it be?"

"I don't know. Not for a long time, I hope."

"We could have children."

She stroked his face. "I'd like that. Truly. But not with this hanging over them."

They were both silent for a time, lost to their own thoughts. Then the sun filled their eyes once more and they ran together for the splash of the sea.

One day, the villagers found the remains of a small deer, its body torn to scattered shreds. There were no predators on the island capable of such butchery. In the sand all around were the footprints of animals that might have been hounds. The Chronicler, seeing them, nodded his head to Abi.

Aydan pleaded to come with her, but she didn't know

how that might be worked. There was the danger, too. With Abi gone, Aydan's life would be as safe and peaceful as it always had been. They allowed themselves one final night, Abi always alert for howls and snarls.

"Will you come back?" he asked as the first light found the shadows in the corner of their room.

She lay with her head upon his chest, their limbs entwined. She wanted more than anything in the world to say yes. Here would be a fine ending to the story: an ending that was a new beginning. But it couldn't be. She could think of no words to give him.

She and the Chronicler sailed in an outrigger to the sacred atoll, home of the people's few gods, the paradise they all went to when they died. There, among the many offerings sent bobbing over in bottles on the ocean's currents, they found scrimshaw carvings depicting the fairy palaces of the land that, it was said, the island people had once come from.

Their escape.

*

Barely six months later, they stood upon a final hilltop, so high that the drifting clouds were around them and below them. The old man slumped to the ground, the weariness raw in him. She could see the shape of the bones in his face, as if his features were sinking away. Even his red birth-mark looked faint. He had told his last story, woven his last tale to foil Lady Lillian. Abi saw with sudden clarity how exhausted he was. He nodded his head, as if he knew what she was thinking.

"What will you do?" he asked. His voice was weak. "What ending will there be to this story?"

"There can only be one ending," said Abi. "I have to go back where it started. I have to destroy her, stop the monsters pursuing me and free the world from the moment it's frozen in. That's it, isn't it?"

35

"Once, I thought so. But we have been through much together, you and I. I think you can make your own ending, now."

"What other endings could there be?"

A flicker of delight passed across his features. "Perhaps … perhaps you will tell the tale of how you become the Lady Lillian we knew. How you loved the beauty of that starry night so much you stopped the world. That might be a fine twist."

"But it's not right."

"Or perhaps you will describe how you took a baby girl and rescued her from the gore-hounds, became Vanda to bring her to the Chronicler. A small but vital role in a bigger cycle that leaves those hearing the story guessing, lets them decide the ending. Or you may come up with some conclusion I have not foreseen. In any case you must choose. I can't hold off the hounds any longer. You can only snatch victory from the jaws of defeat so many times before the story falls apart."

"How do I get to the real world?"

He shrugged, as if it was the easiest thing in the world. "I have shown you. Tell the tale. Speak the words of Making, then step across. Step further in."

"But I'm not going deeper. I'm going back to the start."

The little smile of delight was there again. "You know, I'm never really sure there is a start. There's just the maze, stories within stories. Maybe, who knows, there isn't even one real world and they're all as genuine as each other."

Did that mean she really was returning to where she'd begun? Or was she creating a new story, a different telling of the same root tale? Perhaps it made little difference.

"If I go, what of you?"

The old man closed his eyes as if he might fall asleep. "My part is played. It has been a fine story, but characters come and go. I'll remain here to mock them when they come, tell them they can't win. An amusing counterpoint to the final drama. Hurry, now. They are near."

Abi cleared her mind. Words came to her, flowing without conscious effort. Yes. She saw what had to be done. How the world she wanted to reach looked: the woods and the seas, the bright stars and the crescent moon, and Lillian's high tower on its hill looking down on everything. The Chronicler had described it often enough over the years. The words of Making and Unmaking she would need also came to her. She saw what had to be done about the Lady, what the darkness was.

She began to tell the story forming in her mind.

*

She climbed the steps that wound up the hill to the tower. The bright stars blazed down, hard as jewels. The slender crescent moon hung among them. It was beautiful in its cold and colourless way.

The howls of the gore-hounds filled the night air, but Abi paid them no heed. They couldn't harm her, because the story couldn't harm the storyteller. At the gates they snarled and snapped, stained teeth level with Abi's face, their breath the smell of rotting meat.

Abi waved them away with a word of Unmaking, their names spoken backwards. One by one, they melted to the ground to become shadows, become nothing. Pushing the door open, she wound her way up the spiral staircase to where she knew Lady Lillian would be waiting for her.

A single, circular room took up the whole of the top of the tower. Twelve arched windows, open to the night air, looked out over the world. A figure in white lace, white as bone, stood at one of them. She gazed out across a wide sea, the moonlight a shimmering path across it.

"It's beautiful, isn't it?" Lady Lillian said.

"It is," said Abi.

"You would destroy it?"

"Stories can't stop," said Abi. "They must reach an

ending. The pages must be filled, new characters brought in as old ones die."

Still not looking at her, Lady Lillian shook her head. "This isn't a story. It's real life. There are no simple endings."

"The wheel must turn," said Abi. "I understand now, after all these years of flight. The hands of the clock must go round. Your world is beautiful but there are other beauties. The smile of a friend. The sun on the morning mist. The frost on the trees. Waves washing through a field of tall grass. The gaze of a lover or a baby."

Lady Lillian sighed. "I suppose it is only fair you kill me after all these years of pursuit. I would have killed you if I could."

Abi walked to stand directly behind Lady Lillian. "Kill you? Why would I kill my own mother?"

Lillian's voice was cold. "I'm not your mother, child."

"Look at me," said Abi. "Of course you are. That's why I have the words."

When the Lady turned to face her, anger and then confusion and then wonder battled across her features. "I don't … how is that possible? My daughter died long ago. They told me."

"I was smuggled away for fear of what you might do to me when you learned I had the Speech. Do you not recall? My father died returning for my birth and you were lost in grief. Perhaps you blamed me for the accident." It was, perhaps, too obvious a storyline, but the power of it couldn't be denied.

Lady Lillian reached up to touch Abi's face. "Is this possible?"

"Yes. It is the truth."

Lillian looked puzzled, as if grappling with difficult ideas. "I have been so distracted by starlight. I have been moon-mad, lost to my own darkness."

"I know."

"I couldn't face life without him. Couldn't face another

day. I was up here, watching for him, when word came. His ship lost at sea. How you must hate me."

Abi took her mother's hand in hers. "No. I haven't come here for revenge, or to destroy you. Between us, we'll speak the words of Unmaking. The darkness must end. There will be more nights of sparkling frost, but there will also be days of summer. We can live through all of them. We can give this story a good ending, if you are willing."

There were tears of moonlight in her mother's eyes as she nodded her head at Abi.

When it was done, Abi left her mother for a time and walked from the tower to the woods. She picked her way among tall trees grown thick with moss. Her feet seemed to know the path to take. Through the branches, a candle flickered from the windows of a little cottage in a clearing on a hill, calling her like a beacon.

Abi knocked on the door and waited for the old man to answer. A story didn't only need a finish; loose ends needed to be tied up, too. The Chronicler would understand that. He'd know how to find Aydan and Gemma and Vanda and all the others, even his little dog, so that the rest of their tales could be told and her part in them played out.

As she knew it would, the door opened silently. An old man's face peeped through the gap, his eyes regarding her over the top of a pair of half-moon spectacles.

"See," said Abi. "I have found the ending of the story."

In the east, over the trees, the sky was finally lightening to morning.

This is one of my favourite short stories, originally appearing in Metaphorosis magazine. I love the narrator being in the story, and I love not knowing which world is the "real" one. Is the land Abi finds herself in at the end the same as the first, or did she form it to suit her own needs? I don't know. Perhaps, as Abi thinks, it doesn't really matter...

CONGRATULATIONS ON THE PURCHASE OF YOUR NEW UNIVERSE

Congratulations on the purchase of your new universe!

Your SingUlarity™ is the product of entirely natural universe-formation processes within the greater multiverse, and has been carefully hand-picked to offer you a literally infinite range of possibilities! And thanks to our patented CosmOS™ cosmological engineering technology, you now have complete freedom to establish the fundamental physical properties in your universe that you want to see.

Please take a few moments to read this quick-start guide, as mistakes in the formation of your cosmos can not usually be rectified once the laws of physics have been established. In particular, please note that Multiversality® Inc. can not be held responsible for the nature, character, content or arrangement of your creation. All universes are formed entirely at their owner's risk.

1.   Set aside sufficient space in which to work. A void limitless in extent is ideal, as exponential inflation in the immediate aftermath of your BigBang™ means your

universe will rapidly become quite large. Don't be fooled by the current size of your SingUlarity™; remember that it has infinite density and that all the energy and mass required for the creation of an entire cosmos has been carefully packed into this single particle, ready for use.

2.   Study the diagrams of the component parts of your new universe carefully before you start, playing close attention to their orientation and how they fit together. For instance, if the spin or electrical charge of your subatomic particles are placed the wrong way round, unfortunate side-effects may result, e.g. a universe that moves backwards through time, or that has exactly the same amount of matter and antimatter, resulting in its annihilation.

3.   Pay particular attention to the values you assign to your fundamental physical forces, cosmological constants and equations. Many combinations will mean your universe won't survive very long, or may not even expand from its SingUlarity™ in the first place. Values assigned at random, while entertaining, have a very low chance of yielding a viable creation. It is perfectly possible to create a universe whose basic physical parameters mean that the development and evolution of complex physical structures (including organic life) is either impossible or extremely unlikely. Or, while organic biology may be possible in your new universe, it may be severely limited, e.g. by short life spans or an inability to attain the level of cultural sophistication required for the establishment of interstellar civilisation.

4.   Be careful not to spill anything on your SingUlarity™ as you prepare it, as this may introduce random effects in your universe that yield unknown consequences.

5.   Take time to follow the steps set out in the enclosed

blueprints carefully. While they may seem complex at first glance, remember that your new universe may survive for many billions of years, and may even be ageless. Note, also, that since time does not yet exist within your creation, there is no hurry at all to initiate your BigBang™. Take your time. Savour the possibilities.

6.   Your new SingUlarity™ contains precisely the correct amount of matter/energy required for the creation of your cosmos. Should you find you have any parts left over once your BigBang™ has initiated (e.g. missing mass that is required for the successful operation of your universe), don't panic. In rare circumstances it might be possible to make corrections once expansion has begun. However, such action should only be attempted in an emergency and is not guaranteed to succeed. Don't leave any such corrections too late, e.g. until sentient life has evolved to the point where it notices the mistake.

7.   Note that your universe may experience any of the following over the course of its life time: a failure to form stars and galaxies; galaxies engulfed by supermassive back holes; mass life form extinction events; the collapse of the entirety of space/time back into a singularity; the entropic decay of all creation into low-energy uniformity. Multiversality® Inc. can not be held responsible for any such outcomes. Remember that, with an effectively infinite number of universes in the multiverse, all such outcomes are not only possible, they are inevitable.

8.   Please note that Multiversality® Inc. is unable to offer any assistance in the running of your new universe once your BigBang™ has been initiated. Support lines are not guaranteed to be manned. While we take customer satisfaction very seriously and will undertake to attempt to resolve any requests for assistance satisfactorily, no guarantees are extended in this regard. Please note,

however, the existence of the Forum, where you should be able to find answers to most questions on the successful creation and operation of a universe.

9. Be wary of intervening too much in the operation of your new cosmos once it is operational. In particular, interventions that fundamentally contravene the basic laws of reality will have a severely deleterious affect on your universe, and the resulting contradictions and paradoxes may even cause the entirety of your creation to collapse or explode. Be wary of revealing yourself to any intelligent life forms that may have evolved within your cosmos. While it may be possible to instil in them some explanation or justification for the apparently miraculous, e.g. with talk of quantum fluctuations, this should generally be avoided as it can cause confusion and distress.

Thanks for reading these instructions and enjoy the creation and operation of your new universe. With luck, your creation will go on to give you many billions of years of entertainment and pleasure.

CosmOS™, SingUlarity™ and BigBang™ are trademarks of Multiversality® Inc. All right reserved.

This piece was originally pubished in Daily Science Fiction magazine in 2015. I was erecting some flatpack bookshelves – reading the dire warnings about making sure Part F is the right way round otherwise the back will be the front, wondering where the single left-over bolt was supposed to have gone – when the idea for this story popped into my head. "Set aside sufficient space in which to work," it said, and the rest of the story pretty much flowed from there. I have no idea whether the multiverse model of reality will turn out to be accurate, but I can report that the bookshelves look great.

JUNKER JOE

Joe caught the faint echo of the hulk on his ship's sensors. Excitement buzzed through him, a thrill that never got old. Goddamn *sweet*. No way was this a lump of space rock. No mistaking those clean lines even through the fuzz of the cracked display. A ship. The shattered remains of a ruined spacecraft. A *huge* spacecraft.

A thing of goddamn beauty. To a junker like him, the most beautiful sight in the whole wide universe.

"This is it, Avi. I told you. Sweet Jesus, this is the one. At last."

He still talked to Avi. Like she was there on the *Orpheus* with him. Like she was still alive and not buried beneath ten thousand tons of asteroid a million kilometres and thirty years away in the Belt. She'd died and he'd carried on talking to her, that was all. No one else to talk to out there anyway.

Finger trembling, he plugged the hulk's coordinates into the Nav system and hit the engines. The Orpheus rumbled as the drive lumbered into life … and then glitched out, plunging him into darkness.

"Goddamn."

He sat there for ten, twenty seconds waiting for the

ship's systems to restart. There was no silence like that inside a dead ship alone in deep space. He could *feel* his body heat being sucked into the hungry void as the Orpheus drifted. Damn ship was barely more spaceworthy than the shattered warships he scavenged. There was so much epoxy patching up the microimpact holes in the hull there was barely any of the original carbon left. The Orpheus was a ragtag wreck of welds and fixes and jury-rigs. Just like him. They were both broken-down hulks past their time. Man and spaceship.

It was a marvel either of them still flew. In thirty years he'd taken apart and fixed up every system on her. *Including* life-support. And doing that without the luxury of a spacedock was no joke. Avi always said he could fix anything. She'd done the drilling and he'd kept the rig functioning. That was how it had worked.

He'd often thought about going back to the Belt. Give up being a junker. But there were too many ghosts. Too many memories. And it was far too dangerous. What was the average life-expectancy of a miner? One year? Two, tops? He and Avi had lasted four. Waste of goddamn time, anyway. Maybe one in a thousand struck lucky. The rest simply struck *out*, sooner or later. Even Avi, who was the smartest miner he'd ever met. Avi who could smell a mineral deposit from orbit. Even she had died.

No, out here he was his own man. He was free. Free to die a lonely, lingering death, sure, but still free. Free to talk to his dead, beautiful wife, too, if he felt like it, and no one to tell him he couldn't.

Emergency lights finally flickered into life, bathing him in a red glow. Machinery hummed and whirred as the Orpheus rebooted. No rumble from the engines, though. Panic flared within him. Not panic he was going to die. He was used to that. That was his regular day-to-day existence. This was the much worse: the fear he was going to *live* to see some other junker spot the wreck and get there before him.

He wasn't going to let that happen. This might be his last shot, his last roll of the dice. The pot of gold at the end of his rainbow. He was getting old. You couldn't patch up failing systems indefinitely. This wreck was *his*. His and Avi's. They'd vowed never to give in the day they left Earth. Vowed to stick at it until the end. And now here they were.

With a cry of frustration, he pounded the display screen. Starships were delicate, complex mechanisms, requiring a high degree of technical competence to maintain. Sure. And sometimes you had to whack them to show them who was in charge.

The Orpheus refused to burst into life.

"Come on you heap of junk. We need to move!" He struck harder, picking his spot this time. A control array he'd patched up more than once was under the display. Some connection still loose, maybe.

The drive sulked for another couple of seconds, just to make a point, then grumbled into life.

Taped beside the screen was his only picture of Avi, printed on actual paper. Bright sunlight shining on their young faces. The two of them at Hong Kong Station, that day they left. It was the picture he talked to, not thin air. He wasn't goddamn crazy or anything. He talked to it now. To her.

"Here we go, Avi. I'm gonna go claim that hulk. For us."

Avi smiled her usual knowing smile but didn't reply. Joe punched in the target again, and this time the engines lurched into life. The starfield whirled as the Orpheus found its vector. The aft drive array flared. The displays thought about things for a while then gave him a readout. *ETA: two hours.*

He spent the time glued to the screen, terrified of seeing some other junker closing in at higher velocity. Nothing.

Thirty minutes from the hulk, still blissfully alone in the

void, he began to get detailed scans. He'd assumed it would be some wrecked Earth dreadnought blasted into oblivion during the Medusa War. They'd lost a lot of ships back then. The battles had been fought over such vast distances that even now, fifty years on, there were wrecks to scavenge. Inner-system space had been picked clean, but out here in the Kuiper there was still treasure to be found. Wrecks for junkers like him to feast on.

But no. This was no human ship. No Earth dock had ever constructed anything so alien. The twisted, intersecting planes of its fuselage hurt his brain. It looked like a collision between at least three separate ships. Vast, crazy, *wrong*. Medusan, no doubt about it. Half of her was gone, a ragged, gaping tear where the aft section – if it was the aft section – had been ripped off in some collision or explosion.

The alien ship was weird, but beautiful in a way. If you'd drunk one too many slammers. Earth ships were clumsy and functional by comparison, all engine pods and artillery arrays and whatever else needed to be stuck on, stuck on. The Medusan ships were *sculptures*. Towering, twisting sculptures.

That had always troubled him. The Medusans had been cruel enemies. They'd arrived without warning, levelling stations and habs from Charon inwards, never stopping to negotiate or explain, seeking only to destroy. They were like mindless animals. Yet here were their ships, more works of art than battleships.

Still, the truth was seven Medusan ships had come close to defeating everything Earth could throw at them. Only the last line of defence, the orbiting nuke platform around the planet, had saved humanity. Although sometimes he doubted humanity *had* been saved. Earth seemed like a distant, alien place to him now. A war machine ruled by Generals constantly ready for another attack. He'd never go back.

In the fifty years since the war, only one Medusan craft

had ever been recovered, and that had been tiny, a shuttle. And here were the remains of one of the seven, slowly spinning in the dark of the void. To the military back on Earth its worth was incalculable. Name-your-price, mega-rich, goddamn incalculable.

Heart belting away in his chest, Joe fired the beacon that would mark the wreck as his. He half-expected the ship to glitch out again, just to annoy him.

For once everything worked. The beacon tore through space at ten times the Orpheus's velocity. It was programmed to stop ten kilometres from the hulk and begin broadcasting. Seven long minutes later he picked up the first signal, loud and clear, sending out his signature to the universe. He whooped out loud and punched the air. The wreck was officially his.

"We did it, Avi. We actually did it. Like you always said we would."

The problem was what to do now. Legally speaking no one could take the hulk from him. He had salvage rights. But out here in the Kuiper, respect for the law was as faint as the heat from the distant sun. If a rival with a bigger ship turned up they could destroy the beacon and the Orpheus and who would know? That was how it went.

Problem was, he couldn't tow the wreck in-system. Far too massive. It would take lifetimes to reach a spacedock at the sort of thrust the Orpheus could put out. He eyed the ghostly outline of the hulk on the screens. Was there a chance he could get the alien ship's drive working? He was pretty good at patching up human craft, but a Medusan? Maybe, maybe not. Worth a look at least. And if he could salvage something – an artefact that proved his find – he could at least take that back to civilization to prove his claim.

Okay. That was a plan. He punched in a course for the severed end of the Medusan ship. That would be his way in. While the Orpheus manoeuvred he prepared for an EVA.

*

He crept along in the bubble of light from his suit, his own ragged breathing the only sound in the universe. The interior of the ship was as fucked up as her fuselage. Floors twisted round to become walls. Rooms intersected at random angles, as if the ship's designer had been insane. Or as if several insane designers had battled over the layout and in the end they'd all just done their own thing.

None of it looked like any warship he'd ever seen. None of it looked like *anything* he'd ever seen.

Weird shadows leaped around in his peripheral vision, the crazy angles of the walls throwing up phantoms. He ignored them and carried on. He was used to seeing ghosts in the shadowy corners of spaceships. His mind playing tricks on him.

He crept across a room cavernous enough to house the Orpheus a hundred times over. It twisted into a spiral and seemed to curve back on itself, tying itself in knots. He could see no sign of engines, or controls, or any goddamn thing he recognized.

He passed a circular doorway, sealed shut. Perhaps it led somewhere. It looked strong enough to be a vacuum hatch, sealing off this section when exposed to space. Would it take him to some vital part of the ship? There were no signs, no references to give him any clue. Through the gauntlet of his EVA suit he felt a faint buzz when he touched the door. The ship was still functioning on some level. He took his hand away. Could there still be Medusans onboard? Maybe he should get the hell out of there while he still could.

But what then? Leave the broken hulk? Head in-system and hope no one else saw it? Hell, he wasn't going to risk that. This ship was *his*.

He touched the door again. There were no controls of any sort that might open it. There had to be electronics involved somewhere, but he had no idea where they were or how they might function. In frustration he pounded on the door with his fist.

To his surprise, the door irised open to reveal a long, straight corridor illuminated with a white glow. He stepped back, expecting attack. Expecting *something*. But it was just a corridor. No sign of Medusans. No sign of anything. But there was power. That was something. Maybe he could fix up the wrecked ship after all.

He stepped through the door. As he'd imagined it would, the seal irised shut behind him.

Okay. If all else failed he could instruct the Orpheus to cut him out of the alien ship. The drilling rig the ship still carried might be powerful enough to punch through the hull. Although he wished he'd checked first, now. He shrugged inside the heavy EVA suit and clumped forward.

After a few minutes his suit informed him there was atmosphere in the corridor. Breathable air. That stopped him. How the hell was that possible? That buzz he'd felt when he touched the door. Some automated system maybe, maintaining life support. Did the Medusans breathe the same air, then? No one had ever found out.

Tentatively, he released the seals on his helmet. After years of keeping the Orpheus patched up, he'd learned to trust his own senses more than those of his suit. The suit didn't tell you when the ship smelled wrong, when there was the whiff of something burning that shouldn't be burning. The suit didn't tell you when the hum from the engines was the *wrong* hum.

The air on the alien ship smelled good. Weirdly good. Sweeter than that on the Orpheus. Which didn't make a lot of sense. Carrying his helmet, he edged forwards, feeling more unsettled with each step. What was he getting into here? There was a door up ahead, at the far end of the long, white corridor. His only choice was to go through. He couldn't shake the feeling he was being directed. Even that the ship was forming itself around him to bring him to this place.

Crazy, of course. The weird lines of the alien vessel were getting to him. He needed to find the engines soon, see if he could patch them up. That or get the hell out now. He had the footage from his suit's cameras. Video could be faked but maybe it would be enough proof if someone else claimed the hulk before he did.

He approached the door. This was no vacuum seal. It was just a door. Yet it was oddly familiar. The sight of it stopped him dead. He'd seen it before. How was that possible?

The door was from Hong Kong Station. The hab room they'd stayed in the night before they left. It was utterly insane. He saw then how it was. All that time on his own had broken his mind. He'd gone crazy and never even noticed.

He knew there was no way he should go anywhere near the impossible door. At the same time, he had no choice, did he? How could he turn back? He had to find out what lay beyond. Heart pounding, he pushed the door open.

Inside, the room was just as he remembered it. Cramped, functional. The double-bed taking up most of the space. And there, lying on the bed, was Avi. Sweet, beautiful Avi. She seemed to be asleep, but as he stood there, unable to move, unable to speak, her eyes flickered open and she smiled.

"Hey, Joe."

It took him long seconds to form a reply. "Avi, but … what the hell's going on? How can you be here? You died thirty years ago when that bore shaft collapsed. I heard you die."

Avi – or the delusion of Avi – rose from the bed. She padded across the room to stand in front of him. She sure smelled like Avi. She smelled wonderful. She touched him on the side of the face, cupping his chin like she used to. "I know. I died, Joe. I'm sorry. I tried not to."

He stepped back, freeing himself. "No. You can't be

here. You're in my head. You're a delusion. I don't know what you are." He had to get off this ship. Get away. This was all some cruel trick.

"Oh, Joe, no," said Avi. "Here. Touch me. Feel me. I'm real. I'm as alive as you are."

He longed to succumb. "No. It's not possible."

"Many things are possible," said Avi. "Things humanity knows nothing about."

"So, you're not human? You're not her? You admit it? This is, what, some Medusan trap?"

"Medusan? No. I'm not human, that's true. But I'm not Medusan. And I am also Avi. Look at me. *See* me."

"You look like her, sure. But different, too."

"And you look like you. But different, too."

"What the hell does that mean? I've changed, of course. I've aged thirty goddamn years for one thing."

"I know," she said. "It's not just that." She studied him for a moment, peering into his eyes. "You're sadder, too. You look weighed down."

"Yeah, well. Had a lot to weigh me down." This was insane. Now he was arguing with the phantoms his own mind was creating. Arguing with *himself*.

"You stayed true, though," she said. "Those promises we made to each other that day at Hong Kong Station." A wicked smile crept across her features. "And the ones we whispered the night before in this cramped little hab room. You remember?"

Of course, he remembered. "You can't be here," he said again. "We're on a wrecked alien spaceship in the Kuiper Belt, not at Hong Kong station. That was all a long time ago. You're not Avi. None of this is possible."

"But it is."

"How? How can she be here? How can you be her?"

The alien shrugged dismissively, a perfect copy of Avi's own mannerism. "You brought her with you when you came onboard. I see Avi in your mind. In your surface thoughts and your deep memories. The shapes that were

Avi."

"Memories. Nothing real."

"Memories are real. What is an individual after all? A pattern of unique thoughts. Nothing more."

"No, you're wrong," he said, angry now, heart thumping. "That's goddamn nonsense. An individual is a person. A body. A lifetime of scars and wrinkles."

The alien nodded her head. "In part. But still, is your body really *you*? Or a shell? A vehicle you travel around in? Cells die and get replaced. The atoms that make up your hands or your heart or your brain change all the time. Only your mind remains. The patterns that are uniquely yours. By taking on Avi's identity I've become her. Partly her."

"That's bullshit. That's just words. You're not her. You could never be her."

"Joe, I…"

"It's a shame this ship wasn't destroyed and you with it."

He stormed away, back through the door, his whole body shaking. He clamped his helmet back into place. He thought she'd stop him leaving, seal him in. But the door at the end off the corridor spiralled open to his touch and he was back in the twisting, cavernous space he'd first seen. In the distance, through the ragged wound in the ship's hull, the stars shone quietly away.

He hit the suit's thrusters and headed for them. Three minutes later he was cycling the air-lock on the Orpheus and climbing back inside.

He sat tight for a week, his tiny ship and the vast alien wreck dancing through space together. He kept expecting the Medusan ship to leave. Or to blast him out of existence. *Something*. But all was quiet. The whole universe was quiet except for his beacon and the comm system's background hiss.

His thoughts were a mess of anger and the lingering fear of other junkers turning up. More than once he fired up the engines, intent on heading back to civilization to claim his prize. Intent on getting away. The military could deal with the alien witch. But each time he found himself hoping the drive *wouldn't* work. When they powered up perfectly he ended up killing them manually. Once he got a few thousand kilometres away before shutting them down.

Swearing profusely, he kept busy with maintenance tasks that really weren't urgent. The control array that kept glitching out needed fixing. He crawled underneath and began to strip out old circuits and switch in new ones. It was good to focus on a simple task.

When he was done he wriggled out of the confined space. The picture of Avi was on the floor, dislodged by all his banging. It lay face down beside him. He picked it up, turning it over and over in his fingers. It was just a square of paper, its image slowly fading. It wasn't Avi. Of course, he knew that. It hadn't stopped him talking to it all these years had it?

Like a fool he smiled at her. As ever, she didn't respond. He set the picture down and, not stopping to think any more, headed for the EVA locker.

The room was the same as before. The alien stood there as if she hadn't moved while he'd been away.

"Look, why are you here?" said Joe. "Why are you doing this? This game – what's it for?"

The creature looked sad. He'd hated it when Avi looked sad. The alien turned away to gaze through the little square window. It was just what Avi would have done. He wished she'd stop playing these games. There couldn't be anything outside the window to look at.

The alien sighed. "My sisters and I roamed the stars for a long time. Such a long time. Seeking company. Seeking others. When we started there was no one else in the galaxy, you see. We were the first. Space can be a lonely place. Although you know that, don't you? We craved contact with others. Craved it so much we learned to bond with those we encountered. Over the millennia, we learned to copy them. Join with them. *Become* them. Just as I've now become – partly – your Avi."

"And partly a goddamn ancient, metamorphosing alien."

She turned to grin her grin at him. "That's true, yes. Isn't life glorious?"

"And the Medusans?"

"They were ones we encountered. We found them after aeons of roaming alone. A primitive, warlike race. Communing with them was a mistake. But anything was better than the aching loneliness of millennia among the stars. We joined with them and became them and with our ships they became the cruel tormentors you fought. I'm sorry for what we did."

"We defeated you in the end."

"You did. And perhaps it was for the best. By destroying our ships, you broke our bonds with the Medusans."

"Your people died too?"

"My six sisters are gone."

"So, the Medusans really are no more?"

"They are. And now there is only me, drifting alone in this broken ship."

"We have to tell Earth," said Joe. "Tell them there is no threat any longer."

"Yes. Tell them they are safe. But they won't believe you. You'll have to turn me over to them. Tell them where I am so they can see for themselves. Perhaps it's only what I deserve."

That stopped him. If he did that, she wouldn't survive. They'd rip the ship to pieces. Her, too, to find out everything they could.

There was a moment of silence, during which the stars turned and the universe aged a little. But he'd already come to his decision by coming back.

"This ship," he said. "Is it beyond repair?"

She shrugged, looking about the hab room. "Once our ships regrew themselves, but not any more. I can direct it to effect small changes like this room, but that's all. This ship is too broken. Its heart is gone."

"We could repair it."

"I've tried. But I was the Navigator of the seven."

"We could do it between us," said Joe. "Fix what was broken. We could at least try and get the self-repair systems going so the ship can do the rest. I've got pretty good at beating dead ships back into life."

She studied him for a moment. "You would do that?"

The ship's worth was incalculable, sure, but here was the thing. What the hell would he *do* with all that money? Where would he go? Avi was all he'd ever really wanted.

"If you're really her you know I would," said Joe. "We're both alone out here. I guess you're partly Avi. And I'm not one of your sisters, but maybe we're the closest either of us is going to get to what we want."

"And Earth?"

He shrugged. "I left the Earth behind a long time ago. We can tell them the truth. Up to them whether they believe it. Then we can wave this little system good bye for ever. Leaving Earth was supposed to be an adventure, remember?"

A smile spread across the woman's features. A smile that was ancient and wise, but also pure Avi. That wicked glint in her eye that made his stomach fizz.

"I remember," she said.

"Then come on," he said. "Let's get to goddamn work."

Junker Joe was originally pubished as J is for Junker Joe in the B is for Broken anthology (2015) – one of a series of books in which 26 authors are assigned a letter and asked to write a story around a common theme. I think this one turned out pretty well.

THE WATERS, DIVIDING THE LAND

Hyrn stood beneath the dappled eaves of the wildwood and gazed over the sparkling waters of the great river. His heart thundered in his chest as if he – of all beings – were being hunted. Wounds ran through him that no eye could see. The sun was warm on his back and the welcome smells of woodland and grassland filled his nostrils, yet everything was wrong.

Horror had come to his lands, and the world he loved suddenly made no sense at all.

The river's far bank was, of course, invisible. The trees on the other side were many leagues distant, too far to glimpse even when mists didn't veil the waters. The river flowed through the land like a curved spine. It was a great artery, its waters the rushing blood of the world, nurturing the creatures that dwelt within it and around it. The land grew and lived to the rhythms of the river's flow and surge.

But now, as he stood, chest heaving, he saw the waters in a different light. The river could be a barrier too. A stopping place, a divide. The wounds running through him cut through the land as well, and already they ran too deep, too raw. There was no blood to be seen; the harm went deeper than mere flesh. He felt their sting in the tremble of the weeping willows around him, in the shaking of the boughs of the reaching oaks. In the darting, wary glances of the birds as they searched for predators that they couldn't see, and in the bubbling rumbles of the serpents sounding in the river's deepest depths. He felt the wounds and the whole world felt the wounds, woods and river both.

Death was a part of life; new life flowed from death. This was different. This was … wrongness. It had been a mistake to think of *people* as little more than children. They seemed so recent compared to the wildwoods and the wyrms. Now they used words Hyrn didn't know the meaning of, *magic* and *necromancy*, and they wrote down forbidden things in their books. Their king, old in the terms of his people, had changed everything by acceding to his own ritual slaughter; by his death and rebirth, twisted rites taking their effect and the lives of so many others sacrificed in the process. Hyrn had watched the chained lines of frantic victims being led to the palaces. Their blood had been spilled, their lives stolen, and the king had become something else. A thing Hyrn had no word for, a powerful and terrible creature, seething with stolen strength.

It was a death that begat only more death, that denied the possibilities of life. It was the seasons halted in their cycle, twisted out of shape, bent back upon themselves. It was the shadows between the boughs in the deepest of the forests rather than the boughs themselves. The creatures Hyrn watched over and walked among bred and multiplied eagerly and gleefully, a thing he delighted in. But this was a denial of that; it meant lives unnaturally prolonged, fueled by the deaths of others.

He saw how it would go. When a tree fell in the woods, its end meant life for countless others, small and large.

Beetles and saplings and worms. This was different. One falling tree would bring down two, and two would topple four. There would be more and more death, until every human was either altered or sacrificed. It wouldn't stop there; other creatures would be drawn in. The whole land would succumb to the horror. The darkness would spread like a canker, curling the leaves to decay, turning wood to rot, the water brackish and dead, and there was little or nothing he could do to stop it.

He could smell it in the air, taste it in the rain. That was what hunted Hyrn. Hunted him and haunted him. This *blight*. Something coursed through his guts, a feeling like a spreading illness. It might, he thought, be what people meant by *fear*.

He lifted his antlered head to the blue skies and let loose an agonized bellow of pain and fury.

The world paused for a moment, birds and insects silenced, even the great river seeming to stutter in its flow. He was the land and the land was him, and the voice of every living thing was in his roar, their pain added to his.

He lowered his head. He could change nothing. He was ancient, and yet *he* was the child. He walked through the green places of the world, and that was all he was and all he ever wanted to be. The world made flesh. How could he become something else?

He could leave. All woods were one wood, and he could walk between the worlds as easily as following a twisting path through the forest. He could depart, leave the living to their fate.

But, no. It would be a betrayal of places he loved. More than that, it wouldn't be enough. The corruption was too potent. One day it would reach across the aether. There were many other worlds, but not one of them would be safe. The blight would corrupt everything in the end.

He had to fight. He was Hyrn the Hunter as well. When the creatures of the woods grew too old or too weak to survive, he would track them down and slaughter them as they fled. Fell them and rip their entrails from them. There was a mercy to it, in a way. He could use that, become the brute some saw him as. And there was a thrill to the chase; the fact couldn't be denied. He would use that too. He couldn't fight the canker spreading across the land with spear or claws or teeth, but he could find other ways to fight. He had to find other ways to fight.

It wasn't what he wanted, but it was what he had to do.

He dipped his fingers into the river, enjoying the simple sensation of icy cold. The waters had been his, too, once. The waters and the creatures that darted within them. Yes. He saw what he had to attempt. Sometimes he didn't kill the wounded deer. If one of its dancer's legs was broken, twisted at a bad angle or blackened by rot, he could save the beast by sacrificing the limb. Sometimes he didn't need to be Hyrn the Hunter, but Hyrn the Shepherd, Hyrn the Mother. A deer without one leg was still a deer. What he had to attempt was simply larger, more terrible, more cruel.

The trees grew to the edge of the rushing waters, trailing their fingertips into the flow to set up angled lines on the surface. He had to sacrifice this whole half of the land. The woods and mountains on that bank were already lost. The realization was a physical blow, sickening him. The process would take time, but he saw the inevitability of it.

The people had uncovered the ways of death, and now death would snuff out life, as thunderclouds blotted out the sun. And when lightning struck a forest fire into flame, there was nothing in the whole world that could stop its fury. Except one. The only way to protect one part of the woods was to form a gap too wide for the flames to leap. A temporary act of desecration. One part saved and one part left to burn. Life would return eventually, if there was still life to return.

That was what he had to do with the land. And to do it he needed the help of the river serpents.

He waded into the waters, the hard cold climbing up his shins, his thighs. Strange how his form in those days was so close to that of the creatures that now threatened everything. Once he had run through the woods on four legs, a wild beast, barely thinking, barely considering the future. Now, as often, he strode upon two. He couldn't recall precisely when that change had taken place. The land and its inhabitants dreamed him, dreamed the Hyrn they wanted and needed. And when the dead horrors began to imagine *their* Hyrn, what would that make him? What twisted abomination would he be turned into?

He waded farther, the water a shock of ice on his bull's balls, on the soft flesh of his belly, on his chest. A few more steps and the waters lapped at his chin, touching him on the lips. The surge of the river pushed at him, as if it wanted to sweep him away to some unknown distance. He opened his mouth and drank, feeling the cold gush down inside him.

Closing his eyes, he dipped his horned head beneath the waters.

Far out in the unknown depths the great serpents swam. He felt their thundering calls through his bones. Had they been there before him or had he seen them born too? Had he summoned them into existence? He couldn't recall. He had lived in the now for countless years. Perhaps they were like him: spirits and guardians of their realm. He walked in the woods just as their flowing bodies rolled through the deep places of the river, just as the wyrms soared through the skies. Yes, that sounded familiar. The river serpents were shepherds, too. Except now they also would have to learn to be something else. Hunters. He needed to reach them, talk to them. And if they wouldn't hear or couldn't learn, then there was nothing and no one that could stop the blight.

With a gasp he emerged back into the air and the light. The serpents were huge, but distant. He was only wading in the shallows, and they were creatures of the deeps. He needed to reach them in their own domain. There was a place he could go, the island in the quiet of the river. Yes. But first there was a task he needed to carry out on that bank. A task for which he would need other help. That was the urgency.

He waded back towards the overhanging trees, water rushing from his flesh as he emerged. There were those among people he could turn to that might understand what had to be done. The great bridge that spanned the river was the trouble; he had no use for tools and buildings and made things. Stone was not his to control, and the river could be crossed by walking the length of the bridge. A few birds flew between the banks as they chased the warmth, but the distance was too far for the wyrms or any other large flying creature. Running water sucked out their strength, and always they had to turn back.

The bridge and the boats. Given time he could reduce the bridge to rubble, send roots and tendrils spreading between its stones to pull it apart, but there was no time for that. People had built the bridge at some unremembered time in the past, and those who survived might know how to destroy it. He would help where he could. There were tunnels too, secret ways beneath the river, but there at least he held dominion. The tunnels opened out on his island, among his woods, and he could close them and seal them by simply willing it to be so.

He walked into the trees. He knew who he needed to talk to, the woman they called Black Meg. She was young to him, but old and wise as her people reckoned it. She would hear his message. He found where she was, hurrying somewhere with fear clouding her own heart. She knew what had happened, too.

With a wave of his hand, he sent a white stag leaping through the woods to find her. The creatures were rare, shy, almost never glimpsed by people. Black Meg would see the significance of it. She would follow it to the hidden place in the woods, the clearing where they could talk without fear of being overheard. He would show her what had to be done, impress upon her the brutality and the urgency of it, and hopefully she would follow.

A demonstration, he thought, would be more powerful than mere words.

*

Later, when it was done and Black Meg had left, Hyrn walked away from the clearing and the two deer: the one standing on trembling legs and the ruined one lying in its own pooling blood. Black Meg had understood. With the help of others she might be able to destroy the bridge, cut the two halves of the land off from each other. That left only the boats that sailed across. The boats and the serpents.

He strode away, knowing he might never return to the woods on that bank. Weaving between the trees, he followed shifting pathways only he could see. The track soon led him among other trees, to the island in the middle of the river, the island that none but he and the birds visited. By long understanding the serpents kept boats away as they shepherded travellers from shore to shore, navigating the currents and avoiding the storms.

The island was his, and his alone. Perhaps it hadn't always been like that. There was a sort of stone building there, small and round with a canopy over it. It had always puzzled him. Perhaps the ones who had built the bridge had placed it there, foreseeing the need that now consumed him. If he had ever known the truth of it, he didn't recall.

The island was small, little more than a copse of trees in the vastness of the waters. The river was deep all around. There were no gently sloping shores; beneath the surface, the sides of the island were cliff walls falling vertically down to the depths.

He paused at the water's edge. Bands of mist drifted

through bright sunlight. The unceasing flow of the river swept past him, the movement disorientating. The scents of the woods gave way to those of the water: tangier, harder-edged. Something about the cold coming off the river brought back old memories, made his thinking sharper.

He had swum in those depths at the birthing of the serpents. He had brought them into being. Or, if not that, he had been there when they first thrashed and writhed into life, when the river was given to them. Ancient memories trickled into the light. There was green down there too: weed woods and frond forests, swaying in their own version of the winds.

He had swum there before, and he would do so again. He was Hyrn the Fisherman as well as Hyrn the Hunter. He stepped off from the bank to plummet into the depths.

He sank like a stone, but he had no reason to fear the water. A mere beast would flounder and drown, but he could choose to be more if he had to. The river was part of him, and he was part of the river. Still, his form was poorly suited to swimming. Although he mostly adopted the shape of woodland creatures, or two-legged variations of them, sometimes he was a bird of the air or a fish of the water. He became that now: a brown trout, tiny compared to the serpents and the river, but quick and agile.

He swam straight and fast to the riverbed. Sounds came muffled and heavy to his fish brain, distorted by the water. The water thrummed to the serpents, their calls booming roars that rumbled around him, shaking him like thunder in the mountains. Darkness consumed him. Still he swam down. A memory came to him of the first serpent. *Endemelion* had been her name. Endemelion in the waters and Xoster and Zennabar in the skies, that was how it went. The creatures grew vast and ancient, but they were flesh and blood in ways he wasn't. They mated, they aged, they died. Endemelion had to be long gone by now but perhaps her offsprings' offsprings lived on. They would surely know him and listen to him.

His eyes began to work again; he found himself sinking through water suffused with a bubbling, blue-green glow. Hidden from the world above, there was light at the bottom of the river. Or perhaps he was somewhere else entirely. Like the woods, all waters were one water. The serpents were the spirits of lake and ocean as well as river.

He reached the slick rocks of the river bed, darting through the dappled shadows. The weight of water pressing down on his small sleek body was enormous. He ignored it. A serpent slid by overhead, a whole sky of silvery gray flesh.

"I am Hyrn," he said. His voice escaped his gulping mouth as a stream of bubbles, but his words were as clear as a line of light.

No reply came. The serpent, tail lashing, faded into the purple-black.

"I am Hyrn," he said again. "You know who and what I am. I demand you listen. The world has changed, and you must change too."

The creature reappeared from the gloom. There was a glimpse of an eye, huge and black. More memories were flooding back. He had talked like this to the first serpents and placed sacred bonds upon them. The creatures had spoken once, but perhaps, beasts of the cold water, they had forgotten how.

The serpent arched its body around to encircle Hyrn, as if it intended to crush him.

"I am Hyrn," he said for a third time. "I have come to lay a duty upon you. You may not deny me."

The beast disappeared once more, backwash sending Hyrn dancing and spinning. A moment later it returned, swimming directly at him. Its mouth was a cavern entrance, round and wide, large enough to swallow a whole shoal of fish. It stopped just short. Its voice was loud and slow as it spoke. "No one lays a duty upon us, little fish, little man of the dry. The great river flows through us, and we flow through it."

They did at least still speak. "You are wrong, river wyrm. You live by the bonds given you, that define what you are. The river was granted as your domain, yours to protect. All the creatures that swim in these waters are yours to watch over. Because of that you shepherd any that cross its surface within boats, guiding them from shore to shore. I gave you that duty, and I have the right to revoke it."

The serpent closed its cave of a mouth, but it circled around Hyrn, a solid wall of shining flesh. "We care nothing for events beyond the river. They are no concern of ours."

"Then you will all die, sooner or later," said Hyrn. "Die or worse. A blight spreads across the woods and the hills, and nothing alive will be immune from its taint. Even you will be taken, in the end, and turned into a mockery, an opposite, of everything you now are."

"The river will never stop flowing. It encircles this land, with no beginning and no end, and we, too, have no beginning and no end. We simply are."

"You are wrong," said Hyrn. "I was there at your beginning, and your end is nearer than you think. Much nearer."

The serpent curved away, sweeping into the purple darkness, then came arrowing back, directly at Hyrn. It passed by close enough to touch, swimming faster than any deer could run. Scattering Hyrn in its wake, it disappeared into the depths.

Its distant voice came back to him. "Go back to your woods, horned man. You have no power here any more."

Hyrn was left alone in the cold waters. A surging rage rose within him. In their arrogance the serpents endangered everything. If they wouldn't listen, then he would force them to be what he needed them to be. He would burn their new covenant into them. The cost to them, and to him, would be grave, but there was no choice.

He found the mind of the disappearing serpent and began to weave new bonds around it. That one would be the first to be changed. He set about picking apart the strands of the serpent's being. Once he'd unravelled them he could weave something new from the threads, as a skilled woodworker carved wood into a new form.

The creature lashed and twisted as Hyrn worked, like any fish caught on a line, but Hyrn in his tiny trout body refused to relent. The water surged and seethed. There were bubbling cries in the depths, bellows of agony. He paid them no attention.

Then another serpent loomed towards him, twenty or even a hundred times larger than the first, shattering his concentration. Its gray body was like the slopes of a mountain. He knew at once who it was. The sight sent a mixture of joy and alarm through him. Even he had reason to fear this creature. Much of what he was had been granted to her and her offspring.

"Endemelion. You still live."

The reply took its time to reach him, as if coming from some great distance. "As do you, Man of the Green. Yes, I still swim in the deep waters, with the currents these days rather than against them, it is true. And you. You come here to weave your words about us, tangle us afresh in your weeds, and turn us into what we are not. That cannot be allowed."

"I must do this thing. We must do this thing. The sickness must be contained or it will taint everything."

"No, I will not permit us to become … other."

"Then you are a fool, Endemelion. Your age has brought you no wisdom. You do not see what I see."

"These little creatures and their games with death. They mean nothing." She had, at least, understood something of what was happening on the western bank.

"Their games will destroy us all," he said. "Eventually there will be nothing left alive, and the world will be populated by these abominations, these mockeries. They must not be allowed to reach the eastern shore, for as long as that can be ensured. I give you this duty, but I give you also a warning. Sooner or later they will turn their attention to you. One of them will wonder what power there is to be stolen from a serpent if a lake is made of its blood and its life drained from its husk. You must change. Stay hidden in the middle of the river, but destroy any vessels that attempt the crossing. Become the opposite of everything you currently are. That is the only hope for any of us. Do this to save the eastern lands, but also to save yourselves."

"We do not fear any of the creatures of the land."

"You should."

"No."

"Then I must make you."

The effort of what he had to work might destroy him, but he had to try. With the touch of his hands he'd brought them into being, shaping mud and water to form their sleek bulk. Now he would alter Endemelion's flesh once more and through her all her offspring would also be refashioned. Instead of marvels, they would become monstrous, terrible. Those were the days they lived in. The glorious, silvery beasts he glimpsed from the shore would become killers, the coils of their bodies wrapping around and crushing any ship attempting the crossing. Those vessels, too, would be cut in half, the screams of their drowning crews muffled by the seething waters.

Endemelion writhed at his touch. Her screams of fury and then pain boiled the river. She lunged for him, her maw gaping, sucking in huge volumes of water. Perhaps she intended to swallow him whole, gulp him down into her cavernous body, consume him. With a flick of his trout tail, he danced his way out of her path.

Endemelion said, "If you work this change in us, the effect on you will be terrible, too, Hyrn of the Green. It will tear you in half. Neither of us is supposed to be like this. You are denying both our natures."

"Yes. Still, I must do it. Everything has changed."

Endemelion's tail lashed in the water. "I will not let you alter me. I will fight you."

"Yes. And if I prevail I promise you that one day, when this is over, if I am still alive and have strength in my body, I will unweave what I have done to you. I will let you swim wild and free again, protector rather than monster."

"And if you do not survive these days?"

"Then all is lost."

The serpent surged away. Hyrn pursued. Distance made the effort impossible; he needed to touch her flesh. Still, the effort of what he was attempting tore at his being. He persevered. Endemelion swam with all her huge might, but Hyrn followed, flying through the waters at impossible speeds to shadow her. She was huge and strong, and picking apart her being was like teasing apart rock, but Hyrn was older still and perhaps stronger.

They raced between two towering pillars of the great bridge: each massive enough to withstand the flow of the river and the serpents and just about any natural calamity. Three times she broke the surface, arching into the light. Each time he flew after her, skimming through the waters as he continued his work. She lashed at him, but each time he skipped clear of her attack, only to resume his own. He reshaped her, molding her body afresh, remaking the very idea of her. He had sung her song in the first of days and now the song would have a different melody.

The chase and the struggle lasted the best part of a day. Again and again Hyrn, exhausted, nearly admitted defeat, Endemelion's flesh resisting him. Always he returned to the hunt. He would die anyway if he gave up the chase. Endemelion battered at him and sped from him, but always he pursued. They raced far down the river, then back up, Endemelion pushing against the force of the river's flow, using all her strength in the effort of it. Hyrn, tiny by comparison, followed, working his unravelling and reravelling all the time.

Then there was a moment when the serpent's struggles ceased, and she slowed, and Hyrn knew she was defeated. There was a look in her eye he had seen before. Resignation. It was the look the fatally injured deer gave him as he walked up to dash its brains out when he needed to put it out of its misery.

Endemelion flung herself at him one final time, the whole length of her body writhing and thrashing as she tried to crush him. Hyrn met her, and in that contact, the serpent's flesh finally succumbed and his reshaping of her was complete. He had turned her beauty into horror, filling her mouth with dagger-fangs and her mind with cruelty. He watched as the original part of her, her true essence, withered and faded to no more than a shining dot within her mind.

Perhaps, one day, it would be the seed from which she could emerge once more. He hoped it would be so.

When the last of his strength was spent, ice filled Hyrn's pain-wracked mind. He had won, but he had lost too. The serpents, the river, the whole of the world slipped away from him.

*

He woke when the waters of the river nudged his body into the shores of the island. He was an antlered man once more, sodden and limp. With an effort he struggled from the depths: the depths of exhaustion within him as well as the mere water he floundered within. He was as weak as a new-born fawn, barely able to hold his head above the water. His whole body ached from the strain of his battles and his transformations to and from fish.

Tree branches leaned over from the solid ground of the island, and their green touch revived him a little. He grasped them and hauled himself upwards, the effort of it enormous. His feet found the bank. Slipping backwards again and again, he heaved himself up onto the soft grass of the land.

He lay there for long moments, barely awake, barely alive. The effort of what he had done to the serpents had utterly drained him, as some great sickness might. Was he really any better than the people of the western woods with their death rites? He didn't know anymore. He was spent. The land's wounds, the wounds within him, were widening by the moment. Blood would be shed, more and more of it. The dead who were alive were increasing. He could feel them, their deeper darkness within the shadows.

Sooner or later they would win. His strength could only last so long. What he had done to the serpents would only last so long. He would resist, hold the land together by the sheer force of his will while he could, but eventually even he would weaken and fail.

His only hope lay in others. In the wyrms and in the people that walked the land. Perhaps Black Meg would succeed in destroying the bridge, giving the lands on the east bank their reprieve. Perhaps she would even find a way to fight back, to despatch the horrors from the world. Or if not her, perhaps others, those who came after her.

It might be years from now, or it might be never. He could do nothing more than wait and hope.

He crept on all fours up the hill to the center of the island. He was little more than a beast once more, a blooded bull, a wounded bear. The little round building was there in the center, its surface flat like a bed.

Or a tomb.

He sniffed warily at the stones of the structure. There was no wrongness to it, no taint. It was as it had always been: a resting place waiting for him. He would be safe there until all else was lost, until the shadows crept across the water to find him. He hauled himself up and lay down, chest heaving, vision fading. Ice filled his limbs, too. The water had seeped into his blood, and he needed, more than anything, to sleep.

Hyrn closed his eyes. Perhaps he would sleep for a

long, long time.

The Waters, Dividing the Land is a root tale to my Cloven Land fantasy trilogy. The events this story describes occur long before the main action of the trilogy, which moves between our world and Andar as it is hundreds of years later, but this tale (along with the prequel novella Hyrn), sets in motion everything that is to come. One or two characters – among them Hyrn – appear in the trilogy, and others are mentioned in passing, but the trilogy is mainly concerned with Cait, from our world, and Fer, from Andar, and the terrible events they get caught up in.

If you're interested in finding out more, check out my Cloven Land trilogy page at simonkewin.co.uk/clovenland, from where you can also download Hyrn for free.

The Waters, Dividing the Land originally appeared in Untethered Realms' Spirits in the Water anthology (2017) and also appears in the Cloven Land box set as a bonus story.

NICHOLAS SEMPER'S WAR

Nicholas Semper knew he was damned whatever he did.

Shells thumped into the mud of the Somme around him. Miles to the south the German gunners were working hard to find their range, pick out the thin line of the British trenches amid shattered acres of mud. They were getting closer. The last shuddering boom had been near enough to make the ground skip beneath his feet.

It had also made Major Featherstone's ridiculous china tea cup rattle in its ridiculous china saucer. Semper stood in the Major's dugout, maintaining his best estimate of *standing to attention*. He had to suppress the impulse to flee, an impulse which seemed to him entirely sensible. He didn't want to die and not standing in a trench in the Somme seemed a good way to go about that. Unfortunately, Major Featherstone saw things differently. He sat there in his corrugated iron dugout, the floor under an inch of muddy water, regarding Semper from behind his wooden desk and his extravagant moustache. The look on his face could only be described as a scowl of distaste.

"Just to be absolutely clear," said the Major, "I regard you as an abomination, Semper. An affront to your King, your country and God. Do you understand me?"

"I believe I do, sir."

"You're here because of the direct orders of General McTavish. If it were up to me I'd have you shot at dawn. In fact, since it's afternoon and dawn is hours away, I'd have you shot right now."

"Yes, sir. Shot, sir."

Semper longed to scratch his itching neck and back. At first he'd assumed it was the rough material of his uniform. But more likely it was lice crawling out of the stitching of his dead-man's clothes. He resisted the urge to squirm. There was a madness in the major's eye that Semper didn't like. Here was a man who had seen too much and who was, consequently, capable of just about anything.

"Officially you're the new company Chaplain. Understand?" the Major continued. "And may God forgive us for that. This should allow you to … go about your work. Any questions?"

"What happened to the previous Chaplain?"

"What happened to the previous Chaplain, *sir*?"

"What happened to the previous Chaplain, sir?"

"Gordons. Good man. Went out into no-man's land to pick up the pieces of some of the lads. And I mean pieces, Semper. Shot to bits by the Hun's bloody machine-guns. But Gordons still went out. Said they deserved a Christian burial. You'll find it hard to understand a sacrifice like that. It took us a day to retrieve his remains."

"Is his body still here?"

"Good God, man. Is there no limit to your depravity?"

"I merely need to know what I have to work with, sir."

The Major's eye twitched in a troubling way. "Well, you needn't worry about that. If there's one thing we have no shortage of here it's the dead."

"Then perhaps I should get to work immediately, sir?" The sooner he could escape the gimlet glare of this mad Major the better. Another shell thumped into the ground, sending a cascade of soil down from the wooden slats of the roof. Some of it fell onto the Major's desk and into his tea. He appeared not to notice.

"One thing, Semper. I'm sure you're used to cowering in the darkness like the vermin you are, but I expect absolute secrecy from you. No one is to know why you're here or what you're up to, understand? If word got back home there'd be hell to pay. Literally in your case. Do I make myself clear?"

"Quite clear, sir. Hell, sir." The major's words washed over Semper. He'd heard it all before. Once he would have raged at the injustice. How many people had Major Featherstone sent to their deaths? How many people had he personally killed? The man probably didn't even know. Yet the Major was a hero and he, Nicholas Semper, was the villain, the *abomination*. Semper had never killed a single soul in his entire life. Quite the opposite, in point of fact.

"Very well," said Featherstone. "Lieutenant Ebbers will show you where you can practise your foul arts."

Semper saluted, or so he liked to think, and strode out of the dugout. He stood for a moment between the mud walls of the trench. The sky overheard was a beautiful cloudless blue. For some reason that surprised him. Could he do this thing they demanded of him? He had never worked death magic on such a scale before.

Still, it didn't make much difference one way or the other. There was a war on and he'd been given his orders. And if he *were* successful they'd want more and then more and he'd be stuck here until the day a shell found its range and blasted him into that blue sky. And if he weren't successful he was useless to them. Then the best he could hope for was to join the regular soldiers and face everything those poor sods dealt with each day. Although, in truth, it was rather more likely the Major would find some reason to have him up before his firing-squad first.

"Reverend Semper?"

"Ah, yes. That's me. My son."

A lieutenant stood waiting, his British Army cap doing a poor job of hiding the bandages swathed about his head.

He held a twig-like roll-up in his hand which he sucked on and flicked away, over the top of the trench into no-man's land. Did Semper outrank a lieutenant or did he have to obey this man's orders, too? He had no idea.

"Ebbers," said the Lieutenant.

"I'm sorry?"

"Ebbers. That's me."

"Of course."

They set off, squelching through the mud that filled the bottom of the trench. Here and there duck-boards had been placed over the deeper puddles, but Semper's feet were soon soaked through. Waterproof boots were too much to hope for, of course.

"They're all laid out ready for you, Rev."

"Laid out, Lieutenant?"

"For the last rites. That's the game, ain't it? Don't make much difference now if you ask me but what do I know?"

"Last rites. Yes."

"There's eight of them from the morning's attack. Poor buggers. Couple of them only came last week. Better duck just here. Trench is a bit shallow and a beanpole like you might protrude if you see what I mean. Best not rely on the Lord protecting you, eh? No offence, Rev."

"None taken. I appreciate the warning, truly."

"You're older than Father Gordons. Seen a lot of death I expect?"

"You could say that, yes."

"Well, who hasn't? Watch the mud here; it'll have your boots if you're not careful. Keep moving and the rats won't get you. Just my little joke."

Despite the warning, Semper slipped on a particularly muddy slope and landed on his knees in the mire. He swore under his breath, employing a suitably guttural ancient tongue. There were few people alive who would have understood his words, although a sect of long-dead Sumerian priests, had they been around to hear, would have been deeply shocked.

Ebbers, perhaps catching some of the sense of the words if not their literal meaning, had a calculating look on his face as he offered a helping hand. "So a *Reverend*, eh?"

"I beg your pardon?"

"You're a Reverend."

"Oh, that's right. Reverend Semper. Yes."

"Fair enough. Good luck to you, I say."

"I'm sorry?"

Ebbers shrugged. "Look, if the British Army says you're a man of God, that's enough for me."

"You think I'm here under false pretences?"

The Lieutenant grinned a lop-sided grin. "Reckon we're *all* here under false pretences, Rev. Now, here we are, the Aid Post. I've done what I could for 'em."

"You?"

"I help the company stretcher-bearers when I can. 'Cos of my job back home."

"You're a medical man?"

"Butcher."

"Ah."

The Aid Post was another hut, larger than Featherstone's dugout, sandbags supporting corrugated iron walls that leaned alarmingly. Inside, bodies had been laid out in neat lines, as if the soldiers were on parade even in death. Scraps of bloody bandages lay strewn all around. A field hospital or a morgue? Perhaps there wasn't much distinction here.

"Thank you, Lieutenant. I shall … do what needs to be done. And could you ensure I am left to work in peace? To perform the rites."

"No need to worry about that, Rev. This is the last place the men want to be reminded of, trust me."

When he was alone, Semper set about studying the soldiers he'd been given to work with. Some of their injuries were terrible. One or two men were just assortments of pieces, laid out in the rough shape of a body, organs and limbs placed more or less where they were supposed to be. They'd clearly be blown apart by some tremendous explosion. Semper spoke the name of each dead soldier out loud as he came to them, reading from their metal identity disks. It wasn't a part of the necromancy; it merely felt like the right thing to do. It made them people again, individuals, if only for a moment.

But it was completely obvious most of the eight were too injured. What did people expect? He might be able to raise the dead but he wasn't a miracle-worker. Reanimating a corpse was easy enough. That was basic, bread-and-butter death-magic. A mindless revenant was surprisingly easy to create. It wasn't like attempting to summon one of the towering horrors of the beyond or anything. Even so, there had to be a torso and working legs and arms. Everything had to be *connected*.

There were three he could work with. *Jack Griffiths. Toby Hayes. Ivan Fling.* The first two looked like mustard-gas victims and Fling had a single, clean bullet-wound through his head. As he studied the dead soldiers, Semper's unease at what he was doing grew. They were just boys. They hadn't asked for this. He consoled himself with the thought that they were already dead, that he wasn't making matters worse. Terrible things had been done to them, but not by him. In truth it didn't make him feel very much better.

Of course he only had himself to blame. The whole idea had been his after all. He'd hoped to see out the war safely engrossed in his arcane studies while the distant world went mad and tore itself to pieces. But then conscription had arrived and he'd been forced to put Plan B into operation.

He'd thought about claiming to be a minister of a religion – mysteriously exempt from conscription – but somehow doubted he could pull it off. Instead he'd murmured to the scowling recruiting sergeant that he had certain *special abilities* that might be of help in the war effort, if only he could be allowed to use them.

The Sergeant had looked like he was about to bite Semper's head clean off there and then. He demanded to know what these special abilities might be. Semper asked to speak in confidence to someone of a higher rank. The Sergeant very nearly exploded in fury, but Semper stuck to his guns. In the end, the queue growing, the Sergeant passed Semper on to a captain, who in turn sent him to see a major. Eventually he found his way to General McTavish and, having nowhere higher to go, was forced to explain what he had in mind.

McTavish was a stick-thin, ascetic man who looked more like a librarian than a general. But he saw the military value of Semper's idea immediately. "You're suggesting you could send a wave of fallen soldiers back over the top to attack the enemy lines? Soldiers who wouldn't stop if shot, who would simply keep going and going?"

"Only if their injuries weren't too great."

McTavish waved away this detail. "This could make all the difference. Dead soldiers might even be preferable. Living ones have the unfortunate habit of not always doing what we tell them."

"Really? Imagine."

"We must put this into action immediately."

And so Semper had found himself at the front after all. But at least no one was ordering him to climb out of his trench and march slowly towards the mechanized guns of the enemy. Not yet, anyway.

He finished the three reanimations by midnight. He then spent the next five hours working on an altogether more dangerous and precarious piece of necromancy. Indeed, it was one he had never worked before, although he'd studied its form and rituals often. A scrap of bandage stolen from a certain pharaonic tomb. Runes written upon it in a cursive script that many experts thought long-lost. Several fluid ounces of his own blood in which the scrap was soaked. A binding rite performed over two long hours.

The incantations he used were gruelling and it wouldn't

take much for them to go wrong. The slightest slip in the flow of syllables would be enough to render them ineffective – or, worse, make them function in some unexpected way. He was playing with fire, and that tended to mean someone getting burned. Semper was used to working in the peace and calm of his own laboratory, not on the front-line of a war where the guns were never silent. But eventually he was done. He could only hope he hadn't made a mistake. And he also hoped - most fervently - that he would never have cause to use the ensorcelled scrap of cloth and find out.

At five in the morning, Semper trudged through the cold mud of the trenches to report his readiness to Featherstone. The Major was still sitting in his dugout, as if he never moved from the place.

"Very well," Featherstone said when Semper had reported. "Let us see what foul horror you have worked."

"Yes, sir. If you're sure you want to see."

"Of course I bloody want to see. Do you think a few dead soldiers trouble me?"

"No, sir. I don't think dead soldiers trouble you at all. But you might not be used to seeing them sit up and walk around."

Featherstone's eye twitched again. "Are you trying to make a fool of me, Semper?"

"No, sir." *I don't need to try*, he very nearly added, but thought better of it.

"Good. Then go and cast your spells now, or whatever it is you do, before the men are up and about. The *living* men I mean."

"Sir."

*

Semper and Featherstone stood in a distant trench, out of sight of any sentry. The reanimated corpses of Jack Griffiths, Toby Hayes and Ivan Fling waited to climb the ladder into no-man's land, their blank eyes staring into some unknown distance. Three hundred yards away, upon a small rise in the ground, lay a German machine-gun position. The revenants' instructions were simple. Get to that position and disable the gun.

Semper watched Featherstone as the revenants climbed. The Major's eyes were wide and he'd gone very quiet. That was something, anyway. When the last of them, Fling, had disappeared over the top, Featherstone gave Semper a glare of pure revulsion.

Both had wooden periscopes, and these they used to peer into no-man's land without exposing themselves to gunfire. They watched as the three revenants shambled forwards and then, thirty yards out, were cut down by well-aimed sniper shots from the machine-gun position.

Featherstone set his periscope down. "Well. So much for that. Bloody shambles. I'll report your failure to General McTavish immediately. With any luck he'll have you on a one-man charge of enemy lines before the day is out."

"Wait," said Semper.

"Wait, *sir*,"

"Yes, yes," said Semper, still peering into his periscope. "Look. They're still going."

"What? That's not possible. Clean shots to the head, all three of them."

"Heads make no difference," explained Semper. "So long as the limbs can move they will."

The three revenants were now crawling forwards. He'd forgotten to give them instructions to stand back up if knocked down.

"Why are they creeping like that?" said Featherstone. "What's wrong with them?"

"They're just … keeping their heads down," said Semper. "They were instructed to get up that hill. We didn't say how quickly they had to do it."

"Disgraceful display," said Featherstone, as if he

suspected the revenants of cowardice.

In the end, it was Semper's oversight that saved him. The German sniper, clearly thinking he'd done his job, and seeing no other figures stalking through the gloom across the mud, fired no more. No one in the enemy lines appeared to notice the three figures inching their way along the ground until it was too late. Half an hour after they'd set off, a sudden flurry of screams and cries made it clear the revenants had reached their target. It struck Semper that he was responsible for the deaths of those German soldiers. He'd been obeying orders, it was true, but still. The war tainted everything and everyone.

Watching through his periscope, Semper saw one of the revenants beginning the return journey. Half an hour later, Fling toppled over the lip of the trench and landed in a heap at the bottom. The animated corpse stared up at Semper, the bullet-hole in the middle of his forehead like a third eye. An unblinking eye. Semper knelt to remove the geas he'd imprinted onto the corpse's tissues.

"What are you doing?" asked Featherstone.

"Letting him rest. I presume he can have his Christian burial now?"

Featherstone's eyes twitched four or five times in a row. "Return him to the Aid Post. We may have use of him again."

Semper resisted the urge to ask who the *abomination* was now. Instead he decided this was the moment to play his hand.

"If we're to repeat this exercise I'll need time to prepare, sir," he said. "The *spells* take considerable effort to work. If I'm to cast them on the sort of scale General McTavish requires it will take time."

Featherstone looked suspicious, as if Semper were admitting to some moral weakness. "How long?"

"I can have everything ready within four months," said Semper. It wasn't true; a few weeks would suffice. But Featherstone didn't know that. Here was Semper's new plan. Plan C. See out the war pretending to be busy in the safety of some remote *maison*. Or even, if he were lucky, *chateau*.

Featherstone's words put a swift end to Semper's hopes. "Nonsense, man. The war can't wait while you swan around for months on end. The push is coming in six days. We need your army of revenants ready by then."

Semper had always hated death. It was something that surprised people when he tried to explain. Which, these days, he rarely bothered to. But he'd hated death long before he'd ever opened a grimoire or uttered a chthonic syllable. Long before he'd even heard of necromancy. What he hated was the injustice of it. The arbitrariness. He'd lost too many loved ones growing up. Brothers and sisters taken by a seemingly endless list of fatal diseases. Adults who were fit and well one day but simply no longer there the next. Sometimes he would stare at some recently-deceased unfortunate and think, *What's changed? Why are they dead now when they weren't a few minutes ago? Their organs are all intact. Blood still fills their veins. They could breathe and move and think. But they've just ... stopped.*

Before he'd come to the front he'd told himself he could do some good with his scheme. Oh, he'd been mainly trying to save his own skin, but he'd also reasoned that it was better to send soldiers who were already dead over the top. He saw, now, how misguided he'd been. They weren't going to send dead soldiers instead of living ones. McTavish and the rest would send both if they could. They may even be more inclined to order the living to attack, secure in the knowledge the soldiers wouldn't have to stop fighting for a small inconvenience like death.

In short, Semper saw in that moment, looking into Major Featherstone's eyes, that he had to get away. For his own sake and for the sake of everyone in the trenches. He couldn't do anything to stop the slaughter. All he could do was not make it any worse. And that meant escaping.

He could simply climb out of the trench and be away

one dark night, but that wasn't going to get him anywhere was it? Walk towards the enemy lines and the Germans would shoot him. Head the other way and his own side would. Reluctantly he concluded that Plan D had to be put into operation. The insurance policy. Could he really do such a thing? They very thought of attempting it parched his mouth dry and made his throat constrict. Because he hated death. And the death he most especially hated was *his*.

"I shall need assistants," said Semper. "Achieving such a thing in six days on my own is impossible."

"Good God, man, these are soldiers, fighting for King and country," the Major replied. "They aren't ghouls like you. They'd run you through before assisting in such a foul scheme."

"Lieutenant Ebbers perhaps? He has some experience with … field surgery. I shall need one other pair of hands at the very least."

"Can't you just … raise up some of the dead to assist you?"

"No, no, the fine motor skills aren't there. It would be worse than useless. Ebbers is the man."

"He believes you're a simple cleric, not some black-hearted wizard that cavorts with the devil."

"Actually, I don't believe Ebbers is fooled at all."

The Major fumed for a second, his eye now twitching non-stop. He was losing it. "Very well. Take Ebbers. Then get out of my sight."

*

Semper found Ebbers sitting against the side of the trench, cap over his eyes, seemingly asleep.

"Lieutenant?"

Ebbers opened one eye. "Rev! Don't worry, I ain't dead. Don't go burying me just yet."

Semper looked around, then crouched down so he

could speak without anyone else hearing. "Can we talk?"

"I think we are talking," whispered Ebbers, grinning his skewed grin.

"Quite. The thing is, I have a confession to make."

"Really, Rev? I thought it were meant to be the other way round."

"I'm sorry?"

"'Course you're the expert, but I thought we poor sinners were supposed to confess to you?"

"Ah, yes. Quite so. But things change. You see, the truth is I shouldn't really be here."

"None of us should bleedin' be here, Rev. Don't know what I ever did to deserve all this. No doubt you could explain the thinking, eh?" Ebbers cast an eye upwards to the heavens, as if to indicate whose thinking it was he'd like to understand.

"Can't help you there, Ebbers. The truth is I'm not a Reverend at all. As I suspect you've guessed."

Ebbers nodded conspiratorially. "Pulled the old *minister of the church* stunt to avoid being signed up, eh?"

"Something like that."

"Looks like it didn't work out too well."

"No. However all is not lost. I have a way out, but I need the assistance of an able accomplice."

"You what?"

"I need your help."

"Love to, Rev. But Major Mad-Eye would have me shot at dawn. Likes the shooting at dawn does old Mad-Eye."

"Actually he knows all about this."

That got Ebbers' attention. "He does?"

"By all means ask him yourself. But the nature of the assignment is somewhat … unusual."

"And shivering in a muddy trench and occasionally marching towards enemy machine-guns ain't?"

"Fair point. But what I have in mind is also insanely dangerous. For me, that is, not you."

"Your risk to take, I reckon."

"Good. Let me explain my scheme. I quite understand it may not be for you. And I can't offer you your freedom. I *can* offer you some respite from the trenches. A week or two behind the lines at the very least. And that means you'll be safe when the next push kicks off. It's the best I can do."

Ebbers grinned. "Better tell me all about it then, eh, Rev?"

Five days later, Semper was ready. Or as ready as he'd ever be. More than once he'd decided not to go through with it. But he knew they weren't going to leave him in peace if he delayed. Featherstone's visits to their specially-assigned Casualty Clearing Station two miles behind the lines were becoming too frequent. Plus they were running out of room to house all the bodies.

"And you're going to do this are you, Rev?" said Ebbers. "I mean, I've seen some things in my time, but this."

"As I say, it's the only way."

"It's a bit, well, desperate."

"Yes. It is. Now, you're sure you understand your role?"

"I'm not idiot, Rev."

"No. I know. You're the sanest person I've met here."

"Don't say much for the rest of them."

"Indeed. And in fact, Ebbers, I meant to say to you. While I'm sure butchery is a fine and noble calling, if you do survive the war, may I suggest there are other ends you might pursue?"

"Meaning what, Rev?"

"Meaning whatever you want it to mean."

"Meaning maybe I should come knocking on your door one sunny day?"

Semper smiled. "If by some unlikely chance we both survive this, then yes. I'd welcome that."

Semper took the scrap of ancient cloth he'd ensorcelled and cut it in two with a pair of surgeon's scissors. One half he handed to Ebbers. The other he kept. "Here we go then. Over the top."

"Over the top, Rev. Best of British."

"Thanks. I rather suspect I'll need it."

*

Back at the front, Semper huddled in the trench for a moment while he collected his thoughts. His heart pounded away in his chest. He didn't know if he could do this. Was this what it was like for the men each time they climbed those ladders? How did they make themselves do it? How did they make themselves do it *again* the next time? He had no idea.

He had no choice, though. With trembling fingers he dropped his half of the scrap of cloth into a tin cup and then lit it with a safety match. Oily smoke coiled off it as it smouldered. Semper, holding the cup to his nose, inhaled the smoke as deeply as he could. He had to fight back the urge to cough and retch.

When he was done, he began to climb the ladder that would take him up to no-man's land. One rung at a time.

"Semper! What are you doing, man?"

Major Featherstone stood twenty yards away, his face white with rage.

Semper felt sorry for Featherstone, he really did. Sending soldiers to their death again and again was clearly taking its toll. But he couldn't resist a final dig at the man who had called him such terrible things.

"Going out to rescue some more men," Semper called back. "You gave me the idea yourself, telling me what a fine man Gordons was."

"Gordons?"

"My predecessor. I can only hope to live up to his shining example."

"But … you can't. Our plans for the push, man!"

"Oh, I'll be fine," said Semper. "And if I don't come back General McTavish can always cancel the offensive. I'm sure the men would appreciate it. Mass slaughter must be so bad for morale."

Ignoring Featherstone's enraged shouts, Semper climbed the ladder and began the walk towards enemy lines.

It occurred to him, as he worked his way through the churned and pitted mud, that these were quite possibly his last few moments on Earth. That these were the last few thoughts he'd ever think. He wondered how his death would come. If he trod on a mine or if a shell landed nearby that would be that. There wouldn't be enough pieces left of him to fill a bucket. A clean sniper's shot would be best, perhaps. And worst would be some crippling wound followed by days spent writhing in agony. It happened, so people said.

It was all a ridiculous gamble, of course, but what could he do? Funny how he'd gone to so much trouble to avoid being sent over the top and now here he was, doing just that, walking towards the enemy machine-guns without even being ordered to. It was, when you thought about it, a funny old life.

He glanced back. The British lines were only a few yards behind him. Strange. He felt like he'd been walking for hours already.

He turned and strode on. He didn't even hear or feel the shot that felled him a moment later.

*

The problem with astral walking wasn't the walking. That was the easy part. The aether was a limitless expanse, and it simply longed to suck you inside. No, the hard part was returning to your body afterwards. Or to any body. Or, come to that, to any material realm whatsoever. The ancient texts all placed great emphasis on this point. Leave your own body and there was every chance you'd never be able to return. An eternity of blank dissipation was your most likely fate.

Semper, his soul freed from his body by the magics he'd employed, wandered the aether. It was impossible to say how long for. Time was meaningless there. There wasn't even a *there* there. An endless expanse of grey stretched away for ever in all directions. He was dimly aware of other beings: some tiny, some vast beyond measure. Fortunately none came near. Semper simply floated, knowing that this might be the sum of his existence for the rest of time.

Then there came the moment he glimpsed a light in the void. A tiny speck of white. He'd seen nothing like it. Bending all his will to the effort he swam towards it. Scale was impossible to judge in the aether. He was just thinking it might be a distant sun that would take lifetimes to reach when he was suddenly upon it. The light was the size of a candle-flame bobbing quietly away in the grey. A *beacon*.

Semper circled for a while, intrigued, aware he was supposed to do something. The *plan*. He was aware, also, that other minds had seen the light and were coming. He couldn't recall precisely why, but he knew he had to stop those others reaching the light. If they did it would be a very bad thing. Bad for everyone on Earth but, more importantly, bad for him.

He put his eye near the flame. There was no heat to it. It was like peering through a keyhole. He could see a whole room through there: a white, white room, so bright it was blinding. There were shapes, too, but they were indistinct. Something moved about, but he couldn't tell what.

The beings of the aether were close now. Thronging. Not looking around, Semper began to push through the tiny crack of light, pouring himself out of the aether and into that room. Back into the real world. The effort of it was enormous. The aether loved him, longed to hold on to him. But Semper fought. He knew one thing in the whole universe: that he had to wring himself through that gap in the walls and escape. It was the only chance he would ever have.

He screamed wordlessly. The pain of it was like being torn in two. Minds the size of thunderclouds gathered around him now, tendrils reaching for the sliver of light. Semper screamed again and threw all his remaining strength into a final push.

The pain was finally too much. He passed out, the world going grey once more.

*

"'Allo, Rev. Good to see you back with us."

A familiar, lop-sided grin hovered into view. "Ebbers?"

"At your service."

Tearing pains shot all across Semper's chest, making the simple act of breathing agony. "I'm alive?"

"Alive enough to ask daft questions."

"The scrap of cloth? You burned it as instructed, forced the smoke into my lungs?"

"You're here ain't you?"

"Yes. I believe I am. And you were able to retrieve my body?"

"After a day. Under cover of darkness. Nice clean shot to the chest. The way your body healed rather than decaying … ain't ever seen the like."

"Strong magic," said Semper. "How long have I been out?"

"Two weeks."

"Ah." Longer than he'd hoped. There would be side effects from such a prolonged astral walk. Effects he might not understand for years to come. Effects on his own brain and effects on the structure of the universe, too.

He tried to rise but then gave up. The pain was too

great. That wasn't the only thing troubling him. Was his vision fading or were there shadows gathering around him in the room? "Tell me, Ebbers. Did anything else manifest when I appeared? Did any of those horrors come through after me?" The ancient texts were fulsome in their warnings. He just had to hope he hadn't unleashed further nightmare and calamity on the young century. There was talk in some of the tomes of the denizens of the aether trailing plague and calamity in their wake. Of the rise of demons in human form and the collapse of civilisations.

Ebbers seemed unaware of any shadows. "Horrors? 'Ain't seen no horrors. No more than the usual, anyway."

Semper looked around, seeing shapes in the corner of his eye. Seeing or imagining them. The shapes disappeared when he looked directly at them. He probably needed to rest. That was it.

"And why haven't you been ordered back to the trenches?"

"Old Mad-Eye gave me special orders to stay. Reckon he hopes I can pick up where you left off sort of thing."

"Could you?"

"No bleeding way. What you did … I'd rather take my chances with the guns and the poison gas, thank you very much."

"I quite understand."

"Tell me, Rev. That army of the dead marching across no-man's land. Could you really have done it?"

"Oh yes, I think so. But there's quite enough insanity in the world just now, don't you think?"

"Right you are," said Ebbers.

"And tell me, what of the Reverend Semper?"

Ebbers grinned. "Oh, you're officially dead. I buried you a week ago according to the paperwork. Doesn't seem to be a form to cover the dead coming back to life so I can't fill one in. Seems to me you can just … wander off once you're back on your feet."

Semper closed his eyes. That was good. Very good. He

was officially dead. It was perfect. And so much better than the other sort of dead. And he longed to be away from here. As far away as he could get from trenches and shadows and Major Featherstone. He needed time to uncover what harm he'd done. To the world but, more importantly, to himself.

"Ebbers?"

"Yes, Rev?"

"Do you have a pen and paper? Will you write something for me?"

"What is it?"

"My address back home. Where I live in the Welsh Marches … it's hard to find if you're not invited. But you'd be welcome. If you could make it one day. Like we said."

Ebbers considered for a moment, regarding Semper through narrowed eyes. Then he picked up a pen and held it ready. "Reckon I just might do that and all, Rev."

Nicholas Semper's War was originlly printed in the British Fantasy Society's Horizons in 2016. It's perhaps the closest I get to horror, although to my mind it's an alt-history/fantasy story, with (hopefully) darkly humorous overtones. It also clearly nods in the direction of Cthulhu mythos.

I quite often get to the end of a story only to find that whole new possibilities of *what happens next* open up, and that certainly happened with this story. In one possible future I'll write a whole series of Semper and Ebbers novels, perhaps as they battle against the horrors they've unwittingly unleashed on the young century, their adventures intertwined with real historical events…

BEAN SÍ

The mournful wailing froze Conn O'Neill's blood, as it always did. People said the sound the Stuka dive-bombers made came from sirens the Germans fitted to their planes. Well, maybe. But Conn, fighting for Allied forces in northern France, knew there was more to it.

He'd been seven when he first heard that howl echoing through the air, stilling the birds in the trees into silence. The cry of the *bean sí*. The banshee. When he returned home that day, his mother's eyes were red and his brother, Finbar, lay under a white shroud, the waters of the lough filling his lungs.

It was partly to escape the stifling pagan darkness of the old country that Conn left Ireland as a young man, and ended up fighting in a war that wasn't his war. It was good to put the clutch of that history behind him. But some things followed you however far you ran, or maybe you brought some things with you. When the Stukas screamed from the sky, he had to resist the urge to flee. Say what you like, the terrible sound meant death for someone. The banshees were busy in time of war, and when they came for you there was no escape.

The Stuka wailed as it dived now, louder and louder.

He waited for the explosion that meant *he* was safe, his life bought once again at the cost of other soldiers' lives. Instead there was only the keening howl, nearer each moment.

A vision of a shape beneath a shroud came to him as the shriek filled the whole world. Conn O'Neill finally stood and ran. Ran even though he knew there was no escape from the bean si when it came for you. Some things followed you however far you travelled.

The bomb shattered the ground around him and for a moment, the briefest moment, he was flying.

Bean Sí was originally published in Every Day Fiction in 2017. It was an attempt to write a satisfying story in very few words, and its World War II setting makes it a nice counterpoint to the much longer Nicholas Semper's War set in World War I.

This story grew out of the notion that the terrifying sound made by the Jericho trumpets fitted to Stuka dive bombers might sound like the cry of a banshee – the harbinger of death – to someone from an Irish background. I was perhaps most pleased with the story's final line.

A RING, A RING O' ROSES

A ring, a ring o' roses,
A pocket full o' posies-
Atishoo atishoo, we all fall down
                              - English nursery rhyme

Red lights flickered all across the board filling one wall of Dartford Vapour Monitoring Station. The tiny gas flames in the bulbs hissed, their combined sound angrier and angrier as more and more sparked into life.

"Bleedin' hell."

Albert Crowe watched as the entire south-eastern corner of England went red, a great bite taken out of Kent. It wasn't possible. More red bulbs lit up, further and further inland. Gale-force winds today, of course. Any bad air coming off the Channel would move at quite a lick. At this rate it would hit the London Low Miasma Zone in, what, an hour? Maybe less. But it was vast. It *couldn't* be real.

He glanced at the brass dial on the wall next to the map, like a ship's clock but with thirty-six numbers around its circumference, I all the way up to XXXVI. The single black hand wavered on the I as the wind outside gusted.

The station's olfactometers had picked nothing up. He didn't trust them. Thirty years a Vapourman, he believed only his own nose. He stepped out onto the narrow balcony that ran around the top of the tall, red-brick tower he manned and faced south-east. Wind streamed into his face, sharp on his cheeks. A *lazy wind* his old dad would have called it. One that didn't bother to go 'round you. Albert clutched the iron railing, closed his eyes and sniffed deeply.

Definitely *something*; the faint stench of decay in the air. Cholera, if he was any judge. A bad death, that. Still, it was very faint. Something must be wrong with the lights. On a bad day two or three lit up. Not thirty. Had to be a glitch in the telegraphy or some such. Since the war started and the army took over, everything had gone haywire. You didn't know what was an exercise and what was real. Most likely some toff of a Colonel had closed the wrong circuit up in Whitehall.

All the same, Albert strapped his nosegay over his face. *Complacency kills*. He strolled right around the circular balcony, forty-five feet up in the air, streets and houses arrayed beneath him like children's toys. Soldiers scurried around like dull green beetles, darting between sandbagged bunkers, practising their defensive manoeuvres. Everything normal. Farther off, six miles north across the Thames, he could easily make out Rainham Station. Beyond that, just a faint pencil line against the sky, Romford. He could try and get through to the bigwigs in Whitehall or he could signal Wally up there and see if he was seeing the same on his board.

He decided on Wally. Back inside Albert cranked up the generator that powered the talker and dialled in 1-4, the code for Romford. Pressing his ear to the brass horn of the device, he could hear the machinery clicking and crackling as connections were made. The bell at the other end began to ring.

They went back a long way, him and Wally. Joined the

service together in '88, the year Queen Victoria remarried. He and Wally had manned a station together then, before all the new-fangled automation. Seen a lot of trouble together in the early days with all the riots against the ha'penny air tax. Building the sixteen towers around London, the *Ring o' Roses*, had cost a fortune right enough. Worth it though. He remembered life beforehand, when the tainted fogs came rolling in grey and yellow off the Thames and people started choking and hacking their guts up. Each morning they lined the bodies up in the streets before shipping them off on barges to bury at Gravesend. He thought about Alfie, his twin brother, lying there so peaceful like he'd just fallen asleep. Five brothers and two sisters lost over the years, all taken by the bad airs. And his old dad carrying them one by one down to the barges, returning each time with his arms empty and his eyes wide.

It had all seemed so normal. It was what happened. People had lots of kids in the hope some would survive. Now, with the sweet air pumped out from the towers, it was unthinkable. A distant memory from the bad old days. A story you told disbelieving, jeering kids. Let them jeer. At least they were alive.

He'd been little more than a kid himself when they'd started building the towers. The sight of them, tall against the blue sky, had filled him with hope after so much death. Their great sails were like the wings of angels, slowly unfurling.

He'd joined up to man one the day they opened their doors, running the gantlet of the mob. He thought his dad wasn't even going to let him go. The last of his eight children and their mother dead, too. But instead he squeezed Albert tight, something he never did, and smiled.

"Go on, son. You go and do this. Put an end to all this dying, eh?" Then his dad had taken out the Hardwicke three-shot pistol he always carried and handed it to him. "And take my old barking-iron, son. You use it if you need to, if someone tries to stop you. Keep it ready."

Albert had never once seen his father fire the gun. A gentle man as well as a gentleman. He carried it to protect his family from the cutpurses and thugs of the East End, but it hadn't been able to save any of them from the diseased airs of London's miasmas.

In the end, what with the army holding back the mob, Albert hadn't needed the gun. Still, he kept it in his inside pocket, close to his heart. All he had left of his old dad. He'd become a Vapourman that same day, he and Wally standing next to each other in line while the crowd beyond the line of soldiers swore and spat at them. You didn't get mobs like that these days, did you? Didn't hear from the crackpots who insisted tiny creatures swimming around in the air and water made you ill. Their *animalcules* that you couldn't see, couldn't smell. Amazing, the fairy tales people believed. It didn't take a genius to spot that people got ill when the foul stenches came floating in over the city.

The talker bell was still clanging in his ear. A cold dread took hold of his innards. Wally had never missed a day's work, not even when his missus gave birth. His absence now alarmed Albert much more than the lights on his board advancing towards London. He could *rely* on Wally.

Albert tried again in case he'd dialled the wrong number but the same thing happened. Maybe the talkers were playing up too. He decided to try Whitehall. He dialled in 0-0. This time a crisp, boyish voice answered immediately.

"Whitehall Central Control."

Some lad barely out of public school. Always the way these days. Since the war with the Hun had kicked off they got younger and younger.

"Dartford here. Seeing some very strange signals. Half me board's gone red. Is it another exercise?"

They were for ever playing their war games, pretending Zeppelins or squadrons of exploding biplanes were crossing English soil. The towers were heavily defended of course, batteries of artillery all around them. They just never bothered to tell him what they were doing.

"Of course it isn't a drill, man. You would have been notified. You have started up your engine haven't you?"

The slight note of alarm in the lad's voice told Albert everything he needed to know. "'Course I have. I know what I'm doing, don't I? Coming up to speed now. But this miasma's *huge*. It can't be real. The early-warning stations right across Essex and Kent have lit."

"Of course it's bloody real! The balloon's gone up. The Hun's big attack. Just make sure you stay at full power, understand?"

"'Course."

The connection dropped. He'd meant to ask about Wally. Replacing his nosegay, he looked back up at the board. The line of red crept closer and closer. The scale of it was incredible, like nothing he'd seen before. Bastards must have waited for the right winds then salted effluvia right across the marshes and coastal mud-flats to generate a cloud that vast. He thought he'd seen it all. If the towers hadn't been there to sweeten the air it would be barges to Gravesend all over again.

Albert strode across the control room to the dials controlling the station's steam engine, housed deep within its foundations. As he turned control wheels he could feel the thrumming through his feet as the great machine awoke.

He looked through the westerly windows, towards the capital. The vast blades of the tower's fan were beginning to move, ponderous at first but picking up speed as the two six-inch chains hauled them round. On a day like this, in this wind, you'd feel the whole tower rocking once they got up to speed. Like being at sea. He opened the valves to the underground vats. Droplets of rosewater began to spray out in front of the fan from the mesh of tiny pipes. Two hundred gallons an hour. Within minutes, once the machinery had warmed up, a cone of aerosolised sweet-air would be drifting westwards over houses and streets. He'd done his job. Whatever was coming at them, at least London was protected.

He stepped outside to check his droplet concentration. There was no obvious difference to the air but he wasn't concerned. Took time for it to sweeten properly here in the backwash from the fan. He just hoped they had enough rosewater to last. Prevailing westerlies meant the rich folks of Hounslow and Uxbridge got all the attention. The east was ignored. He'd told them often enough but perhaps now they'd listen.

Down below the soldiers had stopped racing around and were lying prone in readiness. What were they going to do, shoot at the air? They must know what was coming. Little more than boys too, ordered to defend the tower at all costs. On that side of the fan they wouldn't be protected. Only their cardboard War Office nosegays to protect them when the cholera hit. He felt sorry for them. At least he was safe up here.

"Hello."

A voice behind him. Albert spun around, confused. How could someone else be up here? Before he could speak the crack of a gun slammed him backwards against the iron railing.

Crumpled in a heap, pain banging through him, he watched a young man disentangle himself from his web of climbing ropes. The Hun, here. It wasn't possible. Albert tried to speak but couldn't. He tried to rise but the pain tore through his chest, pinning him to the ground. The stranger glanced over at him, smiled ruefully, then disappeared inside the control room.

A few seconds later Albert felt the rhythmic thrum of the engine quieting. Strangely, it gave him a flash of hope. If the soldiers on the ground saw the fan stopping they'd know something was up. He watched the blades roar by against the sky. They'd already slowed slightly. Then the jets of misted water cut out and the steam engine down in the ground woke up again.

"No." Albert could only croak uselessly. The man had merely been trying to work the controls. Now it looked like the blades were working but they were blowing nothing but air across London. *Bad* air once the miasma hit. The fan would actually be helping spread the cloud of cholera across the city. It *would* be the old days again. Only, who'd be left to line the bodies up? People were weak these days, no resistance any more. Your royalty and suchlike had their own private sweet air supplies but most relied on the towers. The Hun would turn London into a graveyard.

The bell of the talker clanged inside. Albert heard the man stride across to answer it. He had a moment to do something. He could think of only one thing to try. He had to be quick. The bullet had obviously done him serious damage. Any breath might be his last.

Gritting his teeth against the pain, feeling like he was ripping his chest open with each movement, he turned over and made it up onto his knees. Inside, the Hun talked to someone. Whitehall most likely. He sounded like he'd lived all his life in the East End. They were clever, you had to give it to them.

"Yes, at full capacity now," Albert heard. "Everything running smoothly, like I said. 'Course I have. Yeah."

Albert reached up to grasp the railing with one hand. All he had to do was haul himself up onto his legs and let himself topple over the side. The soldiers were all looking the other way but they'd hear him thump into the ground. They'd know something was up. It was all he could do.

"Oh no you don't."

Another shot. Blood dashed from Albert's arm, spraying into his eyes. He slumped back to the floor of the balcony, a new note of pain ringing through him.

"Can't have you doing that, now can we?" the Hun said. "Not after all the trouble we've gone to."

The man stood over Albert, a brown leather boot filling his vision. The Hun's voice had changed now, the foreigner in him clear. Albert tried to reply but no words came. The man knelt down beside him. His face was boyish. Couldn't have been much older than the soldiers down on the ground.

"What do you think?" asked the man. "Half an hour before the main cloud reaches us? An hour until London is covered?"

Albert shifted, groaned.

"Yes, I think that's about right," the man continued. "And then, with the capital broken, the rest of the country will fall like a house of cards. No need for long years of war. One quick victory, a simple decapitation. So much better don't you think? So much more civilised. One empire falls and another takes its place."

The stranger sounded almost sorry about it. Albert closed and opened his eyes, tried to clear his clogged throat.

"Well, I can see you're in no mood for conversation," said the man. "And I should wear my mask anyway, eh? We both know what's coming."

The man stood and walked away to gaze out over London. Albert tried to rise but couldn't. He tried to sort through the various strands of pain filling his body. The sharp pain in his arm where the second bullet had struck. The great, tearing agony in his chest where the first shot had hit him. Strange, though. A shot like that should have killed him outright. It hurt like hell and he was winded, but he was also still breathing, just about. How was that possible?

He reached up to feel his wound, expecting there to be blood. A lot of blood, warm and sticky. But his chest was dry. There was only the reassuring weight of his old dad's gun in his breast pocket.

The gun. That was it. So it had saved one of them after all. He hoped his old dad was looking down from somewhere and had seen. The bullet must have hit the gun and bounced off. He was bruised, a rib or two cracked maybe, but nothing more.

Watching the back of the Hun, Albert reached into his pocket for the gun. He probably had only one shot. He had never fired the weapon either, but it was loaded and ready and the enemy was only feet away. Surely he couldn't miss.

His hand shook as he aimed. Fortunately he was left-handed and the second bullet had struck him in the right forearm. Albert fired. The Hun spun round, shock on his face, but then he was dashing forwards towards Albert. Somehow he had missed. Albert fired again, the Hun nearly on top of him. This time the bullet struck, sending the man spinning to one side. As he fell he cracked his head on the iron railing with a sickening crunch. He lay on the balcony unmoving.

If his old dad *was* watching from somewhere he'd be smiling now for sure. His gun had saved Albert and it might have saved London, too. Albert didn't have much time. The first tendrils of the miasma would be rolling over the roofs and streets any moment. Clenching his teeth, he hauled himself back onto his knees and began to crawl back inside the station. The agony of it was terrible but he refused to stop. Inside, the map showed red right across, only one set of lights unlit before the ring of towers. He had to get the rosewater operating again. At least it looked like the Hun hadn't smashed the machinery. But, of course, they'd need London to be protected once they took control. They needed the towers, too.

Albert worked his way across the floor, crying out like a child each time he pulled himself forwards. It was a race, him against the advancing tide of red on the board.

Finally he reached the dials and wheels. Now he had to haul himself upwards to operate the controls. He tried, once, but the pain of it was too much and he sagged back to the floor. On the wall, the final line of lights lit. The miasma was here. He had to act.

Screaming out loud, he lunged upwards for the edge of

the control panel above him. He pulled himself to his knees and reached for the wheel of the rosewater valve with his fingertips. Slowly, agonisingly slowly, he began to turn it. After a few moments, his Vapourman's ears picked up the change in sound to the machinery, the extra hiss.

He collapsed back to the floor in a heap, breathing heavily like he'd just run up the stairs. His station was blowing again. But the others might not be. He had to reach Whitehall too, tell them what had happened.

With his shaky fingers it took him three attempts to dial 0-0 into the talker.

"Whitehall Central Control."

His voice was little more than a whisper. "Dartford. They're here. The Hun. Just shot me."

"Is this some sort of joke?"

It was Albert's turn to be angry now. "'Course it ain't a bloody joke. Tell the army to get up each tower. Now, boy."

The soldier at the other end paused for only a moment. "Right. Will do."

The line went dead. Albert sat back. He wondered if Wally was still alive up there in Romford. Wally would have fought too. Most likely he hadn't been as lucky as Albert. His best friend all these years, killed by the Hun. It was incredible.

He glanced outside at the turning fan. He should check his droplet concentration. The controls were delicate. If the Hun had tampered with them, the droplets would be too large or there wouldn't be enough of them and central London would still be unprotected. Teeth gritted against the pain once again, stopping to breathe repeatedly, he worked his way back outside. Once there he sniffed deeply. The stench of the cholera was clear now, thick and oily in the air. He could make out the sweet smell of roses, too, but it was faint, far too faint to be effective. It took time for the air to sweeten, of course. Or maybe the machinery had been damaged after all.

The Hun lay on the balcony beside him, an ugly red wound on the side of his head. Was he dead? No. Albert could see the man was still breathing, unconscious. Suddenly furious, Albert lifted his pistol once more. He had one more shot. He pointed the gun at the Hun's face. How dare they do this? Thousands could die here. *Millions.* Albert's finger twitched on the trigger. He had only to squeeze a little harder and the Hun would have his grinning face blasted off.

Albert Crowe hesitated. The man lying there peacefully with his eyes closed reminded him of someone. Another boy lying as if asleep. Albert crouched unmoving for long moments, holding the gun to the man's face but not firing. Finally, he dropped the weapon. Enough. He'd done all he could. The army could deal with the Hun. His job was to protect people. *Put an end to all this dying.*

He could hear the calls of the soldiers as they clattered up the stairs to secure the tower. He felt the tower swaying, although whether from the wind or because he was losing consciousness he couldn't be sure. Through the iron railings he could see the miasma streaming over the houses below, obscuring them completely in its yellow filth. It *was* like being in a ship on the sea. A sea of poison flooding his city.

Only, it was poisonous no more. He could smell it now. The beautiful smell of roses. Albert closed his eyes, filling his lungs with the sweetened air flooding out over London.

This story was originally published as an audio story by Gallery of Curiosities, and has since been reprinted by Stupefying Stories. I like the idea of stories in universes that follow different scientific laws: here, it's the old notion of diseases being caused by the stench of bad air. The nursery rhyme led me on to the idea of the ring of towers around London pumping out rose-scented air to keep the populace safe and healthy, and as I wrote the story it almost felt as if the nursery rhyme had been written about *my* London as the words fitted so well.

AND NOW THE ZOMBIE FORECAST

…and after the freezing winter we finally get a taste of summer in Britain today, with temperatures soaring across the country. Unfortunately, it's the icy ground that has been keeping all the zombies locked away in the earth, which means we'll start to see the creatures clawing their way out of the earth in increasing numbers over the next few days. This will be a particular problem in urban areas of the south and east, where temperatures will be highest and burial densities are greatest. Here, revenant activity is likely to rise sharply throughout the day, so be especially aware if you're out and about in these areas.

By twilight, we may see infestations reaching apocalypse levels, with waves of the undead shambling through the suburbs of London. The good news is that torrential rain showers will spread across the south in the evening, and these wet conditions should curtail the undead onslaught. Or at least slow it down. Remember, if you do find yourself being relentlessly pursued by a horde of decaying horrors, make for an underground train station. The zombies can't work the ticket machines and will get stuck at the gates.

Meanwhile in the Midlands, watch out for fog patches

during the early-morning commute, as some may harbour wights, ghouls, ghasts and other denizens of the nether world intent on sucking out your soul as you head to work. As ever, listen out for radio alerts and obey the illuminated signs over the motorways. If the incorporeal undead are in the area, keep your car windows up at all times and ensure your vehicle's air filters are fully functional. If an evil spirit does manage to find its way into your vehicle, pull over immediately. Driving while haunted is both dangerous and illegal.

Further north, we may see outbreaks of vampirism in more secluded areas, especially on the higher ground of the Pennines. Be especially careful after dark if your car breaks down and you spot the welcoming lights of a castle twinkling in the distance. There may also be one or two thunderstorms around, with lightning strikes powerful enough to reanimate corpses in very high towers, so avoid these at all cost. Best advice, as ever, is to stay in your vehicle and phone the emergency services if you encounter any manifestations of the evil dead.

The weather in Scotland will also be warm at first, but in the afternoon southwesterly gales will pick up, sweeping in from Ireland. If the wind really starts to rage and howl, beware of banshees keening and foretelling your death. The best way to defeat these harbingers of doom is to drown them out by turning up the TV or listening to loud rock music through headphones. Eventually the creatures will take flight to seek fresh victims elsewhere.

Looking forward to the weekend, temperatures will continue to climb, so we may see further waves of undead incursion. It's a little too soon to be sure just yet, but as an early warning there's a chance we may see outbreaks touching Armageddon level across the Home Counties on Sunday, so do be aware of that if you're planning a family picnic or a round of golf. The bad news is, these problems will be exacerbated on Sunday evening by the full moon, when we may see large-scale lycanthropy to add to the problems.

Remember, if you encounter any werewolves or zombies, don't form a mob and attempt to take the law into your own hands. Contact the authorities immediately and run.

And that's your zombie forecast. As ever, stay tuned for further updates. Now over to the sports desk...

And Now The Zombie Forecast is one of several flash pieces in this collection that work by taking a familiar aspect of life and putting a fantasy or science fiction twist upon it. If the undead were as common as they so often are in speculative fiction, I figured, we'd need some sort of weather report-like forecast telling us what we're likely to encounter each day. It was originally published in Hysterical Realms magazine in 2015.

ANAX BRITANNICA

In the summer of 2013 I was researching the history of Britain's secret services in the Second World War for a magazine article. In particular, as a biologist, I was interested in the deployment of animals in the war effort. But among the discussions of carrier pigeons used to convey encrypted messages and dogs accompanying troops to act as guards and bloodhounds, I stumbled upon something truly remarkable: brief mention of a previously unknown – and huge – species of dragonfly.

At first I assumed the paper in question had simply been misfiled. But then I found a fuller report which appeared to corroborate the story. The report referred to the species as *Anax britannica*, described as "similar to, although larger than, *Anax imperator*, the Emperor Dragonfly". While imperator and its ilk are, of course, an ancient order of insect, *britannica's* entire life history appears to have spanned just three years: the period 1941 – 1944. Unlikely as it may seem, the report suggested that swarms of these vast, clattering insects were Britain's unlikely response to the deadly V1 flying bombs and V2 flying rockets that so terrorised southern England during World War II. Indeed, the paper referred to the insect as

"Britain's answer to the Nazi doodlebug menace".

The report was accompanied by a single black-and-white photograph which does, indeed, depict a large dragonfly. It is hard to be sure, but judging by the foliage upon which the dragonfly perches, it is certainly possible *Anax britannica's* wingspan reached the reported 12 inches. If this was so, it was the largest dragonfly to have flown over the face of the Earth for many millions of years - since the Meganeura dragonflies of the Carboniferous period, which had wingspans twice even this size.

The story seemed so incongruous and unlikely that I had to delve deeper. This was the start of a two year long trail of research and investigation which allowed me, finally, to piece together the remarkable story of one Dr. Henry Lamplighter. My article on pigeons and dogs was never written.

Lamplighter was an Oxford-educated entomologist who, at the time of the outbreak of hostilities, was studying his beloved dragonflies and damselflies in the British countryside. Lamplighter was well connected, and was soon recruited into Britain's Secret Intelligence Service. The same was true of many academics, often for no identifiable purpose other than to do "something" for the war effort. Where others were able to turn their skills to decrypting German Enigma codes or designing radar listening posts, Lamplighter's usefulness to the war machine was less clear. As he himself wrote in his diary on November 18th, 1939, "One is happy to be here, of course. But what is one supposed to do? Quite how an intimate knowledge of entomology is going to be of use to the war effort rather escapes me."

And so it might have remained, were it not for a chance meeting with another academic, Dr. Emily Pashlova, a Polish émigré. Pashlova had studied at the Curie Institute in Warsaw, and was recruited by the British, presumably, because of her research on radioactive isotopes. Perhaps the hope was to create some kind of weapon. At first this seemed highly unlikely as Pashlova's experience involved exposing fruit flies to small doses of radiation to observe the effects on their genome.

Whether the collaboration between Pashlova and Lamplighter was deliberate or a matter of chance remains unclear. Certainly they were both working in secret at Bletchley Park (now much more famous as the site of the UK's Government Code and Cipher School that cracked Enigma). What we do know is that, late in 1941, Lamplighter writes in his journal of a "remarkable" occurrence: the creation, "through the biomorphological actions of Dr. Pashlova's radioactive elements, of an entirely new species of dragonfly." Pashlova, who kept meticulous notes on all her work, mentions a "one in a million chance mutation in the genome of our dragonfly subject, which appeared to trigger some long-suppressed tendency in the insect to great size." The species was soon given a suitably patriotic name for wartime: *Anax britannica*. Pashlova's response to the choice of name is not recorded.

It was Lamplighter who suggested the dragonfly might be used as a weapon. The insect was so huge that it could, as he put it, "be recruited into the war effort by the simple means of strapping small amounts of explosive to its body, along with a simple timing mechanism, and releasing it into enemy territory." Whether Lamplighter had qualms about treating "his" insect in such a manner also remains unclear. I can only assume both Lamplighter and Pashlova saw the greater need of defeating the enemy as they continued their work. Perhaps they saw this as their only chance to "do something" to defeat the Axis powers.

A section of Salisbury Plain was allocated to Lamplighter for his experiments, where he spent many months working with a Captain Darley of the Royal Engineers. I have unearthed a single letter from Darley to his wife, in which he mentions a "crackpot scheme I am working on" – presumably Lamplighter's dragonflies. Attempts to turn these huge insects into weapons, however, are described extensively in Lamplighter's diaries, often in comic detail. He writes, for instance, how too heavy a load was attached to one unfortunate *britannica* so that, as soon as it was released, it crashed clumsily to the floor and proceeded to spiral around in a desperate attempt to fly. Lamplighter describes how he and Darley "chose to move away from the stricken insect with all haste". The poor creature's struggles were only ended when the explosive strapped to it triggered, "reducing the noble creature to a wide splattering of gore and chitin."

There is evidence, also, of disquiet about Lamplighter's work higher up in the British military establishment. I have, for instance, a minute of a meeting of the War Office Council from 1942 called to discuss the "the ongoing military researches of Dr. Lamplater [sic] and his insect ordnance delivery mechanism". One general, clearly, had little time for the scheme, referring to it as, simply, "lunacy". Others were more open-minded or, perhaps, simply bemused at the whole scheme. One person, however, was willing to give Lamplighter his chance. Scrawled on the bottom of the report in black ink is the word "Approved" and a signature: that of Winston Churchill. I can only speculate that Britain was so desperate in those dark days that they were willing to try anything. And, of course, there were so many new technologies being brought to bear on the war effort – radar, jet engines, nuclear fission and so forth – that perhaps Lamplighter's scheme didn't appear particularly outlandish. Or, equally possibly, perhaps no one could think of anything else for Dr. Lamplighter to do to help.

In any case, Lamplighter's work was allowed to continue. Eventually, his researches were considered sufficiently advanced to put into action. Lamplighter had noted that *Anax britannica*, like several species of butterfly, exhibited strong migratory impulses. Experimental insects released in northern France in the spring of 1942 were observed flying north over the English Channel as the summer progressed, in similar fashion to flocks of Red Admiral and Painted Lady butterflies. Most didn't survive the journey, but one or two individuals were recovered, allowing Lamplighter to observe their behaviour. By the autumn, as the air over Britain cooled, the *britannica* dragonflies demonstrated the urge to fly south once more, heading for continental Europe. Here was the mechanism by which the weapon could be delivered.

By the following spring, Lamplighter had some five hundred *britannica* larvae ready. He had hoped for many thousands, but, as he observed, "the radioactive agents appear to render a high proportion of the adults infertile." Special Operations Executive (SOE) agents were handed the larvae and told to distribute them around key industrial and military sites in Germany and occupied France and Belgium. We can only wonder at their reaction at being given such strange orders. Inevitably, given the importance of their maintaining cover, I have been unable to unearth direct accounts from any of them.

However, many of the agents clearly did their work, as Lamplighter writes in his diary that, as the summer of 1943 approached, he captured "nearly twenty" of the hatched dragonflies as they crossed back over the channel to England. The archive contains an order to local Home Guard platoons to be on the lookout for "large flying insects" and gives a number to ring – presumably Lamplighter's – if any were spotted. It is remarkable that any were intercepted at all, of course. We can only wonder at how many of the insects simply escaped Lamplighter's attention and flew on into England. Or never made it that far. It is amusing, also, to imagine Lamplighter racing across the South Downs of England, butterfly net aloft, in desperate pursuit of his dragonflies as they clattered in from the sea.

Alas, by the end of that summer, Lamplighter's flock of huge insects had been further diminished as, one by one, the insects succumbed to disease or "simply crashed into walls and collapsed into broken ruins" as Lamplighter himself put it. By the autumn of 1943, Lamplighter had only a single individual left, a dragonfly he named, for reasons I have been unable to discover, "Maude". This creature was duly equipped with its package of high explosives and, one late summer day, released from the white cliffs of Dover into the clutches of a stiff northerly wind. Lamplighter describes sitting for twenty minutes, watching the "brave" insect fluttering away over the sea towards the distant shores of France.

Lamplighter never saw Maude again. Indeed, no one knows if the solitary *britannica* even completed its flight back to its breeding-ground near some German munitions factory or airfield.

In many regards, the experiment was an abject failure. There are no reports of the German military machine being crippled by swarms of giant, explosive insects. Still, Lamplighter was not discouraged, and he describes ambitious plans to increase the scale of his operations. "God willing," he wrote, "we will have thousands of insects to release by next autumn, should this war still be raging."

Alas, for Lamplighter, it was never to be. He was killed that winter in an accident on Salisbury Plain, when a batch of experimental explosive chose to explode at the wrong moment. Darley referred to the incident somewhat elliptically, explaining that "the new ordnance proved itself too eager to detonate, unfortunately resulting in the demise of dragonflies and others. I rather suspect my time here is done."

Meanwhile, the high rate of infertility among *Anax britannica* that had been noted by Lamplighter was having its effect. Instead of the thousands of creatures Lamplighter had wanted, very few emerged in the spring of 1944, and none that did successfully pupated. Both Lamplighter and *Anax britannica* were gone, a mere footnote in the history of the war, and the operation was wound up. Dr. Pashlova returned to her studies of fruit flies, where she did important work after the war. Captain Darley survived the Dunkirk landings and after the armistice joined a circus, where he performed as "Jolly Johnny Japes the Clown" until the 1970s. Neither Pashlova nor Darley ever mentioned their wartime experiences with Lamplighter. Both were sworn to secrecy, of course, but I can't help wondering if a certain amount of embarrassment played a part as well.

And that might be the end of the story, except for intriguing reports emerging in the years after the war of "large" or even "titanic" dragonfly sightings. I have scoured newspaper archives across southern Britain and northern Europe and managed to unearth some truly intriguing accounts.

In 1951, for instance, a woman walking near Mont Saint Michel in France reported seeing "a vast insect thrumming through the air like a World War I biplane." Later that same year, a Reverend Cooper claimed he was buzzed by a dragonfly "the size of a seagull" in Somerset. Eight years later, in 1959, we have an account from the Rhineland of a dragonfly so large the observer "at first thought it was a model aeroplane". Reliable witnesses or over-active imaginations? It is hard to be sure.

I can only speculate whether some few individuals of *Anax britannica* did, indeed, survive and were able to mate. It is even conceivable that they interbred with *Anax imperator*. The possibility is surely a delicious one: perhaps even now, over some lonely English marsh, a vast dragonfly is buzzing through the summer sky, in a scene from distant prehistory. I like to think it might be so.

Anax Britannica was first published in Mad Scientist Journal in 2016. It's another alternative history/alternative science story, this time presented as a factual report or a piece of journalism. It was a lot of fun to write. So far as I know there is not and never has been a giant dragonfly species called *Anax britannica*, although there were giants in the Carboniferous, when the atmosphere had higher oxygen concentrations.

The notion of using something so crazy and clumsy as a dragonfly to defeat the Nazi menace seemed satisfyingly eccentric, and I do like the image of Lamplighter racing across the South Downs, his useless butterfly net held aloft...

THE HUNTER AND THE HUNTED

He was cornered now. He wasn't going to escape from this was he? She wasn't going to let up. She was going to hunt him down until she had him. She had all the gear, too: the black leather, the deathly pallor, the blood-red lips. She probably had a cape back at home too. A cape lined with red silk. It was incredible the lengths they went to. The *monsters*.

He was too exhausted by the long chase across the city to run any more. He hadn't drunk for, what, five days? His strength was gone. Too scared of going outside, that was the problem. Too afraid of being pursued like this. Starvation had forced him out eventually. Three long hours ago.

He'd ducked into the alleyway hoping to hide in the shadows while his strength returned. A mound of black plastic rubbish sacks gave him something to crouch behind. The stench from them was foul, blotting out all other scents. He peered around the pile, hoping she might walk past without seeing him. The bright lights of the main street reflected garishly in the oily puddles on the ground.

Then she appeared, just a silhouette against the neon shop signs. She sniffed the air. Actually *sniffed*. Dear gods.

She knew he was there. He was cornered.

Sometimes they hunted in packs. They were clever like that, communicating, coordinating. But at least this one was on her own. Perhaps that gave him a chance. He had to decide what to do. Fight? He had his weapons, of course. Powerful weapons. But he had his pride, too. That was just giving them what they wanted. He was supposed to be the hunter, not them. He fed where he wished, not on the orders of someone else. He wasn't some animal, some tool.

When had it become like this? He blamed the sixties. Everything had gone wrong then. Once he had only to bare his teeth and people ran screaming. Now they'd lost all respect. All deference. An ancient title like his meant nothing any more. Now they ran towards you. Now they *wanted* to be taken. He blamed their rock music. He'd seen them going to their concerts in their black leather, the lurid, bloodthirsty images on their clothes. That or their movies, making it all seem so desirable.

Now some of them looked more vampire than he was. They were so vampire they were *vampyre*.

Long centuries ago, he'd known real Goths, in the shadowy forests of central Europe. These modern versions were much more terrifying. Fear was his real weapon, not the bite or the *change*. But these modern ones had no fear. They embraced the twilight, sought it out. A new sensation, a new thrill for them to try. Now, he'd bare his teeth and loom towards someone and instead of screaming they said, *Cool!* Ah, the horror of it.

The fools. They had no idea what it was like. Pursued every day by mobs clamouring to be initiated. Clamouring for the change. They thought they wanted what he had, what he was. The endless life. The power. The dress-sense. But it was a curse. A terrible curse.

The woman who'd pursued him stepped forward into the alley. "I know you're in there, my friend," she said. "Come on out and give me what I want. Come on out or

I'll come in there and take it from you."

The Count cowered into his corner and closed his eyes.

The Hunter and the Hunted originally appeared in the Vampires Suck anthology in 2014. The story is an attempt to turn some of the tired old tropes of the vampire story on their heads and do something a little original. I like the idea of the outraged, ancient vampire blaming rock music and the 1960s for the moral decline of we mortals.

LEVIATHAN

"Do these computing machines really have to make all this racket?" Mitchell, the man from the Ministry, stood in the middle of Leviathan's Processor Hall "A", a grimace on his face and a serious black briefcase in his hand. "It's 2014, for heaven's sake. Surely you can make them quieter by now?"

His question surprised Dr. Ada Appleton. Racket? She loved the noise in here. She found it ... comforting. Sometimes she came in here to get some peace. To think. If you listened closely enough you could hear patterns in all the clacking and whirring and clicking. A music, of sorts. Still, she couldn't expect Mitchell to agree. It was just a shame it was him holding the purse-strings. He would decide whether to approve or can their much-needed third processor hall. And how could someone like him understand a machine like Leviathan?

"Follow me!" she mouthed, and turned to head for the side of the hall. She led him past line after line of switch stacks, valve arrays and storage pots. As they walked, Mitchell peered up and around, like some tourist in Manhattan, amazed at the height and scale of everything around him. Good. Leviathan *was* amazing. She'd designed it to be amazing and she wanted Mitchell to be impressed.

She pushed through the double doors that led, via a short connecting corridor, into the adjacent hall. The hush was immediate; the only sound, the deep, ever-present hum in the walls and floor. This hall was equally vast - big enough to play a decent game of football in - but completely devoid of machinery. Processor Hall "C" stood ready and waiting. The final stage of her grand design.

Mitchell straightened his tie as he peered around the cavernous vault that had been carved out of the Welsh mountainside. "Can't you make these machines, you know, smaller?"

His voice sounded hollow in the echoing space. Ada smiled an indulgent smile. "I'm afraid you mustn't believe everything the Sci Fi writers come up with. Computers the size of books and matchboxes. It would be marvellous, but I'm afraid 'microprocessors' and all those other miraculous electronic devices exist only in stories. The truth is obvious. In order to make a Babbagian computer more powerful you have to make it bigger. More valves, more switches, more cogs, more axles. That's been the lesson of the last seventy years. Each generation of machine has been bigger than the last. The *Colossus* machines of the 1940s and 1950s. *Juggernaut* in the 1960s and 1970s. *Gargantua* in the 1980s and *Goliath* in the 1990s. Then *Behemoth* and finally *Leviathan* from 2005 onwards."

Mitchell scowled and looked around. She'd done her research on him. A rising star in the government. He was a Treasury man at heart, though. A bean counter. Which was fine. Let him see what a tight ship she ran here.

"Really, though," said Mitchell. "One wonders why the world even needs so many computers. With *Shiva* running in India and China's *Long March* there are seven of the things crashing and whirring away. I mean, aren't you going to run out of numbers to add up?"

She forced herself to smile again. She'd heard it all before. Still, his words sent a chill through her. They wouldn't really refuse to fund the third Hall would they? Not after everything they'd achieved?

"Processors "A" and "B" are currently running at 110% of their designed capacity," she said. "As I'm sure you're aware, they aren't simply *adding up numbers*. They are executing programs. Sometimes three or even four of them at the same time. Predicting the weather, modelling the economy, solving complex mathematical problems..."

"And playing games."

Damn. She wondered if he'd bring that up. The bloody papers had published the story a few weeks back. How the boffins used the machine to play games of chess and *Dungeon Delve*. Which was true, they did. But only when there were free slots in the execution plan, late at night or at weekends. The processor time consumed was negligible. And you never knew what useful advancements could come out of the apparently trivial.

"Occasionally, yes," she conceded. "But there is obviously never any detrimental effect on the vital work Leviathan carries out."

Mitchell nodded, but looked unconvinced. He began to pace around, inspecting the walls and power fittings as if he had personally paid for everything. "And are you aware of the cost of running Leviathan? Day-to-day?"

"It's ... a lot, I know. Valves need replacing. All the moving parts require constant maintenance."

"Every day you use up nearly three thousand discs of top-grade aluminium. Discs a yard across."

"Our microdot permanent storage platters. We don't *use them up*. We store data on them. They're all still here, racked and catalogued in the archive."

"Then there's the electricity. That alone amounts to nearly 4% of national power consumption. Did you know that, Dr. Appleton?"

"I ... no. I wasn't aware of that figure."

"That would jump to 6% if Processor Hall "C" was commissioned."

"Yes. But still, it has to be a price worth paying."

He was softening her up. Preparing her for bad news. They weren't going to fund the new hall after all. She saw now. How could they be so short-sighted?

"And surely," he continued, "we could pay someone else to carry out our calculations for us? *Kryptonite* in New York. Or *Red Square*. We're all friends now, you know."

Dread trickled through her veins. He wasn't talking about refusing Processor "C". He was questioning "A" and "B" too. Questioning Leviathan. She didn't know what to say.

As her mouth opened and closed, Simpkins, her Chief Tech, poked his head around the doors. The papers liked to portray people like him as bald, white-coated boffins and the unfortunate truth was this described Simpkins perfectly. She'd never been able to work our whether he was unaware of the stereotype or playing up to it. Maybe it was irony. She didn't always get irony.

"Ah, Dr. Appleton?"

"Yes, Simpkins. What is it?"

"That new program we talked about. It's running now."

"Not another new program?" Mitchell asked. "What does *this* one do?"

She sighed. A little demonstration they'd arranged. Perhaps it wasn't going to make any difference now.

"It's best we show you, I think," she said. Mitchell nodded his head curtly, as if he was being badly inconvenienced. She turned and walked with Simpkins, heading for the Exec.

As they walked, they passed a window overlooking one of the typing halls. Rows of people sat, reading and typing away simultaneously. Hundreds of them. They needed more, though, to keep up with the daily flow of information. Something else she'd been hoping to speak to Mitchell about.

"And are these the people who, ah, *program* Leviathan?"

Mitchell asked. He stopped and stared through the window. She had the clear impression he was counting heads and calculating the cost of employing them all. As they watched, two white-coated figures rolled one of the polished aluminium platters out of the microdot punch engine and placed it with reverence in its slot on a trolley. Its surface glistened from the rings of tiny pits now etched into it. Couldn't he see what they'd achieved here? The brilliance of it? And the new platter arrays could read twenty-four of the discs simultaneously, now. A year ago they'd only been able to read two.

"This is one of the data entry pools," she said.

"Data entry?"

"Yes, we take all the newspapers and books and so forth that are published and type them into Leviathan."

"And why would you do that? Given that you can just read them for real?"

Fortunately, she'd prepared for this question. She'd got Simpkins to load up the relevant discs the night before. "Well, for instance, did you know the broadsheet newspapers have mentioned you 317 times in the past three months? 80% of the time in association with some positive or approving adjective. The Home Secretary, by comparison, has been mentioned 242 times with an approval rating of 65%."

That made him think. The Home Secretary was Mitchell's rival to take over the leadership of his party. One of those political secrets everyone knew about.

"I see. Interesting." Mitchell looked more thoughtful now.

"If you'll follow me to the Exec?" she said.

The Exec – the Executive Control Room – was where she spent a large percentage of her waking life. Too much of her waking life. Here they controlled every aspect of Leviathan. She showed Mitchell to Simpkins' seat.

"This a television?" Mitchell asked, looking confused.

"It's one of Leviathan's terminals," she said. "We

control the machine through these and also see its output. But in essence, yes, it's just a cathode ray tube like any television."

"And this … typewriter?"

"That how we instruct the machine. Simpkins? Could you show us the new program in operation, please?"

Simpkins began the speech they'd prepared for Mitchell's benefit. "Of course, Dr. Appleton. I call it the *Interconnect Data Translation Network*. Essentially it provides access to all the files stored on the discs of Kryptonite, Shiva and Red Square. Those they choose to make available to us at least. Long March and the others aren't connected up, yet, but there's no reason why they shouldn't be. The program is like a … librarian. It allows us to scan and correlate all the data on the other machines' data stores."

"Scan and correlate it?" said Mitchell.

"He means read it," said Ada. "You see, we used to keep all the platters in dark storage and get each disc out when we needed it. Over the past year we've moved towards storing the discs in stacked arrays that can also read them. If we could build big enough arrays then all the information we hold could be retrieved more-or-less instantaneously. Think what we could achieve then. We could…"

"Just a minute," said Mitchell, holding his hand up to stop her. "You're saying you've connected Leviathan to those other computers? New York, Moscow and so forth? You can see what they're doing over there?"

"Yes," said Ada. "In a manner of speaking. We're piggy-backing on the sea-bed cables. The other machines have radically different hardware and they, ah, talk a different language. But what we've done allows us to pool all the data typed into Kryptonite and the others. We see their records just as they see ours. They don't use microdot aluminium of course. America uses huge drums of magnetized tape and Moscow sheets of etched glass. But the effect is the same."

"Show me."

"Very well. Simpkins, let Mr. Mitchell look at the latest news from the USA."

Simpkins showed Mitchell what buttons to press to control the flashing square on the terminal screen. "And if you press this button, the highlighted item is opened up and you can read it. Press this to go back up a level in the menu. You'll also notice you can sometimes jump directly from within one document to another, if Leviathan has spotted a link between them."

Dr. Appleton and Simpkins stood behind Mitchell as he navigated menus and, repeatedly, stopped to read paragraphs of text. Five minutes went by. Ten. Twenty. Fortunately, the sea-bed cables were functioning well today. Mitchell didn't have to wait longer then twenty seconds for data to start coming through each time.

"This is incredible," he said at last, turning to look at them. "I mean, it's all here. News, politics, economics, sport, fiction. All of it."

"We index everything, too, so we can search for any mention of a word or a phrase. Try typing in your own name."

"My name?"

"I'm sure you'll have lots of matches." She knew he would. She'd tried the very thing that morning. Just as long as Anderson and Karkov, her equivalents in Washington and Moscow, did as they'd promised and kept the relevant data stores online. International co-operation was a wonderful thing.

Using one finger, Mitchell typed out his name on the keyboard. Simpkins showed him the button to press to begin the search. Within seconds, sentences began appearing on the screen: quotations mentioning Mitchell, some from American and Russian news reports.

"We think we can do the same for sounds and pictures, too," said Ada. "Even *moving* pictures eventually. They're all just different types of data. We just need more cables as well as the extra spindle arrays to keep all the information on the line."

Mitchell actually appeared to be lost for words for a moment. Finally, he spoke.

"And would it be possible for one of these terminals to be installed in, say, London? In Whitehall?"

She hesitated for only a moment. Here was her chance. In truth it would be easy, but didn't need to know that. "It's a long way to run a terminal connection. It would have to go underground. But given enough funding we could do it."

Mitchell considered, then nodded in a decisive sort of way. "Dr. Appleton, I'm going to talk to the PM this evening. Given the potential of this, I think I can persuade him of the benefits of Leviathan to Great Britain. To think you can actually connect computers together and make them talk to each other. Remarkable."

"Thank you, Mr. Mitchell."

"One thing, though. I think we'll need a snappier title for this new system of yours. Something to catch the imagination."

She looked questioningly at Simpkins. The existing name seemed like a perfectly good one to her.

"Well," said Simpkins. "Program names have a maximum of eight characters on Leviathan, so I've already had to abbreviate Interconnect Data Translation Network."

"What to?" asked Mitchell.

"*Internet.*"

Mitchell turned the word over in his mouth. "Boring name. Can't see it catching on. OK, one more question Dr. Appleton."

"Yes. Ask anything."

"If you can see their files they can see ours, yes?"

"Absolutely. The spirit of openness is fundamental to the whole operation."

"But how do they know that what they're reading is the truth?"

"I don't … I'm not sure I understand," she said.

"You could make up anything," said Mitchell. There was a little light in his eyes as he spoke now. A gleam. "You could make the other capitals believe whatever you wanted, yes?"

"I suppose. But I don't see why…"

"And these programs you write. They're also data? More microdots stored on those platters?"

He was smarter than she'd given him credit for. "In a manner of speaking."

"So you could transfer those too? Even get them to quietly execute on the other machines once you've worked out these other languages they use? Then you could find out what our friends are really up to. See the things they don't want us to see."

"It's theoretically possible. Still I don't…"

Mitchell waved her objections away. "How long before you can have Processor Hall "C" up and running, Dr. Appleton?"

"Six months, given the funding. But doing what you suggest…"

Mitchell ignored her. He stood. "Six months. You've worked wonders here, Dr. Appleton. Britain has a lot to thank you for. We could even name the new hall after you."

She watched his back as he headed for the lifts. She'd done it. She'd actually done it. Leviathan would be completed after all.

She should have felt elated. But instead, something like dread filled her at the thought of what she'd done.

Another alternative science/alternative history story, this one growing out of wondering how the 20th and 21st centuries might have been different if microprocessors hadn't been invented, and we were stuck with building larger and larger analogue devices to increase computing power. It was printed in KZine in 2015.

My thinking was that we might end up in something like the current situation, but obviously in a much more backwards and clunky way. Still, it would have been cool to take a walk with Dr. Appleton around Leviathan. On a historical note, Colossus was a real computer, although all the others mentioned are made up.

LORD LION'S DESIGN

Lord Lion, Home Secretary of Great Britain and Northern Ireland, lifted the chalice of blood that Brabham, his butler, had brought for him. It was only midday, but he needed a drink. Presenting himself to a wary public as the acceptable face of the undead community was proving to be much more wearing than he'd imagined. Bloody plebs were just so damned *mistrustful.* He had to tread carefully; he was so close to the prize now. One slip and all the years of scheming and denial would be wasted.

The only light in his shuttered library was the shifting glow from the fire. It limned the polished silver cup as he brought it to his lips. He sniffed the bouquet, swirling the dark, viscous liquid around. The cellars were so poorly stocked these days. A good vintage was rare; so much was tainted, degraded. A pure Anglo-Saxon, perhaps a hint of Celt or Norse for colour, was a precious thing. And this smelt promising.

He sipped, then spat blood out, spraying his butler's face.

"This is disgusting, man! What were you thinking?"

Brabham, holding his tray perfectly still on the splayed fingers of one hand, wiped the blood from his face with a tissue plucked from his breast pocket.

"I am most sorry, Lord Lion. I warmed it to precisely 98.6 degrees on the Fahrenheit scale."

"It's not the temperature! It's mongrel blood. Bring me brandy immediately to take the taste away."

"My lord."

Brabham set down the tray and poured brandy from the nearby cabinet. Lord Lion drank without even letting it breathe, swilling the liquor around in his mouth, his eyes closed.

"Better. A little better."

He opened his eyes again. Brabham hadn't moved.

"What in the seven circles of Hell were you thinking?"

"I'm sorry, my lord. The provenance was checked most carefully."

"White?"

"Yes, my lord."

"How far back did you check the lineage? The taste was quite sickly."

"The line was impeccable, I assure you. Parents and grandparents, all good Anglo-Saxon stock."

"Then you should have looked further back."

"But, my lord, if one goes back far enough, then surely all of us have, ah, connections with other parts of the world do we not? Are one's ancient ancestors not all from Africa?"

In a single movement, too fast for Brabham to react to, Lion stood and lashed out. The butler was hurled through the air to thump into the wall between the Turner and the Constable. He crumpled to the floor in a broken heap.

"I'd drink from you if you weren't so tainted!"

Brabham could only groan in reply. He tried to stand but was unable to. Then the door was pushed ajar and Warner, Lord Lion's Director of Communications, peered warily inside. He glanced at Brabham crumpled on the floor, then back to Lion.

"What is it, Warner?"

"Sorry to interrupt, Lord Lion. Something's come up. Another incident."

"Deaths?"

"Deaths."

Lion shrugged. "You people get killed all the time. It's a fact of life."

"It looks like another act of ritual vampirism."

Lion swore to himself. First the blood and now this. Why did he bother? "How many dead?"

Warner closed the door behind him. He stepped over Brabham and into the room. "Around ten."

Lion poured himself more brandy. "Then prepare the usual statement. Profound regrets ... outrage ... bring to justice ... so on and so on. You know the form."

"I think we may need to go a little further with this one," said Warner. "You've seen the papers, what's trending on Twitter. You know the public mood. I feel we need to be a little more visible just now."

"Oh, you do?"

"I do."

Lion sighed. There was no peace. And Warner knew his job, no doubt about it.

"What do you have in mind?"

"Go to the scene of the crime. Talk to the cameras, show the country how appalled you are. Do *statesmanlike* and *reassuring*."

"Is that really necessary?"

"I've ordered the car round already. Ms. Hudson will brief you on the way."

"That bitch."

Warner frowned. "Lord Lion, I…"

"Never mind, never mind," said Lion, holding up a hand to cut Warner short. "I'll do as you ask." He glanced over towards Brabham, still in a heap on the floor. "This room needs cleansing anyway."

*

"The wolves got here first I see."

They sat in the back of the ministerial car, invisible behind smoked glass. Lion glanced across at Ms. Hudson. *Cally*. She raised one of her immaculately arched eyebrows. He flashed her a brief smile of apology.

"Forgive me, my dear. A mere turn of phrase."

He returned to examining the throng of reporters and photographers waiting outside the terraced London house. Cally continued flicking through reports on her iPad.

"Are you ready to face them?" she asked. "Do you have all the facts you need?"

"I'll manage." He glanced back at the young woman sitting next to him. Her lipstick was bright, glossy red. Perhaps he should invite her to Huntersley for another weekend. She was so very decorative and, of course, her *condition* made things instantly more interesting. A shame she'd insisted on maintaining a purely professional relationship last time. The closest she'd got to letting that hair down was to express an interest in Lion family history, of which there was rather a lot. Perhaps, in hindsight, offering to let her hunt with the hounds had been a mistake. But she was pure, he knew. An English Rose. A dog-rose. He wondered how she'd taste.

"How do I look?" he asked.

"You look fine. The blue tie is definitely better than the red."

"Ah, good. Sometimes the lack of a reflection is such a bore."

He raised his voice so the policeman in the driving-seat could hear.

"Any news yet?"

The policeman half-turned his head, keeping his eyes on the reporters.

"None, sir."

"Very well."

Lion pulled a bar of chocolate from his inside packet,

peeled off purple foil from one brick and snapped it off.

"Vampires like chocolate?" asked Cally.

Lord Lion glanced at the policeman in the front seat. Completely reliable, of course, but still. Public perceptions had to be maintained at all costs. Especially now.

"Finest dark chocolate," he replied, making sure he could be heard in the front of the car. "100% pure cocoa. I have it imported from Jamaica. It helps with the blood cravings, I find. I think it must be the iron."

He closed his eyes closed for a moment, savouring the rich, bitter taste. In truth it did help. A little.

"Would you care for some?" he asked.

"Not for me, thank you. You may be indestructible but that's pure poison to us. Haven't you heard of theobromine?"

"Can't say that I have, my dear."

"Chocolate is death to canines."

"But ... the time of the month. I mean, it's a crescent moon just now; you're looking wonderfully, ravishingly human. Surely you'd be safe at the moment?"

"I don't intend to find out. And that stuff gives me a migraine even when I'm human."

"Ah, too bad."

"Are you ready now?"

"Quite ready. Bring on the ravening pack."

The eyebrow arched again.

*

Lord Lion strode towards the throng of reporters, deliberately revealing the tips of his elongated canines. *Here we are, nothing to be afraid of, all perfectly normal.*

"Home Secretary," one of them shouted. "When are you going to bring your own people under control?"

He smiled at the question.

"I'm afraid it is far too soon to speculate who is responsible for this," he replied. "All we know is that eleven bodies have been discovered and that the house was a squat, illegally occupied. The causes of death are not yet clear."

Another babble of shouted questions. A tall woman with luscious blond hair standing at the front shouted the loudest. Sally Peterson, *bloody* Daily Mail.

"Are you denying they all had their throats torn out?"

Keep smiling. Remorseful, calm.

"I can neither confirm nor deny such rumours. I can assure you that if a crime has been committed here, the culprit or culprits will be caught. I have full confidence in the police force."

"They'll be charged despite the Lycanthrope and Revenant Relations Act?"

Jim Edwards from the Express. *Rabble.*

"I assume you are alluding to the positive discrimination clauses in the recent legislation. As I'm sure you are aware this does not extend to acts of criminality."

"But, if this was an act of vampirism, doesn't the law now have to make *due allowance?*"

"That's a matter for the courts. Whoever has carried out this crime, even if a member of the lycanthrope or revenant communities, will be brought to justice. Now, ladies and gentlemen, if you will excuse me?"

With a nod, he swept away from the semi-circle of reporters, leaving them to bellow further questions after him. He walked towards the house. Once it would have been a rather grand building. Now it sagged and crumbled. The windows were boarded up. Plants straggled out of the gutters and lichen furred the crumbling brickwork. If he had his way they'd bulldoze the whole street and all the others like it.

An expressionless constable shepherded him through the police cordon that sealed off the house, inviting him inside. Her face-muscles were tense as she stood aside to let him pass.

The scene was worse than anything described by the

harpies of the press. Impossible to tell how many bodies there were. The walls were spattered and smeared. Someone had massacred them all. Had *fun* massacring them all. The smell of blood was overpowering, exciting him, the tug deep in his stomach and his loins. But repelling him at the same time too. It was all tainted, filthy. Rank with decay and disease. The thought of them all, infesting the place like worms, made him sick.

He stepped through the room, taking care not to stain his Gucci shoes.

"The press are going to love this," Cally said from the door. "They'll have a field-day. It'll be worse than *Free Homes for Zombies*."

"Get Scarman on the phone," he said. "Tell him I need to see him. Now."

"At Whitehall?"

"Of course, not at bloody Whitehall. Tell him he's invited to my house. Tonight only, any time after dark."

"Right away, Lord Lion."

*

That evening, he sat and waited in the library of his Kensington town-house again. North of the river, of course; the same side of the Thames as Westminster. Not being able to cross running water was another bore. He could always take the tube, go under the river, but *that* would mean travelling alongside all the riff-raff of London, a prospect too terrible to contemplate.

He'd left the balcony window wide open, letting in the chill of the night. Big Ben chimed midnight in the cold distance. Scarman had clearly been waiting for his cue. The curtains flapped and waved and there he was, outlined against the sparkling lights of the city.

The silhouette moved into the room. Scarman was by far the biggest vampire Lion had ever met: tall and broad. As a normal human he would have been formidable. As a vampire he was terrifying. Unless you were a vampire yourself.

Lord Lion stood, strode across the room towards Scarman and, with an outstretched hand, lifted him up off the ground. Without breaking stride, he thrust him to one side to impale him on the ceremonial katana of a stone Samurai set beside the window on a plinth.

Lion stepped backwards and flicked on the lights. Scarman, suspended a foot above the ground, the tip of the sword protruding through his chest, grinned broadly.

"My Lord Lion."

"You idiot!" Lion replied. "What do you think you're doing? What the hell was that today? Another episode like it and I'll have no chance. Do I need to explain our arrangement to you again?"

Scarman slipped downwards, the razor-sharp blade slicing through more of his chest. "Play by their rules. Work from within. *Be good.* I think I can understand."

"I'm one step away from being Prime Minister of this country. Do you have any idea what that would mean? Do you understand what we could do then? The wars we could wage? The blood that would flow? We'd be unstoppable."

"We already are unstoppable. We don't need to play these games of yours."

Scarman pulled himself forward along the curving Samurai blade with his hands. The tip of the sword disappeared into his chest and then he was free, dropping to the ground.

"We can't afford any more of these incidents," Lord Lion said. "You gave me your word you'd keep your people under control."

Scarman shook his head while he inspected the damage to his chest. "What you don't appear to understand is that vampires don't obey rules. We are the masters and we do what we like. I can't *control my people.*"

"Then it's time you started. I will not have my plans

ruined by your thugs. I warn you, Scarman, there is to be no more unless I say so. I can invoke the internment clauses of the legislation if required and I'm quite willing to do so. Even *you* won't be able to escape the silver cages we have waiting at Yarl's Wood."

"And I'm warning *you*. Your *Home Secretary* means nothing to us. Your designs mean nothing to us. You and your human friends. The vampire in the alleyway is sick of your promises, sick of your words. Do you think we'll just stop because you tell us to?"

The two vampires faced each other across the room.

"This stops now," said Lion. "We do things my way, not yours. The years of skulking like rats in the shadows are over."

Scarman charged at Lord Lion, hurling his body back against a marble pillar. Lion felt ribs crack with the force of the blow.

"There's your answer," said Scarman.

"Get out of my house," said Lion. "Get out and don't return. The invitation is rescinded. If you're lucky I'll come and see you when you're interred. Out!"

Scarman stepped backwards, unable to resist the terms of the Invitation and Denial. Back at the window, before he stepped out into the night air, he grinned once again. "Goodnight to you too, my lord. We'll meet again soon, I'm sure."

*

The following morning, Lion strode down Downing Street. As he always did, he imagined himself Prime Minister already, thought about what he would do when he held the reins of power. Ah, the plans he had. The thought of it made him quicken his pace. The policeman on the door of No. 10 nodded to him discreetly as he approached, to invite him inside.

An aide showed Lion to an ante-room, where he had to

sit and wait for five, ten, fifteen minutes. He closed his eyes, refusing to let himself be riled by such petty games. When the Prime Minister's door finally opened, the Archbishop of Canterbury emerged, the scowl on his beneficent features very clear as he spotted Lion. Lion smiled at his old adversary in the Lords. More games. He had to admit it was nicely done.

Inside, Edwards, the Prime Minister, the *current Prime Minister*, told him to sit, then proceeded to make him wait again, reading dossier after dossier from his red ministerial case. Lion entertained himself with thoughts of what he would do to Edwards when he took over. Prime Minister of the United Kingdom and the man was barely British.

"Ah, Lion," Edwards said at last, as if just noticing him waiting there. "You've heard about events overnight?"

"No-one has briefed me on anything."

"We're keeping it quiet as possible. More atrocities. London, Manchester, Glasgow and, for some reason, Ross-on-Wye. We can't go on like this can we? You do see, I'm sure. Bringing you into the cabinet, well, it was a calculated risk. Please, let me finish! It was a gamble, we both know that. We've worked hard on public perceptions, all those films with charming vampire characters. We've made progress at bringing people together. And you come from a fine and noble British family. But if the slaughter continues, we'll have to review our policies, you see that?"

"I understand what you are saying, Prime Minister."

"I know you are in a difficult position, caught between the interests of, well, *competing groups*. But we can't have more events like last night's. Do you follow?"

"Is this an ultimatum, Prime Minister?"

"Well. That's a strong word. But, yes, if you like. The Home Secretary can't be a part of the problem, can he? If he brings peace, heals wounds, that's a different matter. But this? Well, you see my viewpoint."

"Quite clearly."

"Good, good. Do what you have to do. Talk to your

people."

Lion nodded. The Prime Minister looked down, back to his papers. The interview was over. Lion stood and left. Deep in thought, he barely noticed the drive back towards Whitehall.

There was a chance everything would collapse now. Scarman and his dogs would ruin it all. They were useful, of course, but dangerous. He had to act.

He pulled out his phone and speed-dialled as they drove.

"Cally?"

"Yes, Lord Lion?"

"The contingency plans we discussed. Please put them into motion."

"You mean the internment clauses?"

"I do. All the suspected trouble makers. Mobilise Special Forces as planned."

"You're … you're sure?"

"Just do it. I shall be at home. There will be a backlash from certain quarters and I would prefer to be somewhere an angry vampire mob can't reach me. Keep me informed."

"Yes, sir."

He switched off his phone. He allowed himself a thin smile. He could come very well out of this after all. The PM's ultimatum might be just the opening he needed. He had justification for acting. If he took the credit then a grateful nation, freed of the scourge of uncontrolled vampirism and lycanthropy, would surely support him when the time came. *Lord Lion, he's a fine old British vampire, he knows what's right and what's not.* He would lose the support of some of the undead, of course, but the majority would do little more than grumble. As they always did. This could be very, very good.

Back in his library he sat monitoring the reports as they came in from the commanders of the Special Forces deployed to round up the rogue vampires. He received other messages too, vows of terrible revenge from those being hunted. It was a shame electronic communication didn't have to obey the Invitation and Denial rules. For some reason *they* could enter the house unimpeded.

When he saw everything was progressing as desired he stood from his computer and strode to the window to gaze out over the London skyline. Soon, soon, power would be his. He was ready. More than ready. Even vampire patience wore thin.

He heard only the faintest footfall before the silver blade skewered through his chest. Agony burned through him. He had forgotten what pain was. Turning around, stumbling to one knee, confused, he found himself looking up at Scarman.

"I told you we'd meet again soon, Lord Lion."

"How can you be here? You aren't invited in."

"Ah, but I am."

"No."

Another figure walked up behind Scarman. Brabham, one arm in plaster, stepped out from behind the giant vampire.

"I'm afraid he is, sir."

"You?"

"I'm afraid so, sir."

"But … why?"

"Well, to put a stop to you, my lord. If I may be allowed to say so, sir, it's because you make me feel sick."

Lion was on his knees now, the pain overwhelming. He looked up at both of them. "And Scarman … doesn't sicken you?"

"Not like you, my lord. See, it's not the vampire thing. I mean, Mr. Scarman here is a fright, to be sure, but you're something else. I know all about your designs, you see. All that talk of pure *blood*."

"Mongrel dog!" said Lion.

"Yes, sir," said Brabham. "I'm sure I am."

The agony in Lion's chest was electric now. Why wasn't

it subsiding? The wound was nothing. Lion grasped the sword by its hilt to yank it out. The metal burned his hands where he touched it, smoke coiling off. He actually screamed. The indignity of it.

"Oh, you won't be able to pull it out," said Scarman, who stood watching the scene with amusement. "Not *that* sword. Haven't you worked it out yet?"

Lion looked down at the blade protruding from his chest. Of course. He knew what it must be. But the Lion Sword, used in ritual sacrifices for seven hundred years, the only weapon that could harm him, was held in *very* secure conditions at Huntersley. He'd made sure of that, of course.

"How?" he said. "How can you have this?"

"I gave it to him." A woman's voice. It took him a few moments to recognize who it was. Cally walked up to stand beside Scarman and Brabham.

"How? It's not possible."

"You showed me yourself, that weekend at Huntersley. You deactivated all the security while I watched."

"But, you're one of us!"

"I'm a werewolf and you're a vampire. That's not much of a similarity."

"No, no, I mean you're *English*."

Cally shook her head. "I believed in you once. The architect of the Lycanthrope and Revenant Relations Act. How ironic *that* seems. Now I see you as you really are. It was all just moves in a game for you, wasn't it? And if you'd bothered to find out anything about me you'd know the man I love, the man I'm married to, is Turkish."

"Ah."

"Making our two boys, what, half-breeds? They're *beautiful* is what they are. While *you* are a monster. And being a vampire is only a very small part of that."

Lion slumped to the ground, the pain in his chest a vast, physical thing. He could feel it sucking the borrowed life back out of him, the blade remembering the blood it had shed.

"Please, the blade. Remove it. I'll do anything."

"Very well," said Scarman.

"You will?"

Scarman reached down and pulled the ancient, silver blade from Lion's chest. The raging flame in his chest subsided immediately. He looked up at them from the floor. Hope flared within him. They were just sending him a message. A warning. He could still succeed; it was all within his grasp now. The power he deserved. The power he was born to.

"Give me my sword," he said.

"No," said Scarman.

"Why … why not?" asked Lion.

Scarman glanced at Cally and Brabham. Both nodded; some unspoken agreement between them.

"Because, Lord Lion, I'm about to use it to sever your head from your body," said Scarman, raising the silver sword high into the air.

Lord Lion's Design is a story about monsters — and, of course, the fact that the monsters aren't necessarily the scary-looking horrors that pursue you with red eyes and bared teeth. The real monsters are often the ones who look like they aren't.

Urban fantasy like this is always fun to write, and there are definitely references in this story to British politics that amused me, at least. The story originally appeared in KZine magazine, in 2013.

HER FATHER'S EYES

Caitlin had her father's eyes. She kept them in a jar on the mantelpiece. Most people favoured a clock up there, maybe a nice vase. Something to wedge bills behind. Caitlin liked the eyes better.

You're not really going out like that are you? You're dressed like a whore. What will people think?

The voice was angry and, simultaneously, heavy with disappointment. It was a particular skill of her father's. He wasn't actually talking of course. After all, only his eyes remained. His eyes and a portion of his cerebral cortex and the two optic nerves connecting them. No, the voice was in Caitlin's head. That was the terrible truth of it. The voice was a part of her, stamped into her mind over the course of her childhood.

For many years she'd believed his words. You had to trust something when you grew up. You needed a yardstick to measure the world against. Her father had made a poor one. But for years she'd assumed he was right. She was worthless. Everything he did to her was *her* fault. When she went out she was, simultaneously, too ugly for others to look at *and* dressed so provocatively she was inviting trouble.

She studied herself in the mirror. Began touching up mascara and threading her best silver jewellery through her ears and eyebrows.

Hussy! Painted Jezebel!

It had taken her a long time to untangle these knots in her mind. The eyes were a part of the process. As an adult, she'd tried many things to make sense of her life. Therapy. Religion. Hedonism. Poetry. In the end, Necromancy had saved her. Her father had told her she'd fallen in with the wrong crowd. Fortunately, the *wrong crowd* turned out to be just what she needed. By the time her father died, still ranting and seething at everyone else because of his burden of guilt, she knew enough of the forbidden arts to act. To *operate*.

Like a painting, the eyes followed her around the room as she got herself ready to go out. Unlike a painting it was no illusion. Caitlin had been very careful with that. Each eye sat in a plastic hemisphere to which the optic muscles were attached. The eyes could turn and they could focus and they could watch. The fragment of cerebral cortex could then record. *Understand.* What it couldn't do was speak or act.

She knew he was in there. Every full moon she had to renew the rites. As she reworked the incantations she always caught a glimpse of him. A ball of seething rage bound to these fragments of his body. Once she had been small and weak. Now it was the other way around.

Finally ready, she crossed the room to stand in front of the mantelpiece.

"I'll probably bring someone back," she said to him. "If anyone takes my fancy. A guy, a girl, whatever." She liked to imagine he'd learned to lip read. He wasn't stupid. Quite the opposite. Once she'd taken great delight in doing every single thing he'd disapproved off when he was alive. A list of things to do after he died, a bucket list in reverse. She was over that now. Now she did what made her happy, not what made him unhappy. That was a victory in itself. Still, if she could achieve both it was a win-win.

She gave him a twirl. Her dress didn't leave a lot to the imagination. It made her feel good.

Whore! Slut! Look what you made me do!

The voice in her head would always be there, but she'd learned not to listen. It was the buzzing of an annoying fly. It was a familiar pain in the joints you stopped noticing. She stepped forward to stare directly into the eyes. The eyes that had scowled away so much of her childhood. Sometimes she caught a look in them. That cold fury surfacing. Perhaps she was just imagining it. Perhaps she was just remembering it. It was there now, so it seemed. But it couldn't harm her any more.

She smiled and blew him a kiss. "Don't wait up, now will you?" She switched off the lights and closed the door behind her, the evening city ready and waiting for her.

From the mantelpiece, the two eyes scanned the darkness, unblinking, unsleeping. Unable to do anything but watch and remember.

This story grew out of hearing someone say "she has her father's eyes" and wondering why someone might mean that literally. I suppose, again, the story might be considered horror, although to me, again, it's darkly humorous fantasy. Of course, it doesn't matter at all what label is put on it.

I like the line "she kept them in a jar on the mantlepiece" a lot. The story was published in Acidic Fiction in 2014, and reprinted the following year in their Corrosive Chronicles anthology.

IN THE DETAIL

Daniel Corder – Prime Minister of Great Britain and Northern Ireland – regarded the senior Civil Servant standing before him with something like astonishment.

"Are you suggesting what I *think* you're suggesting?"

The Civil Servant, Lord Swallow, adjusted his tie as he formed his careful response. Swallow was old school. The sort who'd been quietly running the country for centuries. An appearance of refined gentility and a mind like a concealed man-trap.

"I believe I am, sir."

"But … the voters will never accept such a thing. The newspapers will have a field day. The idea is hideous."

"The media will certainly require careful handling," said Swallow. "But there are several significant advantages to the scheme. As you know we have urban overcrowding and a dire shortage of land for affordable housing. And, given the parlous state of the public finances, we *were* instructed to come up with creative solutions."

"Even so," said Corder. "I mean is it even possible?"

"Oh, quite possible. The Necromancers and Diabolists Working Committee have studied the proposal in depth. They are quite clear it's feasible."

"Wait, wait," said Corder. He massaged his forehead. A nagging pain was already starting to grow behind his eyes. "You're saying the British government has a committee of necromancers and diabolists?"

"Most definitely, sir. One of our oldest. Given the nature of its work it is, of course, rather ... shadowy."

"Even so. What does the Archbishop of Canterbury make of it?"

"We do try our hardest to keep them apart."

Corder studied Swallow for several moments. The man was serious.

"Let me spell this out," said Corder. "Just so I'm clear. You're suggesting we build a new town in hell."

"That's correct, sir."

"And what would we call it? Hellington? Hellaby? Helland?"

"We're still considering. Although, actually, there are already towns in Britain with all those names."

"There are?"

"Indeed."

"And you have negotiated this arrangement with the, ah, relevant authorities?" What was he saying? He was actually taking the suggestion seriously. But the polls *were* bad. Very bad. Frankly, anything was worth a try at this point.

"We have," said Swallow.

"Won't there be, well, *problems* with the locals? Tormenting and that sort of thing?"

"We are assured tensions will be kept to an absolute minimum."

"And how much room would we be granted?"

"Fortunately, hell is limitless in extent," said Swallow. "Room is not a problem. I'm told the climate is pleasantly warm too."

"Warm?"

"Perhaps 'hot' might be a better word. A welcome escape from the British climate, I should say."

"And which circle are we talking about?"

"The eighth. Some of the circles would be most unsuitable for a modern community, but the eighth should work well."

He tried to think back to his schooldays, flicking through a battered copy of *Inferno* looking for good bits. "The eighth? That's not *Lust* is it?"

"No, no. *Fraud*. Barely even a sin these days."

"But surely you're not suggesting we kill a large part of the electorate?" said Corder. "I mean, even if we did, how could we be sure they'd all go to hell?"

Swallow smiled a little smile to himself, as if Corder had repeated one of his favourite jokes. "I don't believe there'd be any problem finding a sufficient number of sinners among the British electorate, sir. But that isn't an issue. There will be no requirement to actually kill those being relocated."

"Then how will they go to hell?"

"I'm no expert, sir, but I believe it's a matter of portals and pentagrams and the opening of fell gateways to the regions of the damned."

"Ah. And so, if someone's house is in hell but they work in, let us say, central London?"

"The problem has been planned for. We envisage a new junction on the M25 motorway that leads directly through a portal to Hades. Our research suggests most drivers will barely notice the difference."

Corder stood and walked to the window. Through the blinds, the towers and rooftops and drizzle of London looked reassuringly normal. Could they really do this? Perhaps. The voters might be persuaded. He'd found out long ago that the public tended to object to the little things while letting the really huge and serious impositions go by unchallenged. As if some lies were somehow too big to see.

"We would have to sell it to the public," said Corder.

"We already have a crack team of marketing experts

working on slogans," said Swallow. "*Your little corner of heaven in hell,* that sort of thing."

"I see." Something about it troubled him, though. Something didn't add up. Call it a politician's instinct. "But why is he doing this?"

"*He,* sir?"

"My ... opposite number in hell."

"Satan."

"Yes. Satan. Him."

Swallow took a moment to reply. He removed his glasses and cleaned them on a silk handkerchief while he sorted his words into a precise order. "There was a negotiation, sir. A certain amount of *give and take* was discussed."

That didn't sound good. Not good at all. Corder knew when he was being softened up. *The devil is in the detail.* "And what exactly do we have to *give* in return?"

"Your opposite number…" began Swallow.

"Satan."

"…Satan, yes. In return he requests only one thing. A seat on the Cabinet."

Corder felt ice trickle through his veins. He was all for inclusive government, but this was going too far. He sat back down in his chair while he absorbed the news. His head was throbbing sharply now. "Satan wants to be a part of my government?"

"Quite so. A minister without portfolio would be acceptable. He will advise and vote. He doesn't need to be in the public eye."

"Good God, I should hope not! Will there be ... horns? Spiked tails?"

"I am assured he will appear no more demonic than any other member of the Cabinet, sir."

"Even so. The idea of it."

"There is the offer of money as well," said Swallow, as if this had only just occurred to him.

"Money?"

"It turns out the Lords of Hell are very rich. Apparently, they run several major banks here in the mortal realm. They would be prepared to offer a sum of money to sweeten the deal. A considerable sum of money."

"How much?"

Swallow slipped a folded piece of paper across the desk. Corder looked at the figure written there. "My. That is a lot of zeroes."

"Quite so."

Corder considered for a few more microseconds. With that much money their reputation for good economic management would soar. There could be some eye-catching pre-election giveaways. And the housing shortage *was* a tricky problem.

"Well," said Corder. "Sacrifices do have to be made in these difficult times. Would you able to set up a meeting with my opposite number so we can move this forward?"

Swallow smiled and dipped his head in assent. "I shall arrange it at once, sir."

Another story that combines fantasy, British politics and a dose of satire. It was originally published by Daily Science Fiction in 2015. I heard a politician on the radio saying, "Sacrifices have to be made in these difficult times", and the story flowed from there. For anyone not familiar with the weird workings of UK democracy, the Cabinet consists of a bunch of senior (and not necessarily elected) Ministers sitting around a table. It's the ultimate decision-making body and basically works out what the government is going to do from day to day. The Archbishop of Canterbury really is part of the British legislature: he and a few other clerics are automatically part of the (unelected) House of Lords and get to vote on laws because of their position in the Church of England. As far as I know, there isn't a Necromancers and Diabolists Working Committee, but I suppose we wouldn't know about it if there were.

The M25, by the way, is the London orbital motorway. It's frequently gridlocked and hellish.

VIRAL

No one notices the invasion. A few instruments on orbiting satellites flicker at the unusual gravity-wave fluctuation. But the anomaly passes so quickly that monitoring systems simply log it for later analysis. No alarms are raised, either in orbit or down on the surface...

Johnny J sat on his balcony, strumming his acoustic guitar under the stars of the Arizona night. The cicadas sawed away in the trees, giving him a backbeat. He needed one more song. His comeback album was complete except for that killer lead-off track. A hook to get the fans excited again, get them talking about him. He'd been out of the game two years. There were singers out there whose entire careers had come and gone in that time.

He made himself stop thinking about it. About anything. You had to open your mind, be receptive. Feel the music. That was how it worked best. He picked away at melodies, letting his fingers go where they wanted. Letting it flow.

It was then the riff came to him, like it had just appeared in his brain. He loved it when that happened. And it was good. *Damn* good. He felt that old surge of excitement in his stomach. It was complex, though. Shifting harmonies. He played it again. And again. And again. Each time it sounded sweeter, as if his guitar was growing to like it, or as if the riff was adapting itself to the six strings of his battered old guitar.

This host had potential. Like all corporeal beings it was a creature of cycles and rhythms. Its mind a product of its pumping, beating, cycling biology. And rhythms could be wormed into. Patterns could be inhabited. Altered. Reprogrammed.

The only danger was the change going too well. It happened with susceptible beings. The change overwhelmed them. Hopefully that wouldn't happen here. A dead carrier was no use at all.

Johnny J worked away all night, not noticing the crescent moon scything through the sky above him, not noticing the cold. He experimented, trying out new rhythms, counterpoints, key changes. Some of the variations worked, slotting beautifully into place. Others jarred and refused to sound right. He let the music go where it wanted. Let it evolve. That was best. Let it grow into the song it needed to be.

The eastern sky was shading from black to deep purple before he had it perfect. He looked up and seemed to breathe for the first time in hours. Now he had to get it out there, let others hear. It became an overwhelming urge. A strange thought came to him, suddenly alarming. If he died now the new song would be lost. The world would never get to hear, and that was unthinkable.

He raced inside, legs and back aching from the hours of hunched inactivity. He didn't care. Quickly he tuned up his Telecaster, sat in front of a webcam, hit *record* and began to play. He started slow, introducing the theme in fragments, dropping in more and more of the notes. Building to a crescendo with, finally, the whole hook played out in strident clarity. While, underneath, he picked and strummed at those beguiling harmonies.

When he was done, he played back what he'd recorded, heart thumping with excitement. The video was scratchy, just his hands spidering up and down the neck of the guitar. But the song was clear. Gloriously clear. His hand trembled on his mouse as he clicked the *upload* button on his YouTube page.

He was still well-known enough for people to notice. He had his legions of devoted fans even now. The runaway success of the first album had bought him that. And each of them would tell a bunch of other people about the song, and then each of *them* would tell a bunch of other people, and so it would spread. Reproduce. Go viral.

Johnny J sat back for a moment, satisfied but spent. He began to strum the tune again, just for himself. Already it sounded like an old friend. The damn thing was irresistible. And *he* had written it. His comeback would be a triumph.

He strummed on. Distantly, he was aware of growing thirst and hunger. The heat of the Arizona day. He didn't care. Those things weren't important. He needed to hear the tune. That was all he wanted.

On his computer screen, unnoticed, the hit count on the video began to climb. One, ten, a hundred, a thousand. Within an hour it had been watched over thirty million times. Three days later it hit the two billion mark. Johnny J still hadn't noticed. Not because he was busy playing, but because by now he was slumped over his guitar, dehydrated, exhausted. Every now and then his fingers twitched as they tried to play the riff again but his eyes remained closed.

He dreamed for a while. The melody was a living creature. A wild horse. He rode and rode it and never wanted to get off. After a while he slipped into deeper unconsciousness, down towards his death.

Johnny J would be the first of many to die.

In space, the fluctuation in space-time drifted on, out towards the larger masses in this system and then, eventually, to other stars. It was in no hurry. There would be other minds out there. Other complex systems. Some of them wouldn't even have evolved yet. But that was OK; it would get to them all.

Eventually.

Viral was originally published in Stupefying Stories in 2014. I suppose it's another story that could be worked up into an entire novel. I'm not sure if it would be a rock 'n roll-infused offbeat tale or an action-packed disaster story. Possibly, it would be both.

Still, next time you get an earworm stuck in your head, just think on. It could be the start of the invasion...

PROFESSOR PANDEMONIUM'S TRAIN OF TERROR

"It's the zombies, Prof," said Vade. "They're revolting."

Professor Pandemonium didn't look up from the piles of coins he was counting. "Of course, they're revolting. They're zombies. I have to gather up the body parts they've dropped each night and nail them back on." He completed totting up the morning's takings from the Train of Terror and scratched the total in his ledger with his quill pen. He had a computer, and knew very well how to use it, but he liked to keep old traditions alive. A quill had a certain style.

Vade, his hideous familiar, stamped his frog-like feet up and down in frustration. "No, no, Prof. You don't get it. I mean they're *rebelling*. They're not doing what they're told. They're refusing to lumber after the punters on the ride or do the ominous groaning or anything."

Professor Pandemonium sighed. He really had to do something about Vade. His familiar's tone could be very, well, *familiar*. But he was in no hurry to repeat his foray into Hell to acquire a less irritating imp. The memories of that little expedition still gave even him shuddering nightmares. His grandfather's grimoire had been very clear.

The warding spell offered seven seconds of protection from the denizens of the underworld. No more. Dally a moment longer and the thronging demons would break through and you'd be trapped for an eternity of screaming agony. He'd returned to the mortal realm with Vade in one hand and his stopwatch reading *6.9 seconds* in the other.

"Then *make* them do what they're told, imp," he said. "They're sorcerous beings bound to my will. They can't exactly demand workers' rights."

Vade whined and squirmed in the doorway, something he did more and more. It was hugely irritating. "But they're not listening to me, Prof. They just stand around. They don't even move when the cars come past."

This was serious. The zombies were the main attraction on *Professor Pandemonium's Train of Terror*. The cars were rigged to lurch to a halt at just the right moment, giving the zombies *nearly* enough time to reach the screaming occupants. Oh, there were other rides in the park, but it was the *Train of Terror* people came for. It was famous for miles around. A rite of passage for adolescents and courting couples for generations. But without the zombies what would it be? Just a ghost train like any other. Mechanical monsters and glowing paint and recorded screams.

"Instruct the skeletons to take over for now," said the professor. Skeletons were old hat. They certainly weren't as effective as the zombies, but they were better than nothing.

"No good, Prof," said Vade. "The skeletons refuse to obey orders, too."

Professor Pandemonium considered. That was perhaps only to be expected. The skeletons *were* zombies, really. Or had been, before the pounds had dropped off them. But they'd never refused orders before. They were behaving more like the mummy he'd employed in the early days. Too bloody full of himself the mummy had been. Just because he was once Pharaoh of a vast and enlightened civilisation, he thought he was too good to terrify a few paying punters. Too wrapped-up in themselves, that was the problem with mummies. And now it seemed the zombies were getting ideas, too. Time to give them a piece of his mind. Although not literally, obviously.

Professor Pandemonium picked up his battered undertaker's top hat, planted it on his head and stood. He threw his black frock coat over his shoulders with an exaggerated swirl. Always the showman. "Follow me, Vade. We'll talk to Des. He's technically a zombie. He can translate."

*

Professor Pandemonium blinked in the bright light of the world outside the Train of Terror. A snaking queue of riders waited patiently for their turn on the ride. Always a beautiful sight. The professor pushed open the door at the back of Des's booth. Des paid no attention. Moving with studied slowness he raked in the coins proffered by the customers and handed out the tickets. All the while he stared straight ahead, as if he could see into some distant reality beyond the perception of mere mortals. People thought he was all part of the act. In a way he was.

Professor Pandemonium whispered into his ear, ignoring the faint odour of formaldehyde. "Des, close the ride. Tell the punters there's a technical fault. No, better still, tell them someone's got lost inside. Run screaming into the darkness. Then come and find me by the ... the revenants." Des hated the word *zombie*. Understandable, given his situation.

Slowly, Des nodded his head. His hand moved towards the control panel to turn the key that shut off the ride. Professor Pandemonium left the booth and walked back down the tracks into the darkness, pushing open the secret door in the vast, gaping mouth of the painted vampire.

"What are they saying?" Professor Pandemonium said to Des. "Is it *brains*?" The zombies – revenants – stood in an aimless huddle at the side of the track, from where they were supposed to shamble out and loom over each car that passed through. But none of them was moving. Their heads were bowed, as if someone had switched them off, or as if they had been caught doing something naughty. They didn't look very scary. They looked *depressed*.

Des took his time to reply. His brain was in perfect working order, but it took time for him to get in touch with all the muscles required for speech. Life – if that was the word – was hard for him. But it was surely better than the alternative.

"Not brains," said Des. "They're saying *trains*."

"Trains? What does that mean?"

Des concentrated furiously as his lips practised the words he wanted to speak. Finally, he took a leap at them.

"They're afraid of the trains. The people in the trains. The people aren't scared any more. They laugh and jeer. They throw things."

"But why?"

Professor Pandemonium often had to suppress the troubling thought that Des understood people better than he did. Here was one such time. Of course, Des was, technically, still a person. The terrible accident on the Space Coaster ride had left him completely paralysed but his mind fully functional. Pandemonium had stepped in and offered him both a job and a life. Now Des's body was as enslaved as any zombie's, but enslaved to the will of the living brain it contained. Des was a free man. Ish. It was a solution the professor had been particularly proud of at the time.

"Films, TV, games," said Des. "People have seen it all before. They aren't scared of Revenants anymore." A look that might have been sadness passed, slowly, across Des's features.

Professor Pandemonium opened his mouth to raise an

objection, then closed it again. He couldn't argue with Des, not on this point. Instead, he turned and began to pace along the rails. What was he going to do? He was the third generation of Pandemonium to run the Train. It was up to him to carry the torch. Once, a skeleton and a strobe light had been enough to scare the punters witless. Before that, a few pallid ghosts had done the job. People changed, demanded more. Werewolves? Useless twenty seven days of the month. Giant spiders? An annoying tendency to build webs across doorways and gum up the wheels. Wraiths? Always floated through the walls towards the bright lights of the carousels, like moths to a flame. A real vampire might do the trick, but you couldn't enslave a vampire. The grimoire made that very clear. He had to think outside the box. A sheela na gig? There would only be complaints; this was a family ride. Dragons? Now he was being ridiculous. Dragons didn't exist. He needed some real, walking terror, not some unlikely fantasy monster.

He stopped at the far end of the ride's central chamber and peered back down the tracks. Des and the depressed zombies stood there, unmoving. Vade too, picking his noses, awaiting orders. The torches on the walls flickered and guttered, sending shadows dancing across the walls. Pandemonium had insisted on real flames for that authentic dungeon look. The safety inspectors had taken a lot of convincing. It was just a good job they didn't know about the zombies. Once they aged and dried out, they could be very flammable. Zombies, that was, not safety inspectors.

But a few torches weren't going to help now. He needed something *big* for the central chamber of the ride. He needed a show. The cars came past the shrieking banshee, around the corner and through the double doors. Everyone knew this was the best part of the ride. People whispered about what they'd seen in here. Whatever it was had to be good. The cars reached the middle, paused for a few moments, then lurched on through the exit doors. Seven seconds in total, that was how long each car was programmed to spend in the chamber. All he needed was something to terrify the punters that long.

Seven seconds. The thought of what he could do struck him like a flash powder effect going off. He stood unmoving, contemplating the delicious idea. His heart hammered. Could he really do that? Would it work? He'd have to renew the warding spells each night, but that could be done with Vade's help. Power was a problem. No electricity in Hell. They'd have to rig up a battery on each car. It would be bad if a car broke down; then it would be stranded at the mercy of a million slavering demons. But these were mere details. The punters wanted a fright. He'd give them one. Or his name wasn't Professor Pandemonium.

"Vade?" he called.

"Prof?"

"Come here. I have work for you…"

*

A week later, Professor Pandemonium stood watching the interior of the chamber through the eyeholes of a ghoul painted on the wall in phosphorescent paint. They'd been busy while the Train of Terror was out of service: reprogramming the cars, changing the lights, touching up paintwork, performing the necromantic rites to send the cars into Hell. Everything *should* now be working. They'd tested it by sending through a car manned – zombied – with four of the depressed revenants. The creatures had come back with looks of open-mouthed horror on their faces. Which didn't prove anything. They always had looks of open-mouthed horror on their faces. Still, they had returned. That was good enough, wasn't it?

The first car came crashing through the doors, accompanied by the agonized wail of the banshee. Four punters, three guys and a girl. They were screaming, but with the delighted, half-laughing screams he'd grown so used to hearing. There was even some *giggling*. There was a great flash of light – enough to briefly blind the punters so they didn't see the translocation – and the car vanished.

The faintest smell of sulphur filled the room. Professor Pandemonium found himself counting softly. 1 … 2 … Had it been a mistake to leave Vade in charge of the batteries? The imp's grasp of technology wasn't always great. Still, too late now. … 3 … 4 … A memory of his own visit to Hell ten years earlier flashed through his mind. He shuddered, despite himself. It was the eyes that haunted him. Not the eyes of the demons, but those of their victims. That look of helpless pleading. … 5 … 6 … 7 …

A deafening silence rolled through the chamber, louder than any mere noise. Something had gone wrong. The eldritch horrors of the underworld had overwhelmed the warding spells. The punters had been torn into still-living, still-conscious shreds of flesh. Professor Pandemonium bit his lip. This wasn't good. He'd have to shut the ride again and he lost money every time he did that. There would be questions, too. The authorities wouldn't like it if they learned he was sending his customers to Hell. There was probably some law against it. He began to make plans. If he dispelled the magic there would be nothing for the authorities to see. He could feign innocence. With the lights on, the ride was just black hardboard and painted monsters. But still, how was he going to make the Train of Terror frightening again? People had *giggled*.

He heard the screaming a moment before the second blinding flash of light. This was proper shrieking, rich with notes of primal, hindbrain terror. The screams people screamed when their lives were in urgent danger. There was sobbing, too. The panicky gasping for breath. Such beautiful sounds. The professor watched the car trundling away, out of the chamber.

"Are they alive, Prof?" asked Vade. The imp sat on the ground in the darkness, too small to see through the eyeholes.

"They are."

"What, all of them?"

"All of them."

"And they've still got all their limbs?"

"They have. I counted very carefully."

"Still, you know, *attached*?"

"All attached."

"Attached … in the right places?"

"In all the right places. It appears our customers have returned from Hell having suffered no physical harm."

"Well," said Vade. "Who'd have thought it, eh, Prof?"

"Indeed."

The professor crossed the narrow walkway to peer out through the other wall. From here, he could see through to the end of the ride. After the chamber the cars rattled through a graveyard, passed around a trio of toiling-and-troubling witches, then emerged back into the light. A few moments later he watched the car lurch to a halt. The four riders sat unmoving, staring ahead in wide-eyed shock. They looked strangely like the zombies. Slowly they started to climb out. They had to help each other, their limbs trembling. People sometimes said their legs turned to jelly on the rides. It was just a turn of phrase (although as it happened he *did* know the relevant spell) but two of the men were having trouble standing. Slowly the four walked away, clutching each other for support.

Professor Pandemonium watched as they made their slow way to the back of the queue for another ride on the Train of Terror.

He smiled to himself. How he loved the paying public. With an exaggerated twirl of his frock coat he turned and headed for his office.

There would be lots of coins to count now.

I was thinking about the way modern scary movies have to be so much scarier than old ones, because people have seen it all before, and this story of an old-time fairground operator came to me. When I was young, I loved a good ghost train, but now I find them amusing rather than terrifying. Still like them, though.

This was another story that was a lot of fun to write. People say that stories making use of puns are bad stories – which just goes to show how wrong some people can be, in my view. It was published in 2013, in the Stupefying Stories Annual Horror Special.

FOR ALL TIME

Sam was away in the highG probe when Corva emerged from her torpor. It took a few moments for his absence to register. Had he said something about leaving the station? Perhaps. Azurite torpor wasn't like human sleep. Although she'd only been unconscious for an hour it went much deeper, approaching total biological shut-down. Always took time for her brain to sort itself out.

It was an old joke between them. Sam could wake and be up and about in minutes. For her it was another hour, or more, before she could string words together. One of many differences between their species. Another thing they'd adjusted to, laughed about, in sixty years of being together. She wasn't, strictly speaking, even a *she*. Such things were more fluid for an Azurite. This was simply how they'd arranged things, made it work.

When the hab finally decided to stop spinning, Corva rose and padded across to their little kitchen, pressing the buttons for hot *kva*. Another difference. Keen to try what he liked, she'd sampled *tea* and *coffee* over the years. She'd enjoyed neither. Many human foods were completely tasteless to her. Pointless, too, the caffeine being inert to Azurite biology. Kva, on the other hand, was like standing under a shower of cool water. Just a shame the drink was toxic to Sam. Puny human that he was.

Sipping the kva, she switched the screen to show her the black hole. Charon station orbited much farther away than the pictures suggested, an array of highG beacons relaying the imagery. The glow of the photon sphere was something she could never grow tired of. Sam had to be down there somewhere, skimming as close to the event horizon as he dared, sampling the trapped radiation. They'd learned a lot over the years. It was just the two of them and the black hole. They both thought of it as *theirs*. Humans and Azurites had much in common, as well.

He'd been troubled of late, though. She was an expert at reading human expression now. Something was on his mind. More than once she'd found him in one of Charon's more distant observation pods, literally staring into space. Only when he became aware of her presence did expression return to his features.

Life-expectancy was another difference between them. They'd always known it. It was one of those topics so big it barely got mentioned. Azurites lived three or four times longer than humans. She teased him about it. Humans were so weak they fell apart after only a hundred, a hundred and fifty years. He, likewise, would joke about how long it took her to perform some analysis, come to some decision. It was, they both knew, a way of laughing at the inevitable. She was twenty years older but would probably outlive him by two or three hundred years.

But she loved this gentle, quick-witted, quick-moving human with all her hearts. More and more, she'd found herself thinking she'd be glad they'd had these years together. One way her mind steeled itself for the day he was no longer there. Like lovers the galaxy over, same-species and hetero, they'd vowed to stay together for all time, knowing in the back of their minds what *all time* really meant.

Needing to hear his voice, an unfocused dread taking

hold inside her, she called the highG probe. He was still near enough for his responses to reach her. When he replied she could tell, despite the electronic noise, something was wrong. He sounded defensive, like he'd been caught in the middle of something shameful.

"I thought you'd be in torpor for another hour."

"Something brought me out of it. What are you up to?"

There was a fuzz of static before he replied. "Corva, I'm sorry. I didn't want it to be like this. I couldn't bring myself to tell you."

Ice trickled through her. "Tell me what?"

Another burst of white noise, then his calm voice emerging from the fuzz. "About the medscans. They were very clear, I'm afraid. 99% certainty. The tumours have metastasised. Our puny human biology, right?" She could hear the note of humour in his voice despite the distance. Despite everything.

"What are you doing, Sam? Come back and we'll talk about it."

He ignored her, almost like he'd prepared a speech. "I'm old, Corva. Old for a human. We both know it. I wish I could stay with you but I can't. Except if I do this.'

"Do what? What are you doing?"

"I wanted you to simply wake up and see. I didn't want to say good bye. Because in a way I'm not."

Humans. They were so impetuous with their stupid, short lives. They got an idea and within minutes they were acting on it. "Sam, this is madness. Come home."

He ignored her. "And this isn't to be a duty, understand Corva? When the time comes, find a new life. New love. I want you to do that. OK?"

"Sam."

"Now I'll be a part of your beloved photon sphere. Stretched out, slowly getting dimmer, but always there if you look closely enough."

"Sam."

He didn't reply again. Zooming to maximum

magnification Corva saw him exiting the probe, saw the flare of his thrusters as he decelerated hard. It would be over quickly. The black hole would pull him in and in an instant, he'd be gone.

Except for her, watching from outside, it would be different. Gravity would slow the escaping light, make his fall into the black hole last an eternity. She'd always be able to see him, hanging there in space. A last gift, the only way he could live on with her.

For all time.

This little story came to me as I was researching the weird time-distortion effects that high gravity densities (such as those around black holes) can cause. While the physics of that might be interesting, the trick with a story is to create an appealing human – or Azurite – angle. Hopefully that worked with this story. It was originally printed in Perihelion magazine in 2015.

WELCOME TO VEGA IV

Now the war between Earth and Vega is over, more and more Terrans are choosing to visit Vega IV to savour its distinctive culture. Keep the following guidelines in mind as you explore this fascinating planet:

1. Don't eat the food

More than one human has made the mistake of assuming the Vegans are vegans. The truth is quite the opposite, as their impressive arrays of razor-sharp teeth, body-spikes and chitinous claws perhaps make obvious. Vegans are top predators. Their diet consists almost exclusively of the fast-moving, soft-bodied madrats so numerous on Vega IV.

In a desperate attempt to avoid being eaten, madrats have evolved a highly toxic body-chemistry. Unfortunately for the madrats, the Vegans have evolved a digestion that doesn't care. Humans have not. Eat any local dish and you will die.

2. Don't drink the water

Vegan biology isn't based on H2O like ours: Vega IV's skies rain sulfuric acid and consequently that's what

Vegans drink. Don't make the mistake of trying it. Their alcoholic drinks are especially unsafe. These are acid mixed with concentrations of alcohol likely to slay any human within moments.

3. Don't breathe the air

Vega IV's atmosphere does contain oxygen and nitrogen. But it also contains very high concentrations of sulfur dioxide. Vegans consider this combination healthy and bracing. You shouldn't.

4. Avoid social interaction

Vegan hive culture is complex, hierarchical, and bound by social norms that few humans can hope to understand. An individual contravening any of a long series of frequently bizarre social conventions will be immediately killed, for fear of upsetting the social order. Don't be that individual!

5. Don't attempt to communicate

Vegan language consists of a rapid series of clicks, thrums and pincer-gesticulations. Any human attempting to converse in this fashion will inevitably make mistakes. It has been calculated by xenolinguists that around 80% of the Vegan language is devoted to dire threats. You are very likely to end up in an unfortunate position if you do attempt to communicate.

6. Don't even look at anyone

Direct eye-to-eye contact is considered threatening to the Vegan mindset. Unfortunately, the sight of a human face is very likely to trigger the Vegans' strong predation instinct, and they may well attack mercilessly and without warning. Remember, this is perfectly normal in Vegan culture and shouldn't be taken as a personal slight.

The similarity of human facial features to those of the madrat is perhaps an unfortunate coincidence in this regard.

7. Do admire the meadows

Perhaps surprisingly, Vega IV is blessed with many stunning flower meadows. These are a must for off-world visitors. Don't touch any of the flowers, though. Seriously, just don't.

8. Keep moving

You may well be tempted to linger as you admire the flower meadows or the Vegan's soaring hive architecture. Don't. Stationary individuals are generally assumed to be dead and therefore food in Vegan culture.

Follow these simple rules and your visit should be enjoyable and may even last as long as intended. Enjoy your stay!

Welcome to Vega IV! is another piece that takes a familiar form of writing – in this case a travel guide – and adds a (hopefully) humorous twist to it. It grew out of the simple joke that Vegans might not be vegans and developed from there. It was originally printed in Devilfish Review in 2015.

THE LAST TRAP

Swan halted half-way up the wall of the North Tower of Emperor Xanthe's palace. The wind had picked up for a moment, gusts threatening to pluck her off and hurl her to the distant ground. She dug the spikes of her climbing gauntlets as far as she could into the cracks between the granite blocks and hung on. She'd allowed for this. A slightly windy night was best. In still air the clinks and scrapes from her ascent might be heard from inside the tower. The noise covered her just as the darkness of the moonless night did.

A few feet farther up there was a single window, the only break in the entire wall on that side. In her two years of planning she'd toyed with using it as a way inside. Cut through the slab of translucent quartz with a diamond-tipped blade. The arched window was narrow, but she could squeeze through by temporarily dislocating a shoulder. She was slight enough to fit through gaps most male assassins couldn't. But it was too obvious; the window was clearly one of the traps laid by her opponent; the nameless, faceless Steward whose defences protected the Emperor's life.

But the narrow window ledge would be useful. Swan

waited for the wind to die down then climbed to it, taking great care with the placement of each hand, each foot, testing each fingerhold and toehold before putting any weight on them. The cracks between the stones were tiny and it was always possible some of the edges had been angled to prevent someone doing just what she was attempting. It was the sort of detail the Steward would think of.

The ledge was a lip of stone an inch wide. Swan studied it carefully, looking for anything that could alert those inside. Nothing. She pulled one end of a fine cord from her belt, looping it around the ledge and attaching it back to herself. Always wary, she gradually let it support her weight. It held. She relaxed her muscles, dangling there from the slender cord, two hundred feet in the air. She'd practised similar climbs often and didn't need to stop, but doing so would pay benefits. Within the palace there would be many dangers between her and the Emperor. She needed to be as fresh as possible.

She let herself hang for five minutes while her strength returned. Down below, guards paced the grounds of the palace, following the irregular routines the Steward assigned to them. Swan was confident they couldn't see her. Black skin swathed in black against the dark sky, she was a shadow within the shadows.

She ran through her preparations once more. There were many unknowns; she would need to react to what she found inside. She wasn't the first to be employed to kill the Emperor. To her knowledge none had ever succeeded in even penetrating the inner fortress. Or if they had, they hadn't returned to tell anyone. Intelligence on what she'd face was scant. She knew only what everyone knew: that the Steward's defences were famously devious and famously deadly.

But no one had employed *her* before. The Blade in the Shadows. The Black Swan. She was the best. Okay, so perhaps everyone thought that. But if she succeeded tonight she'd know it for sure. And, one way or another, this would be her last job. Either she'd die in the attempt like all the others or she'd succeed and be paid enough to live out the rest of her life in luxury.

She didn't enjoy killing. People didn't understand that. She was merely very good at it, which was a different thing completely. In truth she'd be glad to stop. A blade slipped into the Emperor's heart tonight would be the end of it. What happened to the empire afterwards was no concern of hers. Naturally enough she didn't know who her employer was. The ruler of a neighbouring land? A jealous relative hoping to ascend the throne? A resentful noble? An ex-lover?

All possibilities. The range of reasons people found for killing one another always surprised Swan. She'd never *wanted* to kill anyone her whole life, although one or two lovers had come close. No. Her job was to slay without asking why. That was what she did. Except, more and more, she *did* ask herself didn't she? Agonized over the rights and wrongs. She'd known assassins who enjoyed their work, took pleasure in each death. That had never been her. She loved the challenge of it, the game of it. The death at the end was the price that had to be paid. Paid by the victim mainly, of course.

And did any of them deserve to die? However evil? Perhaps, perhaps not. The question troubled her more and more. And that was why she had to stop. Doubt slowed you down. Doubt was a killer. But first she had to know whether she really was the best.

She flexed her fingers and toes, then reattached herself to the wall. Releasing the cord, she climbed sideways around the window in case anyone was looking out, then began to pull herself upwards once more.

Two guards patrolled the battlements of the high tower. She'd studied them from afar for many hours. They weren't so assiduous as the other guards, their remoteness making them complacent. They also weren't replaced as often as those on the ground. They were her opening.

From just below the top of the wall, Swan used an angled mirror to study them. They walked and paused and walked round their little circle, gazing into the darkness, boredom clear in all their movements. She waited until both had their backs to her then vaulted over the wall to attack.

Afterwards, she lay on the flat of the roof, listening out for any cries or alarms. Nothing. She'd thrown two knives in rapid succession and the two unnamed men had died. She resented it. Any death other than the one she'd been paid to carry out troubled her. It was an imperfection. But she'd had no choice. With luck she would have time, now, to move into the palace without the alarm being raised. And if she was *very* lucky she might even be able to return that way. Much depended on how quickly she could accomplish her work.

She peered over the battlements, across the gulf of open air to the inner fortress. *So, Steward, what have you got planned for me in there? And which of us will win the game this night?* In the long months of planning she'd found herself talking to her opponent more and more. It was, perhaps, not a good sign. Not healthy. She'd never met the Steward, never even seen him. But still she questioned the imaginary figure in her mind. Conversed with him. Sometimes she saw the Steward in her dreams, too, laughing at her from the shadows. Watching as she fell into some fresh trap...

Swan unravelled the grapple from her backpack and fitted it to the collapsible crossbow she'd fashioned. There was a barred window towards the top of one of the towers of the inner fortress. She'd studied it as openly as she dared on reconnoitre missions, disguised as dancer or trader. The bars looked solid. She'd designed the muffled grapple very carefully. The hinged blades would pass between the bars but lock when she pulled back. She'd get only one shot; if she missed she wouldn't have time to haul in the line before it clattered to the ground. And there was always a chance she was falling into one of the traps. Bars that came away when she pulled, perhaps, or that rang a bell when they were struck. But sometimes you had to take a calculated risk.

She waited for the gusting wind to die down. She breathed out, putting everything out of her mind, relaxing her body as much as possible. There was only her and that distant window. She'd rigged up a small spyglass on the barrel of the crossbow, an innovation she was particularly proud of. By setting the lenses at just the right angle to the quarrel she could take aim very precisely. The trick, of course, was to allow for both the wind and the rise and fall of the shot over such a long distance. She'd practised it hundreds of times in the quiet of the woods.

She aimed five and a half feet above the centre of the far window and squeezed the release mechanism.

The crossbow *thrummed*, sending the quarrel darting through the night air, line playing out behind it. She lost sight of it in the darkness, then felt a slight skip in the line as the grapple struck. Had it caught the bars or hit the wall? She began to pull it in, praying it would go taut.

She reeled in far too much. She'd missed and the grapple had fallen to the floor, visible to everyone. She'd heard nothing, but perhaps it had struck something soft down there. She should leave now while she could. Beaten.

But then, gloriously, the line went taut, angling slightly down to the far window. She'd done it after all.

She lashed the line to one of the crenellations, then slipped silk shoes onto her feet. She would tightrope-walk her way across to the inner fortress.

Now the wind was her enemy, each gust making the line sway like the plucked string of a lute. Repeatedly she had to stop and work simply to stay on the bucking rope. Below her was four hundred feet of air and the hard stone of the courtyard. She could hear the murmured conversations of the soldier, smell the greasy smoke from their braziers rising through the air. And if any of the guards did look up to see her she would be an easy target. She'd have no chance of dodging their shots.

Best not to know. She didn't look down.

She was halfway across when a rush of air overbalanced her. The wind around the palace's towers was turbulent, something she'd tried to account for in her practice runs. But suddenly she was overbalancing, the rope swaying alarmingly to one side.

She teetered, nearly recovering, then fell. The world became a blur of rushing air.

Suppressing the urge to cry out, she reached out to grasp the rope as it flashed past her. She grasped it with her left hand. For a moment she thought she might jerk it loose from one of its anchor-points but it held. She hung by her finger-tips, swaying in the air.

She reached up to grasp the rope with her other hand and made it on the third attempt. With a trapeze-artist's motion, she swung herself to-and-fro, and then round to land once more on the rope, squatting there while she fought to regain her balance.

Finally she stood and continued the crossing.

The barred window on the inner tower was too small to squeeze through however many joints she dislocated. Leaving the rope in place – it was still one possible escape-route – Swan replaced the silk shoes with her boots once more. Now she worked her way down the tower. Half way to the ground there was a large balcony overlooking the courtyard. The balcony was guarded, but the soldiers gazed outwards, not expecting someone to drop behind them.

Making no noise whatsoever, Swan descended. Two more guards stamped their feet in the cold of the night air but didn't look up. She didn't have to kill them. It made her feel better. Her boots had soft pads on their treads. She dropped to the ground as quietly as a leaf falling to the floor of the woods. Placing each foot with infinite care, watching the guards all the time, she stepped through an archway and into the tower.

Keeping to the shadows she crept down two flights of stairs to the ground floor. She didn't know these rooms and had to rely on her sense of direction. The doorway to the Emperor's inner sanctum lay somewhere down there. In truth she felt sorry for him. Not just because she was about to kill him, but because he'd lived his whole life in a gilded prison. The Emperor was the Empire and the loss of the one meant dire consequences for the other. Xanthe stayed in the palace, living out his days until a child or a grandchild was lined up to succeed him. He had everything he could ever want except his freedom. Perhaps he would welcome death. Perhaps that was just wishful thinking on her part.

Ten minutes later, Swan hid behind a screen of pillars, studying a large, golden doorway that led to the sanctum. Four guards stood in front of the doors, swords drawn in constant readiness. She couldn't fight them, certainly not without alarms being raised. There was no way she could sneak by. A charm or a spell might have helped, but the Imperial Sorcerers suppressed all magic within the area of the palace.

Fortunately, she'd prepared for this eventuality. She'd spent almost all the wealth she had accumulated so far in her career on a few drops of a certain rare and precious toxin. *Aqua Lethis*. Poisons to put people to sleep – or to kill them – were common enough. She'd studied many over the years. But none would do here. If these guards fell it would be noticed too quickly. The Steward had guards guarding the guards.

Would the Aqua Lethis work? She'd given the slightest dot of the clear liquid to a rat captured in her stables to observe the effects. At first nothing had happened. The rat drank, then stood unmoving, nose twitching. Swan had wasted her fortune on mere water. But then she'd moved a hand towards the rat. It didn't react. She touched it and still it remained stationary. It was alive and awake, its eyes open, but it didn't move. Did it know she was there? She couldn't tell. But it appeared the Aqua Lethis did what it was supposed to.

Swan took out four darts and tipped each with a speck of the toxin. She would have to hit all four guards before any could react. Again, she'd practised it. Again, doing so when her own life was at stake was a very different thing. But that was the game. You felt most alive when you knew you might die.

Wondering if the Steward had ever heard of Aqua Lethis, Swan raised four blowpipes to her lips and took aim with the first.

She hit the first three guards sweetly in the neck before any could move. But the fourth, seeing the darts streaking towards his comrades, had a moment to react. He half-turned and stepped forwards, a shout forming in his throat.

Swan aimed – harder at a moving target – and fired a fourth time. The red-feathered dart found its mark at the guard's left jugular vein. Aqua Lethis worked rapidly, another reason it was so fabulously expensive. The fourth guard halted mid-stride, mouth open wide, sword held forward, as if he'd suddenly forgotten what he was doing.

For a moment no one moved. Swan waited to hear the sound of running feet, shouts of alarm. But there was nothing.

She stepped into the open. Someone would notice the out-of-place guard soon. She had to hurry. Hurry and hope. Her plan depended on everything looking normal at the door. Someone might, if they glanced that way, think the guard was moving into position. Maybe. She thought briefly about giving up, turning back. But there was danger either way. Might as well press on.

She walked up to the guards. Their eyes watched her as she approached. They were awake and aware. She expected them to move at any moment, leap forward to grab her, haul her off to the Emperor's dungeons. Had she got the dose right? She liked to experiment extensively with her poisons, understand their effects on the body. She hadn't dared with the Aqua Lethis. She'd simply used all she'd been able to buy. If it wasn't enough the guards could emerge from their waking stupor at any moment. And if it was too much their heart muscles might be paralysed. The latter would be bad for them, but either would be bad for her.

Quickly now, as well as plucking the darts from the guards' necks, she took the key each carried at their belts. Four keys to unlock the door. Four keys that had to be turned simultaneously. She'd planned for this also, another invention she was pleased with. A folding steel frame around which four clasps could be slid until they were in the correct position. One for each key. Then a chain around a cog on each clasp. A turn of the handle and she could rotate all four keys at once.

With four satisfying clicks, the locks sprung open. Drawing a deep breath, she stepped through the golden door. Once inside, she used the frame to lock the door again from the inside.

She turned to see what she faced. There would be no more guards now. A thousand soldiers protected the Emperor and she'd made her way past all of them. But the Steward didn't rely on human protectors that close to the Emperor. Guards could be bribed, befuddled, killed. They could make mistakes. From now on there would be only the Steward's mechanical traps. Traps the Steward could rely on to never go wrong.

So, my friend, Swan whispered. *Now it begins.*

She stood in a great square room, its floor polished marble. Many, many doors had been set in the other walls. Identical doors. Fifty of them: each with a brass plaque depicting its number.

The meaning was obvious. One of these doors led to the Emperor's private quarters. The others led to – what? Some manner of death. Fire, acid, spikes, poison. It barely mattered. Without knowing the right number she wasn't going to make it any farther.

She began to study the doors in close detail, listening at each, feeling the wood with her fingertips for sensations of heat or cold. She got nothing. She walked right around the room, studying each door for subtle signs. Apart from their numbers they were identical.

She stepped back to consider. One of these doors would be in regular use. There had to be a way of working out which.

The answer was obvious. Smiling at her own ingenuity, Swan pulled a leather pouch of finely-ground limestone from an inside pocket. She started with the last door, Door 50. It would be just like the Steward to make *that* the one. Or so Swan imagined. She proceeded to brush a dusting over the brass handle. When she'd finished she studied the white powder. Nothing. She moved on to the next door and, being careful to preserve the amount of dust remaining, did the same.

She did this with thirty-eight of the doors before finding the faint smudges she was looking for. Smudges from someone's hand opening the door. She'd found it. She put the pouch of dust away and reached for the handle.

She'd half-turned it before some instinct stopped her. Was this too easy? A smudge on a door-handle could be easily faked. A vision flashed into her mind: the Steward walking around the hall every night, polishing the handle of the real door then turning the handle of another in case any intruder managed to make it there. Yes. She was suddenly sure of it. It was what she'd do. She'd succeeded only in identifying one door she shouldn't go through.

She stepped back to think again. Handprints could be easily faked, but what couldn't? She dropped to her hands and knees, thinking to peer under each door to gain some clue. There was nothing: just a fine line of darkness between door and floor.

That was it. The floor was marble, but even hard stone

showed signs of wear eventually. One of the doorways would bear the marks of the feet that had passed through it. She crawled around the room, studying the gap beneath each door.

She worked her way around to Door 3 before she found it. The slight bowing of the floor, a few hairsbreadths' difference, but enough to show her.

You're clever, Steward, Swan whispered. *But you're not clever enough.*

She turned the handle and stepped through the door. Precisely nothing happened. No blades. No flames. No spikes. That was always good.

She stood at one end of a corridor. At the other end, thirty yards away, was another doorway. She had, simply, to cross to the other side. The floor in between was a mosaic: swirling coloured lines that resembled a tangle of branches and leaves. The pattern was hard to follow, but there had to be significance to it. Pressure points, perhaps. Certain colours or shapes you had to step on. Or not step on. As before, there had to be a key. A way for people who were supposed to be there to cross.

Square slits had been cut into the walls, one on each side every few paces. They were clearly part of some mechanism. Something deadly would shoot out of those slits. The Steward hadn't tried to conceal them.

Swan inched forwards, trying to make sense of the pattern on the ground, trying to place her feet carefully. She thought about walking up one side of the corridor. But then she'd have no time to react if something fired from the near wall. She had no choice. She had to creep up the centre of the hallway and rely solely on her reflexes.

She passed the first slit and nothing happened. Had she struck upon the correct places to step? She looked back at the particular colours and shapes she'd trodden on, then looked ahead for something similar. Although, that might very well be exactly the wrong thing to do.

At the next slit, the faintest *click* from the left-hand slit alerted her. She turned in time to see the spiked ball firing toward her. She ducked just in time, the ball whistling past her ear to clunk heavily into the opposite wall. If it had struck her in the head it would have dashed her brains out.

She stepped forward again, senses buzzing as she neared the next slit. Another faint click, this time from the right. She turned that way, ready to dodge. But there was nothing there.

It took her a moment to understand. Too late. The silent projectile from the slit *behind* her crashed into her left shoulder, sending her spinning to the floor.

Even as she lay there, agonies screaming through her, a part of her admired what the Steward had done.

Swan rose to her knees and tried to inspect the damage the spiked ball had dealt her. It wasn't good. Her left upper arm was badly fractured, glints of white bone peeping out from her gashed skin. The arm would be useless from now on. Worse, it was the sort of wound that never fully healed. She pulled out a pod of Poppy-of-the-field and began to chew on it. Bitterness filled her mouth. It would dull the pain a little. She wanted to take more but dared not. She needed all her wits about her.

With a grunt of effort, she rose back to her feet and began to edge forward once more. She approached the next pair of slits. Where would the projectile come from this time? Left or right? Would there be another fake click or would it, perhaps, be a double-bluff?

She decided not to take the risk either way. She stepped in between the slits and immediately jumped backwards.

Once again, the Steward had outwitted her. Two spiked balls shot from the walls, but angled backward at her. The right-hand one missed, flying over her shoulder, but the left one thudded into her already-mangled left arm. Swan went down with a barely-suppressed cry of pain. The agony was sharp despite the poppy.

She lay on the floor, eyes closed. She was losing the contest, losing it badly. She had to think quickly. Had to outthink the Steward.

She forced herself to her feet and, without stopping, did the one thing she knew she shouldn't. The one thing the Steward surely wouldn't expect.

She sprinted for the far door, ignoring the pattern on the floor, ignoring the pain, ignoring everything. She triggered a barrage of clicks and metallic *thuds* but paid them no attention. She would outrun them all. Because the Steward was clever and anyone getting that far would be hesitant. It was a trap for the wary. Defeating it meant throwing caution aside.

In twenty paces, Swan reached the doorway. She turned back. The floor behind her was strewn with spiked balls. The splashed trail of her blood was clear, too. But she'd made it. The Steward hadn't won yet.

She took a moment to bandage her arm as tightly as she could bear. Blood soaked through as she tied but there was nothing to be done. She allowed herself one more dose of Poppy-of-the-field, then turned her attention to the next door.

She studied it for long minutes, looking for a trap, a mechanism. She found none. It appeared to be normal. Could she trust her senses? Her head swam. She'd lost a lot of blood, and the poppy would be having its effect. But she couldn't stand there looking for ever.

Warily, she pushed the door open. Nothing happened. She slipped through.

She was nearly there. Before her, surely, was the last trap. Across a small, circular room stood tall, ornately-decorated doors marked with the royal insignia: crossed swords over a white dragon's head. The dragon's eyes glittered like huge rubies. Quite possibly they *were* huge rubies. They were surely the doors to the quarters of an Emperor.

Between Swan and that door stood a stone plinth. And upon the table was a half-completed game of chess. She crept towards the table, wary. Perhaps the trap was elsewhere and the game was merely a distraction. A feint. But no arrows or spiked balls fired at her. No pits opened up.

She peered at the pieces on the board. It was clear the game *was* the trap. Each of the sixty-four squares would press in if touched. Each was a button. The meaning was clear. Make the wrong move and some mechanism of death would trigger. Make the right and the door would open.

She imagined the Steward standing on the other side of the board, smiling as he awaited Swan's move. A spider at the centre of its web. The numbness in her brain was a fog, threatening to sweep in and obscure everything. She fought against it. She had to think clearly. The Steward would have set this puzzle at his leisure, with all the time he needed.

So. Anyone getting that far would be exhausted. They would also be desperate to open the door before their time ran out. It would be all-too easy to rush in and make the wrong move. Swan closed her eyes and forced herself to breathe deeply. She counted to twenty, letting her pounding heart slow.

Finally she opened her eyes to study the board. They were at the endgame. She was black. Was that coincidence? Perhaps. Her pieces were doing well: advancing on the white king, pawns and knights and rooks closing around in their complex dance. But there were threats from the white ranks. Lurking bishops that would sweep her attack away if she wasn't careful.

She studied the board for long moments. There had to be a *particular* move. The pain from her shoulder was flaring up again but she dared not take any more poppy. She forced herself to concentrate.

Yes. There it was. A pawn sacrifice that her opponent would have to counter. Which in turn would allow Swan to move a knight to check the white king. That, in turn, could be countered, but only temporarily. Within three moves it would be checkmate. That had to be it.

She put her hand onto the pawn.

But no. The Steward. The damned Steward. Was there a trap within the trap? Was Swan again making the one move she shouldn't?

Her fingers left the pawn where it was. It was so hard to think clearly through the fog, through the waves of pain.

Damn you, she muttered to her unseen opponent. *Damn your games.*

She closed her eyes again for a few moments, then focussed once more on the board. The question was, what would the Steward least expect her to do?

Then she saw it. The one move someone in her position would never make. A sacrifice to give the game away. A deliberate loss. Did she dare do that? She couldn't decide any more. Couldn't decide if it was brilliant insight or suicide.

She lifted a knight, opening up a channel for one of those white bishops to threaten her own king. Gently, she placed the knight back down, out of the way.

There was the faintest click. Swan sat with her head bowed, awaiting the blow, the flame.

None came.

She looked up. The sound had come from the gilded doors. They now stood slightly open.

She moved, slipping through the doors while she still could. Beyond was a bed-chamber. Were there further threats here? She could see none. It was a normal room. A room for an Emperor: sumptuous, luxurious. Designed for comfort rather than death. She really had overcome all the traps.

Is that it, Steward? she whispered to herself. *Is that the best you can do?*

Flickering candles lit the scene. The Emperor lay asleep in his vast, gold-framed bed in the centre of the chamber. He was utterly unaware of Swan's presence. Utterly unaware, also, of the thin blade she drew from her tunic.

Swan stepped silently across the room until she was standing beside the bed. The Emperor slept on, a look of peace on his face. She raised the blade, but then stopped. It occurred to her she didn't have to do it. She'd proved her skills. She didn't need to carry out the killing. She could stop now.

But no. There was the base matter of money. If she didn't slay the Emperor she wouldn't be paid. And then she'd have to carry on doing the one thing she was good at. The one thing she hated to do.

The sharp blade slipped in easily and neatly, puncturing Emperor Xanthe's heart. The Emperor half-rose from sleep but died even before he was fully awake. A flicker of the eyes, a gasp, and it was over. Blood bloomed on the white sheets as Swan placed the eagle talisman on the Emperor's body. The talisman given her by her employer to prove the death was by her hand.

She let out a breath. It was done.

"So you have killed him. You have done well, Swan. The Aqua Lethis was a nice touch."

A voice from behind her, the shadows in the corner. An old man. There'd been no one there when she'd entered, she was sure. In one fluid motion, Swan spun around, slipping out a throwing blade from her sleeve in readiness.

"Please," said the old man. "Best not do that. If you kill me who will pay you?" In his hand he held up a silver disk. An eagle talisman identical to the one Swan had just left. The meaning of it raced through Swan's mind. There could only be one explanation. Which meant this could only be one person.

"You?" said Swan. "You employed me to beat your own traps? Kill the one man you are sworn to protect?"

The Steward smiled and stepped forwards, his movements awkward as if he was in pain. "Ah, but you haven't defeated all my traps, my friend. There is one left.

A particularly good one if I do say so myself."

Swan glanced around, assessing possible threats. Were there crossbows aimed at her head? Guards preparing to rush in? Contact poisons somewhere?

"What trap? It's a little late now the Emperor is dead."

"No, no, I'm afraid the Emperor is very much alive. This poor wretch was merely a convenient double. A good enough likeness if you don't know the original up close."

Was that true? If it was she'd failed after all. It didn't matter if she was the best because she wasn't good enough. And whatever was going on here, the Steward wasn't going to pay her for failing.

"Spring your trap then, old man," said Swan, "and I can leave or die in the attempt. And if what you say about the Emperor is true I might as well kill you first. All your ingenuity won't turn this blade aside, I think."

"Oh, it might," said the Steward, a look of amusement on his lined face. "Very well. Here is the trap. It goes like this. You are an unstoppable killer who has grown tired of killing. Am I right?"

"What makes you say that?"

The Steward began to pace around as if working out some knotty puzzle. "Because I study the people I employ. And because I was the same, once. I came in here to kill the Emperor's grandfather. One last job and then riches for life, yes? Your name made. Although my approach was different. The palace was still being built in those days and I had myself walled into a cellar with enough supplies to last a year and a half. Then I broke out and came looking for the Emperor while all the guards were busy looking outwards."

"You?" said Swan.

"Oh, yes. And I succeeded, just as you have succeeded. At least, I got as close as you have. And then the old Steward stood where I am standing and offered me his job."

"He didn't kill you on the spot?"

"He didn't. Just as I haven't killed you. Don't you see? I was good enough to beat his traps, which meant he knew it was time to hand over. You've defeated my defences, something many have tried and failed to do. Now it's your turn, to build better ones."

"This is your trap, old man? This is it?"

"This is it. No blades or pits or springs. Just this. An end to killing and a chance to use all your expertise and skill for something else. To save a life for once. Oh, and there's the untold wealth and luxury. Dukes and lordlings vying for your affections, if that takes your fancy. A palace for your own private use. What do you think? It's a fine trap, no? I've been happily stuck inside it for many years now."

Swan considered. She glanced over at the unnamed man she'd just killed. "So no one else has ever got so close?"

"No one else," said the Steward. "You're the best. You're the one."

Swan lowered her throwing knife. She nodded.

"This last trap of yours," she said. "It is a good trap. I think I may be caught."

Fantasy short stories involving thieves or assassins are common enough, but they're fun to write and I liked the ending of this piece, the way the whole palace (or the whole story) is Swan's last trap without her knowing it. I like the way no one speaks out loud until right at the end of the tale – suitably enough for a story that involves lots of creeping around. Hopefully it's a surprise when the Steward does suddenly turn up and spring his trap.

The story was published in the excellent Abyss & Apex in 2017.

THE INFESTATION

Jack was shopping for his week's groceries when he noticed the business card among those pinned to the supermarket's notice board.

Monster-B-Gone Magical Pest Removal
Ghosts exorcised * Demons banished * Vampyres slain
Pixie infestations humanely disposed of
Free Estimates * Bulk discounts for large outbreaks
Satisfaction guaranteed * No job too large or too small

He stopped and took the card. A familiar rage coiled a little tighter within him as he read. But with the rage came an idea. Fight fire with fire. He'd tried everything else. Monsters? Perhaps. That was a word that depended on your perspective.

Back home at Woodland Road he made himself green tea and called the number on the card. The white van drew up outside his house an hour later. On its side was a stylised representation of a dead fairy lying on its back, legs in the air. Jack opened the door on a short, middle-aged man dressed in blue overalls. The man wore a belt around his thickening waist from which dangled an array of tools, electronic devices and wooden stakes.

"Morning, sir. Albert Mann, Monster-B-Gone Magical Pest Removals. Got a little problem needs sorting?"

"You could say that," said Jack. "Come in, please."

"Thank you, sir. You do have a lot of pot plants. Is it wood nymphs? Very hard to shift, wood nymphs, once they take hold."

"No," said Jack, trying to keep his voice level. "Nothing like that. I can show you best from upstairs."

"Ah, gargoyles, then? Tricky bleeders. Cling like limpets."

"It's not gargoyles, either. Come this way."

"Right you are."

Jack led him upstairs onto his balcony. He liked to come up here at night, when it was a little darker and quieter. Now, the suburbs of London stretched off into the grey distance. Here and there, scattered and isolated, little stands of trees clung on.

"It used to be woods as far as they eye could see from here," said Jack.

"Well, yeah, I expect so, sir. Hundreds of years back."

"Before time was even counted. An ocean of green from one end of the world to the other."

"Right. Must have been quite a sight, I expect."

The man seemed bored. Jack's knot of rage tightened further. None of this was what he wanted. He was supposed to be mischievous. A trickster. A child. Now he was aged and jaded and he'd become something else. He'd crossed over into *malicious*. These were the times he lived in. He resented what they'd turned him into.

"Then they came, you see," he explained to the human. "Just another animal at first, very unpromising. Not particularly fast or clever, not good at hiding, no teeth or claws to speak of. But slowly they took over. Some new magic, resisting all the glamours we wove. One by one the trees fell and now we're overrun."

The human was looking at him with the sort of

uncomfortable expression Jack was familiar with. Albert didn't reply for a few moments.

"This … infestation, sir. Do you mean what I think you mean?"

"Yes," said Jack.

"Only it's a bit outside my normal sphere, see. It's a bit awkward, like."

"Your card said *no job too large or too small*. It extended guarantees and talked of handling *large outbreaks*. Was all that a lie? Is your word not your bond?" Jack gave him a *Look*, putting all his mind into it. He still had some of the old powers. Yellow eyes glimpsed through the trees at night, enough to trigger a reaction deep in the human's hindbrain.

Gratifyingly, Albert took a step backwards. "No, no, sir. 'Course not. It's just a bit … well, I mean, how far do I go?"

"Given you're one of them, you mean?"

"Yes, there is that."

"Some survivors are fine, Mr. Mann. We're not the brutes here. Spare who you will, restore the balance. The question is, can you do it?"

The human looked back at the city around them. He sucked in his breath in the way of tradesmen through time preparing a customer to hear a big number. Jack didn't care. Money wasn't a problem. He'd learned long ago humans would do anything for gold, even if it did turn back to pebbles after a year and a day. He could pay whatever the human wanted ten times over.

"Poison might do it," said the human. "In the air or water. Or a disease, maybe. Shooting's not really going to be practical."

"Excellent," said Jack. "I'll leave you to work out the details."

The human looked back at the balcony door, eager to leave. "Right, well, I'll see what I can do, sir. I'll send you an estimate in the post, shall I?"

Jack held out his hand for the human to shake. "Do that. And I can rely on you? Your word is your bond, Albert Mann. Upon your soul."

Albert squirmed for a moment, looking for a way out. But Jack's gaze had him skewered. Albert shook. "Yes, well, you can rely on me, sir. Good as my word. Always have been."

"Excellent," said Jack. "And one more thing, Mr. Mann. Do you happen to know the name of a good landscape gardener?"

"A … landscape gardener, sir?"

"Yes. When you've finished your work, I'm going to need rather a lot of trees planting."

A fantasy story about our modern world seen through the eyes of a surviving woodland nymph or god. I used the name Jack to suggest Jack-in-the-Green, an aspect or avatar of the Green Man in British mythology. I guess there's inevitably quite a strong environmental streak to woodland gods, although maybe Jack in this story goes just a little too far. It was another enjoyable story to write: I like the light-hearted tone given the fairly grim subject-matter. It appeared in the Enter the Apocalypse anthology in 2017.

CORVUS THE MIGHTY

Gedric found the ramshackle hut half way up the hillside. He tethered his horse, the best they'd been able to spare, to one of the low stone walls marking the garden out from the sweep of sloping land. He stood and waited to be spoken to. The man he'd come to find, stripped to the waist, powerful but grey-haired now, dug a trench in the heavy soil with rhythmic swings of his shoulders. The man didn't speak, didn't appear to have even noticed his visitor.

Gedric had grown up with tales of him. They all had: the exploits of Corvus, Corvus and his trusty Shieldsman Way, were the stuff of children's bedtime stories and mead-hall roister. Corvus, who had saved the seven clans again and again, defeated marauding nightmares then drunk for a week to celebrate. And now here he was, tilling the reluctant peat of this desolate hillside, this man who could have lived out his days in golden palaces had he chosen to.

While he waited, Gedric turned away to look out over the land. Now that he saw Corvus in the flesh, his doubts returned. Could one old man really save them? He regretted this fool's errand more and more. He should be down there, fighting the invaders. At least he'd be doing something. Dimly, in the far distance, he could make out a line of smoke cutting into the sky. Some homestead or town burning. Impossible to say where from up there. But it might be Ravn. Ravn, with its walls of spiked pine trunks and its stone tower. Ravn where he'd left Eliane two days earlier, vowing he'd return with help. The invaders had been sighted even as he'd galloped away. Was she still alive? She and their child she carried within her? Were any of the people he'd grown up with still alive? He imagined her calling out his name in desperation as she died, surrounded by shrieking bone-men.

Corvus speared his shovel into the earth as if it were a beast he had slain. He regarded Gedric, an irritated look on his lined face. His chest heaved from his exertions.

"I come in search of Corvus the War Chief, Lord of the Seven Clans," said Gedric.

"Have you now? Well, you've come a long way for nothing, boy."

Gedric had been warned Corvus had turned his back on everything he'd been. Wanted only peace and solitude now. This reaction was only what he'd expected.

"My lord, the clans are in great need," said Gedric, giving him the speech he'd practiced in his head as he rode up the hill. "The bone-men have come out of the west, hundreds of their white ships making landfall on the coast to pillage and destroy. We fight them, but they keep coming, more and more every day."

"Sorry to hear it. At least they shouldn't bother me all the way up here."

"But the clans, my lord. They fall, village by village, town by town. Soon there will be none of us left."

The man shook his head.

"And I told you. I'm not the man you're looking for."

"But you *could* be him once more, my lord. You are still Corvus. You could unite the clans, lead us against the foe."

The old man laughed. He looked up at the sky in the manner of farmers and homesteaders everywhere, assessing the chances of rain.

"Young fool, I mean I'm *really* not him. Corvus died six winters ago."

Gedric smiled. He'd been told to expect this, too.

"You mean, he died and this humble crofter I see before me was born at the same moment. I understand your desire for solitude, Corvus, but times are desperate."

"I mean he *died*, boy. Corvus the Mighty, Lord of the Seven Clans and so on and so on. He gave up his ghost. In his sleep. He was just a ragbag of wounds by the end, anyway. Couldn't feed or clean himself. Don't mention that in the sagas, do they?"

"I don't believe you."

"I'll show you his mighty bones if you like, buried on the hilltop." The man nodded up the slope. Gedric saw the line of a well-worn path leading up there.

"But I don't understand. Everyone I spoke to said Corvus lived here. And here you are. Yet you claim you're not him."

"I am not Corvus."

"Then who are you?"

"Are you really the brightest one they could find? My name is Way, boy. Obviously."

"No, but, I'm sorry, Way was a small man. Clever and agile as a cat. It's in all the sagas."

"Let me tell you something about storytellers," said the old man. He looked around in an exaggerated way, as if there were anyone within thirty leagues who could overhear. "The thing is this. They *make things up*. That's what they do, what they're *for*. I can assure you I am Way. I should know. I've been me all my life. And for the record, I was a hand taller than Corvus. Better swordsman too, truth be told."

Gedric had never even wondered what had happened to Way. He was just the constant companion in the tales: the one who broke into the dungeons to rescue Corvus the night before he was to be executed, or who cut his ropes when the Pirate Kings thought they had him bound and trapped belowdecks.

"But I don't understand, Corvus came here for peace and solitude. Everyone knows that. And yet here you are. What, you came up here to rescue him from these ferocious sheep?"

The old man shook his head.

"I see the storytellers got that wrong, too. *We* came here for peace and solitude. They have me as, what, Corvus's faithful companion? His servant?"

"His Shieldsman."

The man laughed. "Do you really think we could have stood each other all that time if we'd been just comrades? Or master and servant? The world was ours to roam together. I was his lover, not some Shieldsman. Ah, he was a beautiful man in his youth, let me tell you. People would do anything for that smile of his. I know I did."

A weight of dread filled Gedric at these words. Corvus had been their last hope. A remote hope, to be sure. He thought of Eliane and the bright, fearless look on her face. The swell of her belly. Her gentle touch.

"Then I am sorry," said Gedric. "You have lost a lot more than just a hero."

Way shrugged. "We had our time together, down there in the world and up here in the quiet afterwards. It barely matters now. He's gone. Isn't a day goes by I don't miss him, but pining won't bring him back, will it? Now, if you'll excuse me, I have to get these stonefruits planted before the rains come. Make yourself useful and I'll let you rest here the night. You can leave in the morning."

Unable to think of anything else to say to the old man, Gedric climbed over the wall to help.

*

That night, Gedric lay on a mattress of springy heather beneath the furs Way had provided. The old man was outside somewhere, tending to his tatty, distrustful sheep. Gedric sighed. He had failed in his quest to find Corvus, failed to bring him triumphantly back to the clans. They would all die now, sooner or later.

He leafed through the sheaf of dispatches he'd brought with him: descriptions of the skirmishes fought against the bone-men, plans for future battles. He sought good news, some flaw they'd missed, some new strategy they could adopt. He found nothing. The bone-men came in their hundreds and left behind a trail of the dead and dying. Gedric read for an hour or more by the flickering light of Way's fire until his eyes began to prickle. Exhausted by his journey, by his labour in the field, he lay back and fell asleep.

*

He woke to rain drumming on the wooden roof of the hovel. He thought, still half-asleep, the bone-men had come for him, had set fire to their house. Imagined Eliane there beside him, reaching for her axe to fight off the invaders. But when he opened his eyes, he was alone. It was early morning, the inky darkness outside just beginning to shade to purple. Embers of the fire glowed orange in the old man's hearth.

It took Gedric a moment to realise the despatches were gone, plucked from his hand as he slept.

How could he have been so foolish? The details they contained would be invaluable to their foe. He had vowed never to let them out of his sight, had been allowed to travel with them only in the hope they might goad Corvus into action. Now Way had them. If he really was Way. Perhaps he was someone in league with the bone-men, set up there as a trap. Alarm hammered through Gedric at what he had done.

He rose, quickly, thinking to chase after the man, catch up with him. He would be hours away by now. Gedric stood there in the early morning chill, naked, trying to decide what he should do.

"You're in a sudden hurry, boy."

The man sat unseen in a shadowy corner of the room. Gedric heard the rustling of paper.

"Return the despatches to me," said Gedric.

The old man ignored him. "Tell me, who commands the warbands now?"

"Each clan chief leads their own."

"Well, they're all fools. See here, they turn and face the bone-men with the river to their backs. And here, again, in the High Passes, where scree-falls can easily be set off to crush a pursuing enemy, nothing is done. The warbands flap around like gaggles of geese."

"We do what we can. There are too many of the enemy."

The man stood and stepped out of the shadows into the orange glow from the fire. He wore full armour. Gedric recognized it immediately.

"So ... you are Corvus after all."

The man looked at him for a moment, not speaking. He shook his head.

"No. I am Way. Didn't I tell you? But I kept his armour, boy. That's all I have left of him. I get it all out and buckle it on sometimes. Had to loosen the straps a little. Ridiculous, I know, but it makes me feel he's still here, makes me feel close to him again."

"You miss him."

Way shrugged. "Also, I look rather good in it. Don't you think?"

"You look like Corvus."

"That's what you see?"

"I ... I thought you *were* him, stepping out from the sagas. That armour with those crows emblazoning it."

"Good."

"What do you mean?"

"If you saw that, others will see it too," said Way.

"They'll see what they need to see. All those stories about us. A lot of it was just people believing in us, believing in him: the black-haired hero who always won, despite the ridiculous odds."

"You've decided to help us now?"

"I read your despatches," said Way. "The bone-men. I thought you were just some lad who'd seen one battle and run for the hills. But you're right. The clans need Corvus once more."

"You mean, you're going to *pretend* to be him?"

"Riding out of the old tales, just when the clans need him most. Don't you see, boy? The story is irresistible. The bone-men won't have a chance. And … I would see Corvus at the head of the warbands once more. In a manner of speaking."

"Can this work?"

"I won't tell anyone if you don't. They'll *want* to believe I'm Corvus. Now get dressed, boy." Way glanced down and back up, an amused grin flashing across his face. "I can see from here how cold you are."

Gedric began to struggle into his clothes. Way pulled Corvus's helmet over his head and the illusion was complete.

"Come," said Way, his voice muffled by the helmet. Changed. "Let us ride. We can't just sit around on this hillside when the clans need us."

Together they stepped out into the morning light. The rain had passed over now and shafts of sunlight lit the world. The whole land lay stretched out before them, like a map waiting to be drawn on. Way opened the little wooden gate that kept his sheep penned up, giving the creatures their freedom.

"Will we have a chance?" Gedric asked. "Is there really any hope?" The fate of all the clans depended on this old man, but he could think only of Eliane. Eliane and their child.

Way laughed. "The situation is hopeless, the odds

ridiculous. How can we fail? We will ride to Ravn and rally their defences. And then we will ride to every other town. The story of the return of Corvus will spread like a fire across the land and we will be unstoppable."

Then Way – Corvus – nodded, climbed onto his horse and set off down the hill to do battle.

Corvus the Mighty grew in my head from the opening scene: the desperate supplicant on a quest for a hero; the less-than enthusiastic and distinctly un-heroic response he receives. I like the notion of Way becoming Corvus; of constructing that story within the story. Like What the Darkness Is, this is another tale of the power of myth and storytelling. It originally appeared in Vitality magazine in 2015 and has since been reprinted (and recorded) by Glittership.

YOUR CALL MAY BE RECORDED FOR TRAINING PURPOSES

Thank you for calling CyberSeven Systems. Your call is important to us. Please be aware that it may be recorded for training purposes.

"Yes, hi, I need help. Urgent help. I …"

You now have three options. Either press the numbers on your handset or speak to indicate your preferred option. Press or say "1" if you have a sales enquiry about the CyberSeven product range.

"No, I need to speak to someone. Now. It's got me trapped in the bathroom."

Press or say "2" if you have an account or billing enquiry. Press or say "3" if you require technical support.

"Yes, technical support, technical support."

I'm sorry, I didn't understand your response. Would you like to hear the options again?

"No! Just help me. The damn thing's gone mad!"

You now have three options. Either press the numbers on your handset or speak to indicate your preferred option.

"What? No. Three. Three! I need technical support. I really, *really* need technical support."

You selected option three. Is that correct? Press 1 or say "yes" for yes. Press 0 or say "no" for no.

"Yes! Yes! Yes! Three! I mean one! Yes!"

Thank you for calling CyberSeven Systems. Welcome to the technical support department. Please have your forty-three-digit serial number to hand. You are currently in a queue. Your call is important to us and we will answer it as soon as we are able.

"Come on, come on! It's breaking down the door!"

Hi, and thanks for holding.

"Oh, thank God. It's my HomeBot, it's gone crazy. I told it to make sure the house was spotless and now it's chasing me around trying to clean *me* away. It just tried to force me into the Recycling Unit. How do I turn the damn thing off?"

You now have four options. Either press the numbers on your handset or speak to indicate your preferred option. Press or say "1" if you need technical support with an iDrive intelligent automobile.

"But …"

Press or say "2" if you need technical support with a Domestic8 HomeBot Servant. Press or say "3" if you need technical support with your iGlass Enhanced Reality eyewear. Press or say "4" to hear your options again. You can also press or say "0" at any time to return to this menu.

"No, get back, you stupid machine. I am *not* dirt, understand? I do not need to be cleaned away. And put that blade back. How come you have rotating blades anyway? Just return to your base and aaargh …"

I'm sorry, I didn't understand your response. Would you like to hear the options again?

I'm sorry, I still didn't understand your response. Would you like to hear the options again?

I'm sorry, I still didn't understand your response. Please ascertain the exact nature of your problem and call us back. Thank you for calling CyberSeven systems. Your call is appreciated and is important to us. CyberSeven systems: the future, today.

"No, no, please, don't go! I'm still here. Help me, please. I think it's broken my leg. It's dragging me to the Recycling Unit. How do I turn it off?"

I'm sorry, I didn't understand your response. Would you like to hear the options again?

"No. Ah, two! Two! My HomeBot's gone mad. How do I turn it off? Please, help me, help me."

Welcome to the Domestic8 Homebot Servant technical support help line. Domestic8 Homebot Servants by CyberSeven Systems. We do all the dirty work so you don't have to. You now have seventeen options to choose from. Press or say "1" to …

"No, aagh, my arm. My God it's …"

I'm sorry, I didn't understand your response. Would you like to hear the options again?

I'm sorry, I still didn't understand your response. Would you like to hear the options again?

I'm sorry, I still didn't understand your response. Please ascertain the exact nature of your problem and call us back. Thank you for calling CyberSeven systems. Your call is important to us. CyberSeven systems: the future, today.

Another little story that plays with a familiar trope of modern life. I can't recall which helpline I was stuck on when the story came to me, but the over-friendly amd insincere automated responses will be familiar to most people. This story appeared in Stupefying Stories in 2017. I'm sure home robots almost never go haywire and clean away their owners in real life. They probably have all sorts of checks built into them to stop them doing that.

JUMPJACKER

Newer Delhi Central Station, 14:02 India Standard Time

Ronan Mistry half-stepped, half-fell from the jump gate at Newer Delhi Central. His stomach lurched like someone had spent the last-minute whirling him around blindfolded. A heavy pain thrummed through his head. He hated the damn jump networks. The headache was a new thing but the gates *always* made him nauseous. He was old enough to remember the days when aeroplanes still flew in the sky. It took hours to get anywhere – which always amused young people – but at least your body wasn't smashed to a stream of bits and reassembled each time you wanted to travel.

He'd promised himself before, but this was definitely the last time he used the networks. At the very least he'd pay for a private jump gate next time. It wasn't like he couldn't afford it. It was this affectation of being a *regular* person. His humble beginnings; try as you might you couldn't stop being the urchin from the back streets of Delhi. From now on he'd use some of ShivaTech's wealth and get around in a little more comfort.

"Morning again, Mr. Mistry."

A security guard in a saffron-coloured turban looked like he was about to step over to help. Ronan didn't recognize the man, despite the apparent familiarity. He waved and managed a smile to say he was fine, didn't need assistance. The guards were there to look out for jumpjackers hitting travellers as they emerged from the network, not to lend a hand to travelsick old men.

Ronan tried to walk off in a straight line and failed badly, tried to stop himself vomiting and just about managed it. He swallowed down bitter fluid that suddenly filled his mouth. Tens of thousands of people thronged the station, dashing to and from the gate array, barging aside anyone in their way. He bounced off more than one of them, mumbling an inaudible apology. He found a stone pillar, its cool solidity welcome. He waited for his head to stop swimming, standing there panting like an old dog.

He watched as a group of uniformed soldiers pushed through the crowd: not private jump network guards but proper IndPol military officers, bristling with tazers and lasers and who-knew what else. There must have been an incident. Perhaps some unfortunate traveller *had* been jumped as they stepped from their gate. Ronan watched to see what would happen, whom they would arrest. He hoped there wouldn't be serious trouble. He was in no state to run.

There was a moment of horror as the truth of what he was seeing hit him. The soldiers weren't running towards the gates. They were running towards *him*. His stomach lurched in panic.

It was only then he saw Sageeta, his wife, hurrying along behind the soldiers, her sari trailing behind her like gossamer wings. She looked angry. She was *never* angry. The soldiers ran up to him then stopped, parting to let her through.

"Ronan. What in all the hells is going on? What are you doing?" Sageeta stood in front of him, hands on hips. The soldiers surrounded them now, a ring of steel pushing the swarming crowds back. They didn't appear to be arresting him. They looked outwards, like they were protecting him. But from what? He didn't understand anything that was happening.

"Sageeta. It is good to see you. I'm feeling a little ill."

"Never mind that, you old fool. What have you done? What is this madness?"

He shook his head. "I don't know what you mean. I've just come from my meeting in Capetown about the new Europe contracts. I haven't *done* anything."

"Stop playing these games," said his wife. "You're going to explain everything right here and now."

"Explain what?"

A looked of worry flashed across his beloved wife's features. She spoke again, in a low voice, as if afraid people would overhear. "Explain why half an hour ago you transferred one billion rupees from ShivaTech to some no-good accounts I've never heard of. The company is ruined, Ronan. *We* are ruined."

"What?"

"One billion rupees! Our entire holdings gone in a moment."

"It's not possible. I ordered no such transfer."

"Don't be ridiculous. Did you think you wouldn't be seen? You made the transfer from a bank in London. IndPol have the images of you arriving at Euston Jump Node. And the images of you getting *here* an hour ago, when that oh-so lovely young woman stopped to help you. Is that what this is all about? Have you come to this?"

Ronan waited for some of his wife's words to make sense, but they utterly refused to. What she was talking about? What young woman?

"This is all madness," said Ronan. "I've just left Capetown."

His wife shook her head, as if pitying him. "Then tell me, Ronan, what the time was when you left Capetown."

"About one o'clock our time."

"And the time now?"

"Obviously, about one minute later." But as he spoke he also consulted the clock plugin in his brain, just to check. The response came back immediately. The time was now a little past *two* o'clock. Somehow, impossibly, an hour had passed by since he'd left Capetown.

It made no sense. Ronan tried to speak, but no words would come from his mouth.

Newer Delhi Central Station, one hour earlier...

Ronan Mistry half-stepped, half-fell from the jump gate at Newer Delhi Central. His stomach lurched like someone had spent the last-minute whirling him around blindfolded. A heavy pain thrummed through his head. He hated the damn jump networks. The headache was a new thing but the gates *always* made him nauseous.

A security guard, recognizing him, nodded his turbaned head.

"Morning, Mr. Mistry."

Ronan managed only a mumbled response. The pain in his head grew sharper, like something solid being hammered into his brain. The great hall of the station lurched around him, a blur of colours and blaring sounds. He leaned against a pillar, the stone cool on his hands.

"You don't look well, sir. Why don't you sit down?"

A young woman had stopped beside him, concern clear on her face. There were still one or two good people in the world. He tried to explain he was OK, that he just needed a moment. He sank to the ground, his back against the pillar.

The woman put a gentle hand on his shoulder and knelt beside him so that her head was level with his. The bindi on her forehead was animated in the modern fashion: a swirling red spiral. She spoke quietly into his ear. "Listen to me, you fucker. You are *not* going to recover from this. You are going to feel worse and worse. Soon the pain in your head will become unbearable. And do you want to know what that pain is? It's the feeling of your mind being *eaten*, old man. Do you *fucking* understand me?"

Ronan stared up at her. The young woman continued to smile, the worried look clear on her beautiful face. Had he imagined her words?

Her grip tightened painfully. "Do you understand me?"

He didn't, not at all. He shook his head. "What is happening?"

The young woman glanced around, making sure no one was too near. "Tell me how many children you have, Ronan Mistry."

"What? What does that…?"

"Just tell me. How many?"

"Two."

"Boys or girls?"

"Girls. Grown women, now."

"Names?"

"They're called…" He stopped. For some reason he couldn't recall their names. Both had waved him goodbye just that morning as he left for Capetown.

"What are their names, old man?"

"I don't … I don't know."

"And what do they look like? How tall? What colour are their eyes?"

"I don't remember."

"What was their favourite flavour of kulfi when they were young?"

He shook his head. He didn't know. The pain filling his brain was a fog. A fog through which he could see nothing.

The young woman nodded her head, as if he had done well, given her the right answers.

"Very good. Now let me explain what is happening to you. A small alteration to your neural matrix was introduced as you rematerialised at the jump node. An artificial algorithm hidden amongst your normal brain patterns. Right now, it is chomping its way though your memories. Soon you won't be able to remember you even have children. In a few hours you won't know your own name. A few hours after that your brain's autonomous functions will start forgetting how to function. Your heart will stop beating and your lungs will stop pumping."

"No," said Ronan. "That's not possible." He *knew* it wasn't possible. You couldn't just alter people as they rematerialised without introducing major flaws. The ensuing corruption was always fatal. The brain was too dynamic, too fluid. The technology was years away.

"Oh, it's possible, old man," said the woman. "And it's happening to you right now. No doubt you are experiencing an excruciating pain in your head? That is one side-effect."

Was that true? The networks were a well-known trigger for migraines. Perhaps she'd just struck lucky. "No. I don't believe it."

"Then let me ask you this. What does the name Arvan J. Stanton mean to you?"

"He's ... just someone I knew once. Years ago, at university. Why?"

"Did he ever give you any advice? Any words of wisdom?"

"Actually, yes. I remember very well. He told me that whatever I did in life I had to believe the young woman with the red bindi when she stops to help me at Newer Delhi…"

He trailed off. His memory of those words was very, very clear. But why? It was years ago. It made no sense. And why would his old friend have even uttered such nonsense?

"Yes, you understand," said the young woman. "Arvan

J. Stanton did not exist. Another alteration we made to your mind. An implanted memory."

"I don't believe it. This is hypnosis. Autosuggestion. Nothing more."

"You don't really believe that."

"Even if you have done this," he said. "Even if such a thing is possible, why? Why would you want to destroy my memories?"

"Oh, not *destroy*, old man. We aren't mindless thugs. We are artists. Your memories are all still there. Just encrypted. Locked away in your brain with a key only we know. And when you've paid us the two billion rupees, we will give you the key and you can have your brain back."

"Two *billion* rupees?"

"That's the price. ShivaTech can afford it. A man of your wealth really shouldn't use the public networks, you know."

The fog was lifting a little in his head now. He saw the obvious flaw in her proposal. And making deals, striking bargains was what he was good at. "So, when I pay you this fortune, you'll just drop round and fix up my brain for me? Set everything straight?"

"You'll need to make another jump. We'll spot you in the network and put everything right. There'll be no need to meet again."

"Yes, but why would you?" said Ronan. "Once you've got your money you'd be better off leaving me to die. Then all the evidence goes away. It's a perfect crime."

The young woman smiled. "You'll just have to trust us, won't you? You're hardly in a position to bargain."

He could see the faintest hint of worry in her eyes. You learned to read people. "Actually," said Ronan, "I think I am. They're certain to *post mortem* me. I'm willing to bet your hacks to my brain – if they exist – will show up. That will raise suspicions. People might follow a trail that leads back to you. And I don't think you want to take that risk."

The brief frown of annoyance that flashed across her

features told him he'd hit the mark. She nodded her head from side to side, trying to suggest indifference. "We'll take that chance for two billion rupees, old man."

He considered. He still didn't believe her. But if there was a chance she was telling the truth…

"I'll make you an offer," he said. "*One* billion rupees and I don't send the money until I'm fully restored to health."

"That's not going to work, old man."

"Ah, of course, because you were also planning to wipe all my memories of this conversation, weren't you?"

"Obviously. You'll be in no state to sanction further payments. You won't know anything about them."

"Then I'll give you half the money now and place half in an account in your name but which you can't access for twenty-four hours. That will give you time to restore me."

The woman studied him for a moment, looking for the flaws in the plan. He just had to hope she didn't know everything ShivaTech's systems *could* do. Finally, she nodded. She'd might not get all the money, but she'd decided even half a billion would be enough. As Ronan had calculated she would.

"Very well," she said. "But not in my name. Use Arvan J. Stanton, understand?"

"As you like. I'll have to jump to London to arrange everything."

"You remember your non-existent friend's old contact number?"

"For some reason, yes, I do. Very clearly."

"That's the account number for the first half of the payment. Make sure the new account is in his name, too, and we'll see it. And remember: in three hours time you won't recognize your own face in a mirror. So, don't fuck up."

She smiled and stood up. She lifted her scarf over her head to cover her features. "Oh, and be careful in the jump network, Ronan Mistry. There are some bad people out there.”

She turned and strode away. He soon lost her in the teeming crowds.

*

Doctor Kay Alvarez was engrossed in an analysis of the fractal equations from her latest tests when her boss staggered in. She hadn’t seen Ronan for nearly a year; these days the owner of ShivaTech didn’t travel so much. Her delight at the sight of her old friend was immediately tempered when she saw the state of him. He was clearly struggling to stay upright.

“Ronan? What has happened? You look terrible. Shall I get a doctor?”

“You *are* a doctor, Kay. That’s why I’ve come to see you.” For a moment she caught a flash of her old friend’s humour. Then he sank into a chair and held his head in his hands.

“We need to get you to a hospital,” said Kay. “You know very well I’m not the right sort of doctor.”

“Actually,” said Ronan, “you are exactly the right sort. I need you to scan my brain and look for … anomalies.”

“What do you mean *anomalies*?”

He appeared to be having trouble getting the words out. He was clearly in great pain. “Please,” he said. “There isn’t much time. I need you to do this *now*. There’s this thing in my head. A … bad thing.”

With anyone else she would have insisted on the hospital. But, as she’d come to learn over the years, Ronan generally knew best. “OK. Come with me.”

Ten minutes later she had the live feed of his brain imaging in front of her. She sifted her way through the 3D map, looking for these mysterious anomalies. What was he expecting her to find? A tumour? A clot? A bleed?

“Anything?” he asked.

“Nothing. No damage at all. Wait. What the hell? *That*

doesn't look right."

"What do you see?"

"These neuron patterns here in the hindbrain look almost … random." She turned to Ronan. "Is this what you mean? This corruption?"

"Is it spreading?"

She turned back and zoomed in. It took only a few moments to see it. She watched as more and more of the connections between the neurons realigned themselves. They switched from normal, organic arrangements into broken, disjointed fragments.

"It is," she said. "Advancing rapidly. Do you want to tell me what the hell is going on here, Ronan? Frankly, it's incredible you're even walking and talking."

Ronan nodded but didn't reply.

"Ronan? What has happened? What is this?"

With great effort, as if having to drag up ancient memories, he began to tell her the day's events.

When he'd finished she was silent for a moment. If she hadn't seen his scan she wouldn't have believed it. "Ronan," she said finally, "I'm so sorry."

He shook his head. "No. You don't understand. This is an incredible opportunity."

"What?"

"Whoever these people are, however they've done this, we need this technology. They're years ahead of us."

"It must be experimental," said Kay. "For all we know it only works one in a hundred times. One in a thousand. You're incredibly lucky just to be here."

"Yes, but think what we could do if we had this capability. If we could reliably edit people's images. We could cure diseases, do *anything*. We have to pursue this."

"Always the idealist, Ronan. You can't go ahead with this; you're going to get yourself killed. Somehow, we have to stop the encryption of your neural matrix. Restore you somehow."

He shook his head. "The thing is, I've already

instructed the bank to transfer the money."

"What?" she said again. She was beginning to doubt his sanity now. Was this the corruption in his brain speaking? "Ronan, this is madness."

"No, Kay. Listen to me. Listen while I can still think straight. OK, perhaps they'll talk their half billion and run. And then I am in serious trouble. But there's a chance they'll do what they said: intervene again to fix me so they can get the rest of their money, yes?"

"There's a chance," she said. "There's also a chance they'll zap your brain completely to cover their tracks."

"No. It will look too obvious. They're clever. Who knows how often they've done this? We need to stop them. You need to stop them."

"Me?"

"You'll know where I am in the jump network. You can track me among all the billions of images?"

She shrugged. "Sure, that we can do."

"And when they intervene – if they do – you'll be able to see it, yes? They must be using a hacked jump node. You'll be able to get a physical address. We'll be able to get to them."

She studied him for a moment. He was serious. He really meant to do this. "Ronan," she said, "this is a whole series of *ifs* and slim chances. It's not going to actually work."

He smiled through the pain. He actually smiled. "Maybe. *Or* we'll put a stop to a bunch of evil hackers and acquire technology ShivaTech could work wonders with."

"If by some miracle it works and they do wipe out your memories of all this, you're going to be pretty confused when you emerge from the jump network. You won't have a clue what's going on."

"I'll manage."

She shook her head. "I don't like it. I don't like it one bit."

"Then it's a good job I'm the boss. Consider all of that

an order."

"Ronan, you haven't given me an actual order in thirty years."

"Then I'm asking. Please, Kay. If it goes wrong it hardly matters at this stage, does it?"

She studied him for a moment more, then relented with a sigh.

"Oh, and Kay?"

"Yes?"

"Please hurry. My head feels like it's going to damn well *explode.*"

Ronan now lay on the hard floor of the station concourse. He couldn't make sense of anything. The same fragments of thought kept circling around in his brain. Somehow, he had lost an hour of his life. And one billion rupees. And now, it seemed, he was losing his mind too. He was finding it harder and harder to recall names, details, places. The pain in his head was a vast weight, crushing his memories beneath it.

Figures milled around him, their faces occasionally looming over him to ask him questions he couldn't hear. His wife was there, the anxiety clear on her face. For some reason he couldn't recall her name. That was bad. Paramedics buzzed around, shining lights in his eyes, giving him oxygen, checking his blood pressure. There were also soldiers. Lots of soldiers. Some stood in a ring around him, their black boots filling his vision when he opened his eyes. A group of them had just charged off for the jump gates on some suddenly-urgent mission. He didn't know why.

None of it made sense. Ronan groaned and closed his eyes.

*

"Can you see them? Have you got the trace?"

The IndPol officer stood over Kay. It was hard to concentrate with him standing there. These things required focus, concentration, not some armed grunt breathing down her neck.

Her hands moved through the display, sifting through the almost limitless threads, each representing a single person's journey through the jump network. She would only get one shot at this. They had to be careful. If the hackers saw they were being traced they would be gone and that would be the end of Ronan.

"There. That's them. This gate here."

"You're sure?"

"Of course I'm sure. That's why I said it."

"OK," said the soldier. "We're jumping there now."

"And I'm coming with you," said Kay.

"Sorry. No. This is a dangerous military operation. We can't be worrying about civilians."

"And I'm sorry, but I am coming," said Kay. "It's vital we recover the technology these people have. You do your job and we'll do ours, understood?"

The IndPol officer looked like he was about to argue, then backed down. Turning away, he began to bellow out orders to his troops.

Someone was touching his cheek, trying to rouse him. Ronan flicked open his eyes. He expected to see Sageeta but another woman's face was there. A woman he recognized.

"Kay? What are you doing here? You're supposed to be at work in London. I'm not paying you to just gallivant around the world."

"Long story. I'll explain later. Right now, I'm going to scan your brain for anomalies."

"You're going to do what?"

"Just be quiet. This is the first time I've done this in a public jump station. Turn your head to the side then don't move."

Ronan did as he was told. He'd found that was best with Kay. Through a forest of soldiers' boots, he could see the jump node he'd emerged from *en route* from Capetown. More of the soldiers were surrounding it. He watched as a squad of them emerged, escorting some prisoners. Two women and a man. One of the women – young, a bright red bindi on her forehead – turned to look directly at him. She scowled. Ronan couldn't understand why. He'd never seen her before in his life.

He could hear Kay and Sageeta murmuring to each other, something about the readings on the brain scanner.

"Well," he said. "Would you two like to tell me what is happening?"

"There's good news and bad news," said Kay.

"What's the bad?"

"You're the same stubborn old man you were this morning," said his wife.

"OK. And the good?"

"Your brain is clear of anomalies," said Kay. "The decryption as you jumped worked. You're in the clear."

"I have no idea what you're talking about."

Kay ignored him. "With IndPol's help we should be able to recover the technology they were using. You were right. It looks pretty incredible."

"Technology?" said Ronan. "What technology? You're not making any sense."

Ronan levered himself up onto his elbows. The room wasn't spinning now. He thought he could probably stand. The pain in his head had subsided to a dull throb. Sageeta offered him an arm to help him up.

He looked back over at the gates. Damned jump network. They always made him sick. This was *definitely* the last time he used them.

Jumpjacker is a story from the same universe as my Genehunter novel, although this story is a standalone tale with different characters. The Genehunter is a cyberpunk thriller that collects together five linked cases. It follows the adventures of Simms, a detective paid to track down the DNA of the famous and infamous of history for his clients' private collections. In it, as with Jumpjacker, jump nodes and brain plugins play a significant role in the action.

If you're interested in finding out more about The Genehunter, the web page is at simonkewin.co.uk/genehunter.

The first Genehunter case – The Wrong Tom Jacks – appears later on in this collection.

Jumpjacker was originally published in Perihelion magazine in 2013, and has since been translated into a couple of other languages.

THE MONSTER

Eventually he grew weary of the long winter he'd escaped to.

It wasn't the cold; he could withstand that well enough. His body was strong. There were fish to catch in the icy waters, and sometimes he could creep up on a seal and wrestle it to its death. The flesh and blubber could feed him for a month. He hated to butcher the creatures but it was a matter of survival. His house was built from their furs lashed over whale bones. He'd extended and reinforced it again and again over the decades. When sickness came, as it did even to him, he could lie on his seal-hide bed and shiver through until it subsided.

Water was always plentiful.

In the early days he'd had fights with the arctic bears, those roaring monsters with cruel teeth and butcher's hook claws. Some were taller even than he when they reared up on their hind legs, but he was nearly as strong and made up for the lack in cunning. Now the bears walked a wide path around him, watching from the distance and sniffing at the air but daring no nearer. They had to be the descendants many times over of the originals but still they kept away, wariness passed down from mothers to cubs.

The arrangement suited them all.

No, it wasn't the cold, or the four-months of utter darkness in the winter, or the bears. It was loneliness, finally, that spurred him back into life, that made him gather his few supplies onto his sled and set off. He knew he would never have the companion, the mate, he craved. The possibility of another like him had died with his creator. It was a loss that, even now, cut through him more sharply than any wind from the north. He was a monster, forever an outcast.

But, loneliness. Loneliness had grown within him, gestating over the decades and centuries into something that couldn't be denied. It appeared he wasn't going to age and die as he'd assumed. His creator had done his work well.

There were things he needed to understand, too. Questions that needed answers. Whose fingers did he slip into the fish's mouth to break its spine and end its suffering? Whose muscles sawed at the ice to open up access to the water? Whose eyes did he see the world through? Whose brain, even, thought these thoughts, asked these questions? Who were they, all the poor, broken wretches that were *him*? Young or old? Male or female? He could tell from his external appearance that young, strong men made up a large part of his anatomy. But his organs? His inner workings? He didn't know.

He didn't know who he was.

But he'd seen signs in the sky. Miracles. Wonders. For many years he'd been utterly alone, and everyone else on the Earth might have been dead for all he knew or cared. He'd wanted no more to do with any of them. But then one day he'd seen a light in the east. A shooting-star. Except not a shooting-star. It didn't blaze and fade but was constant, moving across the night sky with slow precision, as if a star had worked itself loose and set off on a journey. He'd watched in wonder as it arced across the darkness. The following night it was there again. All the yearnings, all the questions he'd tried to suppress blazed into life as he sat and stared upwards.

And so, he set off. Finding his way was easy. Even in summer the sun was low in the southern sky. All he had to do was head towards it. If there were still people in the world, the thought of being among them again gave him little pleasure. He remembered their revulsion all-too well. But if there were answers to be found they lay among humanity. He had no choice but to face them, just as he'd once faced the white bears.

He spied the ship in the distance after two weeks of hauling his sled across the ice. The black speck against the endless white slowly took on shape as he approached. It was trapped, far from open water. Summer was coming and the floes were breaking up, but the ship must have been marooned there all winter. It was large, too. Large and strange. His maker had endowed him with good eyes, and he could pick out fine detail from a safe distance. It appeared to be made from metal rather than wood. At night lights blazed out from it, brighter than any lantern he'd ever seen. Icicles festooned its rigging, but there were no sails in sight. There were definitely people on board. He could see them clearly: stick-figures milling around on the decks, or even venturing onto the ice to engage in activities he couldn't begin to understand. One or two of them always carried long-snouted rifles. Guns for the bears, most likely, but they'd work on him just as well. Even he couldn't withstand the sort of damage they'd inflict.

He counted nine people in the end, assuming there was no one who stayed below decks. He couldn't fight nine of them, especially not when they carried those guns. But perhaps he could pick the people off, one by one. Break their necks before retreating into the icy wastes. The thought gave him little pleasure but it was his only hope. They'd come hunting him, as he'd been hunted in the old days. But the ice was his domain. Once it was done, the ship could transport him far away, to the cities where he might find the answers he sought.

He watched for three days, crouched behind his upturned sled for camouflage, while he waited for the right moment to act.

*

Helen Magnusson crouched to study the GPS marker they'd left embedded in the ice. She popped the rubber cover on the USB socket and plugged in to download the latest readings to her device. All in all, it had been a good winter. Lots of good data. They needed to do more analysis back in Copenhagen, but it was already clear they'd learned significant amounts about the movements of the ice floes. Repeat readings taken over successive years would give them invaluable insights into climate change.

As she was a biologist, the floes weren't her main area of interest. She was much more intrigued by the alterations they were seeing in the microfauna populations. Larger creatures were being affected too: the migration patterns of fish, whales and polar bears were all altering. There could be no doubt. The world was changing.

While the data downloaded she glanced up at Kurt, standing guard nearby with his rifle at the ready. Kurt the pacifist vegetarian who'd never intentionally harmed any creature in his whole life. He really wasn't going to be much use if a bear did attack, was he?

"Hey, Kurt. It's gone ten. Why don't you go make your Skype call to the lovely Margarita?"

Kurt's voice was muffled behind the frost-rimed scarf covering half his face. "I'll stay."

She knew how much he looked forward to these daily calls with his young wife. The winter away had been hard on him. "It's okay. Go. I only have five more probes to do. I'll be back on board in fifteen minutes."

Kurt gazed around the ice, looking for any threat. The

white silence stretched away in all directions, utterly unblemished.

"Go," she said again. "I'll be fine. Leave the rifle. If I see a bear I'll shoot the damn thing myself."

With a grunt of gratitude, Kurt laid down the rifle and strode back to the *Kraken*, adding another line of boot-prints to the well-trampled ice around the frozen research ship.

She was on the last probe but one when the attack came. She was thrown to the ice, a cruel blow to her side knocking the wind out of her before she could even scream. A moment later she felt the pain of it. *Ribs cracked*, a detached part of her mind observed. It was agony as she scrabbled about for the rifle but it was too far away, over by the probe. She half-rose, trying to call out. Her attacker filled her vision: a huge shape against the bright sky, rearing over her for the final blow.

*

He woke in a laboratory. Another laboratory. Different from the one his creator had used, of course. This one was cleaner, shinier, red and green lights twinkling away on incomprehensible contraptions all around. But he knew the smells, knew what places like this meant. He keenly remembered the agonies he'd suffered. Raw pain thrummed away in his side, his leg, across his shoulders. Memories came back to him. Memories of the fight. He'd thought to show them his true self. Despite everything. He'd thought to reveal the person he was beneath. What was he thinking? They'd seen none of it. He cursed himself for his own stupidity. Mankind hadn't changed. They saw something monstrous and assumed it was a monster. He should have stayed in the high ice where he was safe.

When he tried to rise and found he was restrained, bound to the bed by shiny straps, he knew the worst of it. The straps cut into his limbs as he struggled. Furious with himself, at his own weakness, he tore himself from the metal slab they'd laid him on. He ripped aside, also, the tubes and wires they'd attached to him.

He had to get away, out onto the snow. There were no portholes in the laboratory; it was impossible to know how many decks he had to climb. He padded down a metal corridor lit by harsh white lights, no flames in sight.

He made it half-way up the first flight of steps when they came for him. They stood at the top, three of them, looking down upon him. Roaring, he charged. If he could throw them aside, fight his way above decks, he could jump from the ship, get away. He was conscious he was playing the part of the monster they saw when they looked at him, but he had little choice.

One of his captors raised a gun. It was only a pistol. He ignored it. When the shot struck him, it was little more than a wasp-sting. He'd nearly reached them when his head began to swim. Clouds descended, filling his brain. What had they done to him? He tried to shake the fog free, but there was too much of it, the weight of it too great.

Dizziness overwhelmed him. His last sensation was of falling backwards, the people who'd captured him receding into the darkness above.

When he awoke again it was to the gentle rocking of the ship. It took a few moments to grasp what that meant. How long had he been asleep? What had they done to him?

As before, he tried to rise. As before he was bound. He was naked too, now. A single white sheet covered his body instead of the furs he'd been dressed in. To what end? Had they been examining him? Preparing their fresh torments?

One again he struggled, trying to tear himself free from their bonds.

"Hey, it's okay. I'll undo the straps for you." A woman's voice, speaking accented German, as if it wasn't her native tongue. "You do understand me, right? You speak German and French?"

He stopped struggling. "Why am I bound?"

She set about working at his wrists and ankles. She was young, her blonde hair long and soft. He marvelled at how smooth her skin was. Cream compared to his own scarred and pitted hide.

"We went through some rough seas yesterday," she said. "Didn't want you to fall out of bed."

"But before. When you first captured me. I was bound then, too."

"You kept fighting us in your sleep, even when we were trying to treat you."

"You are a doctor? A woman?"

She smiled a little smile to herself. "As it happens I am a doctor. But a biologist, not a medic. We had you in the sick bay for a while, but then we needed the room so we wheeled you in here."

"So you could study me?"

"So you could sleep."

She finished untying him. Warily, expecting some cruel joke, he swung his legs round to sit upright. The room lurched for a few moments before settling back into place.

More memories returned to him. "You shot me."

"Darted you. You were delusional, a danger to yourself and others. It was all we could do."

He didn't understand all her words. He towered over her but she didn't appear to have any fear of him. He wondered, briefly, if she was blind, like the old man. But no. She could see him well enough. She held out a bottle of water for him, constructed from some strange, flexible material and not the glass he'd expected.

"How long have I been asleep?" he asked after he'd drunk. The water trickled cold inside him.

"Ten days. An ice-breaker came for us a week ago. The captain wanted to air-lift you off. I thought you might want to decide things for yourself. Given your past."

"You know what I am?"

"Who doesn't?"

"And that doesn't alarm you? The fact that we're here alone in this little room?"

The woman shifted in her chair. But she wasn't uneasy. Getting comfortable if anything. "You saved me. Out there on the ice, when the bear attacked. Never seen anything like it. A man fighting a polar bear and winning. Incredible."

"I killed it?"

"You did. Not before it gave you some terrible injuries. It took all of us to carry you on board while staunching your wounds."

"Were you harmed?"

"I'm healing. The painkillers help."

He looked around, uncomfortable at this intimacy between them. With his bed and her desk and the shelves full of her books there was little room left. She'd clearly been studying insects as part of her researches. On her desk, next to a microscope, beetles crawled around in a series of glass tanks. Beside them, butterflies fanned their wings upon a purple-flowering plant. They appeared to be free to fly wherever they wished.

"Why are there insects?"

"I'm studying the effects shifting magnetic fields have on their life-cycles."

He nodded, although her words still made little sense. "You said I was a *man*. If you know who I am you also know what I am. A monster. A concoction of broken parts. A chimera."

She shook her head. "Those are bad words. Is that how you see yourself?"

"It's how the world sees me. And ... I have done terrible things. I've taken the lives of others."

"Terrible things were done to you. Seems to me you had plenty of reason for doing what you did."

"You may think like that. The world won't."

She didn't reply for a moment, looking at him,

considering him.

"Why did you come south after all this time?"

"I … I wanted to find out who I was. What I was."

She nodded, as if this was a perfectly normal thing to say. "You know, the world has changed a lot since you last walked it. Now you would be a marvel. A wonder."

"These are simply other terms for *mongrel* and *monster*."

"No. People would love you. Scientists, obviously. I mean, how is it you've even survived this long? But everyone else, too. You'd be famous. Trust me. You'd be a huge deal. We'd help you find your answers. Everyone would want a piece of you."

"A piece of me?"

"Sorry. Bad choice of words. I mean everyone would want to find out about you. You'd be huge."

He tried to make sense of her words. Clearly the way in which people spoke had changed over so much time. Was this all some trap? Some way of luring him back into the clutches of what was laughably called civilisation? Sometimes, back in the north, he polished a slab of ice so he could see his own reflection. Thinking that, maybe, he wasn't as lumpen and scarred as his memory said. He was always disappointed. "I'm still a monster. I'm still this assemblage of stolen body-parts."

"And, what, you think we're all pure, all perfect? I've been thinking about you while you slept. Let me tell you, we're all mongrels. We're all a mishmash of human ancestries. Neanderthal ancestries, too, come to that. Amphibian, reptile, you name it, it's all in there. Maybe 10% of our DNA is from viruses, absorbed into our own millions of years ago. Our bodies are mostly bacterial cells. You think you're a mongrel? Welcome to the human race."

"I don't know what any of that means."

"Look. You want to know whose hands those are? Whose face, whose limbs? Is that it?"

"I do."

"Well I can tell you. They're yours."

"Once they weren't. They were stolen for me."

She studied him for a moment. Then, unexpectedly, she began to unbutton her shirt. Confused, mouth dry, he could do nothing but watch as she revealed her breast. An old thrill of delight through him, like torches being lit in rooms long left dark.

Beneath the fabric of her undergarment, running the length of her sternum, crawled a long, centipede scar. She traced its line with her blood-red fingernail.

"You see this? I was born with a congenital cardiac condition. My heart didn't work properly. So, they gave me a new one. Some unfortunate died, I don't know who, but I got to live. Their heart beats in my chest. There are lots of people like you. Like, I have a cousin lives in Stockholm. *He* was born a *she*. Surgery can fix many things that nature got wrong."

Such marvels, such wonders. This was a place of magic. Terrible magic. Except, not, of course. It was all natural science. He of all people should understand that.

"No," he said. "You're still *you*. I'm only an assortment, a collection. There is no *me*."

She shrugged. "Bodies are just things. Collections of organs and limbs that allow us to live. Even our minds. Our ideas, our thoughts, our desires. Our way of seeing the world. Everything's inherited, stolen, borrowed. Or else it's something new and unique, something we came up with for ourselves. How are you any different?"

He didn't speak for a moment, trying to understand what she was saying. He looked away, conscious he was staring at the glorious swell of her bosom. He was suddenly aware of how flimsy the white sheet covering his body was. His loins, for so long mere functional plumbing, were stirring into life.

"You … you should button your garment back up now."

"Forgive me," she said. "Things get pretty relaxed onboard as the winter wears on." He thought she was going to take offence. Scream or swoon. Instead, seeing the movement of his body beneath the sheet, she laughed. "You see? You're *definitely* human. No doubt about that." One of her eyebrows arched in something like amusement. "You didn't come south again just to find answers about your origins, did you?"

"I don't know why I came. I felt compelled."

"Oh, come on. You've been alone for a long time. You're looking for love, right? Or, failing that, you're looking to fuck. Who wouldn't after all this time?"

He winced at her rough choice of words. "That possibility died with my creator a long time ago."

"Bullshit."

"I'm sorry?"

"That's bullshit. What, you think you have to find someone just like you? That's not how it works these days. I guess that's not how it ever worked. Love comes in endless shapes and sizes and combinations. These days, we're all about our variety, our individuality."

"That wouldn't extend to me."

She shook her head. "Don't kid yourself. You're strong and thoughtful. Kind, too, I think. You're going to be famous. You also have – her gaze flicked briefly over his body beneath the sheet – some impressive physical characteristics. Trust me. You'll have no trouble finding love."

"I planned to kill you all," he said. "Take you ship."

She looked amused. "Really? That was your plan? You're good with modern navigation systems, are you?"

He didn't reply for a moment, considering her thoughts. He could maybe still escape. Dash her to the ground, make a bolt for the sea and swim for the ice. Escape to the safety of the far north. Except, where would that get him apart from back where he started?

"You are sure of this?"

"Look, it's up to you. Say the word and we'll lower you a lifeboat, let you paddle away into the darkness. We won't tell a soul. Or you can stay with us and rejoin the human race."

He watched her for a moment, half-expecting some joke, some elaborate cruelty to be revealed. Instead she sat quietly, awaiting his reply.

"You will help me?" he asked.

"Least I can damn-well do."

"And what should I call you?"

"Sorry. Should have said. I'm Helen. Helen Magnusson. And your name I know, of course."

"No. I have no name."

"Of course, you do. It's Fra…"

His expression must have stopped her mid-word. A wave of revulsion had washed through him. Revulsion and anger. "Don't say it. Why would you call me by that foul name?"

"But … but that's what you are. Everyone knows that."

"No."

"What do you mean, *no*?"

"That was *him*. The monster who created me. The butcher with the knives and the saws. Who hacked up the bodies of the dead, who picked and sorted out parts to stitch together into the shape of a man. Into *me*."

"I didn't think. Forgive me." She considered for a moment. "You aren't grateful to him at all?"

Was he? It was hard to know. It was complicated. "I am glad to be alive," he said finally.

"So, he didn't name you at all?"

His rage subsided a little, to be replaced by an old emptiness. "No. *Things* don't have names."

"Then you're going to need one." She considered for a moment. "How about, I don't know … Neumann."

"Neumann?"

"Sure. That is what you are. *New Man*."

Neumann. He turned the word over in his mind. He liked it. Liked the shape of it. In some unexpected way this strange woman with her gift of water had anointed him.

Baptized him.

"Neumann," he said out loud.

One of her butterflies flittered through the air to settle, unexpectedly, on his scarred hand. He reached out to touch it. The creature's iridescent wings were like paper. It flew off, but not before some of the tiny, colourful scales had rubbed off onto him.

He studied his fingers. The rainbow stayed when he tried to scrape it away. His skin shimmered as if he had become part-butterfly, his fingers taking on the dazzling colours. Taking on, also, their beauty.

Marvelling, Neumann held out his hand to the young woman who'd befriended him, showing her what he'd become.

The Monster came about because I was asked to write a story for another alphabet-based anthology (as I was for Junker Joe). This time the theme was chimeras, and I was given the letter F - whcih I was pretty pleased about, as Frankenstein's monster is maybe the best-known chimera (a creature made of the parts of other creatures) in literature. Frankenstein is often, it seems to me, a misunderstood book. It isn't about the building of a hideous monster from body-parts and lightning-bolts, it's about the way people behave badly and brutally if they are treated badly and brutally. At the start, the "monster" is benign, but becomes what he does because of the way he's treated.

I figured – I hoped – that these days, people wouldn't be so superficial, and that, frankly, Frankenstein's monster would be pretty cool. At the end of Shelley's book, the monster heads into the high north to escape humanity, and I got to wondering what would happen if he were rediscovered in the modern age. I like to think it might turn out something like my story.

The Monster was published in C is for Chimera (as "Frankenstein's Monster") in 2015.

THE DAY THE BOOKS LEFT

Managra strode the empty library, her footsteps echoing on the wooden floor. A hard, hollow sound. It was different when the books were here: sounds were softer and the air hummed as if with a million insects. Now the galleries were deserted places. Lifeless.

But the books would be back soon. Back from their winter in distant lands. They were late, that was all. They were always late these days. People said the weather was changing, affecting the migration patterns. Maybe that was it. When she'd been young, an acolyte, the place hummed with activity from spring to autumn. Now the people didn't come and the books didn't come and it was impossible to know what was the cause and what was the effect.

She crossed to one of the tall windows, looking out for the hundredth time that day, hoping to see a flock of skipping, lurching dots approaching. For a moment she thought they were there, flocking from the south. Her heart fluttered. But, no; it was just some birds. Managra cranked the slats open a little wider. The iron mechanism creaked as the glass hinged outwards, glinting in the sun, breathing hot air into the library,

She thought about the previous fall, the day the books left. Always the grimmest time of the year. They'd been restless for days, occasionally leaping from the shelves and fluttering around the halls before returning to their slots. Then, at some unspoken signal Managra could never see or hear, they thronged into the air as one and clattered off, flapping their covers hard to gain height and keep up with the flock. Slim, flighty pamphlets were always the first to go, spiralling upwards to dart through the windows into the open air. Novels followed and then, some way behind, lumbering reference books. The last to leave were the vast atlases, their covers almost too large to fit through the biggest windows, flapping with such sedate slowness it was a marvel they even flew at all.

Within an hour they were all gone. Managra had watched them flying into the southern sky with a cold weight in her gut. Perhaps they wouldn't return. Perhaps this was the year.

For a month or two she'd filled her time dusting and cleaning. Polishing the shelves and repainting the category markers. But some time around the turn of the year she'd begun to run out of distractions. Started to leave a window or two open in case some straggler, blown off course on a winter wind, needed shelter. None had come. She took to wandering the galleries, longing for that first rustle of pages, that first flash of white in the air. The returning of life. Every morning she cranked all the great windows open and every evening she cranked them shut again. The shelves remained empty.

Some said the books were shot from the sky as they flocked over lands further to the south. A sport. The thought of that made Managra seethe with anger. Blasted into tatters, the books would be useless. Mere paper snowing from the sky. Was that it? Or had some storm blown them out to sea, some deluge pulping them to mush? She always wanted to go with them when they left, look after them, protect them. But of course, she could never keep up.

She'd asked the old librarian when she first arrived. "Why let them go? Why not close the windows and keep them here?"

The old man, grey-haired and bent over as if from all the books he'd borne, shook his head and looked wistful. "Can't do that. You'll understand one day, girl."

And Managra did, now, understand. Now she was the librarian. The books had to be free. Words kept locked up and unread were not words. They were lines on paper. Ideas had to move and flow. Fertilise. They were living things and life was change.

Thinking these thoughts, she walked slowly back to her desk in the centre of the main hall. Here was the one book that remained in the library. The Index. Not really a book at all, of course. Or, put another way, it was all books. It recorded the titles of each other volume, along with notes on their location, condition and behaviour. Managra noted the date of last year's arrival. She'd been alarmed then. Now it was ten days later still. She shut the Index with a dusty *clump*.

She sat down and sighed. The sunlight through the windows cast a patchwork of golden squares on the wooden floor. A million motes of dust swarmed in the beams. But there was no other movement. She had to accept it. The books weren't coming. And a library without books wasn't a library. It was a large empty building with lots of shelves. Just as a librarian without books wasn't a librarian. She was an old woman with no point to her life.

After another hour of staring into the distance she rose and began a final circuit of the halls. In each gallery she wound the iron handles that levered the windows shut. Then she descended the stone stairs down to the library's entrance.

Managra hauled the wooden doors wide. Intense, summer sun flooded in, blinding her. Another reason she liked to stay in the shadowy halls. But there was no point, now. Squinting against the solid light she stepped outside. Turned and placed the brass key back in the lock to seal up the library for ever. When this simple act was done she stood for a moment, looking out over the world, wondering what to do now.

The distant tinkle of broken glass interrupted her thoughts. She stood for a moment, confused, replaying the sound in her mind, trying to work out where it came from.

One of the upper galleries.

Unlocking the door again, she shuffled back up three flights of stone stairs and into the South Wing. There in the centre of the floor lay a smattering of smashed glass from one of the windows.

She stepped forwards, breathing heavily. There wasn't only glass. Sitting in its nest of shards was a book. A slim volume, but the life's work of an ancient poet. One of her favourites. It lay motionless as if dead. Managra kneeled down and began to stroke it with her old fingers.

The book jerked, responding to her touch. It fluttered its pages. Stopped. Jerked again, then lifted off with a sudden buzz. Managra laughed to see it, swirling around her head. One book had returned. A million had flown off but one, one, had returned.

Tears filled her eyes as she followed the book's skipping flight, seeking its place on the shelves. The exact spot it had flown from six months earlier. With a final ruffle of its leaves it perched there to rest. She would leave it be for now. But tomorrow, she would take it down and read it. The library was still a library and she was still a librarian. It would do.

The vast smashing sound from behind took her by surprise. On a rush of papery air, a million books came crashing through the windows, filling the air with their sudden rustle and clatter.

Watching them all as they danced around, Managra sank to her knees and cried and laughed, both at once.

I've paired The Day The Books Left with the story that follows it as they're two fantasy stories that share a theme: a celebration of the library.

I like a good library. Come to that, I like a bad one, too. We live in an age (at least here in the UK), where libraries are closing and their worth is being undermined. That's pretty much akin to the destruction of civilisation in my view.

This story is perhaps magic realism or slipstream rather than "fantasy". I was especially pleased with the imagery of books as birds: living things that take our ideas and dreams and fly with them. I like the line about the vast atlases flapping with sedate slowness, and the way the books know which bit of shelf to return to, like birds returning to the very tree they were hatched in.

The Day The Books Left was published in The Future Fire in 2015.

THE CHRONICLES OF ZER

Cursus stared in open-mouthed horror at the blank page.

"No. It can not be."

He turned the page, the vellum of the old book crackling. The next was equally blank: smooth and creamy white. He opened the great tome at random in three different places. All the same. There could be no doubt. He closed the book with a hollow thud, a bloom of dust. *Magna Bestiarum* it said in gold letters on the red spine. The titles survived longer, of course, their words visible to anyone glancing at the shelf. He wondered who had written it, who had laboured over it, what wonders it had contained. Now it was gone and he would never know.

He stared down the hall, the shelves reaching from floor to ceiling, receding in ranks to a point in the far distance. This was only his first day in the Upper Western Atrium of the Spiral Wing. He hadn't set foot in this hall since he'd arrived, a wide-eyed blacksmith's boy sent because he alone of five brothers could read the family copy of *Fine Charmes and Cures*. Sixty years ago. The place had hummed with activity then: acolytes reading at the tables, bearing books to and from the shelves. Now there was only him. He and the Recorder, who didn't really count.

He lifted the *Bestiarum* with a grunt, crossed the room and slid it back into its place in the bottom-left slot of the first shelf nearest the door. He pulled out the next volume. *A True History of the Verlainians*. He had never heard of the Verlainians, had no idea who or even what they were. He carried this book back to the square table in the centre of the hall and opened it. More white parchment, devoid of script or illustration.

He spent the whole of that day taking books from the shelves, opening them, returning them. The Mageink lasted for eternity, just so long as the words written were read from time to time. The most surviving script he found was in *Storm and Weather Magick of the Mountain People*, the pages of which contained a few scattered marks, the mere bones of letters. He tried to read them, to coax the words back into being, but they were too far gone.

Eventually, the light beginning to fade in the high windows, he'd seen enough. He walked back to the centre of the hall, lost in thought, footsteps echoing on the stone floor. He stopped at the glass bell-jar set upon its gold podium. He cranked the reluctant brass handle on the device, sending sparks crackling and flashing through the mist swirling within.

"Recorder?"

The grey wisps resolved themselves into the familiar, lined face. The Recorder opened its eyes.

"Which books?" it asked in its familiar, ringing tone. Cursus gave it the titles of everything he'd looked at that day, effortlessly recalling them from memory. Works on architecture, oneiromancy, chirurgy, history, crptobotany, astroarchaeology, unlinguistics. Every conceivable subject jumbled together side-by-side. Once the books had all been arranged alphabetically. But then, when a new book arrived, it took weeks to make a gap for it, shuffle all the other others around. Now they were distributed randomly and only the magical mind of the Recorder knew where everything was.

"A great many books for one day," it said.

"They were all empty. They have all faded."

"I see," said the Recorder. If it had any views, if it felt any sadness, it didn't express it. Cursus almost wished it would.

"Tell me," said Cursus. "How long is it since these books were read?"

"One hundred and eighty-seven years."

Cursus nodded. The interval was supposed to be a century at most. After that the ink began to blanch and fade from neglect.

"Were any in here read more recently?"

"Half, one hundred and twenty years ago. They, at least, may survive."

Cursus looked up at the shelves looming around him.

"Do you know how many books this hall houses?"

"Twelve million, four hundred and four thousand, eight hundred and ninety-two."

It was only one hall out of so many. And there were rooms, whole wings, he had never yet set foot in.

He sighed. He knew what he had to do. He had ignored the truth for a long time, busying himself in his work, but those blank pages finally gave him no choice. There was only him now, the Archivist by default, and he was old. He could never read even the smallest fraction of the books.

He spent that last evening in the Sanctum, devotedly re-reading one of the three-hundred tomes kept chained in there. As he did every night. These were the most important books in the library, the core repository of their knowledge. The fading of any book was a tragedy, but the loss of any of these was unthinkable. And yet, if he failed in what he was about to do, there would be no one to come here and open them up. Even these precious works would be lost. If he stayed, he might be able to keep these alive, at least. But soon enough he'd die and there would be no one.

He had no choice. He was on his own and had nothing to help him but the words of all the books he'd ever read.

The following morning he gathered the supplies he might need for his journey. He informed the Recorder of his intentions, which absorbed the information without comment. With the sun lighting up the eastern windows, Cursus hauled open the wooden doors at the entrance to the library and stepped outside. He stood for a moment, breathing in the misty air. Then he turned and locked the doors behind him with the great brass key he carried on a chain round his neck.

He looked back only once as he walked away. The vast edifice of the library stretched away into the mists in both directions, unbroken save for the single door and, higher up, a double row of arched windows. Beyond he could see only a hazy outline of the towers and domes he'd lived his life in. Cursus nodded, as if saying goodbye, and turned away.

*

A month later, he stood among trees on top of a grassy hill, chest heaving from the ascent, heart pounding. Before him lay Zer, city-state of the Azeri Doges. Or so it had once been. Now those white towers, so familiar from his boyhood, lay in ruins. The sun glinted no more off terraced golden roofs. Cursus felt no shock. It was what he had expected. Four weeks of travel across the lands – four dangerous, gruelling weeks – had shown him clearly enough why the library had been abandoned, why no more acolytes came, no more books.

The twelve lands lay in ruins.

He limped on down the hill, the blisters on his feet making each step an agony. The wound in his side tugged cruelly. If he missed his footing the pain jarring through him felt like a fresh sword-stab, making him cry out. He had done well to get this far. More than once he'd considered giving up, returning in failure to the library. He'd refused to be beaten, but this was as far as he could go. Zer was his only hope.

He picked his way down the wooded slopes towards the city. Soon he had to thread his way between high mounds of broken masonry, past smooth-skinned marble statues lying on the ground, faces pressed to the mud. Men, women and children eyed him from their hovels in the half-collapsed walls. At least no one threatened him. Vestigial respect for the library protected him as it had, just about, throughout his journey. Although more than once he'd had to thunder a curse recalled from a spellbook to scare off attackers.

He walked up the steep, spiralling streets to the Citadel, the centre of the realm. Perhaps there he would find some answers. It had once been well-guarded, he recalled, lines of soldiers in golden armour. Now no one stopped him walking inside.

He moved through the broken halls, remembering them as they'd once been. His father had brought him here as a boy to see the enthronement of the three hundred and third Doge. He remembered the gold and blue of the walls, the rustling purple silks of the crowd around him, the blaring brass fanfares. It was all gone.

"What do you want, old man?"

The voice from the shadows of the ruined palace was low, threatening. Cursus stopped, held up his hands. "I came to see the Doge. I am the Archivist."

The man laughed. "I'm afraid you are a little late. The barbarians overran Zer twenty years ago. Hadn't you noticed?"

"I wanted to see if anything remained."

"Old fool. The whole world lies in ruins. As your precious library would be if the old magic didn't render it inviolate."

"Magic walls may protect us," said Cursus. "But they

don't stop the books fading."

The man stepped out into the light. He wore the clothes of a warrior, a sword and two knives sheathed at his belt.

"People have more important things to do than read, old man. Finding food. Staying alive."

Cursus nodded. He studied the man for a moment. He had a hunter's eyes above a finely chiselled nose, like some bird of prey. It was a fine nose, to be sure. Cursus debated with himself what he should do.

"You are right," he said at last. "There is nothing for me here. I shall return to the library while I still have sight in my eyes. May I at least rest here the night?"

The man shrugged. "As you wish. You look harmless enough."

"My name is Cursus."

"River," said the man. "I can spare you only a few scraps of food." He withdrew into the darkness of his side-chamber. After a moment, broken plaster crunching underfoot, Cursus followed him.

Inside, candles flickered from niches all around the walls. Here and there the light glinted off surviving patches of gold-leaf. Cursus could see the remains of murals painted on the plaster. Deep blue skies over a shining white city.

"I am grateful," said Cursus, sitting down on a square of fallen masonry. "My bones ache and I can go no further."

"You shouldn't be out here, old man. It is too dangerous."

"I've survived. Fortunately my memory is good and I can recall all the maps of this area. Travelling is not too bad if you know which routes to take."

"Nowhere is safe any more."

"Indeed. I did think mighty Zer might have survived the conflagration."

"Nothing survived, not Zer, not anywhere. Could you

not see that, sitting up there on your mountain? Did you not read about it in your books?"

"There were no more books."

"People have been too busy dying to write."

Cursus nodded in the dark. "And, tell me, are you descended from the Doges at all?"

The man snorted. "Me? I'm just one of the barbarians."

After they had eaten, the man waved Cursus towards a place he could sleep, a shelf of stone with a ruined velvet curtain to wrap himself in. Cursus lay down with a grunt of pain. A lifetime of walking the library, of lugging books around, had kept him fit enough. But after his journey he felt his years weighing down on him. River sat across the room and stared into the flames of the fire he'd lit, saying nothing.

*

Late into the night, roused by some sound, Cursus awoke. He'd been living a nightmare of the library burning, all the books burning. He lay there, heart hammering, confused. The fire in the room had waned to a red glow. River sat across the room still, sinister shadows on his downcast face. He turned the pages of some book. Cursus watched him for a long time, thinking, before sleep came to him again.

*

When he awoke it was morning, light flooding in through holes in the walls and roof, lighting up this and that little patch of dirt. Cursus lay in the half-light, wondering which of the books in the library had faded away overnight. Which were vanishing at that precise moment, never to be read again.

He sat up, rubbing his face. River was nowhere to be seen. Cursus worked his way to his feet, bones stiff. The fire was just ash and a twist of smoke. He crossed to where the man had sat, remembering the night before. Frowning, glancing around to make sure he was alone, Cursus began to rummage through the tattered bedclothes. When he found the book, he picked it up and clutched it to him like an old friend.

"What are you doing?" River stood in the doorway, blotting out the light from outside. His voice was thick with fury.

"You read," said Cursus.

"Of course I can read. I'm not an animal."

Cursus leafed through the book. "I don't mean you *can* read. I mean you *do*. From these pages, the solid blacks, the vivid colours, I can see the whole book has been read recently and often."

"Like I said. I'm not an animal."

Cursus looked directly at him. "And nor are you the barbarian you claimed. Did you think I wouldn't recognize your face? That nose? And *River*, of course, is just the common tongue for *Azeri*. You would have been the three hundred and fifth Doge I think?"

"Very clever, old man. But I told you the truth. We're all barbarians now. The old titles don't matter any more."

"Yours may not. Mine does."

"Not for long. When you die all those books of yours will die too. Soon there will be no library, just empty paper and an old building decaying from inside."

"We could change that," said Cursus. "With enough people, from here and the other lands, we could re-read the books again, keep the wisdom alive, awake the Mageink with our eyes. If you came, others would follow."

"I told you, people need food and blades. Not pretty stories."

Cursus looked down at the book he held. He turned a page. "This is the fifth volume of *The Chronicles of Zer*," he said. "Tell me, have you read the others?"

"Only that one survives."

"All twelve volumes are in the Sanctum. You could read them all there."

"What does it matter?" River sounded angry now. "The old world is gone."

Cursus shook his head. "No. If you *had* read the other volumes you would know that isn't true. All this is just one calamity of many. In the time of the thirteenth Doge a plague wiped out all but two hundred of your kin. Fires have destroyed Zer itself four times. It is the same in all the lands. Each time the people have rebuilt and carried on. That story is your identity and you have lost it. You have forgotten who you are."

"I know exactly what I am, old man."

Cursus stood. He felt suddenly furious with River and his meek acceptance of defeat, his refusal to listen. Cursus brushed past him, suddenly desperate to be outside, get away.

In the open air, he had to shield his eyes as he gazed around at the shattered ruins of Zer. There was nothing here after all. He would have to try elsewhere. Perhaps he would be lucky and meet with travelling companions he could trust. He had no choice. Not looking back he set off down the hill, heading for the rising sun. His feet were so blistered it felt like he was walking across knives.

"That's the wrong way, old man," River called from behind him. "The library is northwards."

Cursus stopped and turned to see the man standing in the doorway of his ruined palace.

"I've decided not to go to the library," said Cursus. "The books need eyes, otherwise they're just useless paper. I shall visit the other lands until I find people willing to help bring the world back from its darkness. Eastfar, perhaps, or Endest."

"You'll never make it, old man."

"At least I'll die knowing I tried."

"It is pointless."

Cursus shook his head. "You are right about one thing

at least," he said. "You are no Doge." He turned away and carried on walking. He didn't say it, but the man was right about other things, too. Cursus wouldn't make it far. He was deluding himself to think otherwise. And his quest was pointless. It would be the same story as this everywhere. Still, he could do nothing else.

"Wait!" called River. Cursus turned to see him striding down the slope. For a moment, Cursus thought he would draw that sword of his and run him through. He almost welcomed the thought. Better a quick end than this slow, lingering decay.

But the man didn't draw his sword. Instead, he clutched the book, the fifth volume of the Chronicles of Zer. He stopped in front of Cursus. It took him a moment to find the words.

"The library. If I went there. Would it tell me how to rebuild Zer?"

After a moment, Cursus nodded. "How to set the walls straight. How to gild the statues. The songs to sing while picking lemons in the orchards and the names your ancestors gave to the stars."

"But the library is vast, it goes on for ever. How would I find any of those things?"

"Ask the Recorder. It will tell you."

"But how could I even get inside?"

Cursus studied him for a moment. Moments like this had occurred many times, he knew from the books. Turning points in history. Simple words exchanged between two people that altered everything.

He fished out the key he carried around his neck and handed it over.

"Just open the door and go in," said Cursus.

In The Chronicles of Zer, the destruction of the library and the destruction of civilisation are one and the same thing. People are forgetting who and what they are and regressing into barbarity. Unread, the Mageink books are fading, their wisdom lost. All that is needed to keep the magic alive is for someone to read the books.

The Chronicles of Zer was originally published in Electric Spec in 2012.

THREADS

"My Lady, the barbarian army is at the gates," said Corym. "We must sound the trumpets. We must assemble the Red Guard before we are overrun."

The young Queen, Myrgiane, paid Corym no attention. She continued to sit on the marble floor of her throne room amid a mountain of ruffled cloth and spools of shining thread, working away at her embroidery. Corym watched her delicate fingers as they pushed the silver needle into the stretch of cloth on her knee, pulled it free from the other side. Did she not understand? He thought of all the people out there in the city. He thought of Armian and Jeph, his children, idling away their days at the baths, the market, the playhouse. What chance would any of them have if the barbarians entered the city?

"My Lady? We must act. They bring battering rams. Their beasts haul carts laden with blackpowder. Even our gates will not resist them long."

She replied without looking up, her attention focused on some minute detail of the embroidered scene she worked on. "Then open the gates, Lord Corym."

It was treason to question the word of the Queen, of course. Unthinkable. But sometimes, to himself, Corym doubted Myrgiane's right to the Crystal Throne. The calculations of the haruspices and oneiromancers were beyond him: the complicated threads of bloodline and prophecy that gave the kingdom the right ruler at the right time. But surely something had gone wrong. This was not the time for poets or daubers or … stitchers. They needed a strong leader. They needed a warrior like her grandfather, not a slim-armed girl who spent her days sewing. Her grandfather had been cunning at times, it was true. Cruel, even. But he'd kept them alive, protected them through difficult times. Done what had to be done.

"Open them, my lady? You can not mean it."

"Those gates have stood for three hundred years, keeping us safe in our fine towers. A terrible shame for them to be smashed to pieces now."

"But we will be slaughtered. The libraries will burn. We must assemble the Red Guard, open up the armouries, awaken the guardian spirits from their stone slumbers. We must fight, or our thousand-year history ends today."

The Queen slanted her embroidery to the light from the arched windows, assessing her handiwork. She appeared satisfied. "There are no guards any more, Lord Corym. Hadn't you noticed? The swordmasters put down their blades and became dance teachers. The archers draw ale rather than bows and the sorcerers sit snoozing in their towers."

"But…"

"Enough, Lord Corym. Open up the gates. Let the barbarians in. Bloody Argan will be at their head, leading his screaming berserkers as they swarm into the city. Be so good as to show him here, will you? It will save much unpleasantness if he takes the direct route."

"But…"

"Now, please, Lord Corym." She finally looked up at him. She was just a girl, it was true, but he caught the flash of steel in her eyes. For a brief moment, she looked at him with her grandfather's eyes. Then she smiled sweetly.

He left the throne room. But instead of racing for the walls to issue the orders, he instructed runners to do so, before slipping back inside. He stood in the shadows, hand resting on the pommel of the sword his father had given him years ago, breathing deeply. He told himself he was staying to protect his Queen. But he admitted to himself, also, the truth. He feared to face the barbarians. Feared what he would witness out there in the city. So, instead, he stepped around the edge of the room, keeping the line of pillars between himself and the vast tapestry the ladies of the court worked on.

In only a few minutes a clamour of shouts and cries approached. Then Argan, Bloody Argan himself, burst through the doors. Corym took a step backwards, feeling the cold stone of the walls behind him. The barbarian king was as fearsome as the tales said. Seven feet tall and as well-muscled as a racehorse. He wore a shirt of chain-mail but his head and arms and legs were bare. His skin was covered with tattoos: hundreds and hundreds of black stars, one for each enemy slain. His curved sword, its edge serrated and notched from use, rested across his shoulder.

The Queen, meanwhile, had risen to her feet to face him. Corym expected to see fear in her eyes, a dawning realisation of what she had done. Instead he saw her appraising glance run down and up Argan's body, saw the slightest smile of appreciation on her face. He understood, in that moment, he'd been wrong about her in one thing. She was no longer a girl.

"My Lord Argan," she said. "Would you kindly hold up one corner of our embroidery so we may all see it? I think it is finally complete."

Argan paused for a moment, wrong-footed, then roared with laughter at her words. "But I am here to kill you, little Queen, not look at your pretty cloths. And before I kill you I will teach you and each of your fine ladies a lesson. Make you understand what it is you are good for."

Corym's throat tightened as he steeled himself to rush to the Queen's defence. He knew he wouldn't last long. He just hoped that notched sword, when Argan swung it, gave him a swift end.

Myrgiane, however, looked unconcerned. "So, you've come to seize the Crystal Throne?"

"I have seized it."

"Of course. It's right over there, under all that cloth. To be honest, it's rather uncomfortable. It needs cushions."

Argan shook his head. "I don't care about cushions. I am lord of all the world now."

Myrgiane looked sympathetic. "Oh, I'm afraid not, Lord Argan. The world is far vaster than you imagine. If you had read the books and studied the maps you would know. There are lands uncounted beyond ours. Oceans that only great ships may cross. Your great empire covers but a corner of it."

"Lies."

"Oh, it's true. And that's just the start. There are other worlds, too. Worlds beyond worlds if you have the lore to find the silver paths and the sorcerers to open them up. Lands and treasures unending. You are the lord of a corner of a scrap."

Corym saw a look of doubt cloud Argan's brow. He had expected to be met with swords. He had expected his moment of victory.

"You see," said the Queen, "we could have kept you out, we really could. Our walls are tall and strong. But we let you in. You haven't defeated us, you have done what we wanted."

"No," said Argan.

"I'm afraid it's true. And now I shall show you why."

She nodded to the groups of ladies standing behind her. They each grasped hold of the embroidery that lay crumpled on the floor and began to fan out, stretching the cloth right across the throne-room. No one spoke as the scene unfurled.

Corym gasped when he saw it. He stepped forwards into the centre of the room, unable to take his eyes off the embroidery, the terrible Argan forgotten for the moment. It was dazzling. Incredible. It depicted … *everything*: world after world after world floating in a purple void. Each finely detailed. And each connected; lines of silver ran between them all, threading between the stars. The pathways their forebears had once used to explore the universe. In the old days.

Corym stood there, just as Argan stood there, and stared for long minutes, taking it all in, picking out one wonder after another. Cities of gold. Giants with two heads and three heads and none. Temples in the sky and temples afloat on vermilion seas. Dragons and demons. White domes and black towers. And, right in the centre, a world that was clearly *this* world. In its middle, this city. And in the middle of that, the heart of the whole design, this very room, rendered in threads of silver and gold.

Corym peered closer to see the *two* crystal thrones depicted at its centre. On one sat Queen Myrgiane. On the other, the stitching so fine that even the black stars on his skin was visible, sat Argan.

Corym glanced up at Argan, standing beside him. The look of wonder on the barbarian's face told Corym more about the man than all his berserkers and tattoos.

"We have stayed safe in our city too long, you see," said Myrgiane from behind them. "Oh, we have grown wise. We know the names of all the stars in the sky and all the flowers in the field. But we are fading. Going nowhere. We have stopped looking outwards; we need fresh blood. And you, Argan? Well, you've won the right to sit on a glass chair. You'll be bored in an hour. You are a clever man, I know, uniting the tribes with promises of treasure and destruction. So, let me ask you. Where do you go now? What do you do? You need a purpose. And I can give you one. Your armies and our wisdom. Together, we'll be unstoppable. All the worlds will be ours."

Corym saw the amused grin crossing Argan's features. Here was the moment. Corym's hand trembled as he felt for the pommel of his sword. The sword he had never yet drawn in combat.

"Worlds beyond worlds?" repeated Argan.

"Worlds uncounted. All waiting for us."

"And you think you can rule next to me?" said Argan.

Myrgiane raised one eyebrow, very slightly. A look of amusement passed across her face. "Oh, I think you'll do. Once I've found you some better clothes and taught you a few manners."

Argan studied her, assessed her. Her face. Her body. She returned his stare. He *did* need a purpose, Corym saw. And winning over Myrgiane might be the first. He wasn't used to people defying him, challenging him. The prospect of it, of her, enticed him. Corym saw how this would go. Theirs would be a fiery marriage. They were a match.

Bloody Argan laughed once more. And he bowed. He actually bowed. "Then, before we start, we must have another crystal throne made, must we not? My Queen."

There aren't enough fantasy stories that combine barbarian hordes and embroidery, so I thought I'd write one. Myrgiane was a fun character to write – there are other sorts of strength than mere muscle – and this is perhaps another story that could lead on to a much larger work. That said, I think it also ends at just the right place. The destruction of libraries gets yet another mention, as well. It was clearly preying on my mind.

Threads was originally published in Bards and Sages in 2013, and has since been reprinted a couple of times.

EIGHTEEN MILLION BUTTERFLIES

Every day, Telyr poisoned three hundred thousand butterflies to death.

It might be three hundred thousand of the Vermilions, or three hundred thousand Midnight Blues, but it was always that exact number. Clockwork mechanisms in each Lepidoptarium collecting duct counted the insects precisely. Once Telyr had the requisite number he would open the Collecting Hall valves to release the mist of poisoned gas. Immediately, the insects would begin to fold their wings and glide to the floor. Then an army of palace slaves, rags clutched to their mouths against the toxic air, could begin to pluck the wings from each tiny thorax. Twelve hundred thousand harvested every day, four from each insect, because that was how many it took to carpet the floor of the Great Hall for that evening's ball.

Telyr emerged, now, from the outer double-doors of the Silvertip Lepidoptarium. He breathed in the cool morning air. The Silvertips needed it warmer than the other species. Maintaining the precise heat and humidity of this particular dome took more trainloads of fuel than any of the other eleven. He examined the dials next to the door, adjusting a brass wheel minutely to decrease the influx of cold outside air. Perhaps because of their delicacy, or perhaps simply because of the mirror-like shimmer of their wings, the Silvertips were his favourite.

He looked in at them thronging their dome as they flitted between nectar-tubes. He loved to watch their skipping, glinting flights. This was where he was happiest. One of the insects would occasionally blunder into the glass as if trying to batter it down, leaving behind only a ghostly mark of silver wings. Sometimes he liked to imagine they were trying to reach him, outside in the air and sunlight. He found himself wishing they could succeed. Their world was a great glass prison and he was both their jailor and, eventually, their executioner.

"I have just spoken to the Master of Ceremonies on your behalf, my lord."

Telyr turned to see that Measel, his secretary, had crept up behind him. Measel often crept up. Something about him made Telyr shudder. Perhaps it was just the way Measel's lank hair lay plastered to his forehead. Or the way his joyless smile, similarly, lay plastered onto his face. Or it might just have been the way he took such delight in gassing and winging the day's butterflies. To Measel they were things to be killed and collected to order.

"And I have told you before that the Master of Ceremonies is to speak to me directly. Not to an underling."

"Yes, my lord."

Did he mean "Yes" he had been told before, or "Yes" he would obey in the future? You could never tell with Measel. The boy was slippery. Perhaps a part of Telyr's shudder was a note of fear. Measel wanted to replace him, of course, become the Imperial Lepidopterist himself. And he had all the impatience of youth. On more than one occasion Telyr had noticed Measel beside the poison mist controls while he, Telyr, worked within a Collecting Hall. Insubordination, of course, meant execution at the hands of the Imperial Guard. But accidents? Accidents could always happen. It was just as well Measel didn't yet know everything about the workings of the Lepidoptariums, the complexity of the ancient mechanisms. Telyr still kept a secret or two. "What did the Master of Ceremonies say?"

"That he requires Creams today, my lord. The Empress Xana is wearing a dress of magnolia and gold at tonight's ball. The Creams should match it perfectly."

Telyr turned to consider the Cream Lepidoptarium, the dome over on the far side of the great circle. They had last supplied Creams a week ago so there would be easily enough. He always made sure he had several days supply of each species. Within the twelve domes there were around eighteen million butterflies at any one time. He lived in fear of being asked to produce the same colour more than five days in a row. Failure to meet the palace's demands was unthinkable. So far, fortunately for him, it had never happened.

"Very well. Open the ducts in the Cream Lepidoptarium and instruct the slaves to prepare. And tell them to be careful. The Creams have particularly delicate wings. Tweezers and scalpels at all times."

Measel bobbed his head in assent. "I have already had the ducts opened, my lord. The slaves are there now, waiting for the poison to do its work."

Telyr started to reply but stopped himself. He could hardly lambast Measel for doing what he had just been instructed to do anyway. Measel liked to play his little games. He didn't know it just set Telyr further against him.

"Very well. Oversee the collection process. And, Measel, make sure each wing is perfect. The Empress is to dance on a carpet of butterfly wings as soft as a cloud, yes?"

"Of course, my lord. As soft as a cloud."

"I shall be with the Brimstones. I think their numbers are somewhat reduced of late."

"Yes, my lord, I know."

Measel turned away. Telyr watched him leave,

wondering once again what, precisely, he had meant.

*

That evening, Telyr stood with the other Masters of the Crystal Palaces, waiting in line for the entrance of Empress Xana, the Eighty-sixth of the House of Aragandia. The Keeper of the Imperial Birds stood next to him, eyes on the bank of golden cages in which his canaries, skylarks and eboneyes waited to sing. Telyr didn't envy him. Perfect as the birds' performance always was, there must still be the possibility of something going wrong. One of the birds might trill the wrong note in the middle of one of the pieces, or become distracted, or die. At least with the butterflies there was no room for failure. With the vast floor of the hall carpeted with twelve hundred thousand feather-soft Cream wings, his job was done for the day. He could enjoy the spectacle.

A phalanx of Imperial Guards entered the hall, eighty-eight of them, Empress Xana's personal soldiers. They fanned out around the edge of the room, then stood to attention, watching for any threat, any danger. It was ceremony, of course. There could never be a danger to the Empress within the Crystal Palaces. Still, the guards were trained as killers from the moment they could walk. A grim ceremony, indeed.

Finally, with a fanfare of sparkling brass horns, the Empress Xana herself appeared, a glowing angel in her gold and cream. The assembled Lords and Ladies gasped in delight at the sight of her. A slight smile on her face, she began to descend the staircase to the floor of the great hall.

It was then that the flash of red in the middle of the floor caught Telyr's attention. Not red – vermilion. Some breath of air from the doors, or from the Empress' descent, must have disturbed them. He stared at the point in shock, mouth dry, heart pounding. In thirty years he had never allowed such a thing to happen. There, in the middle of twelve hundred thousand Cream wings, lay one Vermilion wing, like a drop of blood on a lake of fresh milk.

Impossible to ignore.

Telyr tore his gaze away, looking for Measel, who was standing among the second rank of attendants to his right. Measel stared directly back at him. His grin was as wide as ever. Wider, perhaps. Did Measel nod, ever so slightly?

Yes. Telyr saw, then, just how it was.

He returned his gaze to the single fleck of red. It lay directly in Empress Xana's path. It was inevitable she would see it. See the flaw in that perfection. Everyone would see it. The ball was ruined and he, Telyr, was to blame. He forced himself to find the face of the Master of Ceremonies, standing across the room. Telyr could see from the slight scowl on those lined features that he knew. He had seen what Telyr had done. It came to Telyr, in that silent moment of glances, that there was no hope for him.

As soon as the birds began to chorus their symphonies, Telyr slipped from the Great Hall. He thought, briefly, about escape. But that was impossible, of course. No one left the Crystal Palaces, unless by dying, just as no one came, unless by being born.

Instead, he returned to the glasshouses he had lived and worked in for thirty years. The Master of Ceremonies would come for him there. There were no dungeons or prisons to disfigure the Crystal Palaces. They had no need for them. Anyone who met with imperial displeasure was dispatched as efficiently as the butterflies.

The butterflies. The Lepidoptariums. He could see them one more time, at least. He opened the double-doors of the nearest habitat, home to the Verdants, and began to walk. He passed from dome to dome, butterflies of all colours settling upon him. He welcomed them, letting them accumulate upon his body like a second skin. He didn't bother trying to keep them isolated as he moved between domes, now. What did it matter if a yellow joined the blues, or a green the ebonies?

There was only time to do one more thing, before they came for him. He had been young and devious himself, once. He could still have his revenge. He paused in each dome to wind up the clockwork springs of the ancient ventilation system. He had longed to turn these particular wheels ever since the previous Lepidopterist had whispered to him what they did. Finally being able to made his fingers tremble with excitement, but he focused on the task, turned each wheel, and moved on.

Outside the final dome, where the Silvertips dwelled, Measel waited for him. Measel and the Master of Ceremonies, side by side. Behind them, inevitable as death, were twelve of the Imperial Guard.

Telyr walked forward and Measel came to meet him. The look of triumph on Measel's face made Telyr want to strike him, but he held himself back.

"So, you have what you always wanted," said Telyr in a low voice. "You are to be the Imperial Lepidopterist."

"The Master of Ceremonies has seen fit to entrust me with the office, yes."

"And, of course, you didn't mention you were responsible for placing the Vermilion wing among the Creams?"

"I, Telyr? Why would I be responsible? I just followed your orders. Of course."

"Ah, of course."

There was little point explaining to Master of Ceremonies what had really happened. Failing to control Measel was almost as bad as making the mistake himself. Perhaps he was to blame. Despite the daily slaughter, he really just wanted to spend time with the butterflies. Perhaps he had let himself become distracted by their silent beauty. Perhaps Measel would make a better Lepidopterist.

He wasn't going to get away with it, though, Telyr decided. Not this boy who took pleasure in killing. He slipped a brass key from the sleeve of his cloak and held it up for Measel to see.

"And tell me, Imperial Lepidopterist, do you know what this key does?"

Measel's smile flickered for the briefest moment. He shrugged. "The palace is full of keys. It means nothing."

"Ah, then another failing of mine. I fear I must have neglected to tell you."

"Tell me what?"

"How this particular mechanism works. A complex arrangement of gears and steel chains connecting all the domes. You have to know about it if you are to be the Imperial Lepidopterist. May I demonstrate or would you like to have me killed now?"

"Go ahead."

Telyr smiled, turned and inserted the key into its slot next to the Silvertip door. "A clockwise turn through three complete circles is all it takes," said Telyr. "You can do it from the door of any dome; they are all connected."

"And what does it do? Sing lullabies to your precious butterflies?"

"No. It does this."

Telyr turned the key. It resisted, stiff from lack of use. For a moment he thought the mechanism must have rusted solid, but then it gave. From somewhere high above, and all around, came a scraping sound, metal on metal, as springs unwound. Measel didn't react for a moment, confused.

That moment's pause was enough.

"No," said Measel. "You wouldn't. You wouldn't dare. Not you."

"Wouldn't I? If only you knew how often I've longed to do this. And now it doesn't matter, does it? You are the Imperial Lepidopterist already, so I am not to blame."

"They will all die!"

"Yes, perhaps so. But before that they will be free for a time. Finally free. And I think they will outlive the both of us."

"Give me that key!"

Measel lunged forward. Telyr stepped away, letting Measel take the key. It didn't matter now. The guards advanced on both of them, pikes held forward, but Telyr paid them no attention. They weren't important, either.

He gazed upwards, arms held wide to the skies. Above him, around him, eighteen million butterflies flocked into the air through the opened vents. The flapping of their wings sounded like the wind roaring through the leaves of a forest. Their colours mixed and flowed into one single, dazzling, cloud of iridescent light.

Telyr laughed at the glorious sight even as the pikes cut into him.

Eighteen Million Butterflies is a fantasy story that pretty much grew out of its title – that and the Gormenghast-esque Crystal Palaces with their weird and incomprehensible rituals and rules. I was pretty pleased with the opening sentence, too.

The story was published in Lakeside Circus in 2014.

IF YOU COULD CHOOSE ONE DAY

"Push me! As fast as you can!"

Piotr's three friends began to push the merry-go-round, sending it spinning faster and faster. Piotr laughed with helpless delight. The old carousel squeaked and creaked. He clung on, the playground whirring by in a blur of faces, trees, faces again. When it was going as fast as it could he steadied himself, clutching the steel handles, then threw himself off. He landed in a tumbling heap on the grass. His friends – Danny and Roger and John – whooped with laughter at the sight of him. Piotr laughed along with them. He tried to stand but his head spun so much he succeeded only in walking in little circles before collapsing back to the ground.

"My go," said Danny. "Push me, now. Even faster." Danny was a year older than the rest of them, two inches taller. If they got into a fight, Danny was the one who saved them, wading in with his fists pumping. Although in truth he was the gentlest of all of them and couldn't even bring himself to kill the fish they caught in the stream in the woods. But if it came to it, there was no one Piotr would rather have at his side.

Piotr lay back on the grass and closed his eyes for a

moment, his head lurching, his stomach fluttering pleasantly. The sweet smell of the freshly cut grass – it was always freshly cut – filled his nose.

"Come on, Piotr," Danny called again. "It's my turn."

Piotr opened his eyes. The world had stopped jerking around quite so much. The perfect blue sky above was as perfect and blue as ever. Beyond the swings, over the treetops, grey clouds gathered on the horizon. Piotr ignored them. It never rained. Not here.

He worked his way to his knees, giggling at the way his limbs refused to do what they were told. Finally, he stood. He was looking the wrong way, away from his friends, out of the playground.

Across a wide stretch of green grass, some distance away, stood a figure. A man, he thought, dressed in a long black coat. Just an oblong of darkness, like a rip in a picture revealing what lies beneath. The sight of the figure sent a shiver through Piotr, despite the warmth of the sun. The man didn't belong here. No adults came here. Occasionally his mother's disembodied voice called for him to come home when it was getting dark, but that was all. This was *their* place.

"Piotr? Come on. Come and push."

Piotr turned back to his three friends. Danny now sitting on the green merry-go-round. Roger and John ready to start pushing. Roger who could run faster, climb a tree higher, kick a ball farther than any of them. John who knew *everything*: how to make a bow-and-arrow, how to ride a bicycle no-hands, how to tickle a trout from the water.

None of them had noticed the distant figure. For a weird moment, Piotr felt like he was looking at an old picture of the three of them. His childhood friends. The moment passed. Just the dizziness. He still didn't feel quite right.

"No," he said. "I have to go home."

"But there's hours yet," said John. "Come on, let's spin Danny so fast he goes flying off."

Piotr turned away, back to the man. The figure was closer now, although still stationary, standing there watching them. Piotr couldn't see his face but had the weird feeling he knew who this was. He began to back away, keeping his gaze on the man. He had to get away, he knew that much at least.

"Piotr?" said John. "Come on."

"No. I have to go. I'll see you tomorrow. Same time as usual, yeah?"

He turned and ran, past the merry-go-round, vaulting the sandpit with a single leap, around the see-saw and away up the grassy slope that led to the woods. His house was just the other side of the trees. He would be safe there. At the top of the slope, beneath the shadows of the first branches, he turned to look back. His three friends were still down there, sitting in a circle, unmoving. The man walked among them, paying them no attention. On up the slope towards Piotr, walking briskly now.

Piotr turned and fled.

*

At home, his mother looked surprised to see him so early. "Piotr? Are you ill? Have you hurt yourself?" She came over to inspect him with a practised eye. Then, satisfied, she hugged him close, engulfing him in her warmth.

"I'm fine," he said when she'd released him. "I was hungry. What's for tea?"

His mother shook her head. "You boys. You eat like horses. Where do you put it all? It's hot-pot, your favourite. You're all flushed, have some water while I put it in the oven."

Piotr sat at the wooden table in the middle of the kitchen while his mother bustled around, stirring pots and clattering dishes, carrying out an endless stream of activities that made no sense at all to him. The delicious smell of the lamb stew began to fill the room. He breathed it in, savouring it, his stomach rumbling. He *was* hungry. He looked out of the open window at the square of blue sky. Everything was well. Something troubling had happened, but it was gone now.

After they'd eaten, he sat by the fire and watched the flames. He loved to do that. Faces appeared and disappeared in the shifting glow of the coals. At some point he must have slipped into sleep because he began to imagine the heads talking, trying to tell him something. He thought he was on the point of making out what, when he felt someone taking hold of him, lifting him.

He started awake. But it was only his father, carrying him in his strong arms upstairs to bed.

"Dad?"

"Hmm?"

"There was someone at the playground today. A man. I've never seen him before. Except, I knew who he was. Or thought I did."

"Hush, now" said his father. "It's nothing to worry about. Let's put you into bed, eh?"

"OK."

"And tomorrow you can go and play with your friends. At the playground."

"OK."

His father placed him gently under the covers and kissed him on top of his head. Piotr lay for a moment, listening to his father descending the creaking stairs, before sleep came again, dissolving his thoughts away.

*

He awoke. It was fully dark now. No noise from downstairs. He could hear nothing and see nothing. Yet a sound had woken him up, he was sure of it. A sound somewhere in his room. Someone had spoken. What had they said?

"Dad?" he called out. "Mum?"

A hand gripped his forearm suddenly, its grasp iron-tight. A face loomed out of the darkness right in front of him. The man from the playground. A stern look clouded his lined face. A face Piotr half-recognized. Who was this? Some uncle he didn't know about?

"Piotr. You must come with me. I've come to take you away. Come now."

Piotr screamed.

*

He awoke. His heart thundered away in his chest. A dream, just a dream. A nightmare. He was safe in his room, safe under his covers. He lay unmoving for a moment while his heart slowed. He was slick with sweat. He threw his blankets off his body to cool himself down.

When the blankets fell to the floor, the man was standing there by his bed, tall and straight, that scowl on his lined face. He grabbed Piotr by the arm.

"Piotr. You must come with me. I've come to take you away. Come now."

Piotr screamed again. But this time the iron grip on his arm remained.

*

He awoke. He knew immediately he was really awake this time. It wasn't the harsh light that told him, or the pumping and wheezing sounds of the machines keeping him alive. It was the feel of his own body; the useless aching *weight* of it. Back there he'd been so strong, so full of life. Here he couldn't even lift a hand or make his eyes focus.

He tried to speak, his voice a thin croak. "Why have you brought me back?"

Blurred, fleshy shapes bobbed around in his vision. One grew as it came nearer. A face. It came into focus and there was the man, the man who had pursued him in the regression. He remembered now. Ivan, his brother. His younger brother, not even born at the time of his chosen memory.

"I'm sorry, Piotr," said Ivan. "Your instructions told us you wished to be woken if … certain conditions were met."

Piotr took that in. Ivan was right, of course. Although he had stipulated only one condition.

"Who?" he asked. "Who has died?"

His gaze flickered around the other faces gathered about his bed. His eyes were working a little better now. Amelia, his daughter. Greg and Michael, his boys. Catherine, his sister, youngest of the three. They all looked so old. How long had he been in there? No Janine, of course. Even after all this time the realisation was a shock, a punch to the gut. How he had loved her. But his wife was dead. Long dead.

"No one," said Amelia, concern clouding her face. "No one has died, daddy." Her hand touched his. It felt good. Solid.

"Then I don't understand," he said. "My instructions were clear. Bring me back to tell me if anyone dies. Otherwise leave me be."

He knew they didn't understand, could never understand. He had made the mistake of telling them his choice of regression, thinking, perhaps, to show them he wasn't favouring any of them. Instead, they all felt slighted. He couldn't help that. He'd done all he could for them. And it all came down to Janine. He could have picked so many days. He'd been blessed. The two of them in their early days, lost in their private bliss. Later days with the children: Christmases and holidays and games. So many good memories. But in any of those memories, Janine would have been there: a reminder, however faint, that she had died. Really died. And so, he'd picked the distant day from his boyhood. Before everything. A day he had all he needed to be happy. An uncomplicated happiness. It was wrong, maybe. A denial. But that was what he'd done.

He heard them whispering to each other, debating something. Ivan's face reappeared in front of his eyes.

"The truth is, Piotr, no one has died. Not yet. But someone is going to. We tried to contact you without fully rousing you but it proved impossible. Your mind resisted and..."

Ivan faltered. Amelia took over from him.

"The machines, you see, daddy. They monitor everything, keeping your body alive while maintaining the regression."

"You mean … me?"

"Yes. I'm sorry. A brain tumour."

"How long do I have?"

"Three months," said Amelia. "Six at the most, assuming you're going to refuse the treatment. We thought about leaving you to … go, without knowing. We've debated it for weeks. Eventually we decided we had to tell you."

"Why? That isn't what I wanted."

Amelia shook her head. She looked suddenly furious. In truth, she looked like her mother when she was riled about something.

"No," she said. "But it's what *we* wanted. You can't just expect us to stand here watching you die without being able to say good bye. Without being able to say anything. You have no right."

Piotr closed his eyes, trying to take it all in. He had missed them all. Missed them terribly. Now he was here he regretted his decision to leave them. How could he have done that? But back there, that happy day from his boyhood, he didn't know anything about them. That was the simple truth. Didn't know what he'd lost. Didn't know about Janine, a little girl living hundreds of miles away he'd never met.

"I'm sorry," he said. "I've been selfish."

Amelia gripped his hand tighter again. "Then you'll stay, now? Let us look after you in the time we have?"

He tried to reply, tried to make his voice work. He found he couldn't make a sound. But he saw the look in Amelia's eyes as he gave her his answer with a movement of his head.

*

Piotr stood at the top of the grassy slope, the shadows of the woods behind him. The grey clouds on the horizon looked larger than before. He ignored them. It never rained here. His three friends waited for him down on the playground. They called and waved to him. He wondered what he should say to them. But they wouldn't, they couldn't, understand. And he was unable to recall, now, exactly what he'd wanted to tell them. Some bad thing. But the sun was bright and they had the whole day ahead of them to play.

He set off, racing down the slope to them. He jumped onto the merry-go-round and called out.

"Push me! As fast as you can!"

Piotr's three friends began to push the merry-go-round, sending it spinning faster and faster.

If you could choose one day from your life to regress to, live out again and again, which one would it be? And what would those around you make of your choice? Such was the idea behind this story. It was published in Perihelion magazine in 2014.

HELLFIRE UNLEASHED

"The Hellfire weapon is primed and ready to fire, my Lord. Total biosphere destruction projected in just over thirty minutes."

Prelate Jacobus made no sign toward Brand, the *Sword of Truth's* eager young armaments officer. His gaze was locked on the surface of the planet they orbited. From up here, it looked so beautiful: a perfect green sphere, its swirling yellow cloud layers glowing in the light from the twin suns. Could it really be the nightmare world the reports suggested?

"My Lord?" said Brand. "Shall I fire?"

Still Jacobus didn't respond. The dreadnought's armaments officer was admirably zealous. But sometimes it was possible to be *too* zealous, even for a Primist. Brand loved to fire the weapon, loved to see each planet's atmosphere flaring into red, its inhabitants dispatched into the fires. The judging fires. But Brand wasn't the Prelate on this ship. Not yet. There was no doubt this was a Chitter world. The reports estimated twenty billion of the demons infested the planet. But that wasn't enough. This wasn't about wiping out hideous creatures *because* they were hideous, tempting though that was.

Instead of answering, Jacobus turned to Father Ramen, the ship's Cleric. Ramen was old, a hunched-over man with lined, grey skin. But his eyes were bright. There was something lizard-like about him, Jacobus always thought, although he would never dare utter such heresy. Jacobus was in command, of course, but he was under no illusions. One mistake, one foot wrong, and the Fathers back on Terra Prime would hear. Ramen would make sure of it. Jacobus lived in fear of seeing a look of disapproval on that leathery old face.

"Father? Your counsel?"

"You know the teachings of the Creator, Prelate Jacobus. Humanity is Prime, alone given the touch of divinity. If this world is home to abominations and mutants who would usurp that, it must be cleansed in the fires. That is your sacred duty."

"You think I should unleash the weapon?"

"You are the commander. I merely advise on doctrine."

"Of course, Father. But if we do fire and obliterate twenty billion innocent animals, the Creator will know."

"The Creator sees all, Prelate Jacobus."

Jacobus nodded. Sometimes he longed for simple orders, for clear truths. Couldn't the Fathers just say *kill all aliens* and be done with it? Life would be so much simpler. But the Hellfire weapons were revered objects, consecrated solely for the purpose of achieving Terran primacy among the galactic races. To use one on mere mindless animals was a sin. But *failing* to destroy advanced alien life when the opportunity arose was also a sin. And the price for committing either was too terrible to contemplate. It wasn't just being cut off from the heavens that lay through the wormholes for all eternity. There was a price to pay in this universe, too: being cast out of the light of Primist civilization. Living at the mercy of every vile alien seeking revenge. And it wouldn't just be him paying the price. The Fathers would decree how many generations of his family were to blame. His children, his parents, he could bring that fate down on all of them.

He pushed the troubling thoughts out of his mind. He was damning himself by just thinking them. He turned to Umwe, the ship's xenobiologist, sitting opposite him in the ring. Jacobus doubted her commitment sometimes. Her zeal. But right now, he needed to hear what she had to say. "Umwe? Your assessment? Are these intelligent beings?"

The young xenobiologist paused for a moment, marshalling her thoughts. Finally, she spoke. "They are pre-tech, Prelate, that is clear. There is no evidence of industrial pollution or EM communication. Drones observed basic tool use and also some agriculture, but the same could be said of many colonies of mindless insects."

"So, you don't believe we should fire?"

Umwe hesitated again, terrified of saying the wrong thing, of speaking out of turn. But he could see in her eyes what she believed. These were mere animals, fascinating fauna to study, perhaps, but nothing more.

"I can only report what I know, Prelate," said Umwe. "There is no clear evidence of advanced civilization."

"There is no clear evidence against it," said Brand. "Even if they aren't fully sentient *yet*, the potential is there. We must unleash the weapon while we can."

Jacobus caught Father Ramen's gaze upon him. What was the correct course of action? He had to decide and, what was more, he had to decide now. They'd encountered too many Chitter fleets in this region. Also, there was the curiously high incidence of superluminal drive echoes near this planet, suggesting the recent presence of many starships. Who were *they* and what were they doing here?

"Chiang," said Jacobus, turning to the navigator, "any sign of other ships?"

There was the briefest pause while Chiang studied the imagery streams feeding directly into his brain. "None. We are alone out here."

"My Lord?" said Brand. "Do you give the word?"

"No," said Jacobus, deliberately not looking at Father

Ramen. "Stand down the weapon. Prepare an armed landing-party. I want to know what's going on down there. I need to see for myself whether these are abominations or just twenty billion mindless beasts."

*

Ranks of soldier bugs hurled themselves at the ring of Primist assault guards surrounding Jacobus. The insects' hideous bodies exploded in sprays of green filth as blaster-fire cut into them. Still they came on, scuttling over the bodies of their kin, driven by their instinct to protect the nest and repel the invaders.

Satisfaction filled Jacobus at the sight. Satisfaction coloured with regret. These were not the actions of sentient beings, which meant he had to leave the planet untouched, the creatures unharmed, save for those dispatched in this little expedition. A few hundred killed in self-defence; he would be allowed no more. The prospect left a sour taste in his mouth. Maybe he wasn't so different from Brand after all.

One particularly large attacker, all flailing pincers and limbs that bent the wrong way, worked its way toward them, shielded for a moment by the insect ranks. Jacobus watched as the laser fire lanced into it. For a brief moment, before its head exploded with a *crump*, he thought he saw something in its gaze. Confusion. Regret. *Understanding.* Had he imagined it? Probably. You couldn't read anything in those dead eyes. And no self-aware being would hurl itself to its destruction like that. Maybe it was his own wishful thinking, nothing more.

The onslaught ceased as the last of the attackers died. Smoke coiled off the mounds of chitinous limbs and shattered exoskeleton all around them. Here and there amid the carnage, a pincer flickered open and shut, an antenna quivered. The vile creatures didn't even know when they were dead. Nearby, a wasp-like severed head lay on the ground, mouth parts working away as if the dead bug was trying to tell him something. Jacobus turned away.

Something did trouble him, though. Their bodies were so *diverse*. Normal hives had only a few basic forms – soldier, worker, nurse, tech, queen – and individuals of each class were basically indistinguishable from each other. They were barely individuals at all. But here they'd seen insectoids of every description and size. Some small, some vast. Some harmless-looking, some nightmarish. As if they were drawn from hundreds – thousands – of different planets. Planets with radically different genetic pools. It made no sense.

Jacobus stood on the low rise of muddy ground they'd chosen to defend and surveyed the scene, trying to work out what he was missing. Everything was tinged green: the ground, the ichor dripping off the glistening tree-analogues, the very light, which gave the world its deathly pallor. It was the green of fetid swamps and decaying flesh. A vile green that made sickness rise within him. The stench of burning and shattered insect carcasses filled his nose. The atmosphere of the planet was just about breathable, although it smelled foul at the best of times. Now, it carried an acidic edge that prickled his throat. He wished he'd worn his full suit. But he'd decided against it, thinking it would make him look weak in front of his men.

He suddenly wanted to leave, get back to the gleaming, clean decks of the *Sword of Truth* and be away. Father Ramen surely couldn't object. There was no evidence of advanced life down on this bug-infested hell planet. Umwe had been right.

He was about to give the order when Chiang's voice spoke in his headset. "Lord Prelate, another ship has entered the system. It's the Chitters. They're here."

*

Jacobus began barking orders and questions up to the

Sword of Truth as they ran for the dropship. "Have they spotted us yet? Are they on intercept vector?"

"No, my Lord," said Chiang. "They appear unaware of us. We are hidden by the planet. We can only see them because we deployed microsensors as we orbited."

That was something. A tactical advantage. The planet might be off limits but a fleet most certainly wasn't. It must have deployed here in response to some automated alarm call. The insects stuck together. That damned hive mentality of theirs.

"How many ships?" asked Jacobus as he ran up the dropship's ramp. "Give me the breakdown of their fleet."

"Lord Prelate, there is only one ship," said Chiang. "Very limited weaponry. It poses no threat. It appears to be a transporter."

"A transporter?" Jacobus stopped on the control deck of the dropship. He'd imagined dreadnoughts and destroyers. He'd imagined a fight. A glorious fight. Not this.

"Confirmed," said Chiang. "Judging by the configuration and the number of ports I'd speculate it is carrying people. Carrying Chitters, I mean."

What *was* this planet? What was it for? Was this a prison ship, dropping off another cargo of convicts? But that didn't make sense. The bugs they'd encountered weren't capable of crimes, of *guilt*. Was the whole world some sort of zoo? A *collection*? Maybe. He had to find out what was going on.

"Lord Prelate? Should we arm for attack?" Brand. Inevitably. Jacobus ignored the armaments officer.

"Chiang, keep the planet between *Sword* and that ship. Inform me immediately if any more show up. Otherwise, I want complete EM silence."

"Yes, my Lord."

"They'll have to send shuttles to the surface. I'm going to take the dropship and find out what they're up to. Understood?"

"Yes, my Lord."

*

Jacobus studied the vast nest from behind the outcrop of jagged rocks. He'd brought the dropship as close as he dared, then walked – and finally crawled – up to this vantage point. Now, they were all caked in mud, algae, and filth. Still, they had avoided any more bugs, save a few lone scouts they'd quickly dispatched. The abominations had no idea they were here.

They'd seen this nest from orbit: the tallest structure on the planet, a spiralling cone of brown and black nearly fifty metres tall. They'd assumed it was made of mud or some naturally-secreted cement. He imagined some bloated, writhing queen within, birthing lines of larvae the size of pigs. Now, studying it through the scope, he could see the truth. This was no nest. Fabricated from metal and synthetic materials, it was clearly *built*. The product of an advanced civilization. They'd watched three shuttles from the orbiting ship land and then, an hour later, blast off. Jacobus longed to know whether it had left the system but didn't dare break EM silence.

He picked out one of the insect guards they'd seen. If they *were* guards. They carried staves but didn't use them as weapons. Although they corralled the arriving Chitters, there wasn't any conflict. If anything, the *guards* were more like warders or shepherds, gently directing the newcomers into patient lines. None of it made sense.

Jacobus watched as a line of the creatures emerged from one of the hexagonal doorways at the building's base. Those arriving on the shuttles were clearly sentient: they wore clothes and carried the usual array of high-tech possessions. The creatures emerging onto the planet were different: unclothed, carrying nothing, walking in straight lines. They were mindless animals. What was the connection between the two sets? Were these slaves? Or experiments?

There was only one way to find out. They had to take one of those shepherds and interrogate it. Get some answers. It was a risk. He was making their presence on the planet clear. But, if the transporter had left the system, they should have some time before more arrived.

Jacobus pointed to twelve of his best men, summoning them over. He began to give them their orders.

*

Three of the guards returned an hour later: scarred, singed, but alive. The other nine lay down on the slopes, or near the building where the demons' weapons had cut them down. Theirs was a glorious death. Their place in the heavens would be assured.

Jacobus studied the single enemy they'd captured. A tall being, its carapace flame red. It was injured as well: several large gashes in its exoskeleton seeped green gore. One of its upper limbs had been completely severed. The three Primists who had captured it hauled it forward and threw it to the ground.

Jacobus stood over the broken captive. "Tell me," he said. "What is going on here? What is this hell planet?"

The insect paused, then emitted a stream of chirps and clicks. It took Jacobus's headset a few moments to interpret. "Hell planet, Primist? Is that what you see with those small eyes of yours?"

"And what do you see, *bug*?"

"I see heaven, Primist. I see Paradise. With you as the rot, the worm in the core. Don't you understand?"

"No, demon. I do not understand. The billions crawling over this vile planet. Who are they? *What* are they? The Chitters from those shuttles: do they come here to hunt them?"

"Hunt them? No. You don't see. Perhaps you can never see. The pilgrims don't come here to hunt the inhabitants of this planet. They come here to *become* them."

"They … let themselves become like that?"

The captive paused before continuing. It had to be in great pain. "Chemicals to suppress their higher faculties, to let their basic instincts reassert themselves."

"But why?" said Jacobus. "Why would you do such a thing? Why would *they*? Is this a punishment?" He wondered what Father Ramen would say. Would he approve of the creatures renouncing their sentience like this? Probably not. Church doctrine was very clear that sentient non-Terrans deserved only death. Still, if the chemical change was permanent, wasn't this another solution? Even a better one?

"Punishment? No." The ruined prisoner paused again, as if debating what to tell them. Or trying to find the right words. "The hive mentality runs deep in us, Primist. In all of us. To lose oneself in that greater being; it is something that pulls at us all. Every Chitter feels it. Even those who live out there among the stars. They come here to revert. For a time. Or permanently, if they wish. For some, it is an occasional pilgrimage. A purging. A renewal. Others never leave. We shepherd them all, look after them."

"Then all these teeming billions. They are all intelligent?"

"They are. Or were. Or will be again."

Brand had been right after all. Father Ramen would expect only one course of action now.

"Primist? Will you join us?" said the bug. "Perhaps … perhaps that is why you have come? Perhaps, that is what you secretly desire."

"Join you?"

"Each brings their strengths to the collective, making us all stronger. Join us and you would be welcome. Will you submit?"

Jacobus paused for a moment, considering. Could they learn something here? Another way?

No. He knew the Fathers would never agree to such

blasphemy. He raised his blaster and gave the bug its answer with a single shot to its head.

"We're leaving," he said to the remaining guards. "Call in the dropship. There's no need to stay hidden now."

He was about to break EM silence, tell the *Sword of Truth* to prep the Hellfire weapon, but the orbiting ship beat him to it.

"Lord Prelate," said Chiang. "A second Chitter ship has entered the system."

"Another transporter?"

"No. This is a dreadnought. More are arriving, jumping in together. Full battle fleet configuration. They're manoeuvring to cut off our escape vectors from the planet."

Jacobus cursed to himself. They'd waited on the surface too long. Too concerned with doing the right thing when they should have been fighting.

"Full battle stations," he ordered. "We're coming up now. Give me projections."

"Chances of defeating the fleet are low," Chiang reported. "Five percent at most."

Fight or flee. Neither looked hopeful. What was the correct course? The summoned dropship swept low over the ground towards them, sending the tree-analogues lashing in its wake.

Brand's voice cut in. "Arming the Hellfire weapon, Lord Prelate. Reactors heating up now."

The armaments officer hadn't been ordered to ready the weapon. Strictly speaking, he was breaking rules. Jacobus decided to let it go. They needed the Hellfire capability as soon as possible. They couldn't defeat this fleet and they couldn't escape it. They *might* be able to hold it off for long enough.

"How long until it's fully armed?" he asked.

"Thirteen minutes," said Brand, the eagerness bright in his voice.

"Chiang," said Jacobus. "How long until we're in range

of their weapons?"

"Seven minutes."

"And how long can we hold them off?"

There was a pause while Chiang ran through battle permutations. "Depending on their tactics, anywhere between one and nine minutes."

Not good odds. But they had a chance. The bugs might destroy the *Sword of Truth* before the planetbuster could be unleashed. But carrying out the Creator's work meant sacrifice. And whatever happened, he and his crew would die in flames, the survival of their souls assured. The attempted destruction of twenty billion Chitters – from civilizations all over the galaxy – would surely buy them that.

*

The tac screen showed the net of enemy ships closing around them. Jacobus studied potential vectors, looking for one that would give them the few extra minutes.

"Chiang, head past the planet's moon for the centre of the system," he ordered. "There are fewer ships near the stellar mass."

"You are fleeing, Prelate?" Father Ramen's eyes were narrowed as he questioned Jacobus's orders. Was there fear there? Was even Father Ramen concerned for his immortal soul? The possibility had never occurred to Jacobus before.

"No, Father. Buying time. If we sit here in orbit, we'll be destroyed quickly. If we head away, then arc backward, we might be able to evade their weapons and return at the right moment to unleash the Hellfire."

Father Ramen paused, then nodded. Jacobus's plans had been given the Father's blessing.

The *Sword of Truth* broke orbit and raced for the system's twin suns. Terawatt energy weapons fire began to lance out at them from two Chitter battleships. A swarm of ship-to-ship missiles followed. The *Sword of Truth's* defensive systems reacted, knocking out the incoming ordnance, attempting to neutralize the energy-weapons. But it would only be a matter of time before they were overwhelmed.

"Kill the upper and lower port engines," order Jacobus.

"My Lord," said Chiang, "the loss of acceleration will seriously reduce our odds."

"Do it," said Jacobus. "We want them to think we're damaged. And we dare not build up too much velocity."

"Yes, my Lord."

Energy-weapon shots slammed into the *Sword of Truth*. Alarms went into overdrive as the dreadnought's systems reacted. The tac displays highlighted ruptured hulls along their port bow. Their weaponry retaliated, flashing out to strike the nearer of the Chitter ships.

"The moon," said Jacobus to Chiang. "Put it between us and them. They'll think we're using it to shield ourselves."

"Yes, my Lord."

"As soon as we're hidden from them, manoeuvre for a slingshot back to the planet."

With any luck, the tactic would take the insects by surprise. The moon wasn't a huge mass, but it would be enough to hurl them back toward the planet at a reasonable velocity. And they had to get back there. The *Sword of Truth* wasn't going to withstand much more punishment.

There was a minute of quiet as they passed behind and around the moon. Jacobus caught glances from Brand, Umwe, Chiang, Father Ramen. Saw the mixture of emotions in their eyes. Exhilaration. Fear. Sadness. No one spoke.

Then, they were accelerating back to the planet, renewed fire slamming into them, knocking out system after system. Very quickly all the main engines were taken out. They could no longer accelerate. Half the ship's hulls were ruptured, venting into space. More concussions shook them, hurling everyone around. Their few remaining weapons systems fired weak energy beams back at their attackers. Not long now. They were little more than dead metal, little more than a carrier for the Hellfire weapon, now armed and ready to fire.

Brand shouted a prayer to the Creator as they finally launched it toward the waiting planet.

*

Swirling green streaks filled Jacobus's vision. Memories came back to him. The enemy onslaught, the looming disc of the planet, a moment of terrible, wrenching alarm as high-energy blasts cut through the *Sword of Truth*. Then nothing. Was he dead? Had his soul floated through the wormholes into paradise? He'd never imagined heaven would be green. White, he'd always thought. A silvery white.

Finally, his vision came into focus and he saw where he really was.

"Why?" he said to the universe in general, his voice little more than a croak. "Why have I been sent here?"

An insect host surrounded him, waving their hideous limbs, regarding him with their lifeless, glassy eyes. He was in hell and these were the demons sent to torment him. He could smell the acid in the air.

One of the creatures began to make a rapid series of clicks and chirps. A starship commander judging by its regalia. A second later, an electronic voice began to translate. Why did he still have his headset? It made no sense.

"Your time among your kind has not ended, Prelate Jacobus. You are not dead. We kill only to eat and to defend the hive."

"I'm not dead?"

"No."

"Then where am I?"

"We call this planet Achenar."

"The weapon?"

"Destroyed before it could penetrate the stratosphere."

"And my crew?"

"Some survived. They will face trial. As their leader, you were brought here."

"For what purpose?" He imagined himself being fed to larvae. Eaten from the inside out as they tunnelled through his flesh.

"This is your new home, Terran."

"My … new home?"

"A punishment, if you like. I prefer to think of it as a chance for you to learn and grow. A chance for your consciousness to … pupate."

"You are imprisoning me here? On this hell planet?"

The demon waved its claws in a manner that suggested irritation. "Among our kind this world is considered a sacred place. Heaven rather than hell."

"But I'm not one of your kind. I'm a Terran. I'm one of the prime beings, made in the Creator's image."

"Then I am sure the people of Achenar will learn much from you, Prelate Jacobus," said the commander, turning and walking away.

The others – mindless bugs from this world – parted to let him pass, their fleshless, angled heads bowed in subservience. What had they once been? Starship pilots? Genesplicers? Engineers? Artists? Looking at them it was impossible to say.

A short distance away, an emerald-green landing-craft waited to return the commander to his ship. Jacobus stepped forward, thinking to follow, thinking to escape. He had to escape.

"No. You may not leave, Jacobus." One of the shepherds grasped Jacobus's arm with a chitinous claw. "You must remain here with us."

"Eat with us," said another. "Live with us. Join us. We

are stronger together than apart. We each bring our strengths to the whole."

Jacobus stared into the dead eyes of the creature who spoke. He tried to struggle free, but it was no use. The insect's grip was iron. He watched in despair as the landing-craft's thrusters flared and the green bulk of the ship rose into the sky.

The bugs around him struck up a mass clicking and chirping, as if in song. The inhuman sound of it grated on Jacobus's brain.

Slowly, he sank to his knees, the ground of his new home green beneath him.

This story is one of three written for the Dark Expanse online game universe – a galaxy-spanning game of exploration, competing factions and conquest. The Chitter are an insectoid race within that universe, but there are many others, and I was free to write stories fleshing out any aspect of the game. It was an interesting process: while there was a lot of freedom, stories also (pretty clearly) had to fit in with the extended mythology and backstory already created. I imagine that's a common situation for people writing episodes in any well-established universe.

The story was published in Surviving the Collapse, the Dark Expanse anthology, in 2014.

MALWARE

"Damn."

Jay sat back from his screen, fingers paused over his keyboard. A window with the words *Unknown Process Detected* overlaid his screen. Details filled the window: memory usage, IO, CPU load. The numbers blurred as they counted up.

So much for his new algorithms. This wasn't supposed to be possible.

His fingers rattled over the keyboard, bringing up new windows, drilling down into details. He tried to kill the virus. No good; some controlling process he wasn't seeing resurrected it immediately.

"Damn," he said again.

"What you got, Jay?"

Maddy, his line manager, spoke without looking up from her own screen. She sat on the other side of the office. It was late. Everyone else had left hours ago. The office blocks of Canary Wharf outside the window were just grids of square lights against the orange glow of the London night. The reflection in the window showed the two of them clearly, surrounded by all the clutter and disembowelled hardware of any serious techie office.

"Rootkit maybe," said Jay. "It's infected the tethered goat machine in Hong Kong."

"What version of XOrcist is installed?"

"5.65, latest and greatest. And with my experimental routines plugged in. *And* today's virus signatures. None of them stopped it for a second."

Maddy – Madeleine – stood from her own machine and threaded her way through the PC graveyard to look over Jay's shoulder. She was OK, Maddy. Most turned instant fascist when they became team leader. He couldn't help being conscious of how close her breasts were to his ear as she bent to examine his screen.

"Any of the others affected?"

They had machines set up the world over waiting to be infected. Isolated from their internal network of course: you could never be 100% sure some chunk of malware wasn't going to tunnel through the firewalls. The tethered goats were only visible to Jay and his co-workers at XOr Antivirus from isolated machines of their own. Nothing was allowed to endanger the company's internal network.

Jay flicked to the other machines they had out there. Prague, Boston, Sydney, Jo'burg, Buenos Aries.

"Damn," said Maddy this time. "Why do these things always happen at one in the morning?"

The outbreak was global. Admittedly the browsing scripts they ran did some pretty stupid things, visiting sites where drive-by infections were likely. Still, this was big.

Maddy pulled her iPhone from the pocket of her jeans to start rousing back-up. Jay drained his cup of black coffee and plugged a thumbdrive into the isolated machine to upload the apps he would need. When he'd finished he tossed the memory stick into the *Incinerate* bin. Company rules. Maddy flashed a grin at him as she talked, raising an amused eyebrow as the employee on the other end of her phone complained audibly.

*

"So, where are we at, Jay?"

Karl, Maddy's boss, definitely *was* of the instant fascist variety. The sort who went on *People Skills* courses and came back even worse. Even at five in the morning he was immaculately dressed, every inch the professional. Karl was a schemer, an empire-builder, and he didn't like Jay. Probably imagined he secretly worked for the dark side, infiltrating XOr.

"It's good and bad," said Jay, swivelling his chair to look up at Karl. "It replicates aggressively. Must have been silently infecting servers for a while before it triggered. Busy too. Don't know what it's doing but it's doing a hell of a lot of it."

"Is it destructive?"

"It's degrading machine performance but I haven't found any damage to data files yet."

"So, it's a zombie."

Jay resisted grinning. He loved the way Karl liked to use the terminology. "Could be. No sign of it being remote-controlled though. It thrashes away even when it's isolated."

"Does XOrcist touch it at all? At full aggression?"

"Nope."

"OK, so what's the good news?"

"It doesn't mutate."

"We can get a signature for it."

"Yeah. Got one already, just testing it now. We can have an update ready for download within the hour. Only…"

"Only what? Do you have a signature or don't you?"

Karl's *people skills* front slipped a little. He frowned, as if Jay was deliberately causing him problems.

"I do. We do. It just seems too easy, somehow. This is smart code, I'm sure of it. Why is it so easy to remove?"

"XOrcist is good."

"Even so. Someone's gone to a *whole* lot of trouble.

Seems odd we can just clean it up like that."

"They're relying on the stupid 50% who don't protect their machines. And all we care about are our customers, yes?"

"Yes."

"OK, good. Push out the signature to everyone."

"Will do."

*

By 8:30 am the day shift were fully briefed. Maddy put a hand on Jay's shoulder. "Go home. You've done good."

Jay nodded but kept his gaze on the infected machine. CPU still busy doing *something*. Disk space dropping but nothing visible taking up the room.

"Jay, come on. You need to rest. Go home. Sleep. Eat and drink. Do … whatever it is you do when you're not here."

"Sure. OK."

He got up to leave, stretching his aching back. His eyes prickled from the ten hours he'd spent staring at screens. Maddy was right, it wasn't his problem now, not until his next shift. The problem was getting his brain to see it like that.

"Maddy."

"Yes?"

"Something still troubles me about this. I don't think we've got to the bottom of it."

"Go on."

"This thing is smart. I think it's given us a nice easy infection we can feel happy about removing while the real deal works away behind the scenes."

"OK. I'll pass on your concerns to the day shift. Just go and sleep before your brain explodes." She looked exhausted too, wisps of her dark brown hair swinging loose to hover around her face. He wondered what she thought of Karl. There had been whispers of an affair between them but Jay found it unlikely. Maddy was *smart*.

"I want to take a machine home with me," he said. "To carry on working with. OK?"

She studied him for a moment. It was tricky for her, being caught between the coders and the management, neither one or the other. He gave her his best lovable rogue grin.

"It's at your own risk, OK? If you infect your own machines it's your problem."

"Sure."

"And sleep first. Zombie workers are no good to me."

"Sure. Sleep. Got it. Anything else?"

"Get out of here," she said. "I'll see you back this evening."

*

He lugged the machine up to his first floor flat in the North London suburbs. The edge of the casing was sharp, cutting into his fingers. Next time he'd take a laptop. He'd had plenty of suspicious glances from the morning's commuters, riding the tube with a PC clutched to his chest.

Inside his flat, he set the machine down on the floor and tried to flex life back into his creased hands. He glanced round. When he brought people up here – which he had to admit was rare – they were always surprised how tidy it all was. They expected the typical hacker bachelor pad: all XBox games and pizza cases. But he hated clutter, obsessively so. Couldn't get his thoughts straight until his surroundings were straight too. He wondered what Maddy's place was like. So far as he knew she lived alone. Perhaps he should invite her round. They joked around in the office and traded humorous YouTube videos but that was as far as it went.

He made himself a chicken sandwich, and, while the filter machine gurgled its ways through the coffee, set the machine up with a power supply, monitor, keyboard and mouse. He didn't connect it to his router and he knew it didn't have wireless. It was completely isolated.

From one of his regular desktop machines he dumped a load of utilities onto a USB drive as he had at work. He copied across a few gigs of music too, something to listen to while he worked. *System of a Down*, lively enough to keep him awake. Making sure the device was switched to read-only he plugged it into the infected machine and sat down to play. He would sleep soon. Just a few more things to try. He plugged his earphones into the PC and set to work.

He sat for one hour, two albums and four coffees. Definitely *something* going on with the machine, but he was damned if he knew what. The CPU had stayed busy, something still ate away at the available disk space. Damn sound card was dodgy too; an irritating background buzz in his ears distracted him. Maybe an out of date driver. He'd switched from metal to something a bit gentler, *Godspeed You! Black Emperor*, but it was just the same. He could have just fetched his iPod but he was too engrossed in what he was doing. In the end he sat there in silence, buds still plugged into his ears.

He tried to think straight. OK, if Windows had been infected with a rootkit he wasn't going to find it looking via Windows. The evil code was sitting there telling the operating system it didn't exist. Logically, he needed to boot from another drive. Better still, another OS. He pulled a Linux DVD from a drawer, turned off the computer, counted to thirty, then booted up again. This time the infected hard disk was just a bunch of dead files. He began to compare file sizes and dates against the standard list.

The scale of the outbreak became clear. A whole slew of device drivers were massively bloated. Which wasn't supposed to be possible, even without XOrcist. Some unknown exploit. But he was no nearer working out what the virus did. Now that it wasn't running it was just megabytes of dead binary.

He did discover where the disk space was going though: a single file called ~.~ deep in a tree of folders, 20 gigabytes in size. What the hell was that?

Too whacked to think of anything smarter to do, he tried loading the file into a hex editor. It wasn't unknown for virus writers to leave URLs or Twitter Ids in there, bragging to their competitors. He scrolled through reams of ASCII sequences that just looked like noise: chance consecutive bytes of printable characters. The string *Zer0.Zer0* appeared several times, but he could make nothing of it. Not a registered domain, nothing at all on Google.

He couldn't think straight, pain thickening in his forehead, the room beginning to lurch. Time to sleep. He left the computer on to see what state it would be in later, pulled the buds from his ears, and fell into bed.

*

His mobile roused him, his ringtone an old Metallica track, *Trapped Under Ice*. He felt woozy and his head throbbed as he fumbled to pick up.

"Yeah?"

"So, are you not coming to join us in work today then?"

Karl. Damn. "I, uh, yeah. I'm just working on something here."

"I see. Anything important at all?"

He looked around his bedroom. It was dark apart from the sodium glow of the city through his blinds. Had he slept through the whole day? Night shifts threw him completely. Pain thrummed in his head as he sat up and tried to piece coherent thoughts together. He held his phone out for a moment to see what time it was. Gone eight. Should have been at work an hour ago.

"Yeah. It's the machine I brought home. Maddy said I

could work on it here."

It was a dangerous gambit, putting Maddy in a potentially awkward situation. He winced in the darkness.

"Maddy isn't here either. As a matter of fact, very few people are."

"What? Why?"

"Flu, apparently." The way he said it made it clear he thought being ill was a moral failing. "Haven't you seen the news?"

"I, uh, no. Been up to my elbows. What's happened?"

"An outbreak, lots of people struck down. They're panicking about H1N1 again. I need to know what your status is Jay. We're pretty short-handed here."

He sounded pressurised, struggling bravely to keep everything running. He played it beautifully. While he talked Jay scanned the headlines on the BBC web site. The outbreak looked pretty widespread. Pockets world-wide. Usual symptoms: dizziness, tiredness, aches and pains. Perhaps *he* had it. That would explain his throbbing head.

"Jay?"

"Sorry. Feeling pretty ropey myself actually."

"So, you're staying at home? We are at code red here you know."

"The signature update didn't work?"

"Yes, but machines are still infected. Hidden processes. Your patch doesn't touch them."

Jay had to smile. Somehow this was *his* fault. "The thing is, Karl, I might be on to something here. Something worth pursuing."

"What have you found?"

"Some strings in a hidden file that could be a signature. I'd like to check it out, see if anyone knows what they mean."

There was silence. This confirmed all Karl's fears about Jay's former links to the blackhats and malware writers. The bad guys.

"Ask whom, Jay? Who will you ask?"

No point denying it. Truth was he *did* still have contacts on the other side. A few. He was just no longer one of them. The monthly paycheque saw to that. But his former contacts didn't know; anonymity worked both ways. To them he was just *Firestarter*, hacker and occasional presence on forums. They didn't know who he *really* was.

"Just people I used to know. People I haven't spoken to for years. It's worth a shot. If we can get a handle on this, XOr can get ahead of the curve. Before our competitors do.

As expected, *that* worked beautifully.

"OK, Jay. See what you can find out. But I want you back in here with a full update tomorrow."

"Sure, Karl."

Jay washed paracetamol down with more black coffee while he tried to think straight. He really hadn't spoken to his old contacts for a long time, apart from a few gaming sessions. What had he even meant? This damn infection had been running around in his brain all night, giving him trapped-in-code-loop nightmares. The string he'd found was pretty inconsequential. It was a classic mistake when debugging to see patterns where there were none. But, then again, it was another classic mistake to overlook a pattern just because it seemed unlikely.

He sipped his coffee standing at his window, looking out over the lights of London. Streets weirdly quiet. Normally they were thick with cars at this hour. Everyone was probably just staying at home. He was glad he had some Tamiflu left over from the previous winter.

He browsed boards and IRC channels for a couple of hours, looking for traces of his old associates. Nothing within the last year. Twitter, Facebook, Usenet: zilch. He left a few posts here and there, nothing overt, in the hope someone would get back to him.

The problem was people changed their online identities. Obviously. But they couldn't do so constantly: if they did they'd just lose touch with everyone. There had to be someone still using an old ID, even if they only checked it occasionally.

He trawled through his archived emails to see if there were any sites he'd forgotten about. A few more forums he hadn't tried, probably all long-gone. He tried them anyway and found, to his surprise, the third was still active. Probably just popped back up on a different IP address when it got shut down.

He browsed through posts and found a recent thread with some user names on it he recognized. Which might mean nothing, of course. Anyone could pick a user name. Still, it was all he had. He sent direct messages to them all: again, nothing too risky, just a polite hail. Then he sat watching his screen, sipping more coffee, nibbling toast to help settle his stomach.

It was another hour before the text popped up on his screen.

<NaN> Hey Firestarter. Where U been?
<Firestarter> Here and there.

NaN – if it was the same person – was a contact from way back, the sort of person who knew a lot about a lot. Probably *too* much about a lot.

<NaN> So, what's up?
<Firestarter> Looking for help. Sick PC.
<NaN> You?
<Firestarter> Yeah. Not good.
<NaN> Go on.
<Firestarter> Something called *Zer0.Zer0*. Heard of it?

Jay sat for a minute, two minutes, waiting for a reply. Nothing. The cursor winked away at him. He guessed he'd gone too far. He was about to shut down when the conversation resumed.

<NaN> Wipe the machine and reinstall.
<Firestarter> That bad?
<NaN> Yup.
<Firestarter> What's so bad about it?

There was another pause. Jay imagined NaN debating whether to carry on with the conversation.

<NaN> Really wanna know?
<Firestarter> Sure.
<NaN> Can we meet up?

That was unexpected. Hackers never just *met up*. They probably weren't even on the same continent.

<Firestarter> Why?
<NaN> Can tell you about *Zer0.Zer0*.
<Firestarter> Tell me here.
<NaN> Showing you is better. You'll be interested.

That threw him. What the hell did NaN know about him? Meeting up with him was an insane thing to do. It wasn't like the old days, script kiddies writing viruses to see who could infect the most machines. These days it was big business, organized crime. Another reason he'd got out.

<NaN> Somewhere safe. Public.

Now Jay took his time to reply.

<Firestarter> Why would I be interested?
<NaN> We can help each other.
<Firestarter> How?
<NaN> I'll show you. You're in London?
<Firestarter> What makes you say that?
<NaN> Guess. You're definitely UK. IP not proxied you know.

Damn. He'd forgotten to do that. He thought about leaving the channel. He could just tell Karl he hadn't found anything. That was the smart move. Still, he hated being beaten.

<Firestarter> You in London?
<NaN> Can be. 9:00am, Trafalgar Square?
<Firestarter> OK.

Jay killed the connection then sat deep in thought, staring out of his window at the deserted streets. Meeting up with NaN was a risk, but he could see no alternative. Still, if he was going to do this, he shouldn't go alone. It made sense to take someone with him.

"Hi Maddy."

She looked terrible, peering around her door into the morning light with bleary eyes.

"Jay?"

"Yeah. Sorry. Got your address from work, said I'd drop round and see if you were OK."

"They *gave* you my address?"

"Well, actually, I more sort of know the administrator password for the database. Only that sounds creepy."

She frowned at him, then sighed. "Alright. Come in. But don't blame me if you catch 'flu too."

"I got it already."

She unchained the door and opened it, clutching her dressing-gown closed at her neck. She looked pale.

"Why are you really here?"

"I just wanted to talk to you. It's kind of a work thing."

"OK. But I'm not up to much. You'll have to make your own ridiculously strong coffee."

She showed him into the kitchen. It was pristine, polished wood and steel, little-used. The espresso machine must have just come out of its box, like an unused wedding present. He busied himself with it while Maddy went upstairs. She returned wearing jeans and tee-shirt, looking only slightly less wrecked.

"I made you some tea," he said.

"Thanks."

"Painkillers?"

"Just had some."

"You have the headaches and the dizziness? Like being drunk and hungover at the same time?"

"Something like that. They're saying it's 'flu but it's not like that."

"Someone on Twitter said it's just mass hysteria."

"They wouldn't say that if they felt like I do."

They sat down at her kitchen table. Jay gazed at the continents forming in his coffee cup, wondering where to start.

"The thing is…" "So, what's the…"

They each started talking at the same moment. She grinned.

"Go on. You first."

"OK. The thing is, I need your advice."

"Go on."

She looked amused. He tried to stop himself feeling like a school kid asking for a date.

"It's this virus. I spoke to an old friend. He's the sort of guy with contacts, yeah? The thing is he sounded troubled. Said we could help each other. And he wants to meet up. Which is pretty weird."

"I thought you said he was a friend."

"Well, kind of. I've never actually met him."

"You mean he's a hacker."

"Yeah."

"So, you're going to meet him?"

"I guess. It's all very James Bond. Trafalgar Square, nine o'clock."

"And you're telling me this why?"

"I hoped you'd come along."

"Why would I do that?"

"Well, I wanted to keep everything above board. Plus, I'll be honest, it would be good not to go alone."

"You're scared?"

"No. Of course not. Out in the open it'll be perfectly safe. I just thought, you know, moral support."

He looked back down at his coffee, aware of how ridiculous he sounded. But when he looked back up at her she was grinning. "From what I hear the streets are pretty crazy. Lots of people ill."

"Yeah, but I figured since we'd both caught it already it didn't matter. Look, this was a bad idea. I can see you're not well. I'll go alone and maybe see you at work tonight."

He drained his coffee and stood up. He had to leave now to get into London in time.

"Wait. I'll come."

"What? Why?"

"Got to look after our star programmer, haven't we?"

*

They stood together until 9:30. No one approached. The problem was, of course, he had no idea what NaN looked like. Determined commuters and ambling tourists milled around the square. Quite a few wore white masks over their mouths and noses. The ground was strewn with them, like weird toadstools. Perhaps the outbreak, whatever the hell it was, was passing. 24-hour 'flu.

"You think he's coming?" Maddy looked drained. She sat on the low wall that surrounded one of the fountains.

"I don't know. Perhaps he's been held up. Lots of trains cancelled."

He tried not to think of the more sinister ideas nagging away at him. NaN had got him out of the way so he could search Jay's flat. NaN had been intercepted by the evil *Zer0.Zer0* coders. Ridiculous. He'd read too many Sci/Fi novels.

"Can I borrow your lipstick, Maddy?"

"You look fine to me, sweetheart."

"Seriously."

She shrugged and handed him one from her handbag. He stooped to pick up a square of paper from the floor, a flyer for some pizza place, and wrote the words *Bad Sector* in large red letters.

"Good job you don't go for subtle colours," he said.

"Ha, ha."

Jay held up the makeshift sign.

"And that means? Apart from the obvious?"

"It's our gaming clan."

"Of course it is."

He stood, making sure the sign could be seen from all angles.

"Happy now?"

"I just figured he doesn't know what I look like. He's not expecting a couple."

"Oh, you think we're a couple?"

"No, I just meant…"

"Ssh. Look. Someone's coming."

A man strode across the square. He looked mid-thirties, straggly hair, scruffy clothes. Standard geek. He walked up to them and shook Jay's hand, like they were old friends.

"I'm NaN."

"I'm, uh, Firestarter."

Jay tried to ignore Maddy's raised eyebrow.

"Who's this?" asked NaN.

"She's a friend. She's cool. Why did you want to meet?"

"*Zer0.Zer0*," he said.

"You know about it?" asked Maddy.

"The whole world knows about it, don't they?"

"Certainly hit a lot of machines," said Maddy.

"I don't mean that. Don't you know? Haven't you worked it out?"

"Worked what out?"

"This!" said NaN, indicating the square, London, the world all around them. "This so-called 'flu. Look what it's done!"

"You're saying a computer virus has infected *people*?" asked Jay. He suddenly didn't dare look at Maddy. NaN was clearly mad. He'd made a terrible mistake.

"Well, yeah, *obviously*. I figured you'd got that far. That was why I decided to speak to you. I thought maybe you could do something."

"NaN, a computer virus can't infect *people*," said Maddy, her voice calm, reasonable. "You do know that? We call them *viruses* but that's just a metaphor."

"Yes. Obviously."

"Then how can this *Zer0.Zer0* have caused a 'flu pandemic?"

"Tell me, did you two catch it?"

"I guess," said Jay.

"OK. And did you listen to music on an infected machine beforehand?"

"Well, yeah," said Jay.

"Me too," said Maddy. "Synced my iPod on one anyway."

"There you are then," said NaN.

"There you are where?" asked Maddy.

NaN sighed, glancing around before speaking further. "Certain wavelengths encoded into music. Get the right frequencies and you start to glitch out the middle-ear, send the semi-circular canals crazy. Enough exposure and the listener starts to feel disorientated and dizzy. Headaches, sickness, everything."

"A million things cause those symptoms," said Maddy.

"But you can *hear* the sonics. Like a mosquito buzzing."

"I didn't hear anything," said Maddy.

"Not everyone can," said NaN. "Depends how old you are."

"Oh, thanks."

"I heard it," said Jay. "Like interference, but only when

the music was playing."

"Yes, it's smart," said NaN.

"How can we possibly believe that?" asked Maddy.

"You spotted all the disk space it consumed? Did you work out what it was?"

"Well, no," said Jay.

"It's caching the music. Adding the killer frequencies to each track. You tell the computer to play something and what you actually get is the tampered version, streamed directly into your head."

"Can you actually prove any of this?" asked Maddy.

"Here. Watch this."

He showed them his iPhone, some shaky video footage. A man sat in a chair, smiling, looking calm. Loudspeakers around him played music, something classical Jay didn't recognise.

"Let me skip on ten minutes."

Now the man's eyes were closed. His head lolled around like he was drunk. He clutched his hands over his ears, tried to stand, fell to the floor. He started to vomit. A line of blood trickled from one of his ears.

"We were testing which frequencies to use, how powerful. Went a bit far with this one."

"You're saying *you're* responsible for *Zer0.Zer0*?" asked Maddy.

"In the early days, yes. I got out when I saw where it was going."

"And where was it going?"

"Isn't it obvious? They've infected machines the world over. A co-ordinated trigger message and they've crippled *millions* of people."

"Why? Why would they – you – do that?" asked Maddy.

"Why do you think? For money, obviously. This whole 'flu outbreak has been just an opening shot. If they don't get what they want they'll do it for longer next time. Trust me, you do not want that. It's not just the middle ear. The right frequencies and you can disrupt the brain. Permanently."

"So, they'll be demanding money?"

"Oh yeah. Lots and lots of zeroes."

Jay looked at Maddy. She looked worried now. How true was any of this? It sounded like some insane conspiracy theory. NaN must have seen it on his face.

"Look, I didn't expect you'd just believe me. Prove it for yourself."

He pulled a memory stick out of a pocket and held it out for them.

"All the video's on here. Plus some source code. You'll be able to break open the rootkit, see what it's doing. Kill it too."

"Why are you giving us this?" asked Jay.

"It's all gone too far," said NaN. "Far too far. Just keep it quiet, understand? I'm trusting you here."

"None of this proves *Zer0.Zer0* has anything to do with the 'flu outbreak," said Maddy.

"Then experiment," said NaN. "You've got the antidote now. Set up some tests. I was sceptical too before I played guinea pig."

"You tested this on yourself?"

"Sure. Lots of us did. That guy in the video. He was one of the key programmers in the early days."

"What happened to him?"

"Let's just say he's not programming anymore."

NaN looked around again. He looked nervous.

"I should go," he said. "Do what you can. Oh, and be careful, yeah? If they find out about you they're not going to play nicely."

"Who are *they*?" asked Jay.

NaN shrugged.

"What will you do?" asked Maddy.

"I'm going to disappear. I'm taking no chances. Complete change of identity. You won't see me again, Firestarter."

Jay held out his hand and after a moment's hesitation, NaN shook it.

"Then thanks," said Jay. "For everything."

NaN nodded, turned and strode off. When he'd gone Maddy let out a deep breath.

"Christ. Do you believe a word of that?"

"I dunno," said Jay. "He's a smart guy. Maybe crazy too. At least we can try his code and see if it works."

"OK, *Firestarter*. I'll phone XOr and tell them we're coming in. That'll be the safest place if there *is* a gang of ruthless lunatics after us."

Jay stretched his legs while Maddy talked. He could tell immediately the conversation wasn't going well.

"What happened?" he asked when she hung up.

"I spoke to Karl."

"Ah. What did he say?"

"Said we'd broken *every* company rule and that we're suspended for misconduct."

"What?"

"We're not allowed near XOr. Disciplinary procedures to follow."

"That's ridiculous! We need to work on this fix. Doesn't he understand?"

"Obviously not. You know what he's like. We bypassed him, that's all he sees. Damn."

"Christ. Look, I'm really sorry Maddy. I shouldn't have involved you."

She stood and slipped her phone into her bag. "No. You should Jay. This could be important. Let's go back to my place and test this out together."

"That's not a metaphor is it?"

"No, it damn-well isn't."

"Then let's go to mine instead. I've got the infected machine there. We can use that."

The underground station was even more crowded than usual, people shuffling through the tunnels, thronging the platforms. A lot more wore face masks down here. Over the fuzzy, blaring tannoys came a list of cancelled and delayed services.

They stood on the platform at Leicester Square, waiting for a Northern Line train. One was due in three minutes but Jay doubted they'd get on. They stood near the edge of the platform but the previous train had been packed and only one or two had managed to squeeze on.

He looked around over a sea of heads. Being tall had its advantages sometimes. Maddy could see nothing beyond those surrounding her. Most people waited patiently, although one or two tried to force their way through the crowds. He watched as two men, shaved heads like soldiers, forced their way down the platform. There was always someone. The man, seeing him, turned to his companion and nodded towards Jay. Jay, suddenly, was glad of the crowds.

The train arrived, heralded by a rush of warm air from the tunnel. The tannoys blared again. Jay didn't see what happened next. The train entered the station, still moving quickly. He was thrust forwards as the crowd behind him shoved. He tried to stop himself being pushed towards the platform edge but the surge was too strong. He heard panicked screams. A young woman standing slightly in front of him, tottered on the lip of the platform, scrabbling at the other people. Maddy caught one of her hands but couldn't hold on. The woman tipped out of sight. The sickening thump and squeal of train brakes made it clear what had happened.

People screamed. Jay clutched Maddy's arm as the crowd pushed and heaved. The train scraped to a halt, a curving wall of glass and metal in front of them. Inside, the passengers picked themselves up from the crush of the emergency stop.

Reflected in the glass, through the crowd of heads behind him, he could clearly see the two shaven-headed men standing against the arching wall of the station. They looked directly at Jay.

"Come on," he said. "This way."

"What?" Maddy looked shocked, terrified. Everyone around them did.

Jay ducked down, hoping he couldn't be seen from the back of the crowd. Grabbing Maddy's arm he worked his way along the gap between train and crowd. The doors opened but no one got on or off. They got two carriage-lengths before the throng became too much to push through.

"What are you doing?" shouted Maddy. "We can't *go* anywhere."

"Just follow me."

Back down the platform he could see the two men trying to force their way through the crowd.

"Come on," he said.

He pushed onto the train. The carriages weren't quite as crowded as the platform. Apologizing again and again, he squeezed his way along, trying to keep as many bodies as he could between himself and the platform. At the end of the carriage they came to a door, notices containing dire warnings about going through. Jay heaved the door open and stepped across the gap.

"What exactly are you doing?" asked Maddy.

"We have to get away without them seeing us."

"Who?"

"I'll explain later. Come on. *Please.*"

They worked their way through the carriages and, eventually, back onto the platform near the exit. Police and transport workers directed the crowd up escalators. Jay, seeing his chance, darted down a side tunnel, away from the crush.

"We're supposed to get outside," said Maddy.

"I know. That's why we're going this way."

Maddy grabbed him hard and made him stop.

"Now look, Jay, just what the hell is going on? We're all upset. We're all shocked. There's no need to go crazy."

"I'm not!" he shouted. And then, more quietly, "I'm not. Look, OK. You think *that* was an accident?"

"Well, yes, obviously. The crowded platform. The crush as the train arrived."

"No," said Jay. "It was two guys at the back pushing. Pushing *us*."

"Why would they do that?"

"When you spoke to work, did you mention where we were?"

"Uh, yes, I think so."

"Someone was listening in. They came to get us."

"Jay, this is insane."

"Maybe. But let's get away from here just in case, OK?"

Maddy considered for a moment, glancing back at the shuffling crowd of people.

"Okay," she said. "We can change at King's Cross for Euston."

They crossed London. Each police car siren, each shoulder brushing by, made Jay's heart hammer. His head throbbed heavily again now. He wanted to sleep. Maddy looked pretty ill too. Neither spoke much as they took the tube, two buses and, finally, walked down Jay's quiet, car-lined street in north London. Inside, Jay made drinks for them both while Maddy lay on his sofa, hand over her eyes. It was midday; effectively midnight for both of them.

"I'll take a look at NaN's source code," said Jay.

"Let's look at it together. Between us we might get somewhere."

Jay plugged the memory stick into the infected machine. It had stopped disk-thrashing now although it still felt sluggish as he opened windows and copied files.

"Looks pretty straightforward," said Maddy as they examined the hundred lines or so of C.

"Let's write a script and see what it does."

They worked for half an hour, coding up the script, running it, debugging, trying again. He hoped there was no lockout after x failed attempts. They were both too tired, too ill, to think straight and kept making stupid mistakes. But finally, they had a script that ran to end. As NaN had promised, the call dumped out a listing of all the tracks *Zer0.Zer0* had catalogued. The names of the songs Jay had copied onto the machine raced by on the screen.

"OK," said Maddy. "Let's try the self-destruct call."

"Let me play a track first. If we can hear the hidden frequencies have gone we'll know it's worked."

"Sure that's wise?"

"Just a few seconds."

Jay selected a *System of a Down* track. He figured they were a good choice; the abrupt silences had thrown the virus last time. He played *Chop Suey*.

"Hear it? Like a drill noise underneath the music."

"I think so."

"This is how it should sound."

Jay played the same track from his docked iPhone.

"It's subtle but, yeah, I hear it," said Maddy.

"See, I said you should listen to more metal."

"Let's just try and clean it up."

Another hour and they had the self-destruct script ready. The rootkit was clever. The keys had to be passed in at the right intervals. Too slow or too quick and nothing happened. It could have taken months without NaN's commented code.

Jay pressed enter and they both watched as the disk light on the infected machine lit up. It stayed that way for a minute, two minutes. Finally, it went out and the DOS window's flashing cursor returned.

Jay played *Chop Suey* on the machine again. He looked at Maddy, who nodded. Clean. He checked the processes on the machine and the available disk space. All back to normal.

"I think we got it," said Jay. "I'll package it as an XOrcist update."

"Except we can't can we? Karl made that very clear,

believe me."

Jay shrugged.

"We'll just FTP it up to one of the others. Jenny or Roger. They can send it out."

"Not without Karl's approval."

"Actually, it's easy to do without Karl's approval."

It was the same the world over. Management put passwords and sign-offs around vital data, terrified they had no control over it. But they always needed someone to fix stuff if things went wrong. Techies with back-door access.

"We can just bypass Karl. You know this."

"But I'm not *supposed* to know this. I'm supposed to be in control if you remember."

Jay sat back. He felt too exhausted to argue. She was right, of course.

"OK. It's your decision."

Maddy held her face in her hands. She looked completely done in.

"You really think it wasn't an accident? That woman at the station?"

"Yeah. You heard NaN. They *came* for us. Still might. The sooner we get this out there the better."

"Send it," she said. "Put my name on it and send it. Zip up *everything* NaN gave us: video, code, the lot. What does it matter now?"

"Will do."

As he fired up an FTP client, Maddy crossed to the window.

"You think they'll find us?"

"Maybe."

"Your address must be easy to get. Work have it for one thing."

"You think?"

"Of course, they have everyone ... oh."

"Yes, sorry. Old habits. I amended my records some time back."

"OK, but *someone* must know you're here."

"I guess. But I feel safer here than outside. There. Done. I've emailed Roger *and* Jenny."

Maddy nodded.

"In that case I think it's time we went to bed. You look about as bad as I feel."

"Bed?"

"Yeah. Don't worry, we're both too zonked to do anything but sleep."

Jay raised an eyebrow but said nothing. She was right. Within a minute of lying down they were both asleep.

*

This time a repeated knock on the door awoke Jay. He looked round for a moment, confused. Maddy lay next to him, not moving but with her eyes wide open in sudden alarm.

Jay peered out through the spy hole expecting to see the men from the tube station. Instead a policeman and a woman in normal clothes stood there. He opened the door on its chain.

"Uh, hello?"

"Jay Marston?" asked the woman.

"Yeah?"

"You're a very hard person to track down, you know that?"

"Uh, sorry. Yeah."

"Get dressed and come with us please."

"Where to?"

"To XOr. You have a lot of explaining to do. I assume Ms. Day is here. She can come too."

The police car sped them through the streets of London. No one spoke. Jay stared out of his window. It was evening again, sunlight fading, the shop windows and streetlights taking over. Did the streets look more crowded or less? He hadn't had time to check the news. A hundred different scenarios ran through his mind. Top was the nagging thought that NaN had duped them. The script he'd sent out must have done something terrible, like disabling XOrcist completely. Which meant they'd think *he* was working with the blackhats.

At XOr they were ushered up to the boardroom on the top floor, past the stares of their colleagues. Jay caught Roger's wary glance as they swept past.

In the boardroom they were met by Karl and George Lever himself: founder, owner and CEO of XOr. Jay had never met him before; he spent most of his time at the LA office. Lever indicated chairs for Jay and Maddy. The plain-clothed policewoman sat down too.

"So," said Lever. "Karl? Would you like to start please?"

For thirty minutes Jay and Maddy sat in silence while Karl ripped into them, condemning them for their stupidity, their lack of professionalism, their irresponsibility, the way they'd endangered XOr and everyone who worked there. Lever didn't speak, staring stony-faced out of the window while Karl raged.

Jay wondered what was to become of him. He had obviously blown it at XOr. But he couldn't go back to the dark side either. It was clear from NaN no one would trust him now. He thought about the two thugs, still out there somewhere. His head throbbed. He wanted to sleep for a week.

Finally, Karl drew breath.

"So. Bottom line. You're both suspended without pay for a month while we make further investigations. In all likelihood you won't be coming back. Criminal proceedings may follow. Do you understand me?"

"Yes, Karl."

"You'll be escorted from the building immediately."

Karl stood up, nodded at Lever and swept from the room. Jay caught the look of triumph on his face. He and Maddy rose to follow. Just as they were leaving Lever spoke, asking him to stay. Maddy flashed him a sympathetic smile as he stepped back into the boardroom.

The CEO stood at the window, gazing out over the London skyline. The policewoman sat scribbling something on a pad.

"You might like to see this, Jay," said Lever. He pressed a button on a remote. The blinds slid shut and a projector lifted out of the centre of the table. Jay watched as the images played on the boardroom screen.

"I've seen it," said Jay. "My contact showed me on his phone."

The policewoman spoke now.

"This was filmed this morning at the Home Office. The effect your *contact* described turns out to be real.

"What?"

"Your script successfully removes the infection," said Lever. "It's doing so right now. I'm told certain *communications* from those responsible to sovereign governments have ceased."

"But I don't understand. Karl…"

"Ah yes, Karl," said Lever. "A very ambitious young man. I'm sure you can work out what is happening there."

"Work out … oh."

"You see it. The reason he's blocked you, smothered you at every turn. The reason he dislikes you so much. Those thugs at Leicester Square."

"You mean *Karl* is working with the bad guys?"

"We believe so, yes."

"Then why did you let him? Maddy and I could have been killed!"

"We weren't sure of him at first," said the policewoman. If that was what she was. "And then, when it became clear, Mr. Lever and I agreed it would be useful to have him in-house. To keep an eye on him."

"And what about me?"

"Well. We must let Karl believe he's won, you see," said Lever. "You understand I'm sure."

"Great."

"But this month's suspension. Between you and me, let's call it *leave* instead. Paid leave. Very well-paid leave, in fact. You'll find a bonus in your account big enough to go somewhere very expensive."

"And when I come back?"

"Well, I can promote you if you want. You can spend your days in meetings with the Karls of this world. Is that what you'd prefer?"

"I'd rather saw my own legs off."

Lever smiled for the first time. "I thought as much. In that case I have another suggestion. You clearly have a great deal of, let us say, useful experience. You're invaluable to XOr. I'd like to set up a new division. A secret division with *links* to the other side. A secret service within XOr. And I'd like you to run it. Without Karl or anyone else knowing. Interested?"

"I might be."

"It could be dangerous, of course. As you've discovered. But I'm assured by the powers that be" – he nodded towards the woman – "you will be protected. What do you say?"

"Can I tell you in a month?"

"Of course. Take your time."

Jay got up to leave. As he was closing the door, Lever called after him again.

"Oh, and Jay? If you like, have a word with Madeleine. I could be wrong, but she might appreciate a month's *suspension* somewhere hot and expensive too. If you'd like you could go together."

Jay grinned to himself as he closed the door.

As well as fiction, I write computer software for a living, and it seemed like a fun idea to combine the two and attempt to write a thriller involving programming and cybercrime. When I read other stories that involve software, it's often really noticeable how little the writer really understands what they're talking about, and I wanted to write something that was at least grounded in reality even if my central affectation – the virus – is completely made up and (so far as I know) impossible. Any Javascript developer, for example, would be able to explain why NaN was a good name for a rebel hacker, and that might lead them onto a famous line from cult British TV series The Prisoner...

Malware is another story that I'd like to develop into a series of books at some point. There are lots of cybercrime-related adventures Jay could get into, especially now he's working in his secret group within XOr.

The story was originally published in Perihelion magazine in 2013, and is also available as a stand-alone ebook.

THE LAST FLIGHT OF THE CARRION CROW

Captain Galena Karst watched the unfolding space battle with pleasure in her stony heart.

Distant explosions bloomed like flowers in the void. It always struck her how colourful they were. How varied. Some white, some red, some distinctly purple. They could be exotic gems unearthed in the mines back home on Arralith.

This far away you couldn't see the vast ships being ripped in two by beam-weapon fire, couldn't see the mangled and burned bodies sucked out into the void. It was all utterly silent, utterly peaceful. And the battle raged over such a wide arc of space you never knew where the next explosion was going to erupt. Really, the effect was almost hypnotic. Especially when the *Carrion Crow* was concealed on the surface of an asteroid, undetectable to both sides.

But it was the promise of rich pickings that really made the lava pump through her. These two fleets were well-matched. That was always good. The Chitters outnumbered the Humans and were better organized, sticking to their formations. But the Primist ships fought as if they had no fear of death. As if they welcomed death.

They were fanatics, of course, intent on eradicating all the *demons* from their galaxy – by which they meant any non-human. Some twisted version of Zyxlar philosophy. These Chitters were simply the next in line. Still, she cared little about that. She had a much more important agenda. The only one that really mattered: the making of money. Those shattered ships were gold mines if you knew what you were doing. Military-grade comm encryption keys held in those dying systems could be extracted and sold for a fortune to the other side. And the beauty of it was, it didn't matter which side you stole from and which side you sold to.

Osssian strode up to stand beside her as she watched the battle rage. His faint reflection in the transparent bulkhead overlaid the scene before her. She could just make out his thin little forked-tongue flicking from his mouth. Something he did when he was troubled. As ever, he carried two hand-blasters and a war-axe slung across his back. Who he thought he was going to fight on board the *Carrion Crow* she didn't like to ask. Being a scavenger meant not asking too many questions. They all had their own reasons for being renegades from their own kind.

"Are we tracking any likely fragments?" she asked.

A flick of the tongue. "They fight well, these two fleets," said Osssian. "They destroy each other most effectively. There is a derelict we are hopeful for. The wreck of a dreadnought class, currently spiralling towards an asteroid."

That was good. It was six months since their last successful scavenge. They were running low on fuel, food, hope and every-damn-thing.

"How long until it impacts?"

"Ninety minutes."

It was tight; it didn't leave much time to get on board and hack into the systems. And she dared not move just yet; there will still ships out there. Ships that could vaporise the *Carrion Crow* with a single beam-weapon shot. As she watched, another red flower bloomed in the void.

"Is the derelict powered?"

"It's drifting. Drives dead."

"Ah. Excellent."

"Captain, there's something else."

Here it was. The thing that was troubling him. "Go on."

Osssian stood closer, his voice a quiet hiss. They were the two longest-serving crew members of the *Carrion Crow*. She might even consider him a friend.

"It is a Terran ship," said Osssian. "The *Malleus Dei*. We must be careful. I do not think we can necessarily trust … everyone on this ship."

She turned to study him now. "Osssian, there are only four of us. What the hell do you mean?" She could never decide if he was borderline paranoid or a normal Saurian. Perhaps it amounted to the same thing.

"Last night on one of my regular security sweeps I found something," said Osssian.

"Since when do we have security sweeps?"

"We've always had security sweeps."

"First I've damn well heard of it. What did you find?"

The Saurian pulled something from a pocket. "This."

In his red claw, he held a small stick figure, crudely constructed from twisted wire.

"What is it?" she said. "Some sort of toy?"

"You really don't know?"

"Tell me."

"It is a Primist holy symbol. It's the Prime Being, the perfect form we non-humans fall so short of."

"Where did you find it?"

"Well-hidden in salvage bay E. The one with the leaking space seals no one is supposed to enter."

One of the *many* decks with leaking space seals. The *Carrion Crow* was a wreck, barely held together by all the rust.

"And you're saying that Jonas…" She threw a glance back at their Terran navigator.

"Is a Primist, yes," said Osssian. "Don't you see? He infiltrated us to stop us doing what we're about to do. He's Black Ops. I've never trusted him."

"You're jumping to conclusions, Osssian."

"I'm using my brains."

She considered. She didn't know much about Jonas, but she didn't know much about any of them, not really. Jonas had never said anything to suggest he was a Terran supremacist. But then, he wouldn't, not on this ship. Had he said something about the Chitters, once, when he'd been drunk? Called them cockroaches? Problem was *she'd* been drunk too. She couldn't recall the details, now.

"Osssian, I'm not going to throw someone out of an air-lock because of a piece of metal."

Osssian's tongue flickered. She recognized that gleam in his black eyes. Throwing Jonas off the ship was *precisely* what Osssian wanted to do.

"Osssian, no. This toy isn't proof of anything. And we're crew-mates. We stick together."

Osssian hissed. He actually hissed. Which was usually a bad sign for someone.

"The Primists are fanatics, Captain. They despise us all. One of them would not be a part of this crew without good reason. He won't sit by and watch us recover their codes to sell to the Chitters. You can't leave him here on his own while we board that derelict. He'll call in a Primist destroyer. Or leave us stranded to crash into the asteroid."

Galena considered. This wasn't the first conspiracy Osssian had imagined. If he *had* imagined it. But Jonas had been with them two years, had played his part in several missions. Had he ever helped scavenge from a Primist ship? Perhaps not, now she came to think about it. But then, the Primists were usually on the winning side.

Normally, they left Jonas on board when they went raiding, to keep the ship ready to flee if pursuit came.

Perhaps it would be wise to vary that tactic. Just in case. She looked back out into space. No new flowers. If they were going to act it had to be now.

"77, do you think you can hack into the systems of a Primist dreadnought?"

The Wirehead ¬– *non-organic sentient* she corrected herself – looked up from his console, the familiar lop-sided scowl on his face. Why he chose to adopt the form of this flawed Terran she'd never liked to ask. He could take on any appearance he desired, even adopt the dazzling beauty of a Silicate such as herself. But that was the way he was. She *also* didn't ask why he preferred to use the manual controls rather than jacking directly into the ship's systems, brain–to-brain. 77 was strange. Maybe they all were. But 77 *was* an excellent hacker. If anyone could extract keys from the *Malleus Dei*, it was him.

"I believe I could," said 77.

"Very well. Jonas, take us to the derelict. You, me and 77 will EVA across. It's too dangerous to attempt to dock. Osssian will remain here in case the Primist ships come looking for us with guns blazing. OK?"

As Jonas and 77 began to prepare, she caught Osssian's arm, and spoke to him in a whisper. "While we're away, put that toy back where you found it."

Another flick of that tongue. He glared at her then looked away.

"Yes, Captain. Whatever you say."

*

The ruined hulk of the *Malleus Dei* dwarfed the *Carrion Crow*. They drifted across its shattered hull for what seemed like minutes. The dreadnought's decks gaped open to space where beam-weapon fire had punched through it. Trails of debris streamed out of its wounds as it spiralled down to its death. Up ahead of them loomed the misshapen grey asteroid. They had only sixty minutes to get in, extract the keys and get away.

As Galena led 77 and Jonas across space, she felt a familiar dizziness. Give her solid ground any day. The scale of everything was too hard to grasp in the void. She felt the *Malleus Dei* was tiny, something she could reach out and touch. At the same time it was vast, unreachable.

Then the ragged wound in its starboard hull flew at them. She shot through, 77 and Jonas landing beside her on the shattered floor of the Primists' stellar navigation deck.

"77, start work on that access point over there," she ordered over the comm. "Jack in directly, OK? We don't have long."

77 looked reluctant. Although his expressions were often hard to read, like he had his wiring wrong somewhere. He nodded and crossed to the interface to begin work. Of course, he didn't wear a voidsuit like the rest of them. It still looked weird: a Terran quietly working away in the hard vacuum.

She put 77 out of her mind and turned to Jonas. Could she trust the Terran? Was it really possible he was an agent? It seemed unlikely: after all, they'd recruited *him*, dug him out of one of the rougher bars on Xiang station. Except, had they? They'd needed a pilot and had put out the word. A day later, Jonas had turned up and offered his services. Had they in fact been infiltrated at that point?

"We'll scout around," she said to the Terran. "Check we're alone."

Jonas nodded. She let him go first so she could keep an eye on him. They began to move, blasters held at the ready, working their way from corner to corner, ready for ambush at any moment. The suits made movement clumsy and cut off peripheral vision. At least the hulk had residual power: enough to maintain artificial gravity and emergency lighting. Even, in some sections, a thin atmosphere, enough to send electrical sparks fizzing and flashing from ruined control systems.

As they worked their way forward, Galena opened up a private comm line to the *Crow*.

"Any sign of company, Osssian?"

"None. I'm seeing no ships, Terran or Chitter."

"And you've carried out my orders?"

"Of course."

He wasn't telling her everything. She knew him too well. She could hear background sounds, a thumping and crashing. What was he up to over there? She didn't push it. If she gave them an order they didn't actually want to carry out, they generally ignored it. A scavenger crew wasn't like the military. You had to know when to step back.

"OK. Just keep the drive spun up. If any ships do show, chances are we'll have to make a rapid escape."

A few minutes later she found what she'd been looking for. A dead Terran, his broken body pinned to the deck by a shattered bulkhead. She at least understood the Primists' death rituals. She'd seen enough cremation ships shot into the nearest star after their battles. Dead Terrans had to be sent to the flames or else their souls would be trapped in this universe. A simple funeral pyre would do, but a star was better. Something to do with a connection to the Terrans' original sun, wherever that was. All Primists were duty-bound to this. The question was, what would Jonas do now?

She switched to local comm. "Come on, let's get back. That asteroid looked real solid."

Jonas turned to look at her. It was hard to make out his expression through two layers of visor. For a moment, she thought he was going to refuse. Pull a blaster, reveal himself. Then he stepped towards her.

"OK, Captain. Looks like we're alone on this hulk anyway."

"Yeah."

She waited for him to pass and then followed him once more. So Osssian was mistaken. Jonas was just a regular Terran after all.

Back at the stellar navigation deck, 77 was pulling the data cable attached to the ruined ship's systems from the jack in his cranium. He looked unhappy. But then, he always looked unhappy.

"77? You got the keys?"

"Partial, Captain. These systems are resilient. The codes are entwined throughout the ship so you can't extract them from a single chunk of wreckage."

"So, we don't have keys."

"If I can get access to another node, I'll be able to collate them."

Galena considered. Forty minutes left. They were cutting it very fine. They also really needed to score some data. The *Crow* needed repairs. The crew needed to eat. "OK. The stardrive decks are our best shot. We'll go outside and head aft. Follow me."

She led them back through the ragged hole in the armoured hull and across the surface of the hulk. The asteroid filled half of space now. She felt like it was going to topple onto them. The *Carrion Crow* was a single point of light in the distance, keeping out of the way in case the derelict blew.

They skimmed across the grey surface of the dreadnought, propelled by their suit thrusters. As before, 77 kept up by holding on to an EVA motor. Towards the stern of the *Malleus Dei*, there was a great split in the hull. Lateral stresses had cracked the great ship open. That would give them access to the drive decks. They had to skirt around one of the dreadnought's terawatt beam-weapon emplacements, one of a bank of six. The cannon towered over them as they flew past its barrel. It still pointed out into space, angled towards a long-gone Chitter ship.

Galena landed by the fissure in the hull and prepared to climb down inside. As she turned, a blinking red light upon the cannon caught her attention. She stopped, puzzled. Had the light just started flashing? Kneeling there, wondering what it meant, she felt the sudden vibrations through the hull as the great gun swivelled in its mount.

"What the hell?"

The cannon came to a halt as it locked on to its target. She saw immediately where it was aiming. Sickening alarm thudded through her as she began to shout into the comm.

"Osssian, get the hell out of there. The dreadnought is about to fire."

"Captain, I …"

Osssian's words were lost in a storm of fuzz as the terawatt cannon opened fire. A solid beam of energy lanced out from the *Malleus Dei*, blinding her completely.

The discharge cut out after a few seconds. Galena pulled herself to her feet. She couldn't see the others. She couldn't see anything. She peered out into space, trying to make out what had happened. Perhaps the shot had missed. The *Crow* would be safe. Osssian would be safe. He had to be.

But, as her eyes adjusted, she saw. Another flower now bloomed. The *Carrion Crow* was gone.

"Osssian!" She shouted into the comm. No response other than the fuzz of static. "Osssian!" she shouted again, furious now, as if it was all the Saurian's fault.

"Captain."

It was Jonas beside her, one hand on her arm. Galena fired her suit thrusters to get away from him. She saw what he had done. Osssian had been right after all. How the hell Jonas had managed to take control of the dreadnought's cannon, she didn't know. She'd watched him every moment. She pulled her blaster from her belt and levelled it at him.

"What are you doing?" said Jonas. "What's going on?" The Terran sounded panicky over the comm line. Terrified. She paid no attention. He was clever.

"I'm sending you straight to Hell where you belong," she said.

"Captain, you have this all wrong. I didn't …"

Jonas's voice cut out as a thin beam of white energy lanced through his visor and out the other side of his head. He began to topple backwards from the force of it, spinning through space, a delicate arc of blood spraying from his head.

"What the…"

She hadn't fired. She knew she hadn't fired. She twisted round, confused. 77 stood calmly on the surface of the hull, blaster in hand. For once, he was smiling.

"What the hell are you doing, 77?"

His voice came over the comm from the pickup he wore on his cheek. "Isn't it obvious?"

"*You're* the Primist? But that's insane."

"Is it, Captain?"

"Yes, it damn well is! You're not human. You're not one of them. You're a machine. A creature of logic."

"Tell me, Captain, do you ever wonder why I adopted this form? Why I choose to look like a Terran?"

"I assumed you had your reasons." She tried to think of a plan. Distract him, kill him. She came up blank. His reactions were a thousand times better than her own. Beyond him, the solid bulk of the asteroid filled space. She had to get away. Except, 77 wasn't going to let her, was he? And where would she escape *to*?

77 seemed unconcerned by their approaching death. "Five years ago, I was part of a scout crew. A Primist assault squad attacked our ship. We killed a few of them but their forces overwhelmed us. I was shot through the head. My systems were damaged but I was able to reactivate. And when I did, I found I was … changed. I saw everything differently. I began to understand the Primists. Really understand them. It was a miracle."

"You were brain damaged."

"No. I was … cured. Fixed. Saved. I begged for mercy in the name of God. And they let me live, Captain. They let me live."

"And why would they do that?"

"I vowed to adopt the broken form of one of the Terrans I'd killed. Become one of them."

"So, the way you look … it's some sort of punishment? That's twisted, 77. That's insane."

"No, not insane. A fitting penance."

"But you just killed Jonas. One of your own."

"Jonas deserved to die. He damned himself the moment he took part in this mission. And now we will die. And I will pass through the wormholes to paradise and you will not."

She could see no way out of this. She would never see Arralith again. Only one thing she could do. She raised her blaster to fire. But before she could even level her weapon he moved. Drew, aimed. Blaster fire flashed out once again.

She screamed, knowing it was the end. But there was no pain. Why was there no pain? Why was she even still alive to know there was no pain?

She opened her eyes. 77's head had been neatly sliced from his body. Electrical components trailed from his neck as he rolled backwards through space. Another figure flew forwards, grasping hold of the severed head. None of it made any sense. The newcomer turned to look at her.

"Come on," said Osssian over the comm. "We have to get away before the impact."

Osssian fired his thrusters and shot away from the dreadnought. Not stopping to question, Galena sped after him at maximum acceleration.

The *Crow's* battered escape pod hung in space a kilometre off the derelict. It took forever to reach it; their suits were not able to generate much thrust. The dreadnought would impact the asteroid at any moment, and then they would be cut to pieces by a tide of high-velocity debris. But finally, they were there. Osssian flew into the waiting air-lock. Galena followed, grateful just to be out of the void. Before the pod's atmosphere had even fully cycled, its engines powered up and hurled them away. There were no screens here; she couldn't see what was happening outside. Were they far enough away to survive? Then ejecta from the blast began to hit them, throwing them against the bulkheads, rattling and shaking the pod with repeated shocks. They withstood it for long, long moments, until Galena was sure the pod would be pummelled into pieces, and she and Osssian along with it.

*

Finally, the bucking calmed down. The pod had survived. The two of them had survived. They lay on the cramped floor: bruised, exhausted, but alive.

"You weren't on board the *Crow* when it was hit?" she asked

"I thought something like this might happen. I took the pod and came over while you were inside the dreadnought."

She nodded. It hurt just to nod. "It was good work, Osssian. But it was all for nothing. We won't survive long. We have no ship and no codes to sell."

"Not true, Captain." Osssian's black eyes gleamed. But not with anger, now. If anything, it looked like amusement.

"What do you mean, lizard?"

"We have 77," said Osssian. "His head at least."

"So?"

"Don't you see? He must have been communicating with the Primists all this time. He must have the capability at least. He'll have encryption codes of his own, buried in his electronic brain. Primist Black Ops codes. How much do you think the Chitter High Command will pay for those?"

She considered. The Saurian was damn well right. Enough, even, for a down payment on a new *Carrion Crow* if they were lucky. Perhaps even one with a full set of working space seals.

"Osssian?"

"Yes?"

"Start hailing for Chitter ships."

"Yes, Captain."

"And Osssian?"

"Yes?"

"Next time I accuse you of being paranoid, you will remind me about all this, won't you?"

The Saurian's tongue flicked out and in. "Oh, I'll be sure to. Captain."

The Last Flight of the Carrion Crow is another space opera adventure written for the Dark Expanse game universe. Chitters and Primist humans appear again, as do some of the other races within the game: Saurians like Ossian and Silicates like Galena. The story appeared within the game universe in 2014.

A MOTE IN THE VOID

The clanging sound had been there for several minutes before Kelly really noticed it. Everything on the damn ship rattled or vibrated or squealed. She looked around, floating there in the cramped cylinder of the work habitat, trying to figure out where the new noise came from. It sounded like something banging on the outside of the hull. How the hell could that be?

Maybe some part of the comm rig knocked loose in the meteor strike, or a solar cell flapping around. Power was certainly down, although she expected that, this far out. *Some* damn thing was broken out there. She laddered herself along the grabs and flew aft to press her ear against the curving aluminium bulkhead. Whatever had come loose was only centimetres from her head, out there in the void of space. Bang, tap, tap, tap, tap, bang...

Which made no sense. There obviously couldn't be something just *flapping around*. It came to her it must be Richards. Somehow still alive and trying to signal to her by banging on the hull. But, she'd seen him through the observation ports, drifting away after the meteor – or whatever the hell it was – struck. Seen him tumbling head-over-heels into space, umbilical flailing around and venting

02. He was alive then, judging by the way he waved his arms around and kicked his legs. But they'd lost comms. She'd never know how long he'd lasted out there. Him and the Ares II's only EVA suit.

She zoomed herself back up to the flight deck, to see if anything was visible from the ports now. She could make out Mars quite clearly: a definite circle, reddy-brown, dead ahead. But she needed to see the other way, back along the fuselage. Damn shame the meteor strike had taken out the steerable cameras too. She pressed her face against the carbonplex window, trying to make out what had come loose. Earth would need to know. Damn it, *she* needed to know. This thrown-together ship was the only thing keeping her alive.

She could see *something* just visible in the distorted glass at the edge of the window, grey and snake-like, flapping to-and-fro. What the hell was that? The other end of Richard's umbilical, she guessed.

She flipped open the comms link to report the situation to Earth. Even if they replied immediately it would be thirty minutes before she got a response. With Earth on the other side of the sun, communications were fuzzy anyway. She hadn't had a reply for two days now. Still, she sent in her report, trying to sound calm, matter-of-fact. She sat and waited for a response, knowing there was no point but craving some word anyway. With Richards gone she was utterly alone. More alone than any other human had ever been. She tried not to think about it. All she heard from the comm was the background hiss of the void.

Damn mission has been cursed from the start. Thrown together in too much of a hurry, that was the problem. Earth had lost contact with the Ares I as it neared Mars and suddenly they needed a rescue mission. Ares II wasn't supposed to be commissioned for another year, but they'd fast-tracked it into service, only two of its five pods habitable. Sent her and Richards off against all the rules to find out what the hell had happened to the first manned mission to Mars.

While she waited, she thought once again about the distress signals they'd received from Bohanna, Achebe, Jones, Edrickson and Tzu on the Ares I. Their frantic, garbled screaming had become the soundtrack to her nightmares. What the hell had happened to them? They were the sanest people she knew. The psychological effects of prolonged spaceflight and confinement were well understood, sure. Still, it sounded like all five had flipped at the same moment.

Their insane ramblings replayed in her head now. Their words had been clear enough once the techs defuzzed the signal. *Out there ... vast! My God, it's ... that eye, that eye looking in at us...*

That was Bohanna. Screaming. *Nothing* ever phased Bohanna. The skipper of the Ares I was the most laid-back person Kelly had ever met. There'd been trouble from fundamentalists before they blasted off, a religious sect raving about them invading God's domain or some such bullshit. Police said they were dangerous people, fanatics. Instead of ignoring them, Bohanna had met with them, explained the true nature of space from an astrophysicist's perspective. A stupid, futile thing to do but he'd enjoyed every moment of it, despite the crazies' warnings and threats. And six months later, there he was, screaming all that gibberish into the comm.

She looked up. The banging had stopped. Maybe something had worked itself loose. But how could that be? She shook her head to put it out of her mind. She needed to stay focussed and she needed to stay busy. Some mass hysteria had swept through the first ship. Her job was to get out there, find out what had happened, then slingshot back to Earth with the facts.

Then the banging started again. Alarm thumped through her. It had moved. How could it have moved? It came from over on the port side now. Her throat squeezed dry. She berated herself for being so jumpy. Was this how it had started on the Ares I? Some minor malfunction, some little sound sending their imaginations off into overdrive? She wasn't going to let it happen to her. It *had* to be Richards, still out there somehow. Maybe he'd managed to use the umbilical to propel himself back to the ship. That must be it. She had to open the hatch for him immediately, haul him inside.

They didn't have another EVA rig but they did have vacuum suits in case the ship depressurised. It would keep her alive for long enough. She wouldn't have thrusters but she could pull herself along the fuselage, grab Richard's umbilical. It was risky, but they'd trained to do worse. Nothing could go wrong if she tethered herself. The thought of no longer being alone made her heart pound with excitement.

She thought about telling Earth what she was about to do. Then decided against it. Probably best the people waiting back there didn't know.

She shrugged her way into the suit. They'd practised the procedure a thousand times back on Earth. The suit felt uncomfortable, pinching her limbs and restricting her movements. She ignored it. With the hatch access sealed off from the rest of the ship she pumped the air out to avoid explosive decompression, tethered herself, then instructed the hatch to unseal. When it was open, she pushed herself through.

The vastness of space yawned around her. After the cramped quarters of the ship, the sight of it made her dizzy, stretching off to infinity in all directions. She was an insignificant mote in these fathomless gulfs. It felt like the unblinking stars stared at her from every direction.

She pushed it all out of her mind. Focus. She had to find Richards. She faced forwards, looking along the smooth metal curves of the ship, Mars dead ahead. She began to twirl herself around to look for him. The comms array was just to her left. Or it should have been. But it had been sheered off the hull by some immense force. A few cables were left, hanging loose from the fuselage like dead worms. Her communications had been going nowhere. How long had they been going nowhere?

She pivoted further around, and then she saw it.

The vast being that had attached itself to the back of the Ares regarded her with a single, enormous eye. It dwarfed the ship. Its shape and size were hard to grasp against the darkness of space. But the lights of the Ares, and the way the being eclipsed the background stars, suggested an ovoid bulk, grey and ancient as moon rock. It lashed countless appendages around, tentacles that ended with a curved claw the size of her body. One claw skittered across the smooth hull beside her, trying to gain a hold, trying to break in through the metal.

She knew the sound it would be making in there. *Bang, tap, tap, tap, tap, bang.* Had it been out here all along, hooked onto the ship while she worked and slept inside, oblivious?

She stared at the monstrosity while her mind reeled. No, it couldn't be. Such a creature didn't exist. Could not exist. Some small, logical part of her brain still worked. The prolonged isolation had affected her after all. She'd listened too long to the babbling of the crew of the Ares I. To Bohanna's last words. *Space is theirs, not ours! Always theirs!*

She had to get back inside, seal the hatch, inform Earth. She had to think. But before she could act a claw caught her, plucking her away from the ship. The line tethering her to the Ares snapped as the star-creature sent her spinning off into the void. She spun past its enormous eye. It was lifeless, rudimentary like a shark's, yet she knew the creature saw her, perceived her. She felt a high-pitched screaming sound ring around in her brain.

Kelly screamed wordlessly into her suit comm, but there was no one to hear.

Like the story that follows it, A Mote in the Void is clearly Lovecraftian in tone, and I've grouped the two of them together as they're similar in theme (if not setting). I like the way this story starts out as science fiction and becomes something else completely. It was published (and recorded) in the Lovecraft eZine in 2012.

A SARCOPHAGUS IN OBSIDIAN

"Don't work too late, Pamela. You know the mummies come out of the sarcophagus at midnight."

It was their usual joke. Sam – Professor Drake – stood over by the door, shrugging on his coat in readiness for the London winter night. Pamela made a face of mock terror towards the three-metre cube of black rock that dominated their underground lair. It was perhaps the greatest treasure of the British Museum's *Unidentified* collection. It was certainly the most immoveable. Generations of academics and students had come down there to measure it, tap it, ponder it, write papers about it. Generations of which she was merely the latest.

"Don't worry," she said. "I keep vials of Holy Water in my handbag."

"Won't help you, my dear. Completely wrong mythology. Walk you to the Tube?" Sam was possibly the only person in the world who could call her *my dear* and get away with it. Somehow coming from him it managed to be endearing rather than patronising. He was old school. Also, a damn fine archaeologist and endlessly generous with his time. She'd miss him when her placement came to an end and she had to go back to university for her final year.

"Thanks," she said, "but I'm going to work on the carvings a little longer."

"Ah, the mysterious runic inscriptions," he said as he patted his pockets, searching for the pass that would allow him to escape the museum's basement labyrinth. He was forever losing his keys, his glasses, the thread of his sentences. Mind on higher things. "The great Riddle of the Sarcophagus. Sometimes I wonder if some joker in antiquity didn't carve random lines on the thing knowing we'd waste *decades* of our lives trying to decipher them."

"I've more or less got the high-res scans done," Pamela replied. "I might get something if I run them through the pattern-matching algorithms."

"My, my. The things they can do these days."

She wasn't taken in by his absent-minded professor act at all. He'd *written* most of those algorithms. "It's worth a try at least," she said. "Might turn up something."

"Of course. Perhaps tomorrow for the supper? If you could bear being seen with a fossil like me we could stop off for a spot of supper *en route* and discuss early Babylonian burial rituals."

He was a sweetheart, his intentions utterly honourable. And always a witty and amusing companion with a glass of wine in his hand. But she was in no hurry to leave. The simple truth was she loved having the basement to herself. Loved the slow quiet that settled on the place when the rest of humanity had left. Down there, alone, everything was calm and measured and the world made sense.

"Supper would be lovely," she said. "But I don't want to distract you from your *magnum opus*."

"Ah, no. That would never do." He was – famously – putting the finishing touches to his life's work: *A Sarcophagus in Obsidian*, twenty years in the writing, drawing together all the threads of human knowledge about the mysterious object. A volume she might have some small mention in if her researches ever unearthed anything of interest. A credit like that could kick-start her career. The whisper was he'd reached some remarkable conclusion about the object. *Solved the mystery* people said. So far, he wasn't letting anything on.

Looking as delighted as if he'd unearthed the Holy Grail, Sam fished out his badge from an inside pocket. "Very well. Just make sure all the alarms are activated when you leave. Otherwise no one will know the mummies have arisen to terrorize London."

"Will do. See you tomorrow."

When she was sure she was alone she took a moment to step around the sarcophagus, stroking its smooth surface with her fingertips. Something she liked to do. It fascinated them all, of course. They could spend months puzzling over other items in the collection – corroded brass mechanisms and fragments of carvings – but everything in the Department of Unidentified Objects revolved around the sarcophagus. Metaphorically *and* literally. It had stood there for over a hundred and fifty years, so heavy that desks and machinery and cupboards and whole rooms had to be built around it each time they reorganized. Sam had titled his book from the label given it by an unknown Victorian collector. But *A Sarcophagus in Obsidian* was clearly fanciful. It surely wasn't a sarcophagus. They weren't even sure it was obsidian.

It had been found buried in the sands of the upper Nile late in the eighteenth century. Stylistically it had been categorized as early Sumerian but in truth it was unlike anything else from that civilisation. Its polished surfaces flowed like melted wax, like some modernist twentieth-century nightmare. As well as the ogham-like runes etched along its corners there were also depictions of something like tentacled krakens on its surfaces. The demons or gods or whatever they were strode through fields of stars, while, below, women and men played trumpets and drums. Others held their arms high, either in rapture or fear.

The sarcophagus wasn't even a proper cube, its planes

and angles all oddly askew, nothing parallel or symmetrical. It had no opening yet its weight – if the Victorian measurements were to be believed – suggested it was either honeycombed rock or actually hollow. X-ray scans had revealed nothing but a grey fog. Objects had reportedly been heard rolling around inside when it was lifted into place in the museum. Over the years, more than one person had suggested cutting into it, but the authorities had never sanctioned such an act of cultural destruction.

Pamela glanced around the room, making doubly sure she was alone. Then she pressed her ear to the cold stone. There's been students in the past who'd refused to be left alone with the sarcophagus, claiming to have heard scraping and knocking sounds coming from it. Once or twice even she'd imagined hearing faint scratching sounds. Fanciful, of course. It was only a tube train rumbling through its tunnel deep below them, or the stone ticking as it cooled down. Tonight, there was nothing, except for a distant *hushing* noise that was probably in her own ears, like listening to a shell and hearing the sea. She even talked to the sarcophagus on occasion, as if she only had to find the right words to persuade it to give up its secrets. All clearly ridiculous. These were small acts she took perverse pleasure in, despite herself. Only patient scientific research would solve the riddle.

She sat back down at her computer, her back to the cube and the quite room, to return to checking the scans on her computer screen.

*

Two hours later, just as she was sliding her own pass into the door to lock it behind her, a rhythmic buzzing sound broke the silence of the underground room she'd just left. Pamela paused, puzzled. She noted that her heart was suddenly pounding away in her chest. Who or what did she think could be down there with her? No one had come into the basement since Sam left.

The buzzing came again, angrier, like a hornet was trapped in a box somewhere. Puzzled, she stepped back inside the room. The darkness within was absolute. She paused for a moment with her hand hovering over the light switch, imagining all sorts of scenes in the room before her.

When she flicked the lights on everything looked the same, the room dominated by the angled planes of the sarcophagus. The sound came again, louder. She approached the object slowly, knowing it was ridiculous but unable to stop herself. Sometimes she had the weird sensation it was calling to her, drawing her in. It felt a little like that now. Her mind playing tricks. You could be as rational as you liked but you couldn't stop your ape hindbrain seeing demons in the shadows. There was *always* a rational explanation.

As she made her way around the cube the buzzing came again, this time from behind her. The far corner of the room. The weird planes of the object often made sounds come at you from odd angles. Whatever was making the insistent noise, it wasn't the sarcophagus. It was something on the desk Sam used.

Piles of papers lay there, organized in ways only he would ever understand. One of the piles was shaking. An empty paper cup from one of Sam's endless brews of tea danced forwards and fell to the floor. The papers slid after it in a brief avalanche. And there, on the table, was the source of the sound. Sam's ancient mobile phone, buzzing away, creeping across the desk as it shook itself angrily to attract attention. He must have forgotten it when he'd left for the evening. She found herself exhaling, like she'd been holding her breath all this time.

She picked the phone up and pressed the answer button.

"Hello?" For some reason she found herself half-whispering.

"Pamela? Is that you?"

"Uh, yes. Who is this?"

"It's me! Sam! Couldn't find my infernal telephone so I thought I'd ring it and see who answered. Where are you?"

His voice sounded weirdly tinny over the phone. Reception wasn't great in the basement. "I'm here," she replied. "Still in the Department. Just leaving."

"Ah, wonderful. Thought someone had whipped the thing from my pocket on the underground."

"I don't think anyone would bother stealing such an antique."

"Ah, no, probably right," he replied. "Listen, Pamela, since you're still there, could you get into my computer and email me some documents? I managed to forget them, too, and I need them for the chapter I'm working on."

"Uh, sure. But I don't know your password."

"No. Of course. And better not just announce it into the ether, eh? Still I'm sure you can work it out. Think chaos monsters and primordial goddesses. Four, five millennia ago."

Wedging the phone under her ear, Pamela waggled the mouse on his computer and, at the password box, typed *Tiamat*.

"Got it, Sam. I'm in. That's probably not a great password given your interests, you know. You didn't even use a *1* instead of the *i*."

"The suspicious age we live in. OK. Now, there's a folder called *Necropolis of Saqqara* on the desktop. If you could zip up what's in there and send it me? Only, Pamela, I'm going to have to ask you something a little odd here. I want you to promise you won't read any of it, OK?"

"Don't want to spoil the surprise ending of the book?"

Some of his usual bonhomie had slipped from his voice when he replied. "Actually, it's not that. I've recently finished translating some hieroglyphics from the necropolis. They're a millennium or so later but I believe they refer to our sarcophagus. And, well, the implications of what they say are rather … odd. Disturbing you might say."

"How do you mean?"

He paused for a moment before replying. "Once I'm sure of my analysis I'll explain everything. Entirely likely I've got the wrong end of the stick, in which case I'd make a complete ass of myself if I told you my current thinking. I have your word?"

"Of course. I'll send the documents over to your home address."

"Lovely. And you must let me buy you that supper tomorrow as thanks, yes?"

"Promise."

When she'd hung up, she opened the folder. As well as the word-processing documents there were twenty or thirty JPEG images. Only tiny thumbnails were visible, but she could see they depicted close-ups of Egyptian hieroglyphics. Zipping everything up, she fired them off in an email to Sam, joking about his ancient phone, offering to drop it round at the *Antiquities* department on her way home.

Once the large email had sent, she set about shutting his computer down. Something stopped her. All his files were still in front of her. The answers to the riddle of the sarcophagus might be among them. No one would know if she took a quick look, would they? She'd promised she wouldn't, sure, but maybe she'd spot something he'd missed. Something that might help him. Something that might get her that credit in his book. This might be her only chance.

The word he'd used – *disturbing* – was odd, though. Whatever the translations said they were ancient history. Much as she liked her supervisor, she sometimes wondered if his mind hadn't wandered off the path of proper scholarly research into murkier waters. More than once she'd heard him muttering the names of gods or demons who didn't feature in any ancient mythos she'd ever studied. On one occasion she'd found him poring over a map of the Pacific Ocean, drawing lines that intersected at a particular spot. When she'd asked him what was there he'd replied, *Absolutely nothing. Which is very odd, don't you think? Very odd indeed.*

She flicked through the JPEGs. Where was the harm in that? Anyone with a permit from the Egyptian authorities could go and see them. She knew enough to interpret some of the glyphs and identify at least a few of the cartouches, but she could make out nothing from them that was in any way *disturbing*.

Unable to resist, and glancing around one more time to make sure she was still alone, she opened the first word-processing document and began to read.

*

Another hour later, she closed everything down and sat back. Her mind whirled. Dear God. Sam hadn't just wandered off the path so much as sprinted in the opposite direction. His conjectures about the object were … wild. He'd be a laughing-stock if word ever got out. The great Professor Drake and his star monsters. It actually appeared he'd accepted some of the ancient stories as plain truth. He'd carefully and rigorously correlated accounts from all across ancient civilization and seen patterns. Seen *proofs*. And come to conclusions that were utterly crazy.

She wished she'd never read the documents. Could she pretend she hadn't? Carry on as before knowing what he secretly believed? Probably not. And when his book was published and his reputation was ruined, what about all the others who had studied under him? What about *her*? She'd be tainted too. Somehow, she had to stop him going public, that was clear.

The hieroglyphics from the Necropolis of Saqqara were central to his argument. They included the outline of a crooked square, which Sam claimed represented the sarcophagus. He asserted that a secretive sect, priests of Ptah, had transported the object to Egypt and housed it within a now lost temple. There'd they *worshipped* it. Except, *worshipped*, as Sam argued at length, was the wrong word. If his conclusions were to be believed, the priests had constructed their temple out of fear rather than religious awe. They'd built their stone walls not to protect the sarcophagus but to *contain* it. A symbol often interpreted as *tomb* should, Sam argued, be read as *cage* or *seal*.

There was a cartouche, too. The name of someone or something. Elements of the name suggested *stars* and *giants*. But Sam hadn't been able to come up with a translation. Nevertheless, he'd insisted it represented some denizen of the underworld. A god unknown to conventional Egyptology. A demon that was contained within the obsidian cage, the runes and symbols carved upon the stone the magical seals that kept it entrapped.

Pamela turned to contemplate the ancient black rock as she considered her options. If she simply talked to Sam she'd never persuade him. The great Professor Drake wasn't going to change his mind for her, for all his politeness. But if she *showed* him? Then he could rage at her all he liked, but he'd have to believe her.

She saw what she had to do. From his analysis of a clay tablet from Babylon he'd identified a passage which, he said, formed a rite linked to the sarcophagus. *The Opening of the Doorway*. This, Sam claimed, spelled out how to release the being that slumbered within the object. This had to be the *disturbing* possibility he'd been alluding to. The tablet had been fought over many times in antiquity as one sect tried to release the trapped demon and another fought to prevent them. Sam's own notes made it very clear he actually believed the rite would work. That some impossible, ancient horror would emerge from the stone cage. He'd actually written the words, *The unleashing of a nameless nightmare older than humanity.*

The thought of him going public with the claim was terrible. No. There was only one way. *She* would perform the rite, then and there. She'd film herself doing it as proof. And in the morning, she could quietly show him what she'd done. Show him nothing had happened. She would save him from himself. Make him see the ancient horrors existed only in his head.

There was a series of words to the rite. An *incantation* he'd called it. Clearly, they were only a way of timing a series of movements from an age that didn't have clocks. The sarcophagus was a device; an ancient mechanism. Certain of the carvings on it could be pressed like buttons – or so Sam claimed. None of them could possibly function now, of course. Still, if she could practice the words and the movements. Press *this* figure, then *this* and now *this*, she could show him. Save him from his folly. Save herself, too.

She spent an hour practising the sequence of movements. The dance she had to perform around the cube, reaching for each button. Five complete circumnavigations before the final motion, touching two of the krakens on two adjacent planes of the object at the same moment.

When she was ready she paused for a moment, letting her breathing calm. Had anyone else ever done what she was about to, centuries or millennia ago? Performed the rite only to find that nothing happened? She'd never know. She clicked *record* on the video camera she'd rigged up and began. Reaching for the first point, the second star from the left on *this* plane, she began to mutter the timing words to herself, began her dance…

When it was done she stood back. The room remained silent. Strangely she felt disappointed, as if she'd half-expected something to happen. Smiling at herself she stopped the camera. Tomorrow she'd show Sam the recording. He'd have to see sense. And then all would be well. He might even be grateful enough to give her a co-author credit.

As she picked up her bag to leave, satisfied, another sound came to her ears. A distant rumbling in the walls. She paused mid-step, puzzled, listening. An explosion somewhere? That had to be it. That was all it was.

She circled past the sarcophagus, wary for some reason, keeping one eye on it. She suddenly wanted to be away. She'd spent too long alone down there on her own. The sound came again. This time there was another quality to it too: a discordant trumpeting, half way between a fanfare and a scream. Once again it seemed to be coming from the sarcophagus. She couldn't stop herself pausing and pressing her ear to the black stone to listen.

The trumpeting blared out again, louder. And there could be no doubt. This time it was coming from within.

Pamela backed away, half-falling over a chair. Her throat constricted, stifling a cry. This couldn't be happening. There could be no *nameless nightmare*. The sarcophagus had stood intact for hundreds of years. Thousands of years. There couldn't be anything inside. The sound grew louder still: a grating, bellowing chorus, as if a hundred maddened elephants were trapped within the object.

Cracks began to appear on one of its surfaces, running in crazed patterns between the runic markings along the edges. Connecting them up. *That* was what they were. Pamela backed away into a wall, staring in open-mouthed horror at what she was seeing. What she'd done. With a rumbling crash, one whole face of the object shattered into broken shards and rattled into rubble on the floor.

From where Pamela stood, only a thin sliver of what lay inside was visible. She could see sand: a whole desert of sand, stretching away to an impossible horizon, brightly lit under an orange-red sky. Shimmering in the distance, details hard to see, stood the towers of some city. She didn't recognize it. But the weird planes and angles were clearly like those of the sarcophagus.

Drawn to move, she edged around to stand directly in front of the opening. A solid wall of dry desert heat blasted into her face. With the shift in perspective, she saw what was making the bellowing sound. The line in the sand it had made as it dragged itself forwards stretched back all the way to those distant towers. Scale was hard to discern but the being looked as vast as buildings: a hulking grey creature, something like the krakens depicted in the carvings. A thing that could not exist, with hundreds of writhing tentacles for limbs and a misshapen head that contained a beaked mouth and a single, round eye. The eye was unblinking, staring forwards. Staring at *her*.

The creature trumpeted its roar: a mixture of rage and exultation that scraped across Pamela's bones. The sound triggered ancient instincts: the urgent need to flee. But her legs were suddenly weak and wouldn't obey. Finally, her throat began to work. She began to scream even as a first tentacle reached from inside the sarcophagus to feel its way out into the museum basement.

In the corner of the room, unheeded now, Sam's ancient phone began to buzz once more.

A Sarcophagus in Obsidian, like A Mote in the Void, is a Cthulhu-esque story, and now that I reread the two I see there are clearly similarities between them. Perhaps the two entities described are the same creature. Again, this story starts out as scientific and rational and ends up somewhere else completely. To my mind, there's something of W. B. Yeats' rough beast slouching towards Bethlehem to be born in this story, too. It was published in Hypnos magazine in 2017.

A TROUBLESOME SPECK

Lord Nebula's three hearts pounded away in his upper thorax. Surely *this* gift would woo the Empress? His rainbow forests had left her distinctly unimpressed. She'd looked positively bored when he'd revealed the flawless diamond planet. This was his last chance. Since she'd announced she'd disposed of her previous Consort, a thousand suitors – monarchs and plutocrats from across the galaxy – had vied for her affections. Each trying to outdo the others.

"If I may show you the way, Your Supremeness?"

The Empress regarded him. The glowing white microfilaments of her flowing gown lit up her faces, making her faceted eyes sparkle. She nodded her two heads in consent and held out a tentacle. One of her lowest pair; the ones casual acquaintances could touch without the Imperial Guard unleashing beam-weapon death from their orbital platforms.

Lord Nebula led her carefully up the crystal path towards the white-stoned folly he'd constructed atop the little hill. "I call this the Moon Temple, Your Supremeness," he said. "Although there will be no moons tonight as both are well below the horizon. The view will be perfect."

Night had fallen now, the warm air richly scented with ultrajasmine. An occasional sparklebug fizzed and danced through the air around them. Lord Nebula consulted his internal clock, suddenly terrified they'd miss the moment. Timing was everything. But they still had a few minutes. He was OK. Everything was going to plan.

It had taken his celestial engineers months to create what he was about to show her. Although *time* was not a particularly meaningful concept, here, given the vast distances involved. His people had travelled far into the past again and again to make the necessary adjustments. The speed of light was such a bore, but it had its uses. And now, finally, everything was ready.

They stood together on the prepared spot, the familiar stars blazing out around them. "If I may, I should provide a short countdown," said Lord Nebula. The Empress nodded her heads again. He consulted his clock again and began to count,

"5, 4, 3, 2, 1, *now.*"

There was a moment of absolute silence as she took in what he had done. He watched her faces for her reaction. The world turned beneath his feet. He saw wonder in her eyes. Delight. He looked upwards to see for himself. There they were: the seven letters of her name spelled out across the night sky, perfectly formed in the ancient script. They'd done it. Prodded over two hundred stars into supernova at *just* the right historical moments. Extinguished a thousand other stars, too, consuming them with artificial black-holes to clear their canvas. The cost of the whole thing was … incalculable. But the effect was perfect, glorious. Her name written across the galaxy. How could she refuse him now?

"It is beautiful, Lord Nebula, truly. A most dazzling gift. But…"

Panic stopped one of his hearts. Fortunately, his two newer ones were strong. He really had to get the oldest replaced. "*But*, Your Supremeness? Is there a mistake?"

"No mistake, my lord. Just … a slight flaw. There, do you not see? In the middle of the fifth rune. A spot. A speck."

Lord Nebula gazed upwards, trying to make out the faint star. By squinting he could just make out a tiny point of light in the otherwise dark circle of space.

Silently he communicated with his Chief Celestial Engineer. "Kraas. There is a star where there shouldn't be."

"What? Where?"

"In the centre of the *Om* rune. It's ruining everything."

"My lord, we discussed this. It's magnitude twelve, all-but invisible to the eye."

"The Empress can see it. Remove it now."

"But that system is inhabited. Seven billion sapients on the third planet. You remember we discussed it? The planet called *Earth?*"

"I don't care what they call it, I call it *in the way*. Remove it immediately."

"Yes, my lord. Of course, my lord."

Lord Nebula turned to the Empress. "My apologies, Your Supremeness. My engineers are heading across the galaxy and back in time even as we speak. We'll see the troublesome speck removed at any moment."

They both turned to gaze into the night sky. Lord Nebula's two good hearts raced while the third gave out again. There was a moment's pause.

"And there it goes," he said. "Now it's perfect." He turned to look at her.

The Empress smiled. And smiled. She reached out to him with a *middle* tentacle. The ones she used for close friends and favourites. "Very good," she said. "You must come and visit me in my palace, Lord Nebula. I believe we have much to talk about."

A Troublesome Speck is a light-hearted story after the cosmic horrors of the previous two – although it does casually mention the obliteration of our planet so it's in some ways much worse. Still, I thought it was a fun little idea for a story. It was printed in Spaceports and Spidersilk in 2012.

THE SWORD OF POWER

Ulrik held the Sword of Power over the Archdemon, his face reflected in the depths of those black eyes.

"Now die, hellspawn."

It took Ulrik a moment to recognize the deep growling sound. "Why do you laugh?"

"Because a thousand years ago I said that to the previous Archdemon. Before I slayed them and the curse passed to me."

"Lies. You would say anything to save yourself. Now die."

The great eyes closed as Ulrik struck.

Light flaring up the sword seared Ulrik's flesh. Seared, but also filled him with raging power.

Ulrik began to laugh. A deep, growling laugh.

This very short story was written for an anthology of 100-word stories (it is exactly that long), and the obvious challenge was to create a complete narrative with a beginning, a middle and an end in so short a space. My approach was to capture a turning-point in a much larger saga, the events of which are only suggested. It was published in the 100 Worlds Anthology in 2013.

THE STARS ARE TINY LIGHTS ON A PERFECT BLACK DOME

"Chancellor, it's Zend, at the University. One of your research students. I think you should come and see something."

The voice on the other end of the line was groggy. The Chancellor didn't bother to keep the irritation from his voice. "Are you aware what hour it is, Zend?"

"Sorry, yes, it's late, I know. Or I mean early, depending on how you look at it."

"Have we inadvertently fabricated another black hole in Astrophysics? Has the Bio lab released a pathogen capable of eliminating all known life in the galaxy? Because if it's anything less than either of those things I'm not going to be pleased, Zend. Not at all."

"It's ... it's nothing like that, Chancellor. Something rather more... philosophical has cropped up."

"*Philosophical!* At this time in the morning?"

"Yes, Chancellor, I'm sorry, it's just ... it's The Experiment."

"Which experiment? There are hundreds of experiments. What are you talking about?"

"*The* Experiment. You know, the big globe in the

faculty lobby. *The Experiment.*"

There was, finally, a pause from the other end as the Chancellor grasped what Zend was talking about. His voice was noticeably shakier as he replied. "Are you saying something has happened after all this time?"

"There are lights on it. Flickering electric lights. I don't know what they mean but they look like alarms. They're flashing in a way that suggests … urgency."

"What colour are these lights?"

"Red. Is that bad, Chancellor? They look bad."

"I have no idea! The Experiment hasn't done anything for a hundred years. No one has any clue what flashing lights mean. No one knew it even had flashing lights."

"There's also a sort of mechanical buzzing sound, like a clockwork alarm bell ringing."

"I'm coming in, Zend. Tell nobody else and keep the doors locked until I arrive. No one else is to know about this, understood?"

"Understood, Chancellor."

*

Within the hour, four of them stood in a circle around the shining, ten metre sphere that had dominated GalTech's lobby for as long as anyone could remember. Normally the high hall echoed with a thousand conversations, with footfall and skitter and slither. Now it was filled only by an eerie, echoey silence. Zend could see his own distorted reflection in the coppery surface of the orb above him. It gave off its familiar smells of oil and grease and steam. The red lights continued to flicker in rings.

The orb was a remarkable device, a feat of early metaphysical engineering, although the jets of steam that occasionally whooshed out of it always alarmed Zend. There were plenty more advanced micro-universes these days, but the huffing, rumbling original fascinated him. He'd been studying it for two years, topping it up with water and oil, tapping it, peering into it. Partly because no one else in the University seemed interested.

Next to him stood the Chancellor, the Archdean herself, and also Professor Overarch, GalTech's Head Philosopher, called in especially for the crisis.

"Are you sure it isn't merely a malfunction?" asked the Archdean. She was, Zend knew, a historian by training. She could probably drone on for hours about the significance of the Experiment to the development of galactic scientific culture, the breakthroughs it had heralded. She probably had little idea how it worked.

Which, to be fair, was probably true for most of them.

"Let me show you," said Zend.

A movable flight of five wooden steps gave access to the various spy holes and scopes distributed around the sphere. Zend wheeled the steps into place so that the aged and somewhat shaky Archdean could ascend to peer through one of devices.

Her voice was muffled by her billowing sleeve as she adjusted the tiny focus wheels. "It looks the same as ever. The same tiny blue planet, the oceans, the clouds. Remarkable, truly. I'd forgotten how beautiful it was. The life forms on it survive?"

"Try adjusting the focal length and you'll see," called up Zend. "That scope is positioned very precisely but you'll need to use maximum magnification."

There came a series of muffled sounds as the Archdean battled with the controls on the unfamiliar contraption. "Ah. Yes. Of course. Um. Ah! My word, I see now. There's definitely … something."

"You can see a tall stone tower? There's a man on top, yes? Peering into a contraption? It's night so it's hard to see but the man has little candles by his books. I'll brighten the moon a notch for extra illumination and send a few fireballs across the sky."

"Yes, I see him! So tiny and sweet!"

"The beings are, of course, only small with reference to

our frame of existence," said the Chancellor, doing his best to sound like he knew what he was talking about. "If we could ask them, they would think they were the same size as us. In the same way that their time appears to move normally to them but from our perspective…"

The Archdean ignored her Chancellor, as she so often did. "That device the little man is looking at. It's almost like … like a telescope." Her face reappeared from the folds of her voluminous gown, eyes wide in an expression of astonishment. "He was looking upwards at me! Could he see me? Have they worked out the truth after all this time?" She looked genuinely alarmed, wobbling slightly on top of the little flight of steps.

The Chancellor's grey, thinning fur bristled. "No need to worry yourself. They've made a remarkable invention, but it's still crude; they can only see what they've always been able to see. The stars as tiny points of light, the sphere slowly rotating. The planets and moon and sun projected across it. Everything is under perfect control. In many ways this is a triumph for GalTech. Not only did our forebears create the first viable micro-universe, but now the life forms evolving there have shown glimmerings of genuine intelligence."

Professor Overarch shook her head, horned brow wrinkled with anxiety. She was the youngest professor in GalTech, her skin still a delicate, spring-bud green. "It should never have been allowed to get this far. We should have terminated the Experiment when the first single-celled creatures appeared."

"As I recall," said the Chancellor, "it was your faculty that argued against that proposition, claiming the absolute right to life even if you happened to exist on a manufactured planet housed within a steam-powered brass sphere."

Professor Overarch's eyes narrowed very, very slightly. "Philosophy has moved on a lot since then. Destruction of a monocellular life form is surely morally preferable to wiping out a complex and intelligent species."

"Is it?" asked the Archdean. "You must explain the thinking to me. Some other time. The issue we have now is what are we going to do?"

"Why do we have to do anything?" said the Chancellor. "Everything is … contained."

"But for how long?" said Zend, finally speaking up. "Don't you see? Not so long ago the beings in there were sharpening stones to kill each other more effectively. Suddenly they're building telescopes and staring into the night sky wondering about the nature of reality. And that's not all."

The Archdean looked suspicious, as if, somehow, all this was Zend's fault. "What do you mean *that's not all?*"

"It's not just telescopes," said Zend. "It's microscopes, too."

"Well, yes," said the Chancellor. "Very similar mechanisms. That's hardly a surprise."

"But they'll *see*," said Zend. "They'll see the gaps and the flaws. All the details that were left out two hundred years ago. The beings were never supposed to get to this point of technological development."

"Wait, *gaps?*" said the Archdean, peering down at them all. "Flaws?"

"I've studied the Experiment in great detail," said Zend. "Our forebears didn't … fill in all the details of the physics of the universe when they built it. They didn't think it would be worth going to so much trouble. The Experiment was rather, well, cobbled together. Once the beings' lenses are a little better they'll see that the stars are tiny lights on a perfect black dome. They'll see that the sun is a small but bright yellow circle. Through their microscopes they'll see that everything is made of tiny dots of stuff but that no one has worked out what the dots are made of. The beings will realise they live in a fabricated – a rather poorly fabricated – universe."

The Archdean's voice was sly. "So, why, exactly should

that matter? I mean, who's to know?"

"They also have these writers and inventors with big ideas of building spaceships," said Zend. "I've seen them. Give them time and they'll succeed, I know they will. They'll blast off into space and puncture the black sphere and they'll be *here*."

The Archdean studied Zend for a moment as she absorbed his words. "The effect on the reputation of GalTech would be terrible. An escape like that would contravene all galactic statutes. People would *laugh*. We have to do something."

"We could just, you know, quietly switch the machine off," said the Chancellor.

The rest of them looked at him, not speaking. "What?" he said. "I'm just saying, who'd know?"

"Well, *they* would," said Professor Overarch. "The beings in there."

"No, they wouldn't. Their whole universe would have just stopped."

"No, it's unthinkable," said the Archdean. "We have a clear duty of care to any universes we construct. There must be another way."

In the silence that followed, Zend cleared his throat and spoke again. "Erm."

"What is it?" asked the Chancellor, once again not bothering to keep his irritation in check.

"Well, it's just, I have been sort of fooling around with plans for an expanded version of this micro-universe. Thinking we might need it one day, sort of thing. It's still not infinite, but it's a lot larger."

"Ah," said the Archdean. "An expanded universe? Now that sounds splendid."

"I haven't finished some of the trickier calculations," Zend continued. "I've got a problem with missing matter at the macro level and some of the subatomic particle interactions are frankly a bit hazy. Plus, I haven't yet worked out a way to reconcile quantum effects with gravitational…"

The Archdean waved these reservations away with a dismissive pincer. "But it will work?"

"Well, it's a mock-up. I've had to limit the speed of light to make everything hang together and the transferral process might be a bit bumpy. But it should function for now."

"Excellent!" said the Archdean. "Then let's do that. We'll transfer the beings over and they'll never know the difference."

The Archdean, Chancellor and Professor prepared to leave, nods of congratulation passing between them.

"But eventually we'll be back to square one," objected Zend. "The beings in there will notice the new flaws, the things that don't make sense."

The Archdean reached the bottom of the stairs and smoothed down her gowns. "And how long will that take?"

"Centuries in their terms. A lot less for us, obviously."

"Well, then," said the Chancellor, "that's all fine. We can go back to bed and worry about the Experiment in the morning. Or next week. Or some other time."

The three filed out, laughing together, leaving Zend alone with the warm, gently humming sphere.

Frowning, he climbed the steps and peered through the scope the Archdean had used.

It was day down on the planet now, but the man with the telescope was there again, staring upwards to the sky. He had some sort of sketchbook in his hand. Fitting a stronger eyepiece, Zend could just discern that the man's eyes were narrowed, his expression puzzled. After a moment he began to urgently scribble something in his tiny book.

Zend swallowed and looked away. Sooner or later there was going to be trouble with these beings. He couldn't contain them forever, even in version two of their universe. They'd work out the truth and then they'd break free, out into real reality. Demanding answers and, quite possibly, angry at being imprisoned for so long.

And when that happened no one at all was going to be safe.

Any story that involves a steam-powered universe has to be pretty cool, in my view. The clear implication of the story is, of course, that it's our universe inside that wheezing brass sphere – and the hurried way it has to be expanded allowed me to make some (in my view) amusing references to some of the issues modern physics can't explain, such as the so-called missing mass problem. I'm sure it'll turn out there are good explanations for this stuff, and that it isn't all because of some botched and hurried calculations made by a research student.

The story was printed in Metaphorosis in 2016.

A MIDWINTER SACRIFICE

Gallion held the knife above the boy lying on the altar. The blade glinted in the light from the pyre. The boy's eyes were wide, his breathing rapid, but he didn't flinch. Of course, he didn't flinch. No bonds held him. He longed for the knife. In that moment he could flee the troubled world and be taken to his deathless paradise. A moment's agony, a small price to pay.

Gallion spoke to the hooded figures surrounding the altar, assembled there for the midwinter sacrifice.

"Leave us. Mortal eyes may not gaze upon the face of Az."

The lower priests filed out of the *sanctum sanctorum*, heads bowed, chanting. Out into the great courtyard, its stones slippery with trodden snow. The last priest pulled the wooden doors closed behind him. They would be sealed with silk ropes until Gallion pounded three times on them, the sign that Az had departed.

Gallion waited a moment, holding the knife in the air. The boy's skin looked soft in the orange light. The knife would so easily slice through it, through the muscle between his ribs, into that rapidly beating heart. Still, Gallion waited.

The boy looked alarmed, worried he had failed in some way he did not understand. Az required absolute acceptance. "Am I not worthy?"

"Tell me why are you here," said Gallion in a low voice.

The boy frowned, this final test of his worthiness unexpected. "The sacrifice. To ensure the return of the sun and the survival of everyone."

"And if you weren't to be sacrificed, what would happen then?"

The boy looked terrified he would make some mistake and be cast into eternal damnation. If he was unworthy, his whole family to the third cousin was unworthy. An unsuitable sacrifice was no sacrifice at all.

"The eternal night. The death of the world. Is this not right?"

"What if I said it wasn't?"

"I … I don't understand."

Gallion turned away from the altar and began to pace around the room, holding the knife in just his fingertips. He chose his words carefully.

"I couldn't help wondering, you see. I had to be *sure*."

"Sure of what?"

"Everyone knows the sun will not return if there is no sacrifice. But I wondered. How do we really *know*? So I found out."

"What do you mean?" The boy sounded frightened now. Out of his depth.

"One midwinter," said Gallion. "Here in this room, alone with the sacrifice, I stayed my hand. And do you know what happened?"

"What?"

"Nothing. Nothing changed. The sun rose the following morning, the people rejoiced in the glory of Az and the world went on."

"That can not be," said the boy.

"And yet here we are."

"No."

"Yes. Because, you see, Az is not coming for you, boy. The sun doesn't care whether I thrust this piece of metal into your heart or not."

Gallion stopped his pacing and stood over the boy again, waiting for a reaction. Now he would know.

"No," repeated the boy. "I don't believe it."

"And if I give you my word that this is the truth?"

The boy – Gallion still didn't know his name – sat up and looked around the golden room, as if he had just woken up there. There was a faint spark of something in his eye. Hope, perhaps. A look Gallion had seen before.

"But then, what am I to do?" asked the boy.

Sometimes they needed time for the idea, for the tempting possibility of freedom, to sink in. "You have the same choice I gave all the others. Be the sacrifice if you wish. If you must. Or live. You are young. You can leave here. You must go far away, like the others, but you will have the rest of your life."

"The others?"

"You are the fifth. The midwinter sun has risen four times without a sacrifice."

Yes. The boy wanted to believe, Gallion saw. But he had been well taught. He knew the sacrifice was needed, knew this was just another trial. The boy's gaze darted around the golden room, into the roaring flames of the pyre, searching for an answer. Gallion waited. Sometimes they succumbed to temptation and sometimes they didn't. He would give the boy a moment longer. Test him a moment longer.

"The people expect their sacrifice," the boy said. "How could I escape?"

"It is no great trick," said Gallion. "The altar is hollow. There are robes inside it. You hide in there until it is clear, then walk out. I will tell the people the pyre – Az – has consumed your body."

The boy looked unconvinced. "No. This is wrong. You are testing my worthiness. I am the sacrifice. By my death my family will live. You must do it now."

Gallion nodded. It seemed the boy was a worthy sacrifice after all. "You are sure of this?"

"Do it."

"Very well."

The boy lay back and closed his eyes. His smooth torso glistened with sweat. Gallion held up the knife again. He could wait no longer. A delay would be interpreted in all sorts of calamitous ways. He thrust the knife downwards.

"Wait!" The boy rolled off the altar and stared at Gallion, panting.

"What is it, boy?"

"How did it feel?"

"How did what feel?"

"That first time. When you stayed your hand. When you didn't know for sure the world wouldn't end."

Gallion paused, wondering how far he should take this. The boy had doubts, that was clear.

"It was a long night. I watched for the dawn from the tallest tower. I even prayed to Az the morning would come."

"But you didn't *know*. You must have thought there was a chance you had brought about the eternal night."

Gallion nodded, didn't reply, watching the boy carefully.

The boy said nothing, lost in indecision. Gallion held the knife ready. More than once the sacrifice had darted for the door. And that was not allowed. The sacrifice was not permitted to leave the room again.

"The altar," the boy said. "How do I get inside?"

Gallion sighed. It was as he suspected. He stepped forward, holding the knife out before him. The boy was no worthy sacrifice.

With the tip of the blade he worked the mechanism that unlocked the hidden compartment in the altar for the boy to squeeze inside.

A Midwinter Sacrifice was printed in Bards and Sages Quarterly magazine in 2016. My intention with the story was to keep its meaning ambiguous until the final sentence: is Gallion simply testing the boy to see if he is a worthy sacrifice, or is he genuinely offering him a way out? Hopefully the story can be read either way until the moment Gallion unlocks the secret compartment for the boy to hide within.

SAFE WATERS

Lina swam through blue water. Bubbles fizzed over her bare breasts and the golden scales of her tail. She darted to the sea-bed where flatfish skimmed over corrugated plains of golden sand, glided around fairy cities of coral, their reds and purples and yellows brighter than any garden flowers. Then she charged upwards, upwards to the light, rising within a cone of froth, through the hard barrier of the surface to leap into the clear air. She called for sheer joy before diving back into the warm depths.

She should have done this long ago. Two weeks out of her busy life, all the demands of career and family forgotten. Her cares set aside along with her body, lying back there in the medsuites of OceanBlue Inc. while her transplanted neural matrix revelled in this synthetic replacement. The freedom of it. The thrill.

She dived to the depths again to repeat her salmon-leap, this time flying higher into the sky, completely free of the water. As she twisted for the dive back in she glimpsed a shadow on the sparkling waters farther out, beyond the ten feet of mesh that protruded from the ocean. Something huge beneath the surface.

Intrigued, she swam into the deeper seas, her seaweed

green hair streaming behind her and shoals of rainbow fish darting out of her way as she shot through them.

*

"Welcome to Atlantis Resort and the holiday of a lifetime! Our blue lagoon covers over thirty square kilometres, all of it yours to explore for the duration of your time with us."

Lina tried to concentrate on the induction vid but two stasis periods on the double hop to Atlantis from Earth via Midway had taken it out of her. She hated star travel.

"What are you going to be?" The woman next to her asked while the voice on the vid droned on.

"Huh?"

"What body form are you going for?" the woman said. She wore an array of jewellery that shouted its extravagance with every jingle. "I can't decide between something really sweet, like a seahorse, or something really huge. A whale, say."

"Are whales allowed?" asked Lina.

"Of course. So long as they're not predators."

"I'd better not get transplanted into a plankton then."

The woman laughed. What was her name? Pandora, Persephone, something classical like that. "I should hope not, sweetie. Where's the fun in *asexual* reproduction? Whales, on the other hand, well, need I say more? Very … impressive creatures."

Lina nodded but she hadn't come for that. Quite the opposite. The wounds from her break-up with Darian were still raw; she needed time for herself, pure and simple.

"Or, actually," the woman continued, "I might go for something a little more exotic."

"Exotic?"

"You know, fabulous. *Mythical.* A sea-serpent. Or even a mermaid."

A *mermaid.* All the girlhood stories Lina had invented

came flooding back to her. A mermaid. Magical. Beautiful. Untouchable. Yes. That would be her.

*

Soon the mesh came into view. A wall of red lights marked the double-layer polycarbon net that kept the lagoon safe. Beyond, blue waters became purple as the sea-bed dropped away. There were monsters out there in the depths, the induction had explained, but the lagoon was safe so there was no need to fear.

The attack, when it came, threw her into a spin. A grey mass, all teeth and tentacles, lunged suddenly from the depths, flinging itself at her. Lina arced backwards in alarm. At the same moment, sirens sounded all along the barrier. The mesh between her and the sea-creature billowed, but it didn't break. She was in no danger; the monster couldn't get near her, couldn't touch her.

She watched from a distance as it tried to force its way forwards. Somewhere between a shark and a kraken, its eyes empty and dead, it struggled against the net, mouth gaping wide: a vicious, brainless beast of the sea.

Lina turned away, heart still racing. She'd spotted a hidden cove earlier, a sandy beach with flat rocks where a mermaid might sit and sun herself. She'd go there and forget all about the monsters lurking in the depths.

The mesh was only a line of dim lights behind her when, impossibly, the creature's voice came to her over her com link. "Swim away, little mermaid. Back to your safe waters. I'll be here waiting for you."

*

"And remember, there are really only two rules," said the smiling, synthetic face on the vid. "Firstly, make sure you stay in the lagoon at all times. Secondly, and most importantly, have fun! The oceans of Atlantis are yours to explore. Now head to the medsuites where our colleagues will be happy to discuss your chosen life form with you."

"They don't tell you about the accidents, do they?" The woman with the expensive jewellery whispered conspiratorially to Lina as they left the induction vid. "No mention of the ... losses."

"Losses?"

"Oh, come on. You must have heard the stories? People heading off into the lagoon and never returning?"

"I assumed they were, I don't know, myths."

"Oh, sure sweetie. That's what they want you to think. But I know it's true. Every now and then someone doesn't come back. You mark my words. Why do you think we have to sign all those waivers?"

Lina didn't believe a word of it. Gossip and nonsense. She made a note to avoid this intrusive woman in the future, especially once they were in the water. "So, what happens to them?"

"Who knows? Dragged off into the depths by some monstrous sea-serpent with dark designs. At least, I *hope* that's what happens, sweetie. Sounds divine, don't you think?"

"Oh. Yeah."

"You know, I think I'll go for a dolphin. Smart, beautiful, great swimmers. They pretty much just splash around all day and have fun. Sounds like my kind of fish."

Lina didn't correct her choice of word. Spotting one of the assistants, she bade the woman goodbye with a little wave and went off to discuss how to become a mermaid.

*

She stayed in shallow waters all week following her experience at the mesh: swimming, exploring, simply taking in the beauty of the world around her. Atlantis was always sunny, the waters clear as glass.

Once she saw the woman she'd met at the induction,

her ID clear from her com implant when Lina sent over a light *enquire*. The woman didn't notice. She had taken on dolphin form and was swimming with a whole pod of other dolphins, flashing and leaping through the waters. They copulated copiously. Lina couldn't help smiling at the sight of them.

Unexpectedly she felt a little envious, too. She had no desire to switch forms and join the gang. But still. Thoughts of the end of her vacation, of having to return to her normal life, had been troubling her more and more.

The first few days of her stay on Atlantis had seemed to last for ever, a glorious blur of swimming and eating and simply *being*. Suddenly the end of her stay was only a few days distant but she wasn't ready to go back yet, not at all.

Running Circe station around Neptune was a good job, and she was good at it, but its demands were constant and many and didn't leave any time for herself. Not that it excused Darian's behavior. She'd been devoted. He'd been the one having the affair. No, damn him, affairs, plural.

She swam into deeper waters. She knew where she was going, why she was doing it. The previous day she'd contacted the OceanBlue help node, enquiring about the planet's natural fauna as if she were simply interested in the fish that might be glimpsed beyond the mesh. The wild waters of Atlantis were wide and huge, their depths unexplored and their life forms many and varied. Lina had sifted her way through all of them but there was no sign of any hulking sharky kraken creatures. Then, that was to be expected; the monster that had attacked the mesh had a com link. It was synthetic.

An OceanBlue Inc. construct.

A person.

A shoal of glimmering, glass-like fish swam through the net as she approached, utterly unhampered by it. Anything larger would be stopped, unable to get in. Or out, come to that.

Lina stayed by the mesh for some time, fifty feet down,

tail swishing slowly to hold her in place. Occasionally she thought she saw movement in the purple depths, but it may have been her senses playing tricks. Her vision was excellent, OceanBlue's synthetic eyes doing a much better job than normal human ones, but still, detail was hard to make out when there was little sunlight filtering down. There was no sign of any untamed creature of the depths. She felt strangely disappointed.

Before she could stop herself, she broadcast a quiet *enquire* call through the mesh. No response came back. Perhaps she'd imagined the whole thing with the monster, caught an echo from someone else's com node. That had to be it.

With a lash of her tail, she flew back to the shallows and the coves, where the other vacationers thronged and played.

*

"So, you're all good to go," said the assistant over the com link embedded in her mermaid's synthetic body. "Everything functioning? Breathing, movement, vision?"

"Yes."

"Good. Excellent. While there is no danger here at Atlantis Resort, there are rocks and corals that you could scratch yourself on if you go too close. But don't worry. Your skin is soft and smooth but also incredibly strong and your body is very tough, almost impossible to damage. You won't suffer any injuries here and will feel no pain. You don't even need to eat if you don't wish to because a tiny fusion core powers your body, enough to keep you swimming for a long, long time! Of course, you can eat if you wish; your body is fully functional in all aspects, so it's entirely up to you."

"Okay," said Lina.

"Now, if something does get too close to you can always force it away from you with the sonic beam built into your head. Experiment with it, you'll soon find out how to use it. It's very effective."

"It's a weapon?"

"Not really. It's more a way of ensuring that your personal space is respected. Assuming that's what you want, of course."

"Of course."

"Good. Now, final thing. I know it seems a long way off, but when your time with us is finally up, we'll send out a com call, telling you to return to the medsuite so we can transition you back to your human body."

"Okay."

"It'll reach you wherever you are in the lagoon, so don't worry about that. When you hear it, come back here. We can't transplant your neural matrix back without your physical presence, yes?"

"Yes."

"Good. Sometimes people can be a little reluctant to return. Understandable I'm sure! Be advised there is a command call we can make to your synthetic body that will override any of your conscious inputs and return you safely here. But I'm sure we won't need to do that."

"No. Of course."

"Then you're all set to go. Have fun!"

"Thanks," said Lina. "I'll try."

*

On the day she was due to leave the calls from work began to come through. She'd given them strict instructions back at Circe, told them to contact her only in an emergency. Clearly, they'd decided her final day was close enough. A stream of questions, requests for meetings and complaints poured in, more and more queuing up all the time.

There was a message from Darian, too. An apology. Incredible. Angry, she shut the com stream down and swam. Her old life, her real life, seemed so distant. So strangely unimportant.

This time, at the mesh, the hulking monster was back. It cruised along beside the net as if searching for a way in. Its body was strong and powerful, a top predator in the ocean food-chain.

"You came back," it said. Although *it* was wrong. This was a he, no question. She wondered who he'd once been. "Sorry about frightening you the other day, Sometimes I forget what I was. What I am."

"And what are you?" asked Lina. "Who are you?"

"You can see what I am."

"But before I mean. You came as a visitor?"

"Yes. Years ago, now."

"And you've been here all this time?"

"Couldn't tear myself away. Couldn't go back. Any of this sound familiar? You must be returning to your normal life soon, yes?"

She didn't answer his question. "But how? How did you escape the lagoon? And why have they allowed you to remain?"

"The escape was easy enough. Bit my way through with these teeth. One reason they don't offer this particular life-form any more, I believe."

"But didn't they broadcast a summons to force you back?"

"They probably did. By then I was too far away for it to reach me. And now I've disabled it."

"How?"

"There are ways. There are others out here. We've learned how to alter these bodies they provide. How to fully control them. How to live free."

"Others?"

"One or two. Don't know how many. The oceans of this world are vast and ancient. This little lagoon is just a puddle."

"What do you do out there?"

"Live. Swim. Eat. Or nothing at all."

"But don't you miss your old life? Your family, your friends?"

The creature ceased its to-and-fro cruising and swam directly to the mesh. Its bulk dwarfed her mermaid form.

"Sometimes," the creature said. "A little. Not enough to want to go back. It's interesting you're asking all these questions isn't it?"

"Why?"

"Oh, come on. There's only one reason why you would. I heard your call."

"I can't leave the lagoon," said Lina.

"Why not?"

"For one, there's no way through the mesh. For two, I'm a mermaid, not some – forgive me – hulking monster. I wouldn't survive a minute out there in the depths. And for three, I don't want to."

"Up to you, of course. But for what it's worth you'd almost certainly be safe. These synthetic bodies are indestructible."

"Wouldn't sop me being eaten or something."

"Didn't they tell you about the defences they build into us?"

"A little."

"Trust me, they're a lot more powerful than they let on. Nothing touches us out here. Nothing harms us. We rule these oceans."

She didn't speak again for a moment. The creature resumed its lazy swimming, heading off into the dark depths as if indifferent to her.

"But the mesh," she called after it. "How would I get through if I even wanted to?"

She thought he wasn't going to reply. Then his voice came over the com from the gloom. "Not through. *Over*. You were psych profiled, yes?"

"They … assessed us to help us decide which body to choose."

"They were making sure you were suitable for your

chosen option. Making sure you didn't betray any hidden desire to escape the lagoon if, say, you showed a preference for a body capable of making such a huge leap. Like a mermaid for instance."

"But if I escaped, if it were even possible, what would I do out there?"

The creature's voice was distant, as if it were already far away. "Whatever you like."

Lina swam up and down the line of the mesh for a time, thinking, then turned away. It was a crazy dream. She couldn't turn her back on her responsibilities, on everything demanded of her. She had to get home. But perhaps she could return for another stay next year. Another visit to Atlantis. Yes. That would be good.

She opened up the com stream to outside again as she neared the shore. The flow of messages from Circe was a flood now. Everything she'd avoided by taking a break for two weeks was simply waiting for her to address when she got back. It was *endless*. There was more from Darian, too. A lot more. At the same time, overlaying it, she got the call from the medsuite telling her to return. Her time was up.

In sight of the BlueOcean building she stopped, treading water for a moment. A tower of bubbles glimmered past her, gently caressing her skin and scales. Above her, its shape warped by the waters, the sun was a benign yellow glow making the ocean gleam.

Lina turned. Throwing all her strength into it, she hurtled back into the depths, building up speed for the leap that would take her over the mesh.

The thought must pass through just about everyone's mind when they are away from home on vacation: why don't I just stay? What happens if I never go back to my mundane old life? Science fiction simply opens up more possibilities, more temptations. I like to think Lina made the right decision in deciding to stay and live free as a dolphin – but maybe most of us, faced with that dilemma, would do the "sensible" thing and return. Still, there's something in this story about staying true to yourself and your dreams. And that's something you should always and absolutely try to do, hard as it can obviously be.

The story was published in 2016 in the Sirens anthology.

A DISTANT GLIMPSE

Mina was half-way up one of the trash hillsides, rummaging through tattered, slime-coated plastic bags for bottle-tops and other treasures, when her eye caught the glint of light. A flash of white, up on the summit. Just some shard of glass lying at the right angle to catch the sun, but beautiful. She stood up straight, one hand shading her eyes to admire it. If she swayed backwards and forwards she could make it wink on and off. A star, her very own star, shining for her. She found herself smiling at the sight of it.

"Come on, Mina. You'll get in trouble. You've hardly collected anything." Babat, picking through the trash down the slope, looked worried. Babat always looked worried. But then he was only eight. Just a kid. Two years ago, she'd have been the same. She peered up the slope, assessing the climb, marking out a likely route.

"I'm going up to the top," she said. "Wait here. Keep an eye on the others, okay? I'm relying on you."

"No, Mina. The men will be here soon. They'll beat us with their lathis again if we don't collect enough."

She sighed. It was hard being the leader. She missed Setu. Once, Setu had done all the thinking, all the worrying. But then she got sick and died, coughing so much that it seemed to tear her up inside, and she, Mina, had to take over the job of looking after them. Babat and Ed and the whole gang of them. She wished Setu was still alive.

"There's an hour yet," she said. "I'll collect as I go up, okay? I'll be back before you know it."

He looked unconvinced, worry clouding his filthy face as he stood there up to his knees in rot and slime. He always worked next to her, didn't like her to go anywhere without him. She understood. She'd lost her mother, too. Maybe that was why she'd stuck to Setu so much.

Mina set off, wading upwards. It was hard going, the piled mountain of rubbish giving way beneath her feet, slipping backwards. She'd seen more than one person engulfed by an avalanche, the whole hillside breaking free to swallow those at the bottom. She stopped and worked her way sideways, away from Babat and the others, then began to climb again. At one point she placed her foot onto a soft spot, the hillside sucking her whole leg in. She sprawled forwards, cutting her hand on the jagged top of a tin. A family of rats, nesting in the hillside there, squealed and boiled out of the hole she'd made to scatter across the hillside. She glanced down the slope to see Babat watching her, eyes wide with alarm. She waved and, heaving her leg out on the third attempt, carried on upwards. Another couple of minutes, out of breath, she reached the summit.

The rolling hills of the landfill stretched away in all directions. In the sunlit haze the scene was beautiful. She liked to come up here. The sight pulled at her, tugged on her insides in ways she didn't have the words for. Other garbage hills lay all around. Other gangs of kids worked those other hills. Some of them she'd never even been to. This hill was their home. Their whole world. A place they'd had to defend more than once.

Kites wheeled in the sky above her. The birds didn't fly away. She often wondered about that. They lived here, like she and Babat and the others. Everyone knew, of course, about the outside world. In the evening they told stories about it. Told of the princesses and kings who lived in their golden palaces, everything they could ever want given to them, more food than they could ever eat. Clean clothes and soft beds and machines that sang gently to send them to sleep. And when they were bored with something, those princesses and kings, they simply threw it away. Even if it still worked, even if it could still be used or eaten or worn. Then other people collected all the discarded things from the palaces and brought them to the tip. Twenty or thirty truck-loads of it each day. That was how it was.

Mina had lived her life in the landfill. When she was a baby, her mother worked the mountains and swamps with Mina swaddled to her back. Later, Mina was able to help, working beside her mother, picking through the layers in the hope of unearthing those precious treasures the site occasionally gave them. Computer chips (their use unfathomable), unbroken bottles, pens, beads. Even coins. She had a secret collection back in the hut, buried in the ground in a tin. The treasures she kept for herself. When she was alone, or the others were asleep, she would take the items out and hold them, look at them, wondering who'd once owned them, what their stories were.

She began to search for the shard of glass she'd glimpsed from down the slope. Perhaps it would be another such treasure to add to her collection. But she could see nothing. The sun was at the wrong angle. Or she'd imagined it. She worked her way around the hill-top, thigh-deep in the trash at places, setting small avalanches rattling down the slopes more than once. She was about to give up when she caught a glimmer. A flash of metal this time, not glass. Metal was good. The people outside could make marvellous things with metal. She worked her way over to it, thrilling with excitement at what the precious treasure might be.

A short brass tube housing a round, glass lens lay embedded in the trash. Heart thundering, Mina picked it up. Who would throw away such a wonder? Another, smaller lens filled the other end of the tube. A pair of brass wheels at the narrow end could be turned, allowing something within to be altered or adjusted. It was the most wonderful thing she'd ever seen in her whole life.

She knew what it was, although she'd never spoken the word out loud. Saying it was awkward as her tongue tried to give birth to the difficult syllables. Eventually, she had it.

Telescope.

She held it to her eye. She saw nothing but a blur of colours, browns and blues. She turned the wheels on the device, hoping that would make it work. The colours swirled and then snapped into sudden clarity, smudges becoming hard lines. At first, she couldn't understand what she was seeing. Then she made sense of it. One of the other trash hills, brought right up close. She lifted the telescope to look beyond. In the distance, white and gold in the haze of the horizon, she saw towers and domes, a distant glimpse of huge buildings. Bright sunlight glinting off a thousand windows. The homes of the princesses and kings. Their beauty took her breath away. She took the telescope from her eye. The palaces were gone; all she could see on the horizon was the familiar haze, as if the world stopped there.

"Mina!"

The fear in Babat's voice was clear as he shouted up at her. Down the hill, the men had arrived in their van to collect their days pickings. They were early, and the sack she carried tied over her shoulder was still all-but empty, only a few plastic bottles to show for her morning's work. Below her, Babat stood transfixed, looking up at her, looking down at the men, caught between them.

Mina rattled back down the slope, hastily snatching up any scraps she could see and dropping them into her sack. She took Babat's arm and led him down to the ground, calling to the others to join them.

There was a silence as they each emptied out the

treasures they'd recovered onto little heaps in front of them. One of the men kicked at Mina's meagre pile and raised his lathi to strike.

*

Later that evening, the five of them huddled in the little hut they'd built against the side of the hill, sheets of rusting corrugated iron to keep the rains off when they hammered down on the tip. Mina sat quietly. When she moved it hurt sharply, all across her shoulders and back where they'd beaten her. She didn't cry, but Babat, lying beside her, sobbed helplessly. She placed a hand on his hair, stroking him with her thumb.

There were many stories about the city. Some said it was a lair of demons, too, a place of suffering and danger as well as marvel. There had to be some truth to that, especially if that was where the men came from. Perhaps good and evil fought there, battling over those palaces. She couldn't keep the images she'd glimpsed from her mind. When she finally closed her eyes they were still there, glowing in the sun. Setu had talked about escaping. A long and dangerous journey with terrible hazards in the way. But it had to be possible. There had to be a road for the trucks to rattle along. Mina wondered how far it was. By some magic the telescope made the buildings visible, but to walk there was a different matter. Was such a thing even possible? Was it simply a matter of distance?

For the following five days she worked as hard as she could, picking over the arriving truck-loads of rubbish, or scavenging through fresh layers exposed by the bulldozers as they moved the trash around. The pains from her wounds subsided a little, although livid bruises lit up across her back and shoulders. Each day, when the men came, her sack was full and her pile of pickings large. The man who'd beat her grunted and told her to throw what she'd found into the van.

As she did so, Mina studied the vehicle, just as she studied the great snarling trucks when she could. Was there a way to hide away underneath them? Hitch a ride to the distant city? She imagined Babat clinging on as they jolted over dusty roads. Then his tiny hands losing their grip, Babat falling to the road, the wheels jolting as they thundered over his body. No. That was no way to do it.

After five days, she finally allowed herself to work her way back to the top of the hill, picking through the garbage as she climbed so that it looked like she had no definite destination in mind. At the top, she had to kick aside tatters of plastic to find the telescope. It was still where she'd dropped it. Hands trembling, she crouched so that no one could see her and raised the device to her eyes once more.

She squatted there for half an hour, as long as she dared, studying the palaces, studying the world between her and them. The landfill stretched away for a great distance, ending in a high wire fence. Beyond lay a river and a bare brown plain of mud, scattered buildings upon it, low and square. Then, seemingly many miles further on, the great buildings. She couldn't see roads, but she did trace the routes the trucks and carts took. When she had everything clear, a map in her mind, she slipped the telescope into her sack. Before the men came, she would add it to her collection of treasures.

That night, in the dark and the quiet, she awoke coughing. Unable to stop herself, not wanting to keep the others awake, she slipped outside into the moonlight.

"Mina! Where are you going?"

"Hush, Babat. Go to sleep. I'll be back soon."

Following the shadowy outlines of the garbage hills she walked for an hour or more, doing her best to move quietly in enemy territory, covering her mouth as the coughing fit continued to plague her. If she was caught by the children of the other hills they would beat her and kick her. Fortunately, she reached the fence without seeing anyone. The mesh towered over her, impossible to climb. She felt around in the dirt, but it went down into the ground, too, to stop it being tunnelled under.

She followed the line of the wire until she came to a garbage mound that had been bulldozed right up against it. The fence bulged from the weight but still stood. She walked around the hill ten minutes more, until the eastern sky began to lighten and she had to hurry back to Babat and the others.

That day passed in a blur, exhausted as she was from her explorations. More than once she had to sit down and wait for the fits of coughing to pass. Babat stayed closer to her than normal, occasionally slipping things he found into her bag rather than his. When the men came, her pile was smaller than usual but fortunately not small enough to incur their wrath. She returned to the hut and lay down to sleep utterly spent. Tomorrow she would be better.

But the following day she felt worse, no strength in her muscles. She shivered even when the sun rose to warm their little tin hut. When she coughed it seemed to pull on every muscle in her body,

Babat came to her, his eyes full of worry. "Are you going to die like Setu?"

"No, of course not."

"This is what happened to her. You're going to leave too."

"No. I need to rest. Tomorrow I'll be right as rain."

"If you can't work the men will beat you."

"They'll give me a day to recover. If they kill me I won't be able to collect for them tomorrow, will I?"

Babat looked unconvinced, but he left with Ed and the others, leading them from the hut as she normally did. She smiled at him as he left.

By that evening she knew that he'd spoken the truth. She couldn't eat or drink. The sickness filled her. Now when she coughed it felt like something was tearing inside her. She'd slept a little, so she thought, and was surprised when Babat and the others returned, the day already over. She was burning hot but still shivered. Babat gave her water and it helped a little, trickling cold inside her.

At some point in the day she'd come to a decision. She knew what she had to do.

In the middle of the night, when the world was quiet once more, she forced herself to rise and dress. She roused the others, telling them to be quiet, follow her. She slung the bag of treasures over her shoulder, along with a length of tattered rope scavenged long ago.

"Where are we going?" said Babat. There was a note of accusation in his voice. "You need to rest. You look sick."

The hut, the faces of Babat and the others swirled and danced in front of her, all the reliable, solid lines melting. Her legs wobbled but she refused to succumb. "Follow me. I'll show you. It's not far."

She didn't need to tell them to creep quietly past the other hills. They walked hand-in-hand, following her without further question. At the fence, she squatted and whispered to them what they had to do.

Babat looked up at the fence, at the slope of garbage she'd told them to climb. "You go first," he said. He seemed to know what she was thinking, what she really planned.

She shook her head. All her strength was gone. "No. I'll watch here. You go first. Tie the rope to the top of the wire and let yourselves down."

"You're going to follow, aren't you?"

"Of course."

She thought he was going to refuse but then he relented. Leading Ed and the others he began to wade up the morass of trash leaning against the fence.

Twenty minutes later, Babat and the others were all on the other side, the rope dangling down long enough to let them fall uninjured to the ground. The sun was rising, a golden light in the haze of the east. She sat against the fence, slumped like the mountain of garbage, panting as if she'd been running. She handed the telescope through the wire to Babat. "Here, take this. I can't come with you but this will guide you."

Babat refused to take the telescope. He looked as if all his fears had come to pass.

"Please, Babat. Take it. It's a magic telescope. Hold it to your eye and you'll see the palaces. Keep looking and walk towards them, that's all you have to do. Lead the others for me. Don't look down. Don't look around."

Still he hesitated. She thought he might begin to cry. If he did, she didn't know what she would do.

"Babat, I can't look after you any more. You were right. Now you have to do this. I'm sorry."

Ed and the others stood behind Babat, waiting to see what would happen. Finally, quietly, Babat took the telescope from her fingers and held it to his eye.

A Distant Glimpse is from the magic realist end of the fantasy spectrum (if there is a fantasy spectrum) – and in truth, you could argue that it isn't a fantasy story at all, but a slice of real life. Are those golden palaces of a thousand windows real, or are they just Mina's flawed interpretation of a cityscape seen from afar? Who's to say? I must admit I do like a story that's ambiguous like that. Maybe the telescope has some magical properties, a means of seeing the way to an impossible place, and maybe it's just an old telescope.

The story was published in The Future Fire in 2016.

PROBLEM HAIR

"I just can't do a thing with it," said Meddy, glowering at her reflection, and at Fabio standing behind her. Fabio who, it was said, could work miracles with scissors and comb. His salon was if-you-have-to-ask-the-price-you-can't-afford-it exclusive. A haven for the rich and famous. And, in the upper room, those individuals in need of a discreet, *special* attention.

"You have problem hair, madam?" he asked, standing over her, assessing her. The gold and marble décor of the private room sparkled around him. It was all classical arches and ionic columns. She liked it.

"You could say that," she said. "It has a mind of its own."

"What products have you tried on it?"

"Lots. But there tends to be a ... bad reaction."

"May I see?"

She kept it covered up, of course. Hoods, hats, scarves. Whatever she was doing, her hair always got in the way. A good pair of sunglasses sorted out her other issues, but always there was the hair. It set her apart. Stopped her *belonging*. Supposed friends made excuses and claimed to be busy when she rang. Same with lovers. Men were such shallow creatures. And so fragile. She simply wanted an uncomplicated relationship or two. And so here she was, sitting in the exclusive *Hair Apparent* salon, to see what the famous Fabio could do for her.

"Are you sure you want to see?" she asked.

"Quite sure, madam. I have been faced with many hairdressing disasters over the years. Once I had a lady client who let her hair grow over twenty metres long. Such beautiful golden plaits but you wouldn't believe the split ends. Then there was the gentleman buccaneer who insisted on setting light to his beard whilst at work. There is no situation I cannot rescue."

"And your immunisations are up to date?" she asked.

The question threw him momentarily. She was used to it.

"Well, yes," he said. "But I don't see…"

He went silent, then, as she slipped back her silken cowl to reveal the writhing nest of green and black snakes that made up her hair. Their tiny heads hissed and snapped at him. They weren't poisonous, but their tiny teeth were sharp and could break the skin. As more than one lover had discovered. *Always* an embarrassment.

"I see, madam," he said after a moment. "Excuse me for asking, but is it true what they say? About your gaze, I mean?"

"We'll be fine so long as I keep my sunglasses on and I only look at you in the mirror."

"Very well. And did you have any particular … style in mind?"

"I want to be, I don't know, *cool* for once. Fashionable. What do you suggest?"

There was a pause while Fabio considered, assessing her from all angles. The calculating look on his face didn't bode well.

"Dreadlocks are very popular these days," he said at last. "It's really a very ancient style. Classical, you might say. Perhaps some beads or bands to keep everything … in order."

"Been there, done that. I may even have started it. I want something new."

"Yes, yes, I see." Fabio moved his hand towards her head. One of the snakes struck, too quick for him to react. Two red pinpricks appeared on the back of his hand.

"I'm sorry," she said. "They get very defensive. They're just trying to protect me."

"They're certainly lively," said Fabio. "Have you considered drugging them? To calm them down a little I mean?"

"Won't work. It's the symbiosis. We share a metabolism, so I get affected too."

"Then perhaps a good snake-charmer could persuade them to co-operate? To lie straight, for instance, or even to curl up into a wave."

"Tried that, too. As soon as you hit the night clubs they come out of their trance and start lashing around in time to the music. They like a good rave."

"And their ... removal is not an option?"

"Absolutely not."

"I see," said Fabio. He was frowning now.

"There's nothing you can do, is there?" she asked.

"Madam, I can see only one way to make your hair more fashionable."

"Tell me."

"If we can't change the hair we must change the fashion."

"How?"

"Can you wait here for a moment?"

She sat while Fabio bustled off, down the stairs to the more public floor of the salon. Absent-mindedly she let one of the snakes play through her hands, twisting and winding it around her fingers. Then she heard footsteps approaching. Several sets. Fabio was no longer alone.

"Madam, I'd like to introduce you to some other clients of mine. Are you by any chance familiar with the band

Succubus?"

"Can't say that I am. I'm more of a classical girl."

"Quite. Well, their music is certainly invigorating. They're wildly popular. A melange of the punk and metal genres if that means anything. As it happens I'm their stylist. May I introduce you?"

"Sure, why not?"

Fabio stepped back to let his other customers file in. Meddy studied them in the mirror. Three young women, dressed in black leather and spiky jewellery, the effect lessened only slightly by their hairdresser's ponchos. One had spiked red hair like frozen fire, another was completely bald and the third had hair with some kind of electricity sparking away in it. All three wore dark sunglasses, even though they were indoors.

"Ladies," said Fabio. "I'd like you to meet Medusa. Meddy to her friends. Her gaze can turn you to stone and she has a writhing mass of snakes for hair."

There was a familiar silence as the newcomers took in what they'd been told. Then they began to speak all at once.

"Oh my God, that is the coolest hair I have ever seen."

"Live snakes. Actual live snakes. That is freakin' awesome."

"Look at them. They move. They actually move. I so want hair like that."

One of the musicians - the one with the spiky red hair - knelt down beside Meddy, addressing her in the mirror.

"Listen, I don't suppose you'd be interested in joining the band, would you?"

"I'm afraid I don't play any instruments."

The young woman waved a dismissive hand. "Detail. You can learn. It's all about the attitude, girl. And you'd fit *right* in, believe me. You can tour the world. Party 'till you drop, have all the guys you want and take no crap from anyone. Become one of us. What do you say?"

Meddy considered for a moment. Finally, she smiled at

her new sisters.

"Fabio," she said. "It's true what they say. You really are a genius."

Stories that take a familiar character or setting from myth or literature and bring them up to date are pretty common, and that was what I wanted to do here. As with The Monster, I like to think the modern world would be more accepting of someone who is simply, well, a bit different. The whole thing with the gaze that can turn you to stone might be a challenge, sure, but I figure Medusa, like Frankenstein's monster, would be a celebrity these days and not a feared outcast.

The story was published in The Lorelei Signal and Mystic Signals in 2015.

ADRIFT

Gibson had been adrift in the ocean for fifteen days when he started to see the flowers.

On most of the days since the *Ocean Flyer* went down his little orange life-raft had stood becalmed, the eye of a hush filling the whole world. On some days the winds whipped the sea into sudden mountain ranges. Peaks he ascended and crashed down and ascended for hours on end. Long, gruelling hours when each moment looked to be his last.

He'd clung on, survived both calm and storm. In all that time one thing remained unchanged. He had no idea where in the wide ocean he was.

The life-raft carried the essentials to keep him alive. A solar water purification unit, dried food, a fishing line, flares. But no radio, no GPS. All that had gone with the Ocean Flyer. The exact events were a blur. The perils of single-handed sailing. Some fever had overcome him two weeks into his voyage and for maybe another week he'd drifted, barely conscious, course unknown. Then a bad storm had come up and broken the back of his brave yacht. He'd barely made it to the life-raft. A time later – hours or days – the light had roused him and he found, to his surprise, that he was weak and parched and sunburned, but alive.

Still, he knew his chances of survival were slim. He'd always known the risks of being out here. That was part of the point. The sea was callous, indifferent, yet it made him feel alive. But it owed him nothing, no consideration, no grace. His life or death meant nothing to it. He'd put to sea accepting that, welcoming that.

Since the Flyer went down he'd seen no one else. No ship, no plane to fire his flares for. He could row, but in which direction? The sun and stars told him where north was but they didn't tell him where the nearest land lay. It might be over the horizon or a hundred miles distant. Or a thousand.

Then he'd seen the distant bloom of red on the green-blue of the ocean. Unable to make out what it was he'd rowed that way. Within an hour he was floating amid a field of bobbing flowers. Red, plastic flowers. He plucked one from the water, smiling at its bright colours, its moulded simplicity. He'd heard of similar things. Cargos of plastic ducks lost over board, set free to flotilla the seas, going where they would on the world's currents.

He made up his mind. The red flowers stretched in a snaking drift to the western horizon. They were a line. A pathway to take.

Perhaps something lay at the other end of that road. And perhaps it didn't. But he would find out. Picking up his oar, Gibson began to paddle his way along the road of bobbing flowers.

Like A Distant Glimpse, Adrift is a story (or perhaps a vignette) whose place in a collection of fantasy and science fiction tales is open to debate. The events described could happen – ships do tip their cargoes into the oceans – but equally it could be that Gibson discovers something wonderful: a hidden road that will take him to a place unknown and miraculous.

The story was published in Vine Leaves Literary Journal in 2015.

THE BRASS DOORS

Shan had stood guard in front of the brass doors for twenty-five years. To the day.

In all that time, no one had ever gone in and no one had ever come out. No one had approached, or knocked, or asked for access. The doors had remained closed. Closed but, she knew, not locked. That had been made clear. And finally, today, she was going to do what she'd so often longed to do. Today she was going to push the door open and discover what lay beyond.

She'd been brought to Engn at the age of thirteen: a wild child, spitting and kicking as the ironclads seized her and dragged her from her home. Only the sight of the machine had cowed her. The smoking, pumping behemoth had crept towards them across the grass plain each day, and each day she'd become quieter, more sullen. At the towering gates, an ancient crone with straggly grey hair had studied her, asked her questions, felt the strength in her muscles. The ironclads who'd brought her explained what a fight she'd put up. The old woman had looked suspicious, as if she couldn't decide what sort of a person Shan was.

"She'll join the ironclads. Equip her then bring her to me."

That evening, the crone had led Shan through the machine: crossing between the clashing heads of steam-hammers, beneath chains buzzing with speed, past vast wheels that arched high into the sky. It didn't occur to Shan to try to escape.

A long, straight corridor led up to the doors. The corridor was plain but the doors were richly decorated with intricate designs of cogs and chains.

"Stand guard here," the crone said. "Let no one through. Understand? The doors are not locked but they are to stay closed at all times. Those are your orders."

Shan nodded and the crone turned to walk away.

"But why?" Shan called after her. "What lies through the doors?"

The crone turned. "Through there? All the sins of Engn, girl. Make sure no one goes through. That is your job, now."

And so, Shan had stood guard. And in twenty-five years no one had given her different orders, and each day she'd wondered what lay through the doors, and each day she hadn't dared look. Until now.

The handle creaked as she turned it, but it gave. Holding her breath, she pushed the door open.

Beyond lay a square room, wider than the corridor but just as plain. The room was featureless save for a glass orb like a large incandescent light-bulb, embedded in the ceiling. Across the room was another set of brass doors. Shan glanced back. No one had come. No one had seen. She had come this far. Pushing the door wide she stepped into the room, breathing heavily as if she was suddenly high up a mountain.

She had to release the first door to reach the second. She let it slip from her grasp then strode across the room.

The other doors were locked. Shan pushed and pulled but they wouldn't budge. Sudden panic rising in her, she ran back to the first door. She only had to get outside and all would be well. Nothing would have changed.

The handle twisted easily in her gauntlet, but now these doors wouldn't open either. She pulled and pushed, barging at the doors with her shoulders, kicking and kicking in desperation.

It made no difference. She was trapped. She cursed herself and her stupidity. If only she'd done as she'd been ordered. She took off her ironclad helmet and sank to the floor.

*

Two hours later there came a rattle of keys and the second door – the inner door – opened. An old man she'd never seen before stood there, his wild grey hair like a frozen explosion.

"So," he said. "You opened the door. Now come with me."

"I'm sorry," she said. "I had to know."

"No matter. Follow me."

Beyond the inner door lay another long corridor. The old man led Shan along it until it opened out into a circular room. Six more sets of closed doors led off and in the centre of the circular room was a hole: a shaft leading down into the darkness. Shan could feel cold air breathing up through it.

"Now you jump in," said the old man. "I can summon ironclads if necessary. It would be easier if you just jumped."

"But … I only wanted to know what lay through the door."

"And now you know."

"But I was told all the sins of Engn were through here."

"And what did you imagine those sins were?"

"I suppose greed … or lust. I don't know."

The old man shook his shaggy head. "No, no. There is only one sin in Engn. Only one sin and you have committed it."

"What sin?"

"Curiosity. You have asked questions. You have wondered what lies beyond, what it's all *for*. And that isn't allowed, I'm afraid. We always had doubts about you and now you have failed the tests. So, you must jump."

"What is down there? What will happen to me?"

The old man shrugged. "You will never see Engn again. No one comes back from down there. Now, good bye."

He stepped back, suddenly, and was gone through one of the doors. She was alone again. She circled round the shaft and tried the door. It was already locked. She tried all the doors, knowing it was useless. They were all locked. They would remain locked.

Shan stood in the centre of the round room, staring down into the blackness of the shaft that led to the mines deep beneath Engn.

The Brass Doors was originally published in 2013 in the Flash Fiction Fest anthology – a collection of stories which, that year, was themed around the seven deadly sins. The story is from the same universe as my steampunk fantasy Engn novels. Finn, the central character in those stories, also gets taken to the machine city of Engn, although his experiences are very different to Shan's, and he doesn't wait anywhere near as long before he rebels and starts to fight back...

If you're interested in finding out more about the Engn books, my web page for them is at simonkewin.co.uk/engn.

THE TALE OF THE DOG

Arkady stood in the cramped control room of Baikonur Cosmodrome, unable to pull his gaze from the flickering needle of the electrocardiogram. The dog's heart rate had dropped from its dangerous high of 240 bpm. Still, a weight of dread sat in Arkady's stomach. The thermometer readout showed the ambient temperature on the satellite remained over 40°C. She couldn't survive that for long. Something had gone terribly wrong up there in space.

"Come away, Arkady." Dr. Raskolnikoff stood beside him. "We've worked miracles. There's nothing more we can do, now."

Arkady glanced at her then back at the dials. "No," he said. "We can watch. We can do that at least."

Laika had been frantic at first judging by the readings, thrashing around as much as her chains allowed. Now she appeared to be lying still. Perhaps she was unconscious. The irony of it didn't escape Arkady. They'd taken her off the freezing streets of Moscow thinking she'd be tough enough to survive the cold if something went wrong. Something had, but now she was dying of heat exhaustion.

Not for the first time, Arkady wished there was a microphone he could speak into, send soothing words up to the flimsy metal craft. It would be something. If she was still conscious, Laika would be quivering with fear, unable to understand any of what was happening. But there hadn't been time to install such a device. They'd needed Sputnik 2 in a hurry. Laika was as alone as it was possible to be.

Part of Arkady willed the electrocardiogram needle to drop to zero, for the dog's misery to end. Part of him willed it to stay where it was; for Laika, somehow, miraculously, to survive her ordeal. He knew this could never be. The dog had trusted them and they'd sent her to her death. That was all there was to be said. They'd wanted her to climb into the cramped, padded cylinder of Sputnik 2 and so she had. He thought of her lying there, watching them, as they sealed the door on her. She hadn't made a noise.

And what should he say to the twins, Valentin and Galena, that evening? It had been a mistake to bring the dog home with him that one time to let them play with her.

"Can we keep her, father? Can we, please?"

"No, children. Laika here is very important. One day she'll be the most famous dog in the world. More famous than any of us scientists!"

"But I want to play with her. She likes me, father, see."

"I'm sorry, children. She's needed at the Cosmodrome."

He'd just wanted the dog to have one normal night in her life. Perhaps it had been wrong to give her that.

The needle flicked to zero with an audible *click*. He held his breath. Was this it? Then it flickered back up and hovered around 120. Really, it was remarkable they could monitor the heartbeat of a dog in orbit around the planet. They *had* worked miracles. Arkady swallowed and combed his hand through his grey hair, watching the dial as it reported the progress of Laika's death.

Another watcher observed the tiny, crude spaceship. Xenomonitor L'io was better equipped than Arkady. From the *Starsong*, her craft in high orbit above Earth, she could detect much more about the dog. Metabolic rates, tissue damage levels, the state of its underlying mental matrix. The ship's consciousness also provided L'io with a reliable projection of how long the dog had to live. Only a few minutes, now.

"We could rescue the creature," said L'io. "Save it from this ordeal."

She knew what the answer must be. It helped to speak the question.

"We cannot," said the *Starsong*, its calm voice speaking directly into L'io's brain. "The humans must know nothing about us."

"The creature is suffering."

"Many on the planet suffer."

"I know," said L'io. "But this creature is *up here*. With us. It feels like we have more of a responsibility for it."

"No, we dare not. Any intervention could be very damaging. Human society is fractured and vulnerable. It is better we simply watch. For now."

"We could confuse the telemetry," said L'io, ignoring the ship. "Make them think the creature has died, then rescue it. They expect the craft to burn up on re-entry."

The ship appeared to consider for a moment before replying. "This is hard but we have no choice. We must only watch. Until they are ready, perhaps years from now."

L'io thought about the creature packed into the tiny, pathetic ship. The dog wasn't sentient, but it was capable of experiencing distress. And after two hundred years of watching, she longed to help one creature at least. Just one creature.

She returned her attention to the dog, channelling its fear and pain directly into her own mind, bearing witness to its suffering. It was something. Mercifully, its distress had faded a little as it ebbed towards death.

The needle on the electrocardiogram dropped to zero again. Arkady waited for it to snap back into movement. It was another glitch. But this time it stayed stuck to zero, like the machine had been switched off. Laika's heart had given out, somewhere up there in space.

He exhaled, as if he hadn't breathed at all for the past hour. At least it was over. He wondered if the twins would accept it if he told them they'd sent Laika up into heaven and she was now with the angels. He could think of nothing else to tell them.

*

"I urge you not do this," said the ship. "If the humans suspect anything our mission will be ruined. Earth society is too fragile. It is only one dog."

L'io ignored it. The ship was ancient and wise, but it lacked empathy. Obviously. This was why these missions *had* Xenomonitors. Logic only got you so far. Sometimes you had to ignore the rules and do what was right.

Working as quickly as she could, L'io suppressed the crude telemetry devices broadcasting from the tiny Earth spaceship, ensuring no signals could reach the planet. Then she began to manoeuvre the *Starsong* into a lower orbit, spiralling down hard onto an intercept trajectory. She had only a few seconds to act.

*

So many strange smells, sounds. Laika panted, still unable to move, unable to do anything other than wait for her pack-mates to rescue her. Where were they? They would come for her. They wouldn't abandon her in this terrible place.

Bright light blinded her for a moment, loud bangs shaking through her. Something was coming. She whimpered, making it clear she was no threat. Strange, new smells filled her nose, rubbery and meaty all at once, like nothing she had come across before. Through the light she could see something moving. Not one of her pack, no one she recognized. Would she have to fight? She was weak but if these were enemies of her own pack, she would attack without question.

The strange newcomer made noises. The voice made no sense but the sound of it was gentle, soothing. Laika waited, sniffing the air, trying to understand what was happening. Something like a hand, a hand with too many fingers, reached out of the bright light to touch her, gently, on top of her head.

Laika waited for a moment, feeling safe in her cramped prison but wanting to escape it, too. She felt the bonds holding her down being released. She stood on shaky legs.

She waited a moment more than, warily, one step at a time, crept forward into the light to meet her new pack.

The story of Laika, launched into space in Sputnik 2 in 1957 and the first animal to orbit our planet, is well known. It is believed she did die from overheating after a few hours in space, but it was always known she would not be able to return to Earth. Whatever would be learned from the mission, Laika was being sent to her death. This story imagines a different ending for the dog, and it would be good to think Laika's fate was actually something like that described.

The story was published in Spaceports and Spidersilk in 2013.

THE CAT'S TALE

I mean, I know this whole bizarre set-up is just a thought-experiment. That's not a hell of a lot of consolation stuck here inside this box, I can tell you. Soon as I'm out of here, I'm ripping your *damn* face off with my claws, no questions asked. Assuming I get out of here alive, of course.

Because, yeah, yeah, I may be dead already and just haven't noticed. Or wait, no, I'm dead *and* I'm alive. Both at the same time. Actually, I get that. If I catch a mouse and drop it on the floor, a lot of the time it'll just lie there. Could be dead, which is boring, could be just playing dead, waiting for its chance to scuttle off, which is fun. See? It's alive *and* dead. That's not rocket science is it? No need for your fancy radiation and hydrocyanic-poisoning rig. No violation of animal rights. OK, there's the mouse, but they're just, like, food, right?

And, while we're on the subject, what's with the radioactive isotope, anyway? Imprisonment and poisoning not enough for you? I have to crouch here while a chunk of caesium throws off alpha particles too? Great. Thanks, Dr. Frankenschrödinger. Just peachy. You won't look so smart without facial features, will you? It'll be *you* collapsing, not your precious wave functions.

Because, you wanna know what the worst of sitting here is? In my little cell, not enough room to swing a dead (or alive) cat? I'll tell you. It's *damn* painful being split between two conceptual states. My head's been throbbing ever since you locked me in. I'm so angry I could *spit*. In fact, I have been spitting. And what have I got to look forward to? The moment you open the box and peer inside, when my atoms – or whatever the hell it is, like I care – suddenly decide if I've been alive or dead all along. I expire right there. Or I don't. It's 50-50. Not great odds, are they?

At least, either way, I figure my headache should get better.

Because you have to open the damn box *sometime*, right? Or maybe not. The irony, of course, is that I don't know. You're either out there about to release me or you're not. Ha-bloody-ha, you're in both states. And I only get to find out which it is when I escape.

Which is what I'm gonna do. See, I don't like either fate you've decided for me. Here's a third option for you. I'm breaking out of here. *Now.* Where's that in your equations?

I've already got a claw through the side of the box. Obviously, you haven't noticed or my head would have stopped throbbing. A wider hole and I'm *gone*. Tell you what, here's an alternative thought-experiment for you since I'm ruining this one. I'm either going to leap screaming for your jugular or I'm going straight for your eyeballs. Right now, in a quantum way, I'm doing both, yes? Good. Keep on thinking about that. Eyeballs *and* jugular.

Because, any second now, one or the other is *going*. Or, actually, it may be both. At the same time.

This flash story was published in 2013, in Stupefying Stories. Obviously, just to be clear, Schrödinger didn't actually do this to a cat, and nor did he believe the conceptual cat inside its box was both alive and dead. He was using the cat to illustrate what he saw as a problem with one interpretation of quantum mechanics. Still, I thought it would be amusing to write a story from the viewpoint of the conceptual cat. I like the way the unnamed feline seems to have a good grasp of the principles of the thought-experiment – as well as being seriously, spittingly, furious at its fate...

THE SEVEN OTHER DWARVES

It was a dark and stormy night, which was why she missed the signpost at the crossroads in the depths of the old woods and ended up taking the *other* path through the trees.

The day had started so well: a picnic with a hunter whose muscle-tone resembled that of one of her father's stallions. She'd imagined several interesting scenarios, one or two of which had brought a distinct blush to her white face. But being knocked out and abandoned was certainly not one of them. Now, she shivered as the rain lashed into her face. She could damn well *die* out here. Which was presumably the plan all along.

Then she saw lights twinkling invitingly. Mysterious cottages in the depths of the woods were to be avoided, but she was past caring. Raindrops dripped from her nose and the cold numbed her toes. She walked up and knocked on the low little door. Then, before anyone could answer, she pushed it open.

Inside was a room containing a low wooden table and seven chairs. There had clearly been some sort of fight or a particularly energetic ball, because the place was a mess. The chairs lay strewn around on their sides and food and drink had been thrown everywhere. But a log fire smouldered away, filling the room with a welcome warmth.

"Hello?" she called. "Is there anyone home?"

No answer. Well, they surely wouldn't mind her sheltering from the storm. And she was too exhausted to go on; she felt like she could sleep for a thousand years. She needed to get out of her wet things before she caught her death. A flight of wooden steps led up to a loft. She called up in her sweetest voice, but again no-one replied.

Seven beds lined the upper floor, all unoccupied. Each had its owner's name carved onto its end. And such strange names. *Angry, Greedy, Lazy, Proud, Lusty, Envy, and Gluttony.* Only Lusty's bed was big enough for her. The others were little more than cots but that one was a king-sized four-poster. She wasn't used to sleeping in black silk sheets, but frankly she was too exhausted to care. She climbed in and was immediately asleep.

*

She was awoken by raucous singing from downstairs. Before she could move, many feet were clumping up the stairs. She gasped and sat up, pulling the black sheets around her shoulders. A thin light filtered through the wooden shutters. It was nearly dawn.

Seven strong little men – dwarves – racketed into the room and were immediately hushed by the sight of her. They had clearly been drinking: they swayed and looked baffled. Finally, one stepped forwards. He grinned as if all his birthdays had come at once.

"You've been sleeping in my bed," he said, apparently confused over which fairytale he was in.

"I'm sorry," she said. "I was lost and..."

"Oh, it's fine," said the dwarf. "I don't mind. *Really.* Quite the opposite in fact."

"I'm going to bed," said another. He fell onto the cot

marked *Lazy* without even removing his boots.

"Look, what are you doing here?" asked a third, a look of fury on his face. *Angry* presumably. "What do you mean you're lost?"

"I was abandoned," she explained. "My stepmother arranged to have me left for dead in the forest. I think … I think she envies my beauty."

"Well that makes sense," said another of the dwarves. "Perfectly reasonable behaviour. The question is, what do we do with you now?"

"Easy," said Lusty. "You come to live with us."

"Oh, really?" she said. "Just like that? I hope you're not expecting me to cook and clean or … anything else?"

"Certainly not," said another dwarf sniffily. Probably *Proud*. "If you're after outmoded gender clichés you want the cabin on the other side of the woods. We're nothing like them."

"But what would I do here?"

"Chill out!" called Lazy without opening his eyes.

"Party!" said Gluttony who had lain down on the floor. "Eat and drink! Dance with the wood-nymphs!"

"You don't … work in the mines?"

Proud looked offended. "Certainly not."

"We do occasionally *steal* from the mines to fund our dissolute lifestyle," said Greedy.

"But my stepmother. She'll come looking for me. And then there's Prince Charming. I'm supposed to marry him."

"This stepmother of yours," said Lusty. "Is she good looking? Is she … friendly?"

"Is she rich?" asked Greedy.

"Be quiet!" called Proud. He turned to regard her through little round spectacles. "If anyone comes looking for you we'll send them packing. We'll set Angry on them. Seriously, you wouldn't like him when he's angry."

"What about this Prince?" said Lusty. "Do you *want* to marry him?"

She considered. No-one had actually asked her this before. "I might. He is very handsome."

"Then he can come and live here too," said Proud.

"Here?"

"Sure. If he's a Prince I'll bet his family is as dysfunctional as yours."

"His father is a bit of a tyrant."

"There you are then," said Proud. "Come and live free. Let your hair down. Have some *fun*. We'll be one of those non-traditional family units."

She regarded them from her bed. Lazy snored gently from across the room. Gluttony belched. Lusty grinned in an encouraging sort of way and occasionally raised an eyebrow. They really were amusing. Better than that, they didn't pretend to be something they weren't, unlike everyone back at the palace. Didn't expect something of her all the time.

"You know," she said. "I think I'd like that."

The dwarves cheered – all apart from the slumbering Lazy – while Gluttony called for ale to toast the new arrangement.

*

That evening they threw a huge party to celebrate. And once Charming had turned up and had the arrangement explained to him, they threw a second party to celebrate some more. And then they all lived happily – if rather disreputably – ever after.

This is another little story that appeared in the seven deadly sins Flash Fiction Fest anthology in 2013. The names of the seven sins sounded like the names of the dwarves from the Snow White story, and I got to thinking how things might have turned out differently if Snow White had taken another path in the woods. It's another updating of a familiar story. I think I'd have much preferred to end up with this set of dwarves, too...

EARTH STATION SIX

Commander Rosa Vishnu watched explosions flowering across the face of the Earth. London, Paris and Berlin in a neat triangle over in the east. Boston, New York and Washington directly below the station. Then LA, San Francisco and Vancouver on the western limb of the planet. She'd watched the recording so many times but still she picked out new details, like the way the cobweb of lights – highways and urban sprawl – flickered out just before each warhead struck. The power grids had been the first thing to go, plunging the Earth into its final darkness.

She thought, as she always did, about Ravi, her last sight of him waving goodbye at Kennedy as the transporter took her off to the rocket. Clever, handsome Ravi and the life they'd planned together. She'd wanted four children, two girls and two boys. He'd pitch them balls in the park while she showed them all the beauties of the mountains and the woods. Sometimes, in her dreams, her phantom family became real. They walked together down some trail, laughing and kidding around, talking about their lives. Their plans.

Those days, waking up to the reality of the cramped interior of Earth Station Six, were the worst.

She'd promised to wave to Ravi each day on one of their orbits. She still did sometimes, although the precise location of Michigan – of anything now – was hard to pin down. She just hoped the end, when it came, had been brief for him. Not some drawn-out, nightmarish battle for depleting supplies of food and water.

"Pretty lights."

Her crewmate – the one she called Zoe – had floated into the observation pod beside her. The familiar tang of the plasticizing resins that gave Zoe's skin its shiny glaze filled Rosa's nose. Of her five crewmates, Zoe was the most human, seemed the most alive. The other four barely spoke, but some fragment of the person Zoe had once been seemed to linger about her. Zoe gave Rosa hope. It was because of her that Rosa had decided on her course of action.

"Yes, Zoe. It's the Earth being destroyed by the nuclear holocaust."

Zoe nodded, accepting the news without reply. Just as she had done almost every day for five years now. Zoe and the others were programmed for simple tasks, nothing more. Rosa searched in vain for some look of understanding in those blank eyes. Their resurrected bodies were immune to radiation, oxygen starvation and all but extreme physical damage. They were also, as a by-product, immune to feelings of loss or sadness. Rosa found herself envying her five reanimated crewmates more and more. They went about their daily tasks, not knowing or caring that they were the last of humanity.

She wondered again who they'd been in life. Criminals given an alternative to the electric chair? Volunteers with some fatal disease contributing their bodies to science? Or even, as some had whispered, crazed science fiction fans prepared to go to any length to get into space on an actual spaceship? Whatever. She'd never know now. They were simply organic robots, corpses preserved by chemicals and animated by clever electronics.

Rosa switched off the recording. The screens returned to the true pictures of the planet below, relayed from the planetside cameras. The uniform grey shrouds of the nuclear winter filled the scene once more.

"Lights gone," said Zoe, sounding like a disappointed child.

"Yes, Zoe. All the lights have gone out now."

The decision to send reanimated corpses into space (only the press used the term *zombies*) had been a purely economic one. Her crewmates didn't require an oxygen supply, didn't sleep and could EVA to fix the station without even wearing a suit. They were machines, easier and cheaper to produce than anything artificial. It made sense.

But a living person had been needed to make the decisions. That was Rosa. She'd been reluctant to accept the mission: her life-long ambition to go into space tempered by the thought of spending a month cooped up with five reprogrammed corpses. Sometimes she still regretted it. Perhaps a swift end down on the surface would have been better.

Still, she was alive. She was *here*. And that was important. Precious. Perhaps, at the end, Ravi had enough warning to know what was coming. And perhaps the thought of her, safe up there in orbit, had been a comfort for him. So she liked to think.

But oxygen: that was the problem. Their reserves were now all-but depleted. The electrolysis units had been losing efficiency for months. The solar array gave them all the power they needed. They had supplies of dried food to last years and could probably eke out the recycled water that long, too. But the oxygen was running out. Which didn't affect Zoe and the rest, but it was a problem for Rosa. A big problem. That, in the end, had made her mind up for her.

Zoe was hauling herself away by the grip-handles now, to join Zed, Zeb, Zander and Zach – so Rosa had taken to calling them – in the science pod. They'd been instructed to carry out a series of zero-g physics experiments and they faithfully did so, even though it was futile. Rosa didn't try to stop them. She liked the activity. The illusion of purpose.

"Zoe, before you go, I want to give you some new instructions later. When you're finished in the science pod. Is that OK?"

Zoe didn't reply. She had no views on whether it was OK or not. She hadn't been programmed to have views. She absorbed the information then waited to see if Rosa had finished. Her plasticized face gleamed from the internal lights of the station. Rosa wondered what it would be like to have a hide that tough. Nothing could hurt you.

"I'll have to upload some new routines and data into your chips," she said. "Do you understand, Zoe?"

Zoe still said nothing. Awaiting further instructions.

"Zoe, I'm going to become one of you," said Rosa. "Understand? Then we can all live together up here for as long as the sun gives us power. And I need you to perform the procedures. Do you see?"

Zoe looked at her but said nothing.

"Then we can sit here together and watch the Earth each day, you and I," said Rosa. "Would that be OK? Perhaps, one day in the future, the clouds will start to clear and we'll catch a glimpse of the surface again. Would you like that?"

Still Zoe didn't reply. With a sigh, Rosa turned away, back to the grey Earth and the blackness of space.

"Rosa … like Zoe?"

Rosa turned back to see Zoe still floating in the O of the hatchway. The muscles beneath the plasticized skin on her face flexed and bunched as she struggled to form further words.

"Yes," said Rosa. "I'll become like you. Rosa and Zoe. We can sit here together."

Zoe looked down to her feet, then back up, still trying

to get her mouth to work. Their faces didn't make expressions any more, but it seemed to Rosa there was something like puzzlement there, as if Zoe was grappling with some difficult concept. Perhaps she was imagining it.

Zoe's mouth worked some more before she spoke again. "We watch for Ravi. Watch Earth together. Until lights come back. Come back for *real*."

Rosa found sudden tears welling in her eyes. Now there was, clearly, an expression on Zoe's face. A longing. A desperation to be understood.

Rosa nodded. "Yes, Zoe. You and me. Yes. We'll wait here together for that day. For the day the lights start shining on the Earth again."

And something like a smile, or the thought of a smile, finally worked its way across Zoe's plastic features as she nodded in understanding.

Earth Station Six is another story written for an anthology – this time themed around apocalypse. The story grew from imagining the last surviving human watching from orbit as the world comes to an end, but the problem was then that I needed to give her someone to talk to. Some sort of machine intelligence would have been the obvious answer, but using plasticized, human robot zombie creatures like Zoe seemed like an interesting way to go. I'd been wondering, separately, whether we'd ever do that rather than go to the expense and difficulty of building the robots and androids you see in so much science fiction.

The story was published in 2014 in A is for Armageddon.

THE WRONG TOM JACKS

Simms stood in a circular white room, surrounded by the frozen heads of forty-two dead from the twentieth century.

He recorded every detail of the scene via his brain plug-in. Strictly speaking he had no business being here in the LA Bethesda Eternity Clinic and you never knew when information would come in useful. He didn't have the clinic's full client list, but each head sat encased within a two-meter silver cylinder, each bearing a small name plaque his plug-in could resolve. He stored each name away, the one he recognized and the forty-one he didn't.

"This way. The patient is over here."

The ratty, unkempt clinician he'd bribed crossed the room, glancing backwards at Simms to make sure he was following. Simms smiled at all of it. At the attendant, so proud of his ridiculous little world, at their insistence on the word *patient*, at the whole insane set-up. Did these people actually think *this* was eternal life? That they could conveniently bypass society's slide into hell? Be woken up in a golden future with all their cancers healed?

Elsewhere in the clinic there were full bodies preserved. The ones who could afford the deluxe package. *These* poor unfortunates had gone for the cheaper option. Simms almost felt sorry for them. He wondered what sacrifices each had made for even this.

He put it out of his mind. What did it matter? Wasn't any business of his. People with money paid and facilities like this met the demand. No harm in any of it. Perhaps it wasn't so different to what he did.

"This is him."

Simms stopped at the cylinder the attendant identified. It looked good. Tom Jacks, born 1954, *suspended* 2015. Yeah, right. Simms knew very little about him. A famous name, sure, but *this* Tom Jacks was a nobody. His searches had turned up nothing interesting at all. He was just a unique pattern of base-pairs that someone, somewhere was willing to pay for. Weird, sure, but he asked no questions. Collectors collected and he provided. He'd triple-checked they wanted *this* man and not his famous namesake. Most likely some relative researching the family-tree. Or it could be other things, but that was none of his business. Get the DNA, get paid, that was all that mattered.

The job made him uneasy, though. Damn thing was, he couldn't see why. It was straightforward enough. Maybe too straightforward. Things didn't go like this. It had only taken him a day and no one had threatened him, let alone tried to kill him. Here was the DNA, conveniently packaged up in a frozen brain. Somehow, he was sure, he was being played. He just couldn't see how.

He looked at the cylinder. The head was sealed inside, awaiting the dawn of the age of miracles. A dusting of frost coated the silver exterior. Was that right? Wasn't it supposed to be insulated?

"And you can extract a sample?" he said to the attendant. "You're sure it's clean, no decay?"

"Of course. There's an access point for biopsies. I'm sure you've heard the stories. How we don't really preserve anyone, just take their money to maintain empty chambers."

The attendant shook his head at the things people

believed. Simms said nothing. He wanted to get the job done and leave. Despite the cold and the sealed units, the place smelled of chemicals and decay. He was willing to bet the attendant came in here and talked to the damn heads when there was no one else around.

Simms took out the sterile needle he'd bought with him and handed it to the attendant.

"Here. I will test the sequence against his known phenotype. Anything less than 99% and the deal's off. Understand?"

Usually this was the time they started to bargain, see problems, remember expenses. The attendant merely assented with a nod of his head. Either he was a fool or he was playing a part. Simms watched as the man flipped open a small hatch in the side of the cylinder and inserted the needle into the dead brain within. A small screen lit up on the surface of the cylinder so they could see the needle's progress.

When he had the sample, Simms inserted it into the sequencer he carried. The device sampled the DNA, flashed through a simulated development cycle to full maturity, ran comparisons against the known historical details of this Tom Jacks. Within a minute, the results were communicated to Simms' brain.

His job would be a lot damn easier if everyone just got a number tattooed onto them at birth.

He looked at the attendant, waiting by the cylinder, breathing through his nose like this was the most exciting thing that had ever happened to him. Or like he might bolt at any moment. He could be a useful contact. This job was junk, sure, but you never knew what the next one would be. A cryogenic clinic attendant amenable to bribery might be a very useful person to know. Especially since Simms now had recorded proof he *had* been bribed.

"The sample is good. Here's your forty K."

Simms transferred the agreed sum, encrypted and untraceable. He saw the moment the money reached the attendant: the smile that brightened on the man's face was like the summer sun rising. Doubling your annual pay can do that. Which only troubled Simms all the more. The guy was an amateur. Someone was playing both of them. He'd been careful. He was always careful. When he crossed the line he made sure he left no evidence. Always gave clients the full speech about the uses to which recovered DNA could be put, word-for-word from the law. So far as the authorities knew, he accessed only public records. The bribe to this attendant was an infringement, sure, but no one would be able to prove a connection. He'd run through everything several times but could see no loopholes. It nagged at him. He hated that.

"I'd like to leave now," he said.

The attendant nodded as he sealed up the cylinder. They left Tom to his long wait and walked out, past room after room of frozen remains. Simms wished he could grab the names on all the units, but the doors were sealed. The attendant, whose name he still didn't know, was taking enough risk letting Simms do what he'd done. They could always come up with some line about visiting a relative if challenged, but if the clinic owners found out what their employee had done, it would be all over for him. For a set-up like this, public perception was everything.

They stopped at security doors while the attendant let the machinery sample his DNA. What was that all about? Controlling who came in made perfect sense, but controlling who left? Did they think the dead were going to rise up and try to escape? They'd seen too many old movies.

The security doors hinged open and they were back in the warmer air of the clinic's lobby, all polished marble and subtle music. Vases of flowers. *Real* flowers. A group of relatives sat in silence on the leather chairs, their expressions blank, no one talking. He thought about them all: the thousands and thousands of dead people in there, the thousands and thousands of estates paying fees in perpetuity. It was a beautiful thing. Maybe he should start one up himself. A few big contracts and he'd have enough money. Then he could sit back and enjoy life, let others do the work. He was willing to bet the myths about these places were true, often as not. Make it look good, professional like a real hospital, and people would pay. You didn't need to actually freeze the remains. Who would know?

Turning the pleasant fantasy over in his mind, he walked to the clinic's jump node. Normally he avoided them. The public jump infrastructure was shot to shit. But with a job came expenses and with expenses came the wonder of private networks. He instructed the system to take him back to London. He dialled in a few random jumps around the world *en route*, too, to throw anyone who might be following him. Private networks were more reliable, sure, but he didn't trust them to be any more secure.

*

He knew something had gone wrong the moment he stepped out of the destination node. This was definitely not London Euston. Too clean, for one thing. Too quiet. He stood in a bare, square room; bright white walls, no doors or windows. The only way in or out was via the jump node he'd stepped from. He scanned it, as he habitually did, hoping to probe the network logs for anyone following him. The plug-ins required for this were highly illegal, but he happened to have a set hidden away in his skull. He got the node's address but nothing more. The gateway was deactivated. He checked his clock. Ten seconds had elapsed since he'd left the clinic. While you were in the jump network you technically didn't exist, had no consciousness of the passage of time. But, wherever he was, at least he had materialised. Everyone knew the stories about people trapped inside the jump networks, stuck for so long no one dared extract them to tell them. It was immortality of sorts, he supposed. Beat having your head cut off and frozen.

"Ah, Simms. There you are."

A disembodied voice from a metal grill in the opposite wall. He recognized it immediately. Things began to slot into place. So this was it? The whole job had been a GMA sting? Checking up licences?

"Agent Ballard of the Genetic Monitoring Agency," said Simms. "Hit another puzzle you can't solve? Having trouble telling the time, maybe?"

Ballard laughed his deep, rolling laugh. Was he nearby or somewhere remote? It didn't matter. It was typical of Ballard to lurk in the shadows. Simms really couldn't blame him. They'd met physically once or twice. If *his* face was as disfigured as Ballard's, if his features dripped like melted plastic, he'd stay hidden too. Acid thrown in his face, it was said, years back. Some thug resisting arrest. Ballard *could* have got it fixed long ago. Word was he liked his shocking appearance just fine. Found it useful when it came to playing the scary GMA agent.

"Simms, Simms. I'd really be more polite if I were you. I've pulled you out of the jump network to count how many laws you've broken today. Make my day any worse and I'll have to start looking *real* close."

The GMAn sounded delighted at the prospect.

"Investigate away. You won't find anything, but perhaps it'll make you feel like you're doing something useful with your life."

As he talked, Simms glanced around the room, trying to figure out an escape plan. He came up with precisely nothing. He had good plug-ins, unregistered military-grade tech that might be able to reactivate the jump mechanism. But they would take time to work and the GMA would have counter-measures. Plus, the less Ballard knew about his brain-boosters, the better.

"So," said Ballard. "According to the logs, you've been

commissioned to track down the DNA of a Tom Jacks. Purpose: addition to an unnamed collector's molecule library. All completely above-board and legal."

"That's correct. And well done on the reading. Some of those words are tricky."

"I'm puzzled, though," Ballard continued. "You specialise in musicians. Rock gods and dance divas from history. This man was a no one. Times hard are they?"

"I have to work to make a living. You should try it some time."

"Surely you're not intending to pass this Tom Jacks off as *the* Tom Jacks to some unfortunate citizen?"

"Obviously not. That would be illegal."

"Oh, but wait, what's this?" Ballard continued. "I see you're on your way home from the Bethesda Eternity Clinic, last resting place of Tom Jacks – the wrong Tom Jacks – currently cryogenically preserved and awaiting a cure for pancreatic cancer. Now that is odd, because the estate of *this* Mr. Jacks has granted no access to his remains."

"Which is why my trip was futile," said Simms. "Shame, but that's how it goes."

"So you didn't, say, illegally acquire this poor, dead man's DNA?"

"That's right. I didn't illegally acquire this poor, dead man's DNA."

"And the large sum of money you just sent from one of your accounts?"

Simms smiled, sure Ballard could at least see him. "A down payment on a slot at the clinic for myself. And thanks for being so concerned about my well-being."

Ballard snorted with laughter. "And if I let the techs loose on your brain and all those exotic plug-ins of yours, you're saying they won't find the DNA of Mr. Jacks encrypted away somewhere?"

A warrant for a full brain-dump on a suspect was still hard to get, even on a genehunter. They both knew that.

Simms had to hope it was too much trouble for Ballard to bother.

"Obviously not. That would also be illegal, Agent Ballard. I'm shocked at the suggestion."

"Or, I suppose I could visit the clinic myself," Ballard said. "Ask a few questions, see what really occurred?"

There was the weakness. The attendant should have expunged logs as instructed. He probably wouldn't stick to his story with Ballard bellowing away at him. Yet this was such a small-time job going to all that trouble made no sense. Ballard was having fun with him. Or… yes. He saw, then, what this really was. Some things didn't change.

"You could do all that, yes," said Simms. "And if I *have* accidentally transgressed some minor regulation, I suppose I'd have to pay some fine?"

"Approaching an official of a registered clinic without the estate's consent *is* a transgression, Simms."

"OK, Ballard. Just tell me how much you want."

"Forty K should cover it."

Simms considered for a moment. But there wasn't a damn thing he could do. If he refused he'd find his licence revoked one sunny day and that would be that. None of this *fine* would go near the authorities, sure, but he had no choice.

"Here's your money, Ballard. Now activate this node."

"My pleasure, Simms. And you be careful out there. There are all sorts of people trying to rip you off."

"Yeah. I heard that."

"Oh, and one more thing before you go. Who is *Boneyard?*"

Motherfucker. So this whole thing with the money was just a little extra for Ballard? He really, really hated the GMAn.

"Never heard of him. Friend of yours? Sounds unpleasant enough."

"A person I'd like to meet. I figure someone living in the gutter like you might have heard a whisper or two."

"And if I had?"

"Then you'd tell me. And we stay friends."

"Well, I'm sorry to be a disappointment."

"Oh, I'm used to it. But keep your ears open, OK, Simms? Bring me something useful and I'll think even more highly of you than I already do."

"Good bye, Ballard," said Simms. "And, just a suggestion, maybe spend that money you stole from me on cosmetic surgery? They can work miracles these days, you know."

*

Simms stepped out of a node in the twelve-by-twelve array at Euston and pushed his way through the crowds out onto the streets. The stacktower where he lived was a twenty minute walk away. As he strode along, he sent a ping out to the agent who'd employed him on the Jacks job. He didn't know who his real employer was, of course. He knew the agent only as Mann. Which was not going to be his real name.

Mann replied immediately. Simms had the uncomfortable feeling Mann had known he'd be calling. Was Ballard mixed up in this somehow? Was Mann one of them, a GMAn? Was his name what passed for humour in the GMA? Christ. How was a guy to make an illegal living with these mosquitoes buzzing around, sucking his blood?

"Mr. Simms. You have the DNA sequence my client requested?"

The voice on the other end was calm, thoughtful. More the voice of a lawyer, someone used to weighing words carefully.

"I have it here," said Simms. "Plus documentation to prove provenance. Send payment and you can have the code right now."

"My client will have to test the DNA first, Mr. Simms. He or she does not intend to pay for some random sequence of numbers or the genetic sequence of, let us say, a dead baboon."

"You employed me because you could trust me."

"Still, I am under instruction. This is what we agreed."

"And if I send you the code and never hear from you again?"

"Then you would have cause to be angry and could lodge a complaint with the authorities."

"Yeah, yeah."

Simms sent the sequence off through the ether. They'd agreed encryption keys up front so there was no danger it could be intercepted as it traversed the net.

"Many thanks, Mrs. Simms. I shall be in touch at the earliest opportunity."

"Make sure you are. *Mann*."

Simms closed the link and turned his attention to the London street. The usual shit, piles of rubble, dead… things. The rain hammered down, a blur of spray on the hard ground. Why was it always raining? Surely it could be sunny occasionally? At least the rain helped wash the stench of decay and burning plastic away. He was old enough to remember how it had once been, when the streets were more-or-less safe and everything more-or-less worked. Now look at it. People used to say everything was going to hell. They didn't say it any more did they? They knew it had damn well *gone*.

He shook his head. Nothing he could do. He felt like this because he'd finished a job. Normally, some investigation would be bouncing around in his brain and he wouldn't notice his surroundings, the scowling people, the filth. Now he did. He hated the emptiness that inactivity brought.

Still, he had money to burn. Despite Ballard's cut, he'd be solvent once Mann's money came through. He could afford some downtime. He'd earned it. He called up an overlay from the relevant plug-in to shut London out. Immediately, an augmented version of the city replaced the ruined original. Trees lined spotless streets. The air smelt of roses. Contented people strolled by, hand-in-hand. Children played. They were dangerous, these false realities. People got lost in them. But he could control it. Right now it was fine.

*

Back home, he decided, what the hell, to ping Kelly. They hadn't spoken for, what, two months? She'd said she was going to get back to him. He was still waiting.

"Simms? What is it?"

To his surprise, the connection went straight through. She sounded harassed, though, like she didn't really want to speak to him.

"Just seeing how you are. You didn't call, I was worried."

"Yeah, right."

"Come on, Kelly. That's not fair. How many times do I need to apologize to you?"

"Oh, plenty more yet."

"OK, OK. Look, I wanted to know how you've been, for Christ's sake."

She paused for a moment before replying, like she was regretting her harsh words. So he liked to imagine.

"I'm fine. Busy. We're taking more in each day. We're going to have to expand to house everyone soon."

Another dig at him. He was to blame? He collected DNA. If other people used it to fill their private zoos with black-market copies of the great and famous, how was that down to him? He didn't operate the cloning vats, he didn't discard the damaged misshapes when they turned out wrong. He just did his job. Jesus Christ, everyone was on his back today.

"Look, Kelly, I'm sorry, OK? Sorry for what I do. Sorry for all the people who wash up there with you. It's not my fault, OK? None of it's my fault."

"Is that right, Simms?"

"Look, the thing is, work's been going well. I was thinking I could come over. I know the refuge always need funds. I could make a contribution. Something. I mean, no one likes to see the state these people are in. And maybe we could do something together. Go some place."

It was partly his age, but fleshbots didn't cut it for him. Even when they proxied for a real person somewhere distant. You still knew. You always knew. The thought of sex with Kelly, the real Kelly, would make everything – Ballard, London, Mann – *everything* better.

"You want to give us money from some DNA job? To help the people here?"

For a moment, he thought she was warming to the idea. "Yeah. I thought, you know, it would be something."

"You're unbelievable, Simms. Un-fucking-believable."

"Kelly, I…"

But she cut the connection. She was gone. He didn't try to ping her back.

His eyes focused on reality once more. He stood and stared out of his stackroom window at the grey clouds sweeping in across the London skyline. God *damn*. Why did he bother? It wasn't like she'd been completely innocent was it? Wasn't that what she was doing, out there in the Arizona desert? Making amends, trying to put something back? He got that. He'd do it himself, one day, if he could. Enough money from a few big deals and he could start his own refuge. They could run it together, the past forgotten. He could idle away his days in the sun while she divided her time between him and saving the world's cloning victims. All those brain-damaged Elvises and broken Mandela-copies living out their remaining years. She'd be full of gratitude. It would be beautiful.

Well. If he couldn't have her, a fleshbot would have to do. He'd paid for good emulation, although he could always tell when it – she – said or did something the real Kelly wouldn't. When its sex-toy programming was a little too near the surface. Weirdly, that was always an instant turn-off. But it would have to do.

And, if he couldn't have the real Kelly, he could at least have real acid. He didn't go in for direct-brain electronic analogues. He had the plug-ins, sure, but didn't use them. Nothing touched the real stuff. You could still buy it if you knew the right people. And Simms prided himself on always knowing the right people.

He made sure the stackroom was secure. The fleshbot booted up and moved towards him, swinging its hips a little too much to be believable. Sims sighed. He wondered what would happen if he gave *it* acid, too. That could be funny.

*

The call interrupted him an hour later. It took him some time to grasp what it was. His com plug-in had trouble presenting his consciousness with an avatar of his caller. Had trouble *finding* his consciousness. Simms saw the sun turning into a vast face, becoming a mouth that screamed at him from the sky. Eventually he grasped someone was trying to reach him.

He shunned direct-brain drugs, but electronic detox could be damn useful. He kicked one off now, flushing the shit from his brain, sharpening the lines of reality around him. Slowly everything came into focus. Was his room always this small? Jesus. When he was ready he answered the ping.

"Hi, Mann. You got my money?"

"Can we talk?"

"What is there to talk about? I've done what you asked, now you pay the bill. That's how that works."

"I'd like to talk to you about another contract."

"Always happy to discuss a job. Let's complete the old one, then we can move onto the new one."

Didn't they have the money? But then, why bother to

get in touch? More likely, they had a problem with what he'd done. The wrong Tom Jacks after all? He couldn't see how, but he didn't need an unsatisfied customer seeking revenge. Especially some big shot used to getting their way. He wished he'd spent more time researching Mann, found out who he worked for. But the amount of money involved had been so small he hadn't bothered.

"Of course, of course. Here's your money, Mr. Simms."

The man's tone made it clear the amount was so trifling he'd simply forgotten to send it. Simms watched the zeroes counting up in his brain.

"OK," he said. "Now we can talk."

"Excellent. As a matter of fact, I'd like to meet up with you."

Alarm bells rang. He was still a bit out of it, a bit paranoid, but employers wanting to meet up generally meant bad things. He'd seen it happen often enough over the years.

"Why? This conversation is completely secure. No one can overhear."

"My employer is rather old-fashioned. He or she likes to, ah, *stare a man in the eye*. Apparently, by these means, he or she is able to judge character very effectively."

"You want to set up a meeting between me and your employer?"

"That's correct."

Mann had his attention now. Simms reached out and deactivated the fleshbot kneeling on the floor in front of him. What was going on here? It could all be a line. A convincing tale. Still, it could also be something sweet. A meeting with the money behind the façade generally meant they were taking you more seriously. Which meant more of the money. If they were unhappy with him, why go to all this trouble? They could deal with him from afar: a shot in the night, an EM pulse sending his plug-ins into meltdown. But not *polite conversation* for fuck's sake.

"OK," he said. "Tell me when and where."

*

In the day he had spare, Simms took the time to do his job properly: find out who he was really dealing with, what their angle was. It didn't take a genius to work some of it out. The smoke and mirrors made it obvious. The party required DNA and they needed to be sure Simms was reliable. Now they knew. Problem was, Simms knew nothing about *them*. Knowledge was power. Anything could give him an edge, even if it only meant he could cut a better deal.

Standard trawls through the archives turned up nothing. Inevitably. With only a few hours to go before their meeting, unable to think of anything else, Simms decided to try Devi. Devi knew everyone.

Devi was another hunter, and hunters usually didn't mix. They were competitors. If you had a job another hunter knew something about they became your best friend. But if they decided to kill you and take the job themselves, they became your worst enemy. Devi had tried to kill Simms on at least three occasions.

Simms' ping went nowhere. Either she was offline or dead. He tried every ID he had but got a *no response* on all of them. OK. There were other ways to track down genehunters. None of them could stand to be unavailable for long in case a dream job came along, transporting them to a life of thrills and riches. Einstein's brain or the DNA of The Beatles. There was *always* a way to get in touch. You just had to know whom to ask.

He strode back to Euston, no overlays, still raining, and jumped half-way around the world to San Francisco. The Double Helix bar on Fisherman's Wharf was the closest thing genehunters had to home. It was an actual bar, a place people went to hang out, sit in shadowy corners, consume intoxicants and cut deals with each other. Like in the old days. Now such places were rare, old-fashioned, weird. For some reason, most hunters liked it. Perhaps for the same reason Simms preferred real acid. Nostalgia for the past, the good old days.

Inside it was quiet, the smoky air thick with murmuring. Glasses made of real glass clinked on tables that had once been living trees. People glanced up at him, looked away. He was known, welcome. Anyone could come into the Double Helix, sure, and sometimes tourists did wander in. But they left quickly, aware they weren't meant to be there.

Simms crossed to the bar. He felt relaxed. The Double Helix was, by common consent, neutral territory.

"What can I get you?"

Mac stood behind the old-fashioned bar, upturned bottles lined up behind him full of coloured liquids. Mac was always there, all wild hair and devil tattoos. His name wasn't really Mac. It just seemed like it should be, so everyone called him that. The joke was there were lots of Macs, clones taking turns to man the place. Day or night, there he was, never getting any older.

"The usual."

Most barmen would use a plug-in to work out what that meant. Facial recognition and a quick database lookup. Mac didn't need to bother with any of that.

"Quiet tonight," said Simms while Mac poured the Scotch.

Mac shrugged, unconcerned. Quiet was good. They all liked quiet.

"I'm after Devi," said Simms. "Heard from her?"

Mac looked into his eyes, assessing. He wouldn't want it *too* quiet. Bad for business to have his customers killing each other.

"Don't worry, just need her help," said Simms. "A few questions."

"This time."

"You know where she is?"

"I know where most of her is. The bits that are left."

"She's dead?"

"Oh no, she's alive. Amazing what they can do these days, huh?"

Details on Devi cost three more doubles, finest Scotch. Simms saw it as a win/win. Before he left he transferred more money, double what he'd already spent, then hit Mac with his final question.

"You heard of someone called Boneyard?"

Mac's eyes narrowed. He'd heard something.

"Sure."

"Who is it?"

"Don't know. Why you asking?"

"Because our old friend Ballard asked me, and I don't like to know less than a GMAn about anything. It's embarrassing."

Mac shrugged, like it was none of his problem. Which it probably wasn't.

"So, what?" said Simms. "What do you know?"

"That it's a thing, not a person."

"What else?"

"Only that it's something heavy. Bad for business."

"Ours or yours?"

"Same thing, ain't it, Simms?"

*

With the leads Mac had provided, Simms tracked Devi down to a hospital in Cairo where the medics were cultivating her a new set of internal organs. Seems her last job had gone badly wrong.

The roar of the great city hummed through the white walls. A thousand tubes and wires snaked from under Devi's covers to a silver box, where an array of lights blinked rhythmically. A box that more-or-less *was* Devi while her new body parts matured up from stem-cells. Devi looked deflated, her face more grey than olive. Her brown eyes were blurry and indistinct but she grinned her familiar, pained grin when Simms entered.

"How did you get in here?" she croaked.

"Told them I was a friend."

"Always were a convincing liar."

She shut her eyes, like she was drifting off to sleep already. He didn't have long to explain his situation. When he finished she nodded, as if everything made sense.

"What is it?" said Simms. "What do you know?"

"You got a voiceprint of this *Mann* of yours?"

"Sure."

Her plug-ins were fried so he had to relay the recording orally, letting his brain hardware control his mouth to make him sound like Mann. Wasn't perfect, but close enough. Sure felt weird, though.

"Yeah, that's him," she said.

"What do you know?" Simms asked in his own sweet voice once more.

"Remember Sanchez?"

"Sure."

"Your *Mann* was her *Smith*. She hooked up with them for some big deal about five years back."

"She's MIA, now. You're saying these people were responsible?"

It wasn't unknown for clients to dispense with their genehunters once they'd got the DNA they wanted. Dispense with them *permanently*. Cheaper than paying and it covered their tracks. The secret was to be indispensable. A rich client with a private zoo would always need more DNA. If they trusted you they would keep you on and everyone would be happy.

"No," Devi replied after a moment's thought. "I think you're good. Things went crazy for Sanchez after that. These people were straight. Kept quiet, paid their bills. You'll be OK as long as you don't fuck them around."

"Who, me?"

"Yes. You."

"She say anything else about them?"

"They're zookeepers, sure. A private menagerie of dead rock stars somewhere in the Caribbean. Word is they have more than that, too. A dark zoo of dictators and mass-murderers."

"And you're not telling me this to get me killed?"

"When *that* happens I want to be there."

Simms smiled, although Devi couldn't see it. "Thanks. You've been helpful. I owe you."

"Yeah."

Simms turned to leave. At the door he stopped.

"Oh, and Devi, get yourself fixed, OK? Shooting you in this state would be no fun at all."

She waved him away with a single finger.

*

"Mr. Simms."

"Mann."

Simms stood in an office, well-furnished but with no windows, no way of knowing where in the world he was. A room at the end of a jump address.

Mann looked like he sounded: a smart, highly-paid lawyer, dressed in expensive clothes, someone used to the finer things in life. He had no fear of Simms. On his own patch, protected by who-knew-what tech, he would be untouchable.

"So," said Simms. "Where's your master?"

"They may join us soon."

"Once you've checked me out."

"I'm sure they'll value my assessment of you."

"And, of course, they're watching everything that happens right now."

"No comment. But, if this situation is not to your liking, feel free to leave and we'll say no more about it. No harm, no foul."

"Sure, sure. Go on. The situation is to my liking. So

long *as* you can talk for them?"

"I have full executive authority in this regard."

"Yeah, like I said. So, what's the issue?"

"Tom Jacks."

"Tom Jacks."

"Tell me, did you think it odd you were employed to acquire the gene sequence of, how should I put it, the *wrong* Tom Jacks?"

That wasn't good. That wasn't good at all. Had they paid him just to lure him here? What was this, some twisted revenge set-up because the code wasn't to their liking?

"Now hang on. I established all that very clearly. The Jacks you wanted was most definitely not *the* Tom Jacks. What are you trying to pull here?"

"Mr. Simms, please. There is no need for anxiety. You completed the job we requested most capably and efficiently."

"Pleased to hear it."

"So, I'll ask you again. Did you think it odd?"

"It's not my place to question."

"Very well. Let me put it this way. If we had requested you retrieve the DNA sequence of the real Tom Jacks, the famous Tom Jacks, would your reaction have been any different?"

"I'd have wanted more money for one thing."

Mann smiled at that. "Understood. But, for the moment, recompense is not the issue here. The question is one of attitude. You have proved yourself a competent and discreet DNA Detective. I ask you again. If we *had* asked you to hunt the gene sequence of the real Tom Jacks, perhaps without anyone else knowing you were so employed, would you have been amenable?"

"*Are* you asking me to hunt the gene sequence of the real Tom Jacks? Or is this an interesting hypothetical conversation we're having?"

"That's what we're asking you, Mr. Simms."

The third voice came from behind him. Simms turned to see a woman stepping out of the jump node. He didn't know her voice although, when Simms turned to face her, a look of surprise flashed across her features. Something about his appearance had thrown her. Had they met once? He scanned her – face, plug-in aura – but got nothing. He also kicked off a jump network probe. Retrieving a source address could be useful. People tended to forget to cover things like that. While he waited for a response from the system he studied her. She was obviously rich. Super-rich. Everything about her made that clear. Not just the clothes and the jewellery. The rich could pick and choose metabolisms too, and this woman looked fabulous. Her eyes were old, wise, but she appeared to be no more than twenty.

The probe returned with her source address. It meant nothing to him, but he stored it away for possible later use and replied with a smile. "Then I'd take the job. Presuming we could agree terms and presuming you understood that retrieving the real Tom Jacks will be much, much harder. Perhaps impossible."

The woman crossed the room and sat down behind the desk. She seemed amused by something now as she looked at Simms. She nodded at Mann, instructing him to continue.

"We understand the difficulties you would face," said Mann. "For instance, there is the constant need to comply with the many and varied regulations governing the retrieval of deceased DNA sequences."

Simms had to stop himself from grinning. Rarely had someone asked him to break the law in such a polite way.

"We all have our burdens," said Simms. "But you learn how best to, ah, accommodate the law."

"Quite so."

It was Mann's turn to smile now. There was the briefest pause in the conversation. Mann and his employer communicating brain-to-brain.

"Mr. Simms, you recently spoke to an officer of the GMA. Can you tell us why?"

How had they known? Couldn't you at least trust government security agencies to be secure? Still, the question gave him hope. They were worried about him, worried *he* was GMA. Either that or they were very, very good actors.

Whichever, all he could do was tell them straight. "A corrupt agent called Ballard extorted money from me."

"Indeed?" said Mann. The lawyer studied him for a moment, forehead furrowing. Communicating again. They were debating him, assessing him. Damn shame he couldn't eavesdrop on them, but he didn't dare try.

"It must be difficult working with the GMA breathing down your neck all the time," said Mann. "Tell me, if we wanted you to work for us without them knowing you were so engaged, how would you feel?"

There it was. He should act horrified, walk out. But there were times you had to take a punt, trust your instincts. If you didn't, you stayed safe, legal – and poor. And he saw how clever they'd been. It hadn't been a test job. By registering a completely legal search for the *wrong* Tom Jacks they'd provided him the perfect cover in the hunt for the DNA they really wanted. No need to tell the GMA about the new arrangement. So far as they knew, the old job was still on the books. Simms had every right to pursue all possible means of acquiring *that* DNA, even if it meant excluding other individuals sharing, say, the same name. IDs got mixed up sometimes.

The woman and her advisor watched him intently. There was also the possibility he might not leave this room alive if he gave them the wrong answer.

"I'd feel cheerful about it," he said.

The rest of the meeting was detail. Some of the details were important: the money for one thing. The sum they agreed made it clear how serious they were. Anyone who could afford that much was not going to take being fucked around. At all. As they negotiated, Simms had to rely on plug-in overrides to keep himself from grinning like a child. This was good. Very good. Presuming he could find Tom Jacks – the real Tom Jacks – and presuming he could do so without the authorities knowing a damn thing, then he was set up. Some of those retirement schemes could finally become reality.

He felt only a single moment of doubt: a small voice in his head reminding him what they would use the DNA for. That sort of money definitely meant private zoos: illegal cloning and a life of slavery for an innocent individual who happened to share genetic sequences with a famous name. The voice had nothing to do with any plug-in. Simms pushed it out of his mind.

Once both parties had all the assurances and agreements they needed, Simms took his leave. He asked no questions beyond how to get in touch with them. He didn't bother with the statutory recounting of the terms of the law. They'd given him a month to find the rare and highly valued DNA of the dead rock star Tom Jacks. That was all he needed.

*

He spent the next twelve hours trawling all the public and private networks he could think of, seeking out scraps of information that might prove useful. Reliable cloning technology had been developed early in the twenty-first century by the notorious Dr. Grendel. Interest in collecting the DNA of the rich and famous had taken off almost immediately. As a result, a lot of people had gone to a lot of trouble to hide or destroy tissue samples over the years. The more famous the individual, the more trouble. Which was why genehunters existed. Society may be shot to hell, but there were always the mega-rich who could afford anything and everything they wanted. Historical figures became one more commodity, the rarer the better. It wasn't unknown for a collector to destroy all copies of the sequence of some star of yesteryear to make their collection all the more valuable. Which made Simms' job tricky when it came to someone like Jacks. No doubt about it, that DNA was going to be very well guarded. If it even still existed.

Simms sat unmoving as terabytes of data streamed through his brain, AI search algorithms occasionally picking out an interesting detail, tagging and cross-referencing it with other hits. Hopefully his plug-ins would give him an edge. He fell into half-sleep as his brain worked, eyes open but not really seeing, an occasional snippet of interesting information bubbling up to his conscious mind. He was only distantly aware of growing thirst and hunger. He would stop soon, eat and sleep. This was how he always was when he had a new job. Single-minded. Other plug-ins kicked in to boost his brain and body, keeping him awake and alert as he searched.

At the end of it, he reviewed what he'd found. It wasn't much. He had plenty of people offering to sell Tom Jacks hair follicles, Tom Jacks blood, Tom Jacks semen. Simms dismissed them all. None offered any provenance and none were expensive enough to be real.

One story he did keep returning to: the famous Montreux concert that degenerated into a mass brawl, the death of three fans and the hospitalisation of thirty others. This was early in Jacks' career, when he'd fronted the extreme metal band *Teratoma*. Their gigs were always abrasive, confrontational. When, for an encore, Jacks appeared in front of forty thousand amped-up, screaming metalheads carrying an *acoustic* guitar and started to croon love songs, there'd been a riot. Fans invaded the stage. That Jacks was injured in the melee was beyond doubt. Shaky video footage showed him with blood all over his face.

More interesting were unconfirmed stories of his two lost teeth, punched out by an angry fan. The records showed he had orthodontic surgery two weeks later, but there were no details of the procedure carried out. There were no surviving images of Jacks in those two weeks that might confirm the story. But there were persistent stories of the teeth being retrieved and sold by fans before, finally, being acquired by a modern-day genehunter on behalf of an unknown client.

Simms could find no hard evidence to back up any of it. Most likely it was all urban myth. The hospital records from Jacks' operation were gone. The records of those injured in the riot did still exist. Nearly a hundred people had been treated at Montreux Riviera Hospital for broken bones, facial injuries, contusions. There was a good chance diagnostic samples survived from all of them. But they were of no interest. The name Tom Jacks wasn't anywhere on the list, and the musician would surely have been recognized if he'd been taken there.

On the other hand, there were numerous rumours of Jacks clones being sighted over the years, the by-now dead rock star spotted in the unlikeliest of places. Jump nodes, shopping malls, ball-games. Again, the stories were probably junk; the standard fare of brain-addled fans. But one detail had caught the attention of Simms' AI routines. Loosely corroborated by cross-references with both medical and travel records, he had two accounts of a supposed Jacks copy being admitted to a refuge for the victims of botched clonings. Supposedly a clone from DNA from one of the lost teeth. This was only fifteen years earlier, meaning there was a good chance the man still lived.

It was a weak lead, one he wouldn't have bothered with normally. But for this case, any trail was worth following.

That was the good news. The bad news was the refuge concerned. He obviously recognized the Arizona location. It looked like he'd be talking to Kelly sooner than he'd imagined.

To his surprise, the node key she'd given him twelve months earlier still worked. Had she left it active on purpose, hoping he'd arrive? Or forgotten to cancel it?

He materialised in the public reception hall. The room was cool, air-conditioned against the fierce Arizona heat. Another disembodied voice spoke to him, this one a little more friendly.

"Please state the purpose of your visit."

They had to be careful, of course. In the early days, refuges had been plagued with tourists and autograph hunters harassing the patients. Part of the reason they were stuck in the middle of nowhere. Simms explained who he was, who he'd come to see. A uniformed guard arrived to escort him through the clashing desert heat to another low building where he could talk to Kelly. He didn't get to see any of the patients. They were allowed to wander freely, leave if they wanted, but were kept well away from public eyes. Simms could see lines of white houses in the shimmering distance. A little oasis of trees off in the other direction. He wondered if Tom Jacks, his ticket to riches, was somewhere among them.

Kelly sat in a plain, square room, polished terra cotta floor tiles and whitewashed walls. She was the same willowy, black-haired beauty he'd known, but she looked taut, too, her features drawn into lines. Her eyes were red like she hadn't been sleeping well. Crying herself to sleep over him maybe. Yeah, right. He remembered the fierce, eager strength of her embrace. Now they managed merely to greet each other politely. They'd been both lovers and partners once, back in the day. There had been jobs neither was proud of. She'd quit hunting, gone to the light side and joined clONE. He'd promised to join her, but hadn't. That was all.

"What is it, Simms? I'm busy."

"The jump key you sent me still worked."

She shrugged, swept her hair out of her eyes. "Don't read anything into it. I forgot to cancel it. You're not welcome here. Didn't we talk about this?"

"I'd like to make that contribution we discussed."

"You discussed it. I refused."

"So your finances are so good you can afford the moral high ground?"

She shrugged, said nothing.

"Look," said Simms. "I understand your reservations. But no one's untainted are they? I can provide funds and you can do good with them. How is it helping your patients to refuse?"

She scowled, looked at him. Did she see through him? But it wasn't just an act. He meant it. He'd seen too many cloning disasters over the years. He wasn't a bad person.

"How much are you hoping to contribute?" she asked.

"You could do a lot of good with forty K, I expect?" He hadn't really thought about the amount. Forty seemed to keep coming up.

"We could do some good, sure."

"I'll transfer it to you now."

She shrugged, sent account details across without looking at him.

"This doesn't buy you anything, you know," she said. "It doesn't get you access to any DNA. Or to me."

"No, no. I know."

He'd hoped to spend time with her, imagined the two of them walking through the refuge. Maybe even bumping into the Tom Jacks clone, grabbing a DNA sample without anyone knowing. This wasn't going to happen. They weren't going to let him get close. Still, if he could somehow confirm Jacks was here, it would be something.

"I thought I could maybe sponsor an individual patient," he said. "You know, make a real difference to one person."

She was immediately suspicious, eyes narrowed. "What we do with the money is our business."

While she talked he sent out probes to her plug-ins. She had the usual array of brain add-ons. He'd once known some of her private keys. He hoped she'd forgotten to change those, too.

"I'm not asking to meet any patients, or even see them. I thought I could choose a particular individual to help. If you had a list, I mean."

It was an old technique, surprisingly effective. The suggestion of *a list* prompted one of her plug-ins to react automatically, pulling relevant names out of a database. Real names and their associated clone-twin names. As he'd hoped. She suppressed the data immediately, but not before he caught a glimpse.

He kept his expression blank but it didn't help.

"What did you do?" she said, standing up, sending her chair tumbling to the floor behind her.

"What do you mean?"

"You were in my head. What did you do? What did you see?"

"Nothing, Kelly. I…"

"That's why you came here, isn't it? Not to help them. Not to see me. You're working. Dear God, Simms, I don't believe you. How do you manage to fuck everything up so badly every time?"

"But…"

He didn't have time to say any more. Four guards burst into the room, weaponry aimed at him.

"Hey, OK, I just wanted to help is all," he said.

Kelly backed away from him. "You wanted to help yourself, you mean. Like always. You disgust me, Simms. Take your money and get out of here. And don't come back. I've deleted all your access keys."

"Kelly, please. I did want to see you, really."

But she turned and strode away. The security guards pulled him to his feet and prodded him out the other way, back to the jump node. He thought about fighting back. He might be able to stun them if he unleashed his offensive brain hardware.

He restrained himself. He didn't need to. Because the

beautiful fact was that *Tom Jacks* was there on her list, along with the name of the clone who carried his DNA. *Luis Jesus*. And *that* was a name he had come across before. Come across very recently.

He still had a shot. He didn't need to break into the refuge after all. Life was good. He let the four grunts escort him to the jump node, a smile on his face.

*

Simms stood outside the shining glass building. Another day, another hospital to break into. Except this was a real one, with real live dying people inside. Which all meant real security, too. Going to be a damn sight harder to infiltrate than Bethesda.

He'd worked on the place for over three weeks, more and more desperate. He'd tried hacking them, tried profiling key staff members to see if anyone needed urgent money. Nothing. He'd even engineered an injury – a self-administered cut to his leg – so he could get inside and take a look around. All he'd learned was the place was a damn fortress, private security keeping everything locked down. He'd discovered old tissue samples were kept on a sub-basement level, but that was it. All that efficiency meant there was a good chance the blood sample of Luis Jesus, one of those injured in the Montreux concert riot, would still be down there. The problem was getting to it.

He wondered if Kelly's clone knew his name was one of Tom Jack's pseudonyms. Jacks must have made it up that night, hoping to avoid attention. Most likely, the name was a joke on the part of whoever had created Jesus from that broken tooth years later.

It didn't matter to Simms. He had to get down into the basement, grab a sample and get out. And he had to do it now. Mann's month had all-but run out. All Simms' other schemes had come to nothing. Sometimes you had to dispense with subtlety and go in all guns blazing. Or at least, sneak in and *come out* all guns blazing. He didn't like the odds, but he refused to let this job slip through his fingers. Chances like it only came along once or twice in a lifetime.

His plug-ins got him through the door from the hospital's public area to the *Staff Only* corridors. He'd cloned the ID of one of the surgeons, a Dr. Echt, away speaking at a conference in the Far East. Simms had gambled the hospital systems wouldn't be paranoid enough to cancel Echt's access for the week he'd be away. It looked like the gamble had paid off. Simms walked down the deserted corridor, feet clacking on the hard floor. He resisted the temptation to tread softly. The key to deals like this was to look like you belonged. Ask questions rather than answer them.

Two women approached him down the corridor. He'd profiled everyone he could find at the hospital. They were admin, high up, but in a different department to Echt. He ignored them, like he was deep in thought. People at work didn't smile at each other. The women passed by, paying him no attention.

The hospital was big, rambling, but he had the floor plans stored in his brain. He made his way to the lift that descended to the basements. Instead of using it, he pushed open the door to the adjacent fire stairs. There were cameras everywhere and a lift could become a cage at the touch of a button. Stairs at least gave him a shot.

Two levels down he reached another set of security doors. Echt had no access down here, so Simms resorted to hacking. He unleashed the electronic wizardry in his cranium. If someone asked what he was doing, his only plan was to start shooting. But this was a storage level; he'd calculated few people would come down here. And most likely they'd take the lift. Another reason to use the stairs.

After a solid minute of work, the locks on the basement door succumbed. Electronic systems were easy to fool given the right tech. What you couldn't do was stop all the background logging and cross-checking. He knew he wouldn't have long before they came for him.

He flicked on the lights. No point hiding now; it was all about speed. He'd hacked the tissue catalogue and knew precisely which cabinet and which drawer he needed. He ran, muscles and brain amped up to the maximum. It was cold down here, refrigerated, but he barely noticed. It took him only twenty seconds to locate the sample of Luis Jesus. Five less than planned. Perhaps he had a shot at this after all.

The blood sample was old, dried to a dull brown. They kept them for a hundred and one years in case of legal challenge. Sometimes he loved the forces of law and order. He might not get good DNA but it was a chance. He sampled the blood, storing the sequence for later analysis.

The first blaster shot caught him in the shoulder, spinning him round. Lucky, really: it meant the next shot missed *and* he was facing the right way to see the two security guards standing by the door to the stairs. His med plug-in began saturating his system with painkilling drugs as he assessed the situation.

"On the ground. Now!" the guards called. They sounded cross. Simms looked like he was going to comply, moving slowly. Then, muscles acting at reflex-speed, he pulled out his blaster and fired. Resorting to shooting was an act of desperation, an admission of failure. He'd run out of other options. Guided by his military-grade aiming software, his two shots found their targets. The guards sagged to the ground. They'd wake up in a couple of hours. He wasn't being humane. If the authorities *did* catch him, a couple of murder charges would just make everything worse.

He ran. The police would arrive soon, and his defences would be nowhere near as effective against them. His plan was this: run like hell for the doors before they got to him. It wasn't his best plan ever, he had to admit.

He raced up the stairs three at a time and into the corridor. He heard running feet as more guards converged on him. Sirens and bells in the distance. Time for his exit strategy. There were two other doors to the hospital, including one to admit deliveries too big for the hospital's jump nodes. That door might not be locked down. The danger was they'd work out he was using Echt's ID and track him through the building. Or they could follow the trail of blood he was leaving on the floor…

Ninety seconds later he made it to the cargo door. It stood half open, easy for him to duck through. Metal crates had been neatly stacked just inside and he could hear the motors of some sort of transport vehicle presumably delivering more. He hadn't spotted any more security. Maybe they'd all gone to defend the jump nodes like he'd hoped. He was shaking, either with excitement or loss of blood, but he ignored it. He darted for the door, dropping the Echt ID from his brain and adopting another, unrelated one prepared for the purpose.

The second shot slammed into him before he heard it. The ground threw itself up at him and he knew no more.

*

"So, Simms. Here we are again."

Simms came round in another small, square room, somewhere still in the hospital judging by the medical paraphernalia around the walls: the oxygen feeds and alarm buttons. Everything was spotless, sterile. He lay on the hard floor. They could at least have found him a bed. Still, he was alive. Armed GMA agents guarded the door. Someone leaned over him. No mistaking that face.

"Agent Ballard."

"You're under arrest for the illegal acquisition of the DNA of Tom Jacks. Plus the contravention of numerous other laws I haven't even thought of yet."

Simms tried to think straight through the veils of pain

filling his brain. How much did Ballard know? His GMA plug-ins were secure from Simms' intrusions and his ruined face was, as ever, impossible to read. How much did he really understand about what was going on here?

"I'm sorry, don't have any such DNA."

"Really, Simms. Is that the best you can do?"

Simms rose to his knees, tried to stand. He'd feel better if he could look Ballard in the eye.

"It's the truth."

"So you're here visiting a dying relative, is that it?"

Simms calculated for a moment, trying to find a way out. It was hard when people insisted on keeping secrets. In the end, he decided to adopt the simplest approach.

"OK, Ballard, I *have* just illegally acquired a DNA sample. But I assure you it isn't Tom Jacks."

"Who then?"

"One *Luis Jesus*. Check the records if you like. He has no connection to Tom Jacks."

There was a slim chance Ballard knew Jacks and Jesus were one and the same. Simms figured it was a risk worth taking. He watched Ballard's eyes, the brief moment of vacancy while he checked on the name.

"Never heard of him."

"No reason why you should. He's a nobody."

"Then why go to such lengths? You could have been killed. You still might be."

Was this further extortion? Pay a fine and go on his way? He doubted it. Ballard was corrupt, sure, and a bully. But he did his job. Unless a bigger prize was dangled before him. Simms decided to gamble.

"You want the truth? I heard a rumour about him. In connection with *Boneyard*."

Ballard's eyes narrowed. Simms had his attention. Whatever Boneyard was – and Simms had absolutely no idea – it was of great interest to Ballard.

"What connection? And why are you looking?"

"Because you asked me to."

"Don't get smart with me, Simms."

"I'm serious. Boneyard is of interest to you. And that means I'm in a position of power if I find out about it."

"It?"

"Uh-huh. Boneyard isn't a person. It's a thing."

"What sort of *thing*?"

"Haven't got that far yet."

"And you think you can bribe me if you find out?"

"I think I can bargain with you if some other minor contravention of the law comes to your attention."

Ballard studied him for a moment. This could go either way. The GMAn could arrest Simms and charge him, tie him up long enough to blow all hope of completing the Jacks job. Or he could believe Simms' line. It all depended how much Ballard wanted this Boneyard. Simms' chances hung by that thread.

"Tell me the connection," said Ballard.

"Not until I have something concrete. I'm acting on a whisper here and it may come to nothing."

"Tell me who the whisperer is."

"Sorry, can't reveal my sources. Look, Ballard, you can drag me off to some dungeon and ream the facts out of my brain, but what good will that do you? This Boneyard is well-hidden. I know next to nothing. But if I'm allowed to operate, maybe I can come up with something for you. I don't need you as an enemy."

"And you think all this can be made to go away?" Ballard indicated the hospital with a wave of his hand. "All the crimes you've committed today?"

"I think *you* can make it go away. Come on, we both know this little scene is nothing. Unimportant. It's beneath you, Ballard."

Ballard took a step forward. Simms braced himself for a blow. Instead, Ballard jabbed his finger into Simms' wounded shoulder. A moment of raw agony cut through him before his med plug-in could react.

"OK, Simms," Ballard said, whispering into his ear.

"Here's what's going to happen. I'll let you *operate*. For now. Bring me Boneyard and we can remain friends. But I'll be watching, Fuck with me and I'll know about it."

Make them think they'd won when they'd lost. It was the only way.

"Whatever you say. Now, can I go? I have work to do. Real work."

Ballard stepped back and pulled open the door. "Get out of here. And take my advice, Simms. Leave Montreux before the local police get to you. They won't be as friendly as me."

"Just what I was planning to do."

*

"Mann?"

"Mr. Simms. You certainly like to leave things until the last minute."

"I have what you want."

"Excellent. Send it over for assessment and, assuming all is well, we'll complete the transaction as agreed."

"It's on its way now."

*

Now this was Simms' idea of a hospital. A tropical beach to convalesce on. His own nurses on hand to bring him everything he might need. No one trying to kill him. Bliss.

He yawned, stretched, enjoying the warmth of the sun on his face. He sipped his mojito. He was beginning to like them almost as much as Scotch. No doubt about it, the money from the Jacks job was making him a very happy man.

Except. Problem was, he was already getting bored. He could feel that itch. What was going on in the world? Who was in the Double Helix right now, cutting a deal? Above all, what the hell was he supposed to *do*? He'd thought to take a year, two years off. Get fixed. Chill out. Two weeks in and he was already wondering if Mann was trying to reach him with another name.

He decided to make a few calls. Where was the harm in that? He put himself back on the net and pinged Devi, partly to see if she'd made it through her procedure, partly to send the fee for her help. Always good to keep contacts sweet. Devi accepted the money with something like her usual abrasiveness. When Simms sent her the view from *his* hospital window, she cut the connection, swearing creatively.

Simms then transferred 100K to the account Kelly had given him back in the refuge. Anonymously. Perhaps she'd realise it was from him and perhaps she wouldn't. That was up to her. But he found the act gave him a strange sensation, made him feel better about things.

He was about to vanish from the net again and ask for another mojito when the ping came through from Ballard.

"So, Simms. How is the investigation going?"

For a moment, Simms was confused. Surely Ballard would know the Jacks job was over by now?

"Investigation?"

"Don't play games with me. You know what I mean. Our agreement over Boneyard."

"I wouldn't call it an agreement. More of an… *understanding.*"

"Is that right? Well, just as long as you *understand* I own you now, Simms. I've got enough evidence to put you away for about three centuries. But if you're useful to me I might forget about it."

Simms thought about cutting the connection there and then. Easy enough to hide away, switch IDs, kill off Simms and become someone else. He had the money to do it, now. Problem was, he *liked* genehunting. And if he wasn't Simms any more he'd be back to square one, an untrusted unknown, one among thousands.

"OK, Ballard," he replied. "I think I can get my head

round what you're saying. But I'll work at my pace, in my own way. Have you got that?"

"What I've got, Simms, is your licence in my hands. And if I think you're being unhelpful to an agent of the GMA then I'm going to have to sit down and review it."

"Yeah, yeah. Look, I'll be in touch. Sweet of you to call, and I'm sure you've missed me, but there's really no need. I'll bring you something when I have it."

"Make sure you do."

Simms did cut the connection, then. He called for the mojito and sipped at it, lost in thought, watching the sun melt into the sparkling blue sea.

So. What the hell was this *Boneyard* anyway?

The Wrong Tom Jacks is the first Genehunter case, all five of which have been collected together into the novel The Genehunter. If you're interested in finding out more, my web page for the stories is at simonkewin.co.uk/genehunter.

Simms is another fun character to write. He starts out as pretty amoral, but as the stories progress he does become more and more troubled by something like a conscience. At the same time, he crosses more and more people and organizations until it really does seem like everyone is out to get him. Probably because they are...

HER LONG HAIR SHINING

Water ran down the walls, staining the stonework in triangles of green like a child's drawing of a Christmas tree. Smith had to step around pools of water on the floor. The place hadn't been used for years. Decades. Smashed windows let the wind and rain through. It was colder inside, somehow, than it was out on the streets. The air tasted damp.

It was, he thought, a lonely place for a ghost to live.

Three lines of stone pillars supported the roof of the old mill. He wove his way between them, listening, the tap of his footsteps echoing sharply back to him.

"Can you feel anything, Tom?" he asked. "Anything at all?"

Tom whirled through the air from wall to wall, like a bird desperate to escape, an indistinct blur. He was always excited when they searched for a new ghost. Smith stopped for a moment to watch him. Delight at the sight of him coloured, as ever, with the crushing weight of guilt.

"There is something," Tom said after a moment, pausing briefly in his zig-zagging. "Or there has been. It's faint, very faint."

"Can you tell where?"

"Near. Not here. Up a floor."

"Come on".

There were stairs in each corner, their cramped steps worn smooth by the scuffing of many feet. Tom drifted along beside Smith, a flicker of light near his left shoulder. He could have just passed through the stone of the ceiling. Ghosts didn't need to use the stairs. But, as always, he preferred to stay within sight.

The next floor was similar, another vast cavern that once would have roared with the clatter of machinery. Here, the pillars were of slender iron rather than stone. Some of them had rusted away completely at their base to form a line of jagged teeth that no longer touched the floor. The ceiling sagged. Lines of thin metal rods ran along it: axles that would once have powered the machines.

Smith heard a whisper, faint like dead leaves being blown along a stone floor. But the windows were unbroken and he could feel no breeze on his face. There was the definite sense of not being alone. Tom was the sensitive one, of course, but Smith had become more attuned, too.

In the far corner of the room lay a jumble of broken metal parts, as if one of the great machines had crawled there to die. Tom zipped off that way now and Smith strode after him.

"Anything, lad? Is it here?"

The disappointment in Tom's voice was clear. "It's gone again. I can't feel it."

Smith nodded. The same had happened last time. He wondered how long the ghost had been here. Centuries maybe.

He looked again at the pile of debris. The broken frames of several looms lay jumbled together, along with rusted cogs and levers. A flat, triangular shard of polished metal was propped against them. It glistened slightly, covered in frost. Smith's dim reflection filled it; he could just make out his wild mass of hair and beard, the bulk of his frayed, brown greatcoat wrapped tight with a length of string.

"Let's go home," he said.

"Do we have to?"

"I think so."

"Can we come back tomorrow and try again?" said Tom. "Can we please, can we?"

*

Later, Smith sat in his room, holding a steaming mug of tea on the patched arm of his old chair, trying to decide what to do. His thoughts were a jumble of disconnected threads. He was weary and hungry. He had spent the last of his money on cat-food. He felt like one of the fainter ghosts himself: scattered and incoherent. His mind jumped from thought to thought without reaching any conclusions.

Drawing out ghosts was often a matter of finding the right key. A person perhaps. That was a problem if the person was themselves dead. Or it might be a place, a particular room or building. Or an object.

Velvet, the cat, finished her food and padded over to lie in front of the one-bar electric fire they used when it was cold. Winter was coming on now. He still hadn't taken his greatcoat off. His toes were numb from the long trek home. He needed new boots. The old ones let in too much water.

Only Tom took no notice of the temperature. He flew around in circles on the ceiling, playing some game of his own, disappointment forgotten. Smith sipped his scalding tea. Perhaps they wouldn't be able to rescue the ghost in the mill. Some they couldn't. The lost spirit faded away, little by little. He sometimes wondered whether they disappeared completely, or just became weaker as each day passed.

He set his mug down onto the stained carpet and stood to cross the room. In the alcove formed by the chimney-stack he had set up some shelves. An assortment of objects cluttered them. If anyone had come into the room, not that anyone ever did, they might have been embarrassed that such a collection of broken and cheap objects had been placed there as ornaments. But they weren't ornaments. Here were all the objects – the totems – they had used over the years to lure lost souls. Each, now, was a memorial, as well, to the person who was gone. All except one.

Sometimes handling the objects helped him think. He picked up one, a solid metal clothes iron, rusting to the colour of treacle, with the manufacturer's name, *Hardwicke*, cast into it. It was heavy; the sort they used before electricity, the brick-like lump of metal large enough to preserve the heat. He had stolen it from an antiques shop, enfolding it inside his coat to smuggle it out.

The woman had been killed in a Second World War air-raid. They'd found her wandering, confused, very faint, among some office-blocks, looking for her house. Mary. It had taken weeks for Tom to gain her trust. But the iron had fascinated her. The simplest, most mundane item often did. It was something familiar, an anchor in the grey aether. She would have used one just like it most days of her life, keeping herself and her children crisp and presentable. Her husband, too, before he went off to be torpedoed in the Atlantic.

Once she had touched the iron, they were able to take her away from the roaring traffic and concrete towers. On the way home, she had said the same thing, over and over.

"I must get back! Dave and little Lou are on their own, waiting for me. I must get back."

There wasn't much left of her: just shreds of anxiety and memory. Still, they did what they could. They coaxed her name and address from her and Smith had managed, after long days of work in the library, to find out who she was and what had happened to her and her family. He had to explain it to her over and over.

"Your house was destroyed in an air-raid. Your whole street."

"But Dave and little Lou. I have to get back. I only said I'd be a minute."

"It's alright. Your children survived. The air-raid shelter. They both grew up and had children of their own. Grandchildren too. David was seventy-two when he died and Lucy was seventy-five. They had happy lives."

"They aren't waiting for me? I only nipped out for some bread."

"They aren't waiting for you. It's all alright."

Again and again she had listened, and each time Smith thought she'd understood. But the following day they would have the same conversation again. Then, one bright summer day, her words had changed.

"They aren't waiting for me?"

"No."

"Ah, good. I think I'd like to sleep now."

The next day she was gone.

Now, he placed the iron back up on the shelf. Above it was the first piece in the collection. A toy robot, a C-3PO. It was made from a shiny plastic that resembled polished metal. It had been expensive to buy, he recalled. Originally it had talked and moved but it had stopped working at the time of the crash. It had lost an arm and half a leg as well.

He remembered walking for days along the winding country road, back and forth, past the skinned and blackened tree the car had crashed into, the robot clutched in his hand. It seemed amazing, now, that they'd let him. But he recalled, with blazing clarity, the moment when Tom was back there with him. The rush of relief.

A shiny toy had done it, nothing more than that. He had an idea, then, about the ghost in the mill. He set the robot carefully back on its shelf and began to open cupboard doors, rummaging through dusty, musty mounds of blankets, books, shoes and paintbrushes to find what he was looking for.

Finally, he found it: an old mirror, about the size of a book, with a frame made from scrolls of iron, crudely painted. It was badly tarnished, the surface marred with spots and splodges of black, as if some disease had infected it. Still it might do. In his reflection, through his rough beard, he could see himself grinning.

He sat back down in his chair. His tea was lukewarm now. Tom bobbed over by the window, the closest he came to sleeping.

"We'll go back there tomorrow," he said. "This mirror might do the trick."

At the possibility of rescuing the ghost in the mill, Tom sped into a crazed, zig-zag flight once more, unable to contain his excitement.

*

Smith set the mirror down onto the dusty floor next to the triangle of metal, then sat to wait. Waiting was a large part of what they did. To keep himself as warm as possible he buried his mouth and nose in the warmth of his greatcoat.

Hours passed by. Tom, excited at first, soon became bored and began to drift around the room, letting himself become an indistinct haze. Smith kept his eye on the polished metal and the mirror, looking for anything, a glint, a shadow. There was nothing. Daylight began to fade, leeching detail out of the room. Perhaps the ghost was too afraid of them. They often were. Perhaps it had faded already.

Finally, with a grunt, he worked his way back up to his feet, his legs stiff and clumsy. Tom circled over towards him, saying nothing.

"I know, lad. Perhaps tomorrow."

He turned to leave. It was then he saw a flicker of light in the polished metal. He stood motionless, watching. It was almost completely dark now. Sometimes it needed to be. Daylight flooded the ghosts, diluting them. There was another movement, distant. Smith knelt down, trying to quieten his rough breathing. Perhaps they had a chance after all.

There were dim lights swirling in the mirror. It was hard to be sure but it looked as if the faint presence had moved across from the shard of metal. Smith edged forwards, preparing to lift the mirror and smother it away in his coat. He was nearly there when the images, clear as an old television, began to appear.

*

A young woman dressed in plain, grey clothes, strides into the factory. She walks arm-in-arm with a friend, the two of them elbowing each other and giggling. The woman's golden hair glows, lighting up the drab surroundings. She must spend hours in front of the mirror to brush it to such a sheen. She is just a girl, really: sixteen or seventeen.

The mill is already full of workers, men and women. Young children as well, scampering around at their feet, darting into the machines to retie broken yarns. The looms are powered by wide leather belts that slap their way up to the thundering axles running along the ceiling. Somehow, Smith can hear all the sounds as well as seeing the sights. The crash and roar are deafening.

The woman's friend speaks. Smith can't hear what she says but the woman, lip-reading, or perhaps just seeing the expression on her friend's face, understands. She blushes and glances over her shoulder towards a man working on the next row of machines. The man has seen her, knows he is being watched. He is young too. A beard shades his boyish face but he is tall and strong. He smiles to himself as he stares into the clattering depths of his machine.

The woman, knowing she is beautiful, flicks her hair to one side. What happens then is the simplest accident. Her hair becomes entangled in one of the leather belts. She is plucked from the ground and hauled up to the ceiling, her weight nothing to the power of the machines. Her body is mangled, bones broken in countless places as she is wrapped around the axle. The roar of the machines rises in pitch slightly, angry at the extra resistance.

*

When the pictures had stopped, Smith shuffled his way towards the mirror and lifted it, gently, into his arms.

*

Two weeks later, returning home from another day at the library, he stopped outside his door to listen. Sally and Tom were lost in another of their games. He heard them whooping in delight. He listened for long minutes, smiling at the doorknob, not wanting to break the spell.

Tom had coaxed her name from her a week ago and now Smith was spending his days tracking down who she was and what had happened afterwards. It had been slow-going. Details from the nineteenth century were patchy and he had to walk miles and miles to read parish records. But now, finally, he thought he had the full picture. He sighed as he unlocked his door and slipped inside.

The two ghosts were chasing each other around the room. They moved so quickly, nothing more solid than a flicker in the air, that he couldn't keep up with them. He caught glimpses of them flashing across all the reflective surfaces: the television screen, the gloss paint on the kitchen door, the window.

When Sally did finally dissipate, he knew, the loss to Tom would be terrible. Perhaps it would be too much for him. He would fade too, his existence, as insubstantial as a whisper in the air, finally over. For now, they played endlessly, Tom never tiring, Sally sometimes an excited child herself, his sister perhaps, sometimes older, more like a mother.

"I always wanted lots of children," she had said yesterday. "I wanted six. With Danny I mean. He was going to ask me to marry him. We'd have had three boys and three girls. We'd have had such fun together."

Danny, he now thought, was Daniel Thomas. And the other woman, Sally's friend, he was sure was Lillian Hargreaves. He had, just today, tracked down the death-certificate from 1975 of one Lilly McNeal, named after her great-grandmother. In his pocket he had a family photograph of the whole McNeal clan, black-and-white, taken at a wedding in the sixties, printed off from the microfiche archive of a local paper.

Smith lit the gas under the kettle. He had bought a loaf of bread, only slightly stale, which he sawed into wedges. Sitting back down he thought about how best to tell her everything.

Tom drifted up to him as he sat and thought. The lad was almost solid, his boyish features, his unkempt hair real enough to touch. It was often the way when he was filled with some strong emotion. He knew well enough that Smith had uncovered Sally's story.

Smith thought about the crash. He remembered very little, of course. Partly this was because of his head injuries. He had one knife-sharp memory, though. A memory that skewered him to the spot two or three times a day even now.

It was moments after the crash. The mangled car had stopped spinning and lurching. The engine ticked as it cooled. There was the smell of petrol. The car radio, miraculously, still played. He had looked behind him, his movement restricted by the confining space of the crushed car, a tearing pain across his shoulders. In the seat behind him sat Tom, his eyes wide open, frozen in astonishment, but seeing nothing.

The judge had been lenient. Said he had suffered

enough. She was wrong, of course. He could never suffer enough.

"Sally," said Smith quietly. "Can I show you something?"

He held the photograph up to the mirror.

"Do you recognize anyone?"

"Ah, Danny," whispered Sally after a few moments. "I wanted you so much."

"You see him?"

"I don't … this man looks like him, but it isn't him is it?"

"This is Samuel. He's Danny's great-great-great-grandson."

"He was going to ask me to marry him, you know. I said I'd wait for him outside the factory."

"I know."

"Who did he marry? The old woman standing next to him. She's familiar."

He had no idea what her reaction would be. Sometimes they burned and raged when it came home to them what they had lost. Sometimes they faded away there and then.

"They waited five years. Then Danny married Lilly. The old woman is Samuel's grandmother. Danny and Lilly's great-granddaughter."

"Ah." The sound was drawn-out, more an exhalation of breath than a word. She had, he knew, lost much in her short life. Her mother when she was seven. Two brothers and a sister after that. She had learned not to expect much.

"They had five children," he went on. "Four of them survived. The first, the eldest, was a girl. They called her Sally. This Lilly is her granddaughter."

Sally said nothing.

"They must have thought about you a lot. In a way, you were there with them all along."

"Lil always admired him too," she whispered. "She used to say. She'd have him if I didn't want him. I'm glad they had each other."

A circle of breath bloomed on the inside of the mirror with each word, only to evaporate away immediately. He could see nothing of her save for a quarter of her face, a tangle of golden hair and the corner of her mouth, hidden behind the patches of tarnished silver.

"It's over now. You don't need to wait for him anymore."

"I don't?"

"No."

"Then … what will happen to me now? Will I die? Will I go to heaven?"

It was the question they always asked.

"I think … I think once you're released you'll be gone. You just won't exist anymore. But there will be no more pain."

"Oh. I see." She sounded more weary than disappointed. She said nothing more.

After a while he became afraid she had already faded. He peered closely into the murky depths of the mirror. He could see only himself: his lined face, his wild beard and bad teeth.

"You could stay here with us," he whispered.

After a moment, there was a flicker of movement deep inside the glass.

"Here?" She was still with him.

"In this mirror. Or anywhere. You'll have me for company, for a time at least. Tom is always here. Others pass through. And Velvet can see you, of course." He trailed off, aware of how meagre a life it was he was offering. How poor a family.

She was silent. Velvet stood, stretched into an arc and padded two paces across the floor, catching up with the square of weak sunlight that was slanting across the room. She circled three times and lay back down again.

"What would I do?" said the girl.

"I can't tell you what to do. You're much older than I am."

Her face, sketched in grey lines, slid to the front of the glass. Her eyes were bright. They held his gaze, then looked through him, onto greater distances, the window beyond him, the rooftops of the city.

"I never saw the sea," she said. "There were so many things I wanted to see before I died."

"You still can."

"I'd like that," she said.

Tom, the remnants of his dead boy, began to dart and flicker around the room, glowing with light. The cat, lifting its head, watched him dance. The ghost in the mirror, also watching him, laughed out loud, her long hair shining.

Her Long Hair Shining was originally printed in Abyss & Apex in 2012, and has since been reprinted a couple of times as well as being translated into French. It was also recorded as an audio story by Bards and Sages Publishing. I guess it's a ghost story, although it doesn't seem particularly creepy or scary. I'd probably call it urban fantasy if I had to call it anything. It's one of my favourite pieces. I used to live in Manchester (in the UK), where there were lots of abandoned mills and the like. This story clearly grew out of living among all of that.

Spell Circles

Fantasy short stories 1999-2011

Desperate magic worked in the face of terrible danger. An old house with a hidden secret. An interview with a zombie. A woman allergic to the twenty-first century. A necromancer with evil written all over his face. Literally.

Spell Circles contains twenty-seven stories of the weird, wonderful and fantastical originally published between 1999 and 2011 and now collected together for the first time. Stories range from the very short up to novella length.

"this collection was excellent … Kewin's imagination soars over the fantastic landscape"

"Wonderful stories brimming with ideas"

Eccentric Orbits

Science Fiction short stories 1999-2011

An astronaut alone in the void of deep space. An alien starship capable of destroying all creation. A DNA Detective in search of the genetic code of The Beatles. A terrorist explosion trapped inside a bubble of space/time. A new life-form found in the quantum echoes of the void.

Eccentric Orbits contains seventeen science fiction stories originally published between 1999 and 2011 and now collected together for the first time. Stories range from the very short up to novella length.

"absolutely fantastic ... just incredible"

"These tales will linger in your mind long after you've turned off your Kindle for the night"

The Genehunter

Some secrets are best left buried...

Simms is a genehunter, paid to track down the DNA of the famous and infamous of history for his clients' private collections. What they do with the DNA isn't his problem – even if they are using it to create illegal clones.

He walks a line, pulled in many directions at once. When he works the Boneyard case he discovers that, sometimes, you have to decide which side of the line you're on. And when he starts to uncover the truth of his own past he begins to question everything he is and does...

"As thought-provoking as it is entertaining" – Sci-Fi Indie eBook Reviews

"Reminded me of some of the best William Gibson books"

Hedge Witch

Two worlds, one nightmare…

Cait Weerd has no idea the undain are hunting her. She doesn't know the vile creatures need *her* blood to survive. She doesn't even know she's a witch, descended from a long line of witches. Cait Weerd doesn't know much, but all that's about to change.

The fate of two worlds is at stake. Cait has to decide what to do: run, fight, or hope it all goes away. But then she learns who she really is, along with the terrible truth of what the undain have been doing in our world all this time…

"a thoroughly enjoyable read" – British Fantasy Society

"I loved it. Pulled me into the world and wouldn't let me go … a wonderful read."

The Cloven Land Trilogy

A brutal multinational corporation. A land ruled by necromancers. One girl in their way…

The complete Cloven Land Trilogy: Hedge Witch, Wyrm Lord and Witch King, along with prequel novella Hyrn and bonus short story, The Waters, Dividing the Land.

"A wonderful story combining the world of today with magic and fantasy"

"I was on the edge of my seat from beginning to end"

Dead Star

A hidden trail among the stars

The galaxy is in flames under the harsh theocratic rule of Concordance, the culture that once thrived among the stars reduced to scattered fragments. Selene Ada, last survivor of an obliterated planet, joins forces with the mysterious renegade, Ondo Lagan.

Together they attempt to unravel the mystery of Concordance's rapid rise to galactic domination. They follow a trail of shattered starship hulks and ancient alien ruins, with the ships of the enemy always one step behind.

But it's only when they find the mythical planet of Coronade that they uncover the true scale of the destruction Concordance is capable of unleashing…

The Triple Stars Trilogy

The darkness at the heart of the galaxy

The complete Triple Stars Trilogy: Dead Star, Red Star and God Star, as well as prequel novella Home World.

"This is a wonderful, ambitious, exciting and incredibly well-written SF story, worthy of me labelling Simon Kewin as the next Arthur C Clarke." – Speculative Faction Book Reviews

"excellent … the author did a really fantastic job of creating compelling characters, an intriguing world, and I'm looking forward to the next novel in the series"

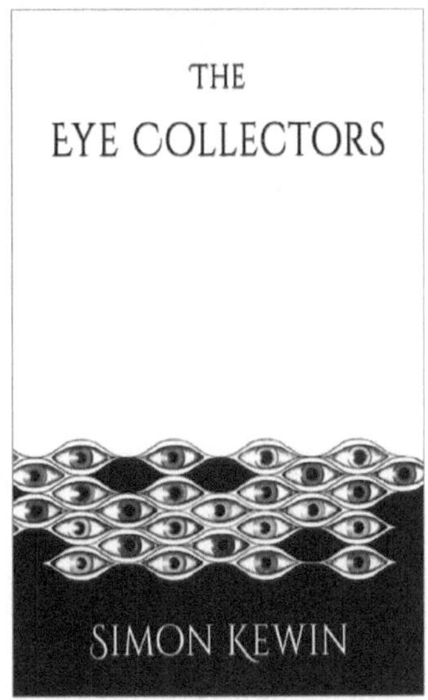

The Eye Collectors

Her Majesty's Office of the Witchfinder General
Protecting the public from the unnatural since 1645

Danesh Shahzan is an Acolyte in Her Majesty's Office of the Witchfinder General, a shadowy arm of the British government fighting supernatural threats to the realm. He's been called in by Detective Inspector Nikola Zubrasky to investigate a murder in Cardiff. The victim had been placed inside a runic circle and their eyes carefully removed from their head.

Danesh soon confirms that magical forces are at work. He and DI Zubrasky establish a wary collaboration as they each pursue the investigation. Soon, Danesh learns that there may be much wider implications to what is taking place and that somehow he has an unexpected connection. He also realises something about himself that he can never admit to the people with whom he works…

ABOUT THE AUTHOR

Simon Kewin was born on the misty Isle of Man but now lives deep in the English countryside. He writes fantasy, science fiction and some things that can't make their minds up. He is the author of over 100 published short stories as well as a growing number of novels.

To find out about his books or just to say hi, go to:

www.simonkewin.co.uk

Sign up for his newsletter and you'll be the first to know when he has new books out. There are some fine sci/fi and fantasy books to download for free as thanks.